PASSION

A young woman [...]
"Sukey" Stone's romantic fate to her. Now, years later, the fiery American schoolteacher still eagerly awaits the coming of her dream lover: a strong, honorable, intelligent man, as handsome and as perfect as a male could be.

RUNAWAY MAGIC

Surely Luke Wyndham is *not* the one foretold. He is, after all, a detestable cad with a murderous reputation—and the most arrogant, infuriating lord ever to emerge from Victoria's England. But something in Luke's blazing green eyes stirs Sukey to her very soul. And the secrets of his guarded heart are drawing Sukey beyond the rumors and shadows into a perilous, rapturous realm of undreamed-of passion and predestined love.

Avon Romantic Treasures by
Deborah Gordon

RUNAWAY BRIDE
RUNAWAY TIME

*If You've Enjoyed This Book,
Be Sure to Read These Other*
AVON ROMANTIC TREASURES

DREAM CATCHER *by Kathleen Harrington*
HEARTS RUN WILD *by Shelly Thacker*
JUST ONE KISS *by Samantha James*
THE MACKINNON'S BRIDE *by Tanya Anne Crosby*
PHANTOM IN TIME *by Eugenia Riley*

Coming Soon

YOU AND NO OTHER *by Cathy Maxwell*

DEBORAH GORDON

RUNAWAY MAGIC

An Avon Romantic Treasure

AVON BOOKS ◆ NEW YORK

RUNAWAY MAGIC is an original publication of Avon Books. This work
has never before appeared in book form. This work is a novel. Any sim-
ilarity to actual persons or events is purely coincidental.

AVON BOOKS
A division of
The Hearst Corporation
1350 Avenue of the Americas
New York, New York 10019

First Avon Books Printing: August 1996

AVON TRADEMARK REG. U.S. PAT. OFF. AND IN OTHER COUNTRIES, MARCA
REGISTRADA, HECHO EN U.S.A.

Printed in the U.S.A.

RA 10 9 8 7 6 5 4 3 2 1

In Memory of Marilyn Slosser Raines

I think you would have enjoyed this one, Aunt Marilyn. We always had such good times together! I'll miss you more than I can express.

Hong Kong is always connected with some fatal pestilence, some doubtful war, or some discreditable internal squabble, so much so, that the name of this noisy, bustling, quarrelsome, discontented little island may not inaptly be used as a euphonious synonym for a place not mentionable to ears polite.

—The *London Times*, March 1859

Chapter 1

Victoria, Hong Kong
October 1871

" **A**nd so the brave and clever physician saved
... the ancient temple from the evil men who
had sought to rob it of its pre-cious secrets. But the
duke who owned the temple—"

"He fell in love with the physician and asked her
to marry him, and they lived happily ever after."

Susannah Stone bent over her audience, a six-year-
old charmer named Eleanor Wyndham, and pressed a
laughing, ticklish kiss into the crook of her neck.
"Who's making up this bedtime story? You or I?"

The girl giggled. "You. But I want a happy ending."

To Ellie, that meant love and marriage. She hadn't
yet noticed that the heroines of Sukey's tales always
wound up with interesting occupations as well as wonderful husbands. "If you'll recall, the duke didn't believe his temple could be in danger, or that anything
valuable was hidden inside. He fought Miss Bright
tooth and nail. So to get them together—"

"Something will have to make him change his mind

and fall in love with her," Ellie finished, her eyes full of mischief. "And then he'll win her over, and they'll be busy and very happy. That's always how your stories go."

The six-year-old had absorbed more than Sukey had realized. She was about to suggest that each of them should invent an ending when the child sobered. "The duke reminds me of my papa, Miss Stone. He's smart and he looks after his family and he works harder than anyone in the world. Papa has been gone forever. I miss him all the time. When is he coming back?"

Sukey's throat tightened. What Ellie was really asking was: Suppose he doesn't return? Suppose he dies and leaves me for good, the way my mama did?

She gathered the girl into her arms. "In two or three weeks, darling, just as he told you. Believe me, the places he's visiting in China are as safe as the towns in England. Before you know it, he'll be here in Hong Kong, and you and William will be settled in your new home." William was Ellie's five-year-old brother, an endearing scamp of a lad. "It's called Number One House, and the taipans of Burns and Company have always lived there. I described it to you last week, remember?"

Ellie yawned and snuggled closer. "Uh-huh. You said it was nice. But once I leave Mr. McClure's house, I'll miss *you* all the time. You're the best teacher I ever had."

Sukey was also the only teacher Ellie had ever had, but that didn't make the compliment any less touching. "Thank you, darling. Students like you make it easy to be a good teacher. But you won't have to miss me. We'll still see each other in school most days, and perhaps your papa will ask me over to visit you now and then."

Another wave of emotion surged through her. Ellie's father was an English gentleman, a breed that had even less admiration for educated and outspoken females than American men did. Suppose he disapproved of her?

She eased the child away from her, then tenderly tucked her into bed. She liked all of her students, but Ellie was special—affectionate, creative, and exceptionally bright. Missing her father as she did, she often slipped into Sukey's room at night for a cuddle and some words of comfort. In the two short weeks the child had been here, Sukey had become deeply attached to her. For the daughter's sake, she wanted the father home, but a part of her wished he would dally in China for months.

"I had better go down to dinner, or I'll be scolded for holding people up." She pecked the girl's forehead. "Since you want the duke and Miss Bright to fall in love, why don't you think of a way to bring that about? And then, tomorrow, you can tell me about it."

Ellie agreed, and Sukey started to leave, only to be stopped by a shy tug on her sleeve. "I have a secret, Miss Stone. If my story was about Papa, you would be the lady he loved. But if he did . . . Would you have him? Or have you vowed never to marry?"

"You mean because I'm twenty-six and moldering on the shelf?" Smiling, Sukey ruffled the child's hair. "I do want a husband and family, but the gentleman and I would have to love and respect each other first. I'm very independent, so it will take a special man to put up with me."

Ellie regarded Sukey through wide and solemn eyes. "Papa is special."

Sukey gave her a final hug and turned off the light.

"I'm sure he is. After all, he sired you and William."

But as she left the room, she thought that a man would have to be more than special to become her husband. He would have to be strong but tender. Honorable and patient. A wonderful father. Intelligent but not arrogant. In other words, as perfect as a male could be.

The description wasn't wishful thinking or a flight of fancy, but a simple statement of fact. It came from her sister-in-law Sarah, who knew things other people didn't. Sukey seldom spoke of the man she was destined to marry—Sarah's special knowledge was a great secret, to be discussed with only a handful of intimates—but she was human enough to think of him often. Indeed, after six years of waiting, she had begun to wonder when this paragon of manly virtue would finally charge into her life.

Fifteen months earlier, when she had left America, she had been sure she would meet him in Hong Kong. After all, Sarah had encouraged her to come here. Her daily diary was full of speculation about her suitors, but her future husband had yet to appear, unless he was someone she had already met, to be revealed to her after some piece of high drama-to-come.

But if not . . . Perhaps a future arrival would capture her heart—Ellie's father, for example. He was the right age, about thirty, and had been widowed for over four years, so it was possible. As she made her way to the dining room, she realized she was curious to meet him, but no more so than the rest of the colony. Indeed, people had been chattering about him for months, ever since he had written the current taipan of Burns and Company, Jeremy Burns, about his intention to take control.

Of course, a certain amount of gossip was only to

be expected. The ascension of a new taipan was *always* a matter of interest to the local residents, and when the trading house changing leaders was one of the principal firms in Asia, the interest was that much keener. If the new chief had never set foot on the continent before, the intense curiosity grew into frenzied speculation.

Luke Wyndham was all those things and more. In a community devoid of noblemen, he was the younger son of an earl, with a pedigree as long as any king's. No English gentleman ever dirtied his hands with trade, so Wyndham's involvement in the rough-and-tumble world of international commerce was both startling and intriguing. But most extraordinary of all, the man had left a trail of dead relations littering the English countryside, and some said he had hastened the demise of every single one.

Sukey supposed that made him an unlikely prospect for a husband, but then, Alex McClure said the talk was pure hogwash, and Alex was seldom wrong. A private investigator, he was an expert at ferreting out deceit. So was his wife Melanie, whom Sukey had known since their childhoods, but Mellie relied upon clairvoyance rather than deduction.

The couple was Hong Kong's most glamorous—the grandson of an English baron and the daughter of a California mining magnate. The colony had offered no school to which they could send their daughters, so they had cajoled Sukey, an experienced teacher, into coming here to establish one. She knew everyone in Victoria by now, and from what she had heard, only two men in town had ever clapped eyes on Luke Wyndham: his partner Jeremy Burns, and Alex himself.

Alex and Wyndham had met while Alex was visiting his family in London, traveling to Hong Kong together by steamer. They had become such good friends that Wyndham had left his children in Alex's custody when they had reached the colony, continuing up to Canton without debarking. He was touring China now, visiting the treaty ports where Burns and Company did business. In the meantime, the members of the McClure household—Alex and Melanie, their three children, Sukey, and Sukey's Siamese cat, Nepenthe—were doing their best to make his offspring feel at home.

Sukey arrived at the table as a crew of Chinese servants set soup bowls before the guests. The rumors Alex had heard about Wyndham upon his return to Hong Kong had so astonished and offended him that he had invited the leading residents of the colony to dine tonight in order to set them straight. Melanie tapped her wineglass with a knife to quiet them all down. The chief topic—the only topic—was Wyndham. "Good heavens, everyone, do you want gossip or facts? I've never heard such a din in all my life. Remember, Alex actually knows the new taipan. They spent over a month at sea together, and—"

"And I lived to tell the tale," Alex said. "Believe it or not, Wyndham didn't even club me over the head, much less try to heave me overboard. In fact, there wasn't a single mysterious death during the entire voyage."

"Probably because none of his relations was on board." The dry rejoinder came from the royal governor, Sir Richard MacDonnell. "As for whether we want the facts or not, in my five years here, I've noticed that the people of Hong Kong only prefer the truth if it's laced with a healthy dollop of scandal."

"A trait I confess I enjoy." The governor's wife

looked hopeful. "Tell me, Mr. McClure, if Wyndham didn't murder anyone, did he at least seduce somebody's wife? Cheat at cards? Drink himself into a stupor and insult everyone in sight?"

"I'm afraid not, Lady MacDonnell. His behavior was impeccable." Alex lazed back in his chair. "Although I have to admit, after what I heard when I first reached London, I expected otherwise. Not that Wyndham had a penchant for vice, mind you, because he was said to be unusually straitlaced, but that he possessed a staggering arrogance combined with all the warmth of a Siberian winter."

Sukey's ears perked up. Alex hadn't mentioned arrogance before. Wyndham couldn't possibly be her future husband, not if he was cold and imperious.

Jeremy Burns, Alex's closest friend among the group, nodded vigorously. "That's exactly right. I met the fellow twice, once when he married my partner's daughter—I mean my partner in Burns's London agency, George MacKenzie—and once after he took over MacKenzie's company. Not only does he refuse to suffer fools gladly; he ignores their existence entirely. The man has ice in his veins. He's an excellent businessman, but if you read our correspondence, you'll see that he's incapable of being friendly or even pleasant."

"At least not to the likes of you and me," James Whittall said, looking amused. Whittall was the head of Hong Kong's most powerful trading house, the British firm of Jardine Matheson. "Sons of peers aren't noted for their cordiality to their social inferiors, Burns, and Wyndham couldn't have been happy when he was thrust into a role no gentleman would willingly accept. From what I'm told, the man is brilliant. He got a double first at Oxford, then earned a master's degree. He was a gifted scientist, perhaps even in a class with Darwin. He was elected to a fellowship at Christ Church . . .'' He hesitated, gazing at Sukey. ''That's the name of a college at Oxford, Miss Stone, not a religious institution.''

She smiled. ''I know, Mr. Whittall. Like Balliol or Trinity.''

He cocked an eyebrow at her. ''How foolish of me to have explained. I should have realized that if any American would have heard of Christ Church, you would. Have I mentioned that you read too much, especially for a female?''

''Frequently.'' Sukey picked up a roll and pretended to take aim.

Whittall laughed and ducked. ''All right, then, you don't read too much. The breadth of your knowledge is a sterling example of the value of education, even for females. I suppose you're even aware of how grand Christ Church is.''

''Naturally I am.'' She set down her weapon. ''Public school boys and noblemen often go there. The dean is appointed by the Crown. When Mr. Wyndham finally alights in Hong Kong, I'll be sure to mention how impressed I am by his academic background.''

''Now there's an encounter I would like to witness.'' Whittall chuckled. ''He'll never have met a woman like you, my dear. Not only a free-thinking American, but a college graduate into the bargain. He'll be polite but condescending, and you'll smile sweetly and tie him in verbal knots, just as you did with me. With all of us, for that matter.'' He paused, then drawled, ''The difference is, there will be no surrender from the likes of Wyndham. After all, he's the son of an earl, whereas most of us at this table are only humble merchants.''

In truth, the traders of Hong Kong were about as humble as Queen Victoria. "Ah, yes. Merchants who believe the Empire exists solely for your benefit," Sukey replied with a laugh, "and who think yourselves superior to everyone from the grandest noblemen to the highest officials. Believe me, Mr. Whittall, if I can handle the exalted taipan of Jardine's, the second son of an earl will be no problem at all."

"Remind me to make a wager with you on that, Miss Stone." Whittall turned to Alex. "So tell us your story, McClure. Where did you meet the Honorable Mr. Wyndham? And how did you gain his confidence?"

"Or even manage to have more than a five-minute conversation with him?" the taipan of an American firm asked. "I realize you're a blueblood yourself, but from what I've heard, nobody but Wyndham's family really knows the man. And before too long, his family will be gone. One by one, he's knocking them all off."

Everyone smiled except Alex. "My cousin introduced us. The new Baron Randall." The previous baron, Alex's maternal grandfather, had taken ill that spring at the age of eighty-six. Alex had reached England in time to visit him, then remained after his death to settle his affairs. "We were sitting in his club one night when Wyndham walked in. He almost never came by, but his brother-in-law was there, and he needed to have a word with the fellow."

"What sort of reaction did he get?" the American asked.

"A cool one. He runs Burns and MacKenzie in much too personal a way for society to approve." Alex's expression hardened. "It's beside the point that the firm would have failed if he hadn't stepped in. That a great many jobs and a huge sum of money would have been lost if he hadn't been willing to solicit business, haggle over contracts, and even go down to the docks when necessary. He's still accepted in society—his mother is immensely popular—but you can almost see the gentlemen of London holding their offended noses when he walks by.''

"Only because he's raised conceit to an art form,'' Burns insisted. "I don't want to make matters difficult for my successor, but there's no point denying what everyone will soon find out. If Wyndham's been snubbed, he has only himself to blame. He thinks he's smarter than anyone else and doesn't hesitate to show it. That antagonizes people.''

"But I thought he was,'' Melanie said artlessly. "Smarter, I mean. More accomplished and better educated. As brilliant at business as he was at science. I can't imagine why society isn't impressed to the point of abject deference, Jeremy.''

Sukey clapped her hands in delight. "Now we've come to the heart of it.'' She looked at the governor. "With all due respect to your personal accomplishments, Sir Richard, we Californians will never understand why a colonial official who owes his position to having the right uncle or a farmer who inherited his land from his family thinks himself superior to a capitalist like Melanie's father, who made his millions on his own.''

The governor waggled a finger at her. "Oh, no, you don't, Miss Stone. I won't be drawn into another argument about democracy. You Yankees won your revolution. I beg you, be satisfied with your social utopia and leave us deluded British to our time-honored traditions.''

In Sukey's opinion, "tradition'' was much too kind a word for a system that deemed a self-made man a pariah while giving its fullest respect to the lazy son of a wealthy peer. She held her tongue only because Americans could be guilty of the same nonsense, and besides, she wasn't going to demolish the English class structure by winning an argument with a middling diplomat. "And if Wyndham had behaved differently? Would that have changed anything, given his commercial activities?"

"Miss Stone, if there's anything we British excel at, it's looking the other way when we wish to," the governor replied. "Wyndham is a younger son. That in itself gives him greater leeway. If he were well-liked, and if he made it clear that he would wash his hands of trade as soon as he could, people would make allowances for his situation. The man was an Oxford rower, for heaven's sake. Do you have any idea of the prestige that confers?"

"I think so. It's the pinnacle of athletic accomplishment. It would excuse a multitude of social sins."

The commander of the Hong Kong garrison nodded in confirmation. "Exactly so, my dear. It's a shame Wyndham isn't more like his older brother, the late earl of Stour. I knew him—Arthur, that is—before he came into the title, when he was here with the Royal Navy. An extremely congenial fellow. He could have broken twice as many rules as Wyndham and people would have exerted themselves not to notice."

"You're right," Alex said, "but Stour is also the one who squandered the family fortune. Eventually, there was so little left that nothing short of a fat dowry could bail him out. And unfortunately for his creditors, he was already married."

"To the daughter of an Oxford professor," the wife of a Scottish taipan put in. "I've heard that Wyndham was the one who introduced them. That he and the girl were all but betrothed at the time. That he's never stopped loving her. Is it true, Mr. McClure?"

Alex shrugged. "That *is* what they say. I only know that since Stour couldn't marry an heiress to replenish the family coffers, Wyndham had to do it. He wanted to be a scientist, but in the end, he was forced to take over Burns and MacKenzie." Alex paused while the empty soup bowls were whisked away and a fish course set down. "You would think he would resent Arthur for that—the arranged marriage, the aborted career—but oddly enough, Arthur is what got us together. I knew him at Eton."

Sukey had heard enough about Alex's past—his brutal father in Scotland, his struggles after he fled to his grandparents' home in England—to know that he disliked speaking of it. He looked down for a moment, then continued, "Eton was . . . difficult for me. I was the son of a Scottish clergyman, with the wrong accent, the wrong manners, and the wrong religion. When my cousin introduced me to Luke, I mentioned how grateful I'd been for Arthur's kindness there. That unlike almost everyone else, he had judged me by what was inside me, not by my speech or my blunders." He paused for several seconds. "We wound up sharing our memories of him. I agree that Luke is extremely controlled, but he's not without feeling. Arthur's lack of responsibility robbed him of the life he wanted, but despite that, Luke loved him. He mourns the loss. That was very clear."

Nobody was smiling now. "And the yachting mishap?" Whittall asked softly. "I know the two brothers were racing against each other when it occurred. I've heard rumors it was Wyndham's fault."

"It was an accident. A storm blew in and the boats grew hard to control. They eventually collided, and

Stour fell from his mast and died. That's all I know. Wyndham didn't offer any confidences about the incident, and it wasn't my place to inquire.''

Alex's tone said it wasn't his guests' place, either, and not even Whittall had the nerve to disagree. But the colony's chief justice was made of sterner stuff. "I understand Wyndham is his nephew's guardian. Lady Stour's trustee.''

"Naturally," Alex said. "He's the head of the family now.''

"Then permit me to say aloud what everyone is already whispering incessantly. If Wyndham was in love with Victoria Stour, he had every reason to want his brother dead. Who else would she have turned to for help and comfort but the man who still loved her? The man who controlled her money and her children?''

"That's true," the governor's wife murmured. "That is, the law might forbid Wyndham from marrying his brother's widow, but—'' She looked at Sukey, and her voice dropped even lower. "Well, you know.''

Sukey rolled her eyes, wishing the people in this colony would stop treating her like a simpleminded schoolgirl. Her female relations—her sister-in-law Sarah and Sarah's daughter Shelby—were seasoned warriors in the struggle for women's emancipation, and frank about the most personal subjects. As a result, she was probably the most unshockable virgin in Asia.

"You mean that from Wyndham's point of view, Victoria would have been the ideal mistress,'' she stated. "He might have been straitlaced, but he was widowed by then, he'd wanted her for years, and she was totally beholden to him. Not only couldn't she demand marriage, she didn't dare make demands at all.

All he had to do was wait. Sooner or later she was bound to drop into his lap.''

''A fine theory,'' Alex said, ''but in point of fact, she's dropped in another direction.'' His disgruntled expression said Sukey had spent entirely too much time with Sarah and Shelby over the years. ''The fellow is a friend of her late husband, a former naval officer named Sir Roger Albright who's now with the Foreign Office. I met him at a dinner party given by Wyndham's mother. He regaled us with his experiences in India and China. Victoria was a guest as well, so obviously he has the family's blessing, including Wyndham's. I assure you, Wyndham gained nothing from his brother's death except pain and a great deal of gossip.''

''And what about his *father-in-law's* death?'' the American taipan asked. ''You can't deny he gained by that.''

''If you're speaking of the money he received,'' Alex said brusquely, ''he would have gotten that in the end anyway, and if you mean the business responsibilities he inherited, he would sooner have done without them. In any event, MacKenzie died of a heart attack. He'd had chest pains for over a year, so it was only to be expected.''

''But his daughter died only six months later,'' the Scottish taipan reminded the group, ''and that *wasn't* expected. Healthy young women don't usually fall off cliffs. They jump or they're pushed. Wyndham only married her for her money, and suddenly he had the money without the woman. That's very convenient, I would say.''

Alex scowled so fiercely that the governor's wife actually flinched. ''If there's one thing I can tell you after spending six weeks at sea with Wyndham, it's that he loves his children. He has no shortage of relations in England, so he could have left them behind. But he knew they would be distressed by the separation, so he took them along. He never would have caused them the pain of depriving them of their mother.''

The chief justice was quick to raise a challenge. ''That's only your opinion, and it's based on emotion rather than logic. Frankly, McClure, I'm disappointed in you. You never stopped to wonder why the arrogant Mr. Wyndham was so cordial to you. To ask yourself what he might have wanted. You're a famous investigator, yet it never occurred to you to use your formidable powers of detection to learn anything more about the man than what you'd heard from the gossips of London.''

''You're correct. It didn't occur to me. What you call emotion, I call judgment, and my judgment says Wyndham is an honorable man who wants what any man wants—useful information, intelligent conversation, and pleasant company. In any event, I'm not in the habit of insulting my friends by grilling them about whether or not they've murdered their closest relations.'' Alex snapped his fingers, and the servants hurried in to clear away the fish plates. ''I suggest all of you judge Wyndham by what he does here, not by the wild rumors you've heard. Savaging his reputation would diminish his ability to function here. While the taipans among you would gain by that, I trust you'll keep the competition fair and play by your usual ruthless rules.''

Given the chilly look in Alex's eyes, nobody could miss the threat behind his words. All these people had secrets they wanted to keep and indiscretions they wished to hide. As a detective and former merchant,

Alex knew a great deal about everyone's activities, and what he didn't know, he could probably find out.

A chorus of "Of courses" filled the air, and then dead, tense silence. Finally Jeremy Burns spoke up. "For heaven's sake, Alex, stop glowering. You'll ruin our appetites." He smiled and shook his head. "We weren't dissecting the man's past in order to discredit him. If you'll recall, I was the first to raise questions, and I would hardly want my own partner to fail here. It was only a harmless parlor game. An innocent bit of entertainment."

"A blood sport, you mean," Alex shot back.

Melanie looked at him reprovingly. "Remember, darling, unlike us, our guests don't have the fun of conducting investigations. They were only indulging their imaginations. Weaving a bit of intrigue around what you must admit is a highly unusual set of circumstances."

"Then everyone understands they were composing fiction here tonight."

The company hastened to agree, and Sukey more or less believed them. She wasn't sure whether the residents of Hong Kong schemed, speculated, and gossiped more than other people did, but she was certain they did so more openly.

Melanie smiled. "There, Alex. You see?"

Alex had better manners than to pursue the topic and ruin everyone's evening. "Perhaps my penchant for sympathizing with the underdog got the better of me. My apologies, everyone."

Much later, however, after everyone but Jeremy had left, Alex admitted there was more to it than believing in fair play. Like Wyndham, he had dirtied his hands with commerce, running off to sea to seek his fortune instead of training for something respectable. When he had visited his grandfather in London, he had suffered much of the same cool treatment as Wyndham had. That shared experience was what had brought the two men together.

"But do you know what galls me most of all? The way an external factor can change the way one is regarded. When Wyndham's nephew was born—when he wasn't the heir presumptive anymore—society felt freer to slight him. When I married Melanie, gained a fortune, and began to donate the fees from my investigative work to charity, I was deemed a gentleman detective and welcomed everywhere."

"Because you'd been a gentleman to begin with," Jeremy said. "As the son of a merchant, I'll never be equally accepted, not even if they make me a knight and a member of Parliament, which I expect they will once I'm back in England. I'm no more fond of the system than you are."

Melanie pointed out that money opened an amazing number of doors. "As everyone knows, Papa's millions even transformed *me* into a lady, and I started out life as his love child by his half-Chinese mistress. So if Wyndham can make you rich enough—" She suddenly frowned. "Speaking of money, Jeremy, what do your records for the third quarter show? Are you still suffering those mysterious losses?"

Jeremy nodded. He had first noticed the problem a year ago, but he hadn't recognized the pattern as suspicious for another six months. Wanting to keep the trouble confidential, he had investigated on his own, but nothing had turned up.

Wyndham had noticed the declining profits, too. Concerned inquiries had given way to pointed suggestions, then curt instructions. Finally, in July, he had announced his intention to come to Hong Kong and take over.

At that point, Jeremy had decided that professional help would be needed. He had wired Wyndham that he planned to bring in a local detective to investigate what might well be a case of fraud.

Wyndham had answered by return wire. There was to be no detective. He would look into the matter himself. Ignoring the order, Jeremy had written Alex in London and described the case. With luck, he'd felt, Alex would be back in Hong Kong sorting things out before Wyndham even arrived.

"I wish you would change your mind and poke around a bit," Jeremy said now. "Nobody would have to know."

"You mean Wyndham wouldn't have to know, but as sure as we're sitting here, someone will tell him. I don't care what excuse we give for my presence at your firm; the gossip will be all over Hong Kong within hours." Alex chuckled. "I'll never forget the way Wyndham blushed when I told him I'd received your letter and informed him I was the detective you wanted to hire. He admitted he'd expected some bumbling backwater bobby. And even though he knew I was anything but, he still didn't want me nosing around his firm. I can't ignore his wishes."

Jeremy, who had been imbibing freely, drained his glass of port. "Why not? You would be doing him a favor. You're experienced at this sort of thing and he isn't."

"He didn't say—he plays his cards as close to the vest as any man I know—but I expect he's worried about the possible financial repercussions, just as you were. As the new taipan, he'll be able to analyze the books and interrogate the staff without questions being asked.''

''Or perhaps he's got something to hide. Perhaps he's even the source of the problems here. After all, there were all those deaths.''

''For God's sake, Jeremy, not you too.'' Alex wearily rubbed his temples. ''Why do you so dislike the man? It can't be his arrogance. There are colonial officials who are far worse, and they don't get under your skin this way. Is it because, without Wyndham's business acumen, his father-in-law never could have obtained a controlling interest in the Hong Kong side of your firm?''

''I admit I wasn't happy about that, but it's more a matter of distrust than dislike.'' Jeremy pulled an envelope out of his pocket. ''This is a wire for Wyndham. I opened it in case it was an emergency. I would swear you all to silence, but the news will have been in the *London Times*, and the pertinent edition will reach Hong Kong any day now.''

He removed the paper inside. ''It's from his younger brother, Hugh. Hugh obviously hoped to catch him along the way, because according to the boy in the telegraph office, it's been to half a dozen cities, always missing your steamer. Wyndham's little nephew, Victoria and Arthur's only son, died of scarlet fever on September tenth. Hugh says that if Wyndham has any instructions, he should wire them back. In the meantime, he's sending out some papers for Wyndham to sign in connection with his inheriting the earldom.''

Melanie's eyes widened. ''Surely you're not suggesting that Wyndham had anything to do with the boy's death. Children often take ill. It's a tragedy, but sometimes they die.''

''Still, the timing is awfully interesting,'' Sukey

pointed out. "The boy must have gotten sick within days of when Wyndham left. You have to admit it would be a clever way to dispose of someone. Find a person who's mortally ill, then pay him to—"

"That's enough, Susannah."

She reddened. "I didn't say I believed it, Alex. I was only quoting what people would think."

"The fact remains," Jeremy said, "that everyone who stood between Wyndham and immense wealth has died. Everyone who stood between him and a grand title has done the same. I'm prepared to believe his relations have been singularly unlucky, but I doubt Hong Kong will see it that way." He tucked the telegram back into his pocket. "Not after this."

Chapter 2

Three and a half weeks later

Sukey never would have resorted to magic if Luke Wyndham, now called Lord Stour, had been a reasonable man, but his refusal to see her or even to respond to her most recent letter had left her no choice. The previous Monday, shortly after his arrival in Hong Kong, he had removed his daughter from her school, writing that he refused to have Eleanor subjected to gossip. Given all the yawns and whispers Sukey had noticed during the past few weeks, the gossip had been real enough—her girls were evidently eavesdropping on their parents late at night—but it also had ended rapidly. She had seen to that.

Unfortunately, her efforts had been in vain. A full week had passed, and Ellie was still at home. In Sukey's opinion, no child that bright and eager to learn should be deprived of an education, and she had explained as much to Stour, very tactfully. But had he listened? He hadn't, not to any of the three very cogent letters she had sent him.

Preparing herself with deep, calming breaths, she gazed around the small chamber where she performed her magic. A clock sat atop the tall, narrow cabinet that held her implements and tools. It was past midnight now, the best time to cast a spell. The world was dark and quiet, and the entities called spirits or elementals more amenable to human enticement.

For eons, people had believed them to be supernatural, but Sukey knew they were actually energy-based beings who dwelled in a higher dimension, beyond the reach of normal human perception. While the reverse wasn't true, they were generally as indifferent to the presence of humans as humans were to the existence of microscopic organisms. Only intense appeals to their senses—certain sights, smells, and sounds—could induce them to come forth. Then, if they wished, they would involve themselves in human affairs. While not particularly intelligent, they had the ability to perceive human intentions and affect human actions.

Sukey's altar, a long, narrow table inlaid with Hong Kong granite, sat in the northern half of the room. Beneath it, the Siamese cat Nepenthe lay dozing. The entities had a special liking for felines. Sukey had taken a ritual bath earlier that evening, and a hint of the seawater she'd added for purification mingled with the stronger aroma of patchouli oil, which helped to increase one's authority. She was ready to begin.

She laid a fragrant rose in the center of the altar, then placed a censer containing frankincense and myrrh in front of the flower and a white candle on either side. Next came a chalice of wine, a bowl of seawater, and her two most important tools: her hazelwood wand and her athame, a ritual knife with a black handle and a magnetized double blade.

Finally—crucially—she placed a purple skull candle on the altar and anointed it with patchouli oil. The candle was specific to the spell she wished to cast, one to persuade the entities to influence somebody's actions. To make it clear whom she wished to control, she had engraved both his name, Luke Wyndham, and his title, the earl of Stour, into the wax.

One also had to elucidate one's goal, writing it on a piece of vellum and setting it beside the candle. Sukey had puzzled long and hard over what to say. Being too general had gotten her into trouble at times, but being too specific was just as risky. The entities could be maddeningly mischievous, fully capable of taking a precise statement such as "Stour will send his daughter to my school each day" and causing him to send Ellie only to fetch her home, or to send her and direct her to remain outside. She finally had settled on "Stour will accede to my wishes about his family and act as I desire." Not only would the request solve the problem at school; it would cover anything else that came up regarding his children.

The next step in the ritual was to mark out a space in which to perform her magic. First, however, she slipped off the white robe she was wearing and draped it atop the cabinet. Beneath, she wore only a silver pentacle on a chain around her neck and a braided red silk cord around her waist.

Her skin prickled. She didn't feel cold, only exposed and vulnerable. Magic, with its deeply sensual overtones, always affected her this way. During her college days, she had been assaulted and almost raped by someone she had liked and trusted, and she had been distrustful of men and fearful of physical intimacy ever since. If she worked nude—what witches termed sky-clad—it was only because the entities were far more attracted to the naked human form than to the clothed one.

They were attracted to human emotion, too, which

was doubtless how displays of affection had come to be included in magical rites. Indeed, the embraces in a ceremony of initiation were so erotic that Sukey had decided to cease her magic on the day she got betrothed. Otherwise, her intended might expect to join her, and the places one had to touch and kiss a lover were utterly mortifying. As for the final step of the ritual, sexual union, she didn't care to contemplate that aspect of the marital relationship.

Rattled by the notion, she breathed deeply to regain her focus, then sprinkled some flour on the floor and placed tapers of brown and pink, the colors of influence, in each corner of the room. She dipped her fingers in seawater and sprinkled some about. "With water and salt, I purify the circle from all anxieties and fears. Come forth, friends. Join me, Luna. Join me, Astra. I welcome you both."

She lit the colored tapers and picked up her knife. Moving slowly, chanting additional words of welcome, she traced a circle in the flour on the floor. Next, after lighting the white candles and incense, she waved her wand and censer around the room and intoned a message of purification by fire and air.

The final preliminary rite was to draw a pentagram in the air with her knife at each corner of the circle, then chant an invocation. Moving clockwise from the east, she exalted the beauties of nature, then asked Luna and Astra to come forth, telling them she needed their help. In truth, she never knew how many entities were present, much less whether they were the same ones each time, but personalizing them helped her to concentrate.

As she returned her knife to the altar, Nepenthe rose and stretched. Humming softly, Sukey picked up the cat. He purred contentedly while Sukey continued to hum, focusing intently now, willing the entities to heed her.

Without warning, a charge crackled through the air. Sukey's normal senses registered nothing, yet in some primal way, she could feel the entities' energy. They had responded to the aromas, sounds, and visions she had provided. With luck, they would be receptive to her requests.

Then she felt something else, and sighed. Amusement. Playfulness. They were in a mischievous mood tonight. Unfortunately, once you summoned them forth, you were stuck with them. They would do as they pleased.

She set Nepenthe on the altar, lit the purple skull candle, and hoped for the best. "Welcome, Astra. Welcome, Luna. Thank you for answering my call. There is a child I need to help. A man I need to control. Please, sense what I have written. Hear what is in my heart."

She pictured Ellie and Stour, meditated on her problem, and thought about the outcome she desired. If she could impress the entities with the gravity of the situation, perhaps they would do as she wished.

Nepenthe began to purr more loudly. The skull candle slowly burned down. The air continued to vibrate. Then, as suddenly as the shimmering had started, it stopped. The entities were no longer manifest. They had retreated beyond her reach.

She sipped some wine, a symbolic alternative to the feast that was supposed to follow the casting of a spell, and dissolved the circle. For better or worse, her work here tonight was finished.

The Victoria Girls' Academy was located near Government House and the Botanical Gardens. Housed in a small building on Caine Road, the school used the rooms on the second floor, above a ladies' clothing shop. Each weekday, Sukey walked there in the company of the McClures' two daughters, Beth and Annie, and their twenty-four-year-old amah, Pearl Douglas. Pearl, who was half-English and half-Chinese, functioned as her Cantonese language instructor and general assistant.

The two women always reviewed the day's lessons during these strolls, but Sukey was distant and silent on the morning after casting her spell. The only thing on her mind was whether it had worked.

The schoolday began at nine and ended at three. For the next six hours, she waited for Ellie Wyndham to scamper up the stairs into the primary room, but the girl never appeared. She was absent the next day, a Wednesday, as well.

That didn't mean the entities had ignored Sukey's pleas, however. As much as they wheedled and pushed, strong-willed individuals could resist them. From what Sukey had seen, Stour wasn't only willful, but imperious and closed-minded. A direct conversation would obviously be necessary, but she was stymied as to how to arrange one. He wouldn't even come to the McClures to dine.

Alex had invited him, of course. He had claimed to be too busy for a proper visit. But his hectic schedule didn't prevent him from dropping into the all-male Hong Kong Club now and then, so Sukey finally had asked Alex to plead her case for her the next time they ran into each other.

To her chagrin, he had burst out laughing, informing her that the men in this world had to endure enough nagging from their womenfolk without suffering the same sort of annoyance from their friends. But in retrospect, she realized, it was just as well Alex had refused.

Taken separately, neither her logic nor the entities' persuasion had been enough to budge the likes of Stour, so she would have to subject him to both at the same time. And since he had made himself as unreachable as a Chinese emperor, she would have to barge into his home uninvited to do it. Even with the entities hovering about, cajoling him to listen, the prospect was a daunting one.

And then her assistant, Pearl Douglas, told her about a gathering that would take place on Friday evening at Number One House. Stour's three top lieutenants at Burns and Company, like Stour himself, had been working like demons these past two weeks. To thank them, he was treating them to a special dinner.

"But in truth, my brother expects to work as much as to relax," Pearl added with a laugh, "even before the dinner itself. Kai-wing says the taipan has some sherries he wishes the men to sample, for reasons of business, of course. If I were you, that is when I would make my appearance. After all, both Shaw and Kilearn would propose to you if you gave them any encouragement, and Kai regards you as a little sister. All the men admire your school. You will have three automatic allies." She smiled slyly. "Why don't I have a word with Kai? Arrange some support in advance?"

Pearl's older brother, Kai-wing Douglas, was the comprador of Burns and Company—the hong's liaison to the Chinese business community and the emperor's officials. Sukey suspected his feelings for her were more than brotherly, but she also knew his sisters wanted him to marry someone Chinese. The other two men, Patrick Shaw and Robert Kilearn, were important partners in the firm. Both had blood ties to the original owners, and before Stour's accession, each had hoped to become the next taipan.

The dinner was so opportune that Sukey suspected the entities had played a role in inspiring it. "That's a brilliant idea. Stour can hardly claim he's too busy to see me when he's sitting there tasting wine." She nibbled her bottom lip. "But don't say anything to Kai. Stour can't be angry at him for mentioning the dinner to his sister, who happened to mention it to me, but he wouldn't like the idea of his top aides scheming behind his back."

Pearl replied that she saw the wisdom in remaining silent, as did the McClures when she asked to borrow their carriage the following evening to pay Stour a call. "Although I must confess," Alex said, "that, like Whittall, I wish I could sneak in and watch. The verbal fireworks should be vastly entertaining. After all, I remember Stour's reaction when I told him about your school."

"But you said he agreed right away that Ellie could attend," Sukey reminded Alex. "Did you fib?"

"Not at all. I was simply too much of a diplomat— or too much of a coward—to tell you the full truth. Now, though, you should know what you're facing. Stour believes you're running a finishing school. In the world he comes from, women with your background and education don't exist. He smiled at my claim that Oberlin was an academic institution much like Oxford. He didn't believe that females could sit in the same classrooms as males and study the same subjects, not if those subjects have any substance to them."

Melanie raised her eyebrows. "Whyever not, Alex? Does he think women aren't intelligent enough to comprehend the same scholarly material men do? That they're too irrational or physically weak to complete an advanced education?''

''I imagine it's a combination of all those things, darling. Like most Englishmen of his class, Stour believes that women are capable of performing only those tasks they already manage—running an inn or a shop, perhaps, or nursing the sick. As for the rare female who achieves something more, he assumes she's a singular exception.''

''Thereby ignoring the fact that it's men like him who keep us in our so-called place,'' Sukey grumbled. ''By God, Alex, I'd like to give the man a lecture about the next two centuries. Tell him about the world Sarah and Shelby come from. About female presidents and prime ministers, and architects and lawyers and even taipans. See what he says to that.''

Alex grinned at her. ''Probably that you're a raging lunatic suffering from delusive visions. Everyone knows that traveling in time is impossible.''

Everyone was wrong, however, and Alex and Melanie were among the few people who knew it. The fact was, Sukey's sister-in-law Sarah had traveled back to the past from the year 2096 under the auspices of a secret time-travel project. But her mission had gone awry and she had gotten lost in 1865. It wasn't until 2102 that her colleagues had been able to send someone back to find her—her daughter Shelby, who had been seventeen at the time.

Sarah had fallen in love with Sukey's brother by then, and in the end, both women had elected to remain in the past. First, though, they had paid a final visit to the future, where they had read about Sukey's fate. The two had been discreet about future events— to reveal too much about the course of history might be to change it for the worse—but they had said enough for Sukey to understand that women would one day do everything that men did.

"Anyway," Alex continued, "Stour isn't as hopeless as all that. His older sister Penelope has turned down any number of marriage proposals to travel around the world and paint rare plants, and he hasn't disowned her for it. On the contrary, he finances her work."

"The man is obviously a saint," Sukey said tartly. She glanced out the window as the coachman drove up with the carriage. "Although why I should expect anything else from an Englishman . . . After all, if your countrymen had any tradition of providing their daughters with a decent education, the way we do in America, you wouldn't have had to lure me to Hong Kong to establish a school. It's no wonder American women will achieve equality long before their British sisters do."

"You're absolutely right. In fact, since you're so eager to enlighten the man, why don't you marry him?"

Sarah had given Sukey permission to tell her future husband as much of the truth as she wished. "It wouldn't be worth the sacrifice," she said. "Anyway, he hardly fits the description Sarah gave me."

Melanie gurgled with laughter. "I think you should stay the course you're on. Give him a long, stern lecture about the superiority of everything American. Once you've humbled him with his English shortcomings, you can whip him into shape."

"More likely, he would throw me out the door," Sukey said with a sigh. She needed to charm and cajole the man, not jaw at him.

Of course, to do that, she would have to keep her temper in check. Thanks to Sarah and Shelby, she had more scientific knowledge in her little finger than Stour had in his whole body, even with his fancy degrees from Oxford. So if he turned out to be as arrogant and condescending as she expected, she would probably have to bite her tongue till it bled.

She rehearsed what she planned to say all the way to the Burns compound in Happy Valley. When Jeremy had been taipan, it had been almost a second home to her, so she knew every servant and employee, and every tree and building. The taipan's residence; the cottages where the partners and griffins, or assistants, lived; the offices and godowns, or warehouses; the shops and inns in the Chinese quarter near the docks . . . Jeremy had departed Hong Kong a few days before, but she still felt a special tie to the place.

Stour, like every new taipan, had inherited a full staff along with Number One House. Sukey's knock was answered by the only majordomo the place had ever known, a diminutive fellow named Tung. As she stepped inside, she heard a gust of male laughter emanating from the library at the end of the hall. The tasting session was obviously going well.

Tung greeted her with a solemn bow, then winked at her. "You come about the child, yes? Little Lady Eleanor. She miss you, Miss Stone. Miss your lessons. Talk about you all the time. Have . . . temper tantrums, His Lordship call them. He very displeased."

So Stour had ignored his daughter's pleas. To Sukey, mistreating one's children was a sin almost as grievous as bumping off one's relations, not that she supposed Stour had actually done that. "And what did he do when she fussed? Punish her for it?"

"He talk. She argue. He scold. She cry. So he bribe her with favorite candy, but she throw it on floor and spit. Oh, very bad girl. Taipan very, very displeased. Send her to her room for many hours.''

"If she's giving him a hard time, he has only himself to blame. He never should have removed her from my school. Still, I would have visited and settled her down if only I'd been invited.''

Tung grinned at her. "But you visit now, Miss Stone. Taipan finally ask you?''

"You know perfectly well he didn't.'' Tung ran this house with all the precision of a crack military unit and had a spy network to rival Bismarck's. "But you know me, Tung. I'm determined to get her back, and I'll fight to get my way. So tell me about the new taipan. Is he a good man to work for? Has he gained your respect?''

"I seldom see. He busy all the time. Arrive and take charge. Very stern, but fair, I think. No problem so far.'' There was another burst of laughter. Tung made the motion of someone draining a glass. "They drink for an hour, maybe more. Talk and laugh. I glad to see. Taipan work too hard. You have good joss, Miss Stone, to come when—''

Tung stopped and frowned, interrupted by a piercing squeal. A moment later, Ellie and William barreled down the stairs, whooping at the tops of their lungs. They were followed by Pearl's cousin Mei-mei, the new amah there. Judging by the dismayed look on her face, she feared her charges' unruly behavior would earn her a sharp rebuke.

Sukey's eyes welled with tears. She raced across the hall, gathered the children in her arms, and hugged them fiercely. They were dressed for bed and smelled delicious, like bath oil and shampoo.

"I saw Mr. McClure's carriage through the window,

and I knew it was you before you even got out,'' William boasted.

''I want you to make Papa send me back to school,'' Ellie demanded.

Sukey sprawled onto the floor and pulled the children onto her lap, unconcerned about the consequences to her carefully pressed olive dress. ''I mean to do exactly that, although from what I'm told about your papa, it won't be easy.''

''I know. Aunt Penny says he's stubborn as a mule.'' Ellie nibbled on a fingernail. ''But he never killed anyone, Miss Stone. I swear he didn't.''

So the gossip still distressed the child. Sukey's heart contracted. ''Well, of course not, darling. I told you, there are so few amusements here that the people get very bored, so they fill up their time inventing ridiculous stories. Your father was new to the colony, and no one knew anything about him, so naturally there was silly gossip. And then he became an earl, which the English think is very grand, so—''

''And I'm a viscount,'' William interrupted, puffing himself up. ''You have to call me Lord Elmsford now.''

''Yes. I know about your exalted new station.'' Sukey raised her chin and looked down her nose at the boy. ''But you're only a child, and besides, I'm an American, young man. We fought a revolution to do things our own way, and that doesn't include having kings, dukes, and earls. Your title is well and good, but you did nothing to earn it, and it doesn't make you any better than what you were.''

Tung coughed softly, momentarily distracting her. She glanced at him to make sure he was all right, then finished, ''If you expect me to 'my lord' you, William, or 'my lady' your sister, you're doomed to disappointment.''

"I'm what?" William asked.

"She means she won't do it," Ellie said.

"Oh. Then I guess she doesn't have to. Since she's an American." A mischievous look entered the boy's eyes. "But what about Papa, Miss Stone? He's a grown-up, and he's not Mr. Wyndham anymore. He's Lord Stour. If you call him *mister* something, that would be a mistake. And I think it would be rude, too."

"You're right," Sukey agreed, "at least by your etiquette in England. I don't believe I care for your customs. They're snobbish and divisive."

The majordomo coughed again, more loudly this time, and Sukey gazed at him searchingly. "You're the picture of health, Tung, but still, I don't like the sound of that cough. I think you should have it looked at."

"Miss Stone—" Tung straightened, and a bland expression stole over his face. "Yes, Miss Stone. I will."

"Good. Now where was I? Oh, yes. Raging against the injustices of the English class system." She smiled at her denunciation, which Ellie and William couldn't have begun to comprehend. "Not that you two children aren't angels, and a credit to your illustrious ancestors, but I expect you to make me proud of you in the years to come. Show me you deserve what you've been lucky enough to inherit. Do you understand that?"

"No," William said.

"She means she wants us to be good," Ellie explained, "but she wanted that before, too, before Papa had a title, so I don't see what's changed. So what are you going to call him, Miss Stone?"

Sukey sighed in defeat. "I'll have to behave myself. Adhere to your hidebound traditions. Abandon my democratic principles in the service of a larger goal."

"What does *that* mean?" William asked plaintively.

"I believe it means that, unlike her idols Washington, Jefferson, and Madison, she's decided to knuckle under to British tyranny and call me Lord Stour." The earl strolled down the hall and stopped by Sukey's side, looming over her. "Is that correct, madam?"

Sukey's heart all but jumped out of her chest, but she managed a posture of impressive nonchalance. If he'd meant to intimidate her by pouncing that way, he wasn't going to succeed.

She pondered the question, then drawled, "I don't know, Taipan." It was a fine appellative compromise, she thought. "If I do, will it get me my way about Ellie?"

"No," he said.

He wasn't smiling. He clearly meant it. She felt a flash of dislike, but it was far outweighed by her intense awareness of his presence. Having him so close made her throat tighten and her body heat up.

Outwardly, at least, he resembled her brother Ty, who was the best-looking man she knew—the tawny blond hair; the firm jaw; the well-shaped, rather thin lips; the strapping build . . . And while the two men's eyes were different colors, Ty's blue and Stour's an eerie yellow-green, she had seen the exact same expression on Ty's face as was currently on Stour's. Her brother, while normally kind and sunny, could be as glacial as the North Pole when he was enraged, and Stour looked just as cold. The difference was, Stour didn't seem angry now, only unyielding. Ice was evidently his natural state.

She lifted the children off her lap and got up, ignoring the hand Stour held out to help her. She wanted him to understand that he wasn't to touch her except on her terms. Her attitude had nothing to do with how he had acted and everything to do with what he was, a virile young male.

"I see." She smoothed her dress. "As you've obviously gathered, I'm Susannah Stone. You have two very special children, Taipan. You must be extremely proud of them." She held out her hand.

He shook it very briefly, and she realized she was wrong about his eyes. For just a second, he stared straight at her, and they heated dramatically. Hostile or not, he was physically drawn to her.

She retreated a step. She had barely turned fifteen when she had realized men found her attractive. Back then, she had reveled in the way they pursued her when she flirted, and relished how they watched her when she sauntered down the street. She had received more than her share of kisses, and enjoyed them very much. But that had been before the attack.

Afterward, she had trusted neither men nor herself. Her manner, though proper, had warned potential suitors to keep their distance. The admirers who had always surrounded her had quickly disappeared, so she had found it a vast relief when Sarah had told her about her future husband.

Either she would recognize him on sight, she thought, or some incident would tell her who he was, and then she could welcome him into her heart. In the meantime, she had met a great many men and found most of them wanting. If they weren't afraid of her intelligence and education, they were as pompous and prejudiced in regard to women as Stour was.

"Usually I am," he said, responding to her comment about paternal pride, "but not at this particular moment." He regarded the children sternly. "I'll remind you of what you were told. Once I bid you good night, you're to remain in your rooms unless you have my permission to do otherwise. I should punish you for disobeying, and punish Mei-mei for failing to stop you."

Ellie looked both alarmed and mutinous. "But that's not fair, Papa. How could we ask permission when we didn't even know—"

"I didn't solicit your opinion, Eleanor."

Ellie hung her head and bit her lip. Sukey wanted to brain Stour for terrorizing the poor child, not to mention for being as rigid as a petrified oak. "For heaven's sake, Taipan, they saw my carriage pull up—"

"Nor yours, Miss Stone."

"—and they got excited. They're children, not trained dogs. Naturally they ran down to see me. They've missed me." She put her hands on her hips. "And I've missed them."

Stour's jaw tightened, the only sign he had heard her. "You are to take the children upstairs as soon as I've finished with them," he said to Mei-mei. "They are to go straight to bed. No treats. No stories. Do you understand?"

She bowed. "Yes, my lord. I am very sorry, my lord."

"Your apology is accepted," he said, and added to his children, "*this* time. But next time, Mei-mei might suffer for your misbehavior. If I were you, I would think twice before I broke the rules again."

Sukey knew she shouldn't criticize a father in front of his children, but she couldn't contain herself. Her sole concession to tact was to use French, a language she assumed an educated man like Stour would speak, while his children wouldn't. "They only did what anyone with a heart and any spirit would do. Only a tyrant would punish them for it. You are unreasonable and very unfeeling."

His icy expression didn't change a whit. Either he was inordinately self-controlled, or he hadn't understood her.

He crooked a finger at his children, who promptly trudged over to him. When he bent down, Sukey expected him to take them over his knee, one by one, and administer some firm whacks on the bottom. Instead, he simply waited—for what, she didn't know.

But William obviously did. "I'm sorry, Papa. I'll try to be better." He pecked Stour on the cheek. "Would you really do it? Punish Mei-mei if we come down again?"

"You never know, William." He ruffled the boy's hair. "If I were you, I would play it safe and behave myself from now on. My patience isn't unlimited. In fact, I've been told I'm an unreasonable and unfeeling tyrant."

The boy looked puzzled, while Sukey blushed helplessly. She suddenly wished she had kept her mouth shut, and not only because you didn't win a man over by insulting him. She was beginning to suspect she had stumbled across a continuing problem here, not just a one-time infraction.

Ellie, meanwhile, was wrapping her arms around her father's neck. Between the girl's easy affection and the twinkle in her eyes, it was obvious she wasn't the least bit afraid. She repeated her brother's apology, then said coyly, "It's boring here, Papa. There's nothing to do. I'll kiss you good night if you let me go back to school."

"Then I'll miss being kissed." He stood, perching

her on his hip. "You know, Eleanor, I might be willing to invite Miss Stone to visit if only you would stop nagging me about her school."

"You would?" Ellie thought for a moment. "She's pretty, Papa. Don't you think so?"

"Yes. Very. But even if she were as pretty as you are, she still wouldn't be able to talk me into changing my mind."

Ellie kissed him soundly. "I know, Papa. Good night." She wiggled out of his arms and scooted over to Sukey, who had been reluctantly charmed by the exchange. After giving Sukey a conspiratorial look, she giggled good night and headed toward the steps.

Stour watched Mei-mei shepherd the children away, then said evenly, "My daughter doesn't seem to understand that the topic of her education is closed. I trust that you do. I'm willing to allow you to see her, but not if you discuss your school with her. As for your visit here tonight, it was a waste of your time to come. If I were going to accept your arguments, I would already have done so. Good evening, Miss Stone."

Sukey wanted to retort that she wasn't a six-year-old, to be manipulated by carrots and sticks, but the truth was, Stour held all the top cards here, including the right to show her the door. "You surprised me just now," she said instead. "You aren't really draconian at all, are you?—only at your wit's end." She thought about the way Ellie had slipped into her room each night. "I suppose they've been staying awake till all hours and coming down here repeatedly. You had no choice but to lay down the law. You're a good father, Taipan. Gentle but firm."

"While praise is never unpleasant, Miss Stone, I have no intention of discussing my actions with you.

Your opinions are a matter of complete indifference to me, including your opinion of how I rear my children. And now, if you'll excuse me, I have guests tonight. I should return to them."

He started toward the library, but Sukey simply followed along. "Yes, I heard. You're tasting sherries with your top assistants. Did I mention I have an exceptionally educated palate?"

He stopped dead. "You don't appear to have noticed that, twice now, I've asked you to leave my home."

"Actually, I did, even though you did it with such wonderful English subtlety that if I were less discerning, I would have missed it completely." She gave him a cheerful grin. "Tell me, Taipan, where did you learn the art of dismissing people? At Oxford?"

"No, Miss Stone. Where did you learn to be impudent and stubborn? At Oberlin?"

She was amused by his quick wit, even if *was* on the sarcastic side. "No. I learned it from my older brother—Tyson Stone, the famous American journalist. I assume you've heard of him."

"Heard of him and his wife, and also read some of their work. I can see the family resemblance. Like you, when they get hold of a topic, they're as polemical as religious fanatics and twice as tenacious. And now, I really must insist that you excuse me."

"All right, then, I'll go," Sukey said, "but first, I'll just pop into the library and say hello to my friends."

Stour went rigid, his eyes growing more glacial than ever. "I beg your pardon, Miss Stone? What did you just say?"

She had gone too far. He wasn't just incredulous and exasperated, but furious with her presumption. And Susannah Stone, who never, ever, used feminine wiles, found herself taking his arm and smiling sheepishly. "Please don't be angry with me, Lord Stour. My older brother reared me, you know, and he used to look at me that way when he was totally out of patience. On more than one occasion, he tossed me over his shoulder, marched me up to my room, and dumped me on the bed. I can see you'd like to do something similar, but I hope that you won't." Her smile faded. "I adore your children, so I would like us to be friends. Please let me stay and try to redeem myself."

He didn't reply, just gazed into space with an expression she couldn't decode. She released his arm. He wasn't angry anymore, that was obvious, but he wasn't receptive, either. After a few moments, he frowned deeply, and she decided he must be mulling the matter over.

A few more seconds went by. He focused on her face, looking straight into her eyes. And then the heat reappeared, so abruptly and powerfully that her heart began to thud and her stomach turned over. She was relieved when he looked away.

"Uh, of course you can stay." He turned to Tung. "Order an extra place at the table for Miss Stone."

The moment the words were out, he seemed to regret them. He looked astonished and befuddled, as if he couldn't believe what he had said. Indeed, Sukey couldn't, either. The last thing she had expected of the arrogant Lord Stour was that he would do such a complete about-face.

And then she realized what had changed his mind. He had invited her to stay because he wanted her in his bed, passionately and overpoweringly, but the feeling wasn't a natural one. The entities had put it in his head, to make him more amenable to her wishes.

The wretched man was bewitched.

Chapter 3

Luke Wyndham, the sixth earl of Stour, waited until Tung had withdrawn, then turned to Susannah Stone and silently offered her his arm. He was keenly aware of how tall and voluptuous she was, of her full breasts and her slender waist, of her wavy chestnut hair and her striking green eyes, but long years of practice enabled him to conceal his feelings behind a bland expression. His loins proved less amenable to such control, but the broadcloth coat he wore mercifully disguised the fact.

In truth, he felt as if a stranger had invaded his body and declared war on the calm and rational being who normally dwelled inside. Miss Stone was the most impertinent female, the most meddlesome female, the most maddening female he had ever encountered. Her letters about his daughter, which had badgered and belabored when they hadn't presumed to instruct, had been brazen enough, but to show up uninvited at his home was the height of insolence.

In London, the spawn of a common clerk wouldn't have dared take him to task for his actions. A half-educated female wouldn't have dared presume to instruct him about what was best for his own child. He should have ordered her to leave the moment he had discovered her intrusion.

But somehow, whenever he looked at her—really attended to her presence—a wave of desire surged through him, leaving him so hot and muddled that he lost all reason. Not only had he allowed her to stay, he had deigned to converse. And then, just when his inexplicable forbearance had run out—just when he had decided to eject her—he had found himself inviting her to dine. He had planned to study his assistants tonight, to assess whether any or all of them might be responsible for the losses at Burns, but instead he would be stuck with Miss Stone and her intolerable nagging for the rest of the evening.

He couldn't make sense of his behavior. Nothing like this had ever happened to him before, not even with Victoria, whom he had loved. The girl was pretty enough, he had conceded that, but he had met the greatest beauties and the most famous courtesans in England without responding this way. On the contrary, if there was anything he disliked, it was a female who tried to manipulate him with her charms—not that any had succeeded. His mistresses had given him more pleasure than he probably deserved, but all in all, he had found science to be far more thrilling than the delights of the flesh.

Miss Stone took his arm, smiling briefly but avoiding his eyes. Her look—her touch—went straight to his groin, but whatever else she was, she was no coquette. Her smile was too strained, her body too taut with discomfort. Her initial reaction had been the same, he recalled. She wasn't enjoying this battle any more than he was.

They started down the hall. A gentleman would have put her at ease with a pretty compliment or some blather about the weather, but Luke didn't say a word. He was never overtly impolite, but he could be aloof and intimidating when it suited his purpose. Even uncomfortable, Miss Stone had been hard to keep in line. Make her feel welcome, and the task would become downright taxing.

After all, he mused, her arrival tonight could be no accident. She must have known his top assistants would be here, and drinking freely. She probably hoped that the wine they had all consumed would make them garrulous enough to champion her cause.

But even if it didn't, their presence would act as a buffer. No matter how outrageous her arguments, Luke would lose face if he couldn't coolly defeat them—if he couldn't control both her and himself in front of his underlings. Of course, not for one moment did he doubt his ability to do so.

He escorted her into the library and smoothly released her. The room, a large one, was lined with bookcases containing thousands of finely bound volumes. Comfortable leather chairs sat in the center, as did a small settee that had become his favorite place to read. Bottles and glasses, most still partially full, were scattered on various tables. Two cases of wine were sitting on a sideboard under the center window—a shipment of six bottles each of four different blends of sherry.

Luke's assistants sprang to their feet and greeted Miss Stone effusively, especially Patrick Shaw, who praised her appearance in the most flowery of terms. Of course, that was only to be expected. Shaw's mother and Luke's father-in-law had been sister and brother, so Luke had been hearing about the man for years. They said he was the foremost ladykiller in the colony.

He was also the most covetous of Luke's position as taipan, though Robert Kilearn, the nephew of Jeremy Burns, ran him a close second. Both were in their late twenties, and both were partners in the firm. Though they weren't related, they looked so much alike—brown hair and eyes, medium height and build, pleasant but unremarkable features—that Luke had come to think of them as almost interchangeable.

Each was competent, but neither was a leader. Their personal codes of honor stopped at the point where profits could be made, but in Hong Kong, that was business as usual. They professed devotion to the firm, but Luke didn't presume that would translate into loyalty to him personally. Only a fool would have trusted men who resented his very existence.

Oddly, the one man he *was* inclined to trust, Kaiwing Douglas, was likely responsible for Miss Stone's visit here tonight. Luke assumed Douglas had mentioned the gathering to his sister Pearl, the McClures' amah, who had passed on the news to Miss Stone. He considered ordering the man to watch what he said to his family, then decided against it. Douglas was honest, intelligent, and well-connected, one of the best compradors in China. If Luke questioned his discretion or integrity, or interfered in his close relationship with his sisters, he might decide to go elsewhere. Luke preferred not to lose him.

He walked to the sideboard and poured himself a glass of sherry, the driest of the blends they were tasting tonight. Miss Stone was quizzing the men about their work, but Luke exhibited no interest in the conversation. He had noticed over the years that people interpreted his aloofness as obliviousness, believing him blind to the subtleties of social intercourse. In fact, however, he missed very little.

The talk turned to Miss Stone and her activities. After several minutes, Luke realized that, where he saw a presumptuous pest, albeit a desirable one, his assistants saw an excellent match. Not only was her brother a famous and influential journalist, when it came to investing, he had a touch even more golden than Luke's own. An utterly uncanny knack for picking silver stocks that proceeded to shoot up in value. An alliance with the sister of such a man would be highly advantageous.

As for Miss Stone, far from simpering and flirting as most females would have, she had erected a subtle but unmistakable barrier around her person. It was remarkable, really. Outwardly, she was perfectly friendly, yet there was something in her manner and tone that kept these men at a distance. Only Shaw had nerve enough to tease her.

Luke decided that her manner must relate to these particular males—that she was signaling that a suit would be rebuffed. And then he noticed that she was only moderately more relaxed with his three assistants, whom she had known for over a year, than she had been with him.

Perhaps it was something about men in general, then. She didn't like them. Didn't trust them. He picked up a bottle of the sweetest sherry. But not all men, apparently. She had seemed fond of Tung, and according to Alex McClure, regarded Alex almost as a brother.

Luke filled a glass halfway, then crossed the room. He had been the object of numerous furtive glances just now, undoubtedly because they were discussing Miss Stone's school. Nobody had mentioned the conflict over Eleanor's education, but Luke assumed the men were aware of it. Tung, who seemed to know everything that occurred on this island, had reported that all of Hong Kong was talking about the dispute. Simple logic would have told the men the reason for Miss Stone's intrusion.

He suggested they all sit down, then escorted her to a chair and handed her a glass of wine. The men were trying not to show it, but her assault on his home had amused them. They probably looked forward to a showdown, especially Shaw, who, as the first cousin of Luke's late wife, treated him in a more familiar fashion than the others.

Luke repressed a frown as he topped off his glass. Hong Kong was a nest of wagging, multilingual tongues, with the masters as bad as the servants. It galled him, but by tomorrow, the news of Miss Stone's visit would be common knowledge, even if he gave orders to the contrary. And if voices were raised—if an argument ensued—the exchange would be repeated verbatim, from the stalls of the Chinese bazaars of Taipingshan to the cribs of the brothels in Happy Valley.

He dropped onto the settee, his mind drifting to his experiences in London. His years there had accustomed him to gossip. He had thought himself inured even to the most scurrilous rumors. But in England, his high birth and family connections had enabled him to respond with stony silence and have it accepted as forceful denial. People might have talked behind his back, but nobody had challenged his authority. Nobody had flouted his wishes.

Hong Kong, however, made no such concessions to his breeding. The only god here was money, and Luke had neither the wealth nor the power to control anyone but his own underlings. His new title, far from helping, had only made matters worse, since people had added yet another name to the list of his putative victims. The truth might have stemmed the flow of gossip, but his whole being rebelled against discussing the most intimate details of his life with strangers. The fact was, he wasn't blameless in all those deaths. There were things in his past that filled him with shame and regret, and some were too heinous to speak of.

He cleared his throat. In addition to everything else, this wretched island was downright unhealthy. He was never ill at home, but he had been under the weather ever since his arrival here. He suddenly longed for the relations who had trusted him, the friends who had discussed science with him, and the fiery and knowing mistress whose bed he had so often shared. The sooner he set Burns and Company to rights and left this colony, the better.

He sipped his wine and forced himself to attend to the conversation, taking renewed interest when Shaw asked Miss Stone how she was enjoying her sherry. In reply, she took a hesitant sip and licked her lips. Every male eye was drawn to her mouth—her full, very sensuous mouth. But even as Luke's manhood stirred, he wondered if the gesture could be nervous rather than seductive. After all, a discussion about wine would reveal the true extent of her knowledge. Perhaps her palate was no more educated than a shopgirl's.

After all the aggravation she had caused him, he relished the possibility of taking her down a peg. "Yes, Miss Stone, do give us your opinion. The producer has offered us an exclusive marketing agreement in Asia in return for charging him a lower fee than normal to ship and distribute, so we'll only make money if we sell—" He looked at Kilearn, who was his chief financial man. "What percentage was it again? Seventy?"

Kilearn nodded. "Yes, Lord Stour. That would be a conservative estimate."

"If we sell at least seventy percent of his output. Tell me, would you serve that particular sherry in your home?"

Sukey put down her glass, looking at Stour from under her lashes to gauge his intentions. He had ignored her for the past twenty minutes and hadn't wanted her here in the first place, so perhaps he was testing her expertise, hoping to catch her in an embarrassing lie. On the other hand, if the wine had mellowed him into a more charitable frame of mind, he might have a genuine interest in her opinion. By all accounts, the man did put business first.

Unfortunately, he wore an expression a poker player might have envied. "Perhaps," she finally replied. "It's a little bi—" She stopped, vexed with herself. Bitter was the wrong term. "Uh, a little dry, but pleasant enough."

"Then you would prefer something sweeter?"

She nodded. "Yes. I would."

He raised his eyebrows. "How surprising—for a fellow connoisseur of wine, that is. You're drinking the sweetest sherry they make. Personally, I found it distastefully sugary. But of course, women have different tastes than men, and females *are* an important segment of our market. What about the brandy content? The balance? Does it suit you?"

Sukey flushed. Stour was obviously no more mellow than a ferret. His only goal was to browbeat her into mortified and permanent silence, but if he thought she was so easily cowed as that, he had another think coming.

"You know the answer to that as well as I do, Taipan. I haven't a clue." She looked at his assistants, all of whom were smiling. "I suppose I should explain. Out in the foyer, I claimed I was something of an enophile—"

The smiles became stifled chuckles. "Then you must do your tasting in private," Shaw drawled, "because in all the evenings I've spent with you, I've never seen you drink more than half a glass of wine."

She laughed. "All right, then, you've caught me in a fib, but I was desperate to angle my way in tonight, and it was the only way I could think to do it." She gazed at Stour with artless sincerity. "You know, Taipan, many of your potential customers will be as ignorant about sherry as I am. Perhaps it would be a good idea to carry something we would enjoy—even if it's more intolerably sweet than this is."

She was skilled at verbal fencing, Luke thought. Shrewd enough to know when to retreat, clever enough to do it with a dash of charm, and tough enough to add some vinegar into the brew. But if she was good, he was better. "This producer doesn't offer anything sweeter, but I'm not surprised you would think that he should. You *are* an American, and it's a uniquely democratic notion, the concept of purveying something inferior in order to please an audience of philistines. In England, and at Burns, we hold ourselves to a higher standard. We believe we should endeavor to elevate the public's tastes, not lower our own and thereby increase the amount of mediocrity in the world."

Sukey was speechless at first, then incredulous. Only an autocrat like Stour would come up with such pretentious, imperious drivel. "The criterion being your own preferences, I assume. After all, who could be more discriminating than a nobleman? More knowledgeable than a fellow at Oxford? Plato's ideal of a philosopher-king must hold a great appeal for you,

Taipan. Tell me, when you envision the perfect world, do you see yourself occupying that lofty position?''

Never in Luke's life had a female attacked him with political theory, but he was too offended by her words to give any credit to the education that had produced them. "No, Miss Stone. I agree with Lord Chatham that unlimited power is where laws end and tyranny begins. I don't for a moment believe myself capable of overcoming that problem, but if I lack the wisdom for the office, at least I possess the manners. Unlike you, I would never be so discourteous as to push my way into a stranger's home, accept his hospitality, and then fling sarcasm at his head.''

Sukey bit her lip in chagrin. She had sworn she wouldn't lose her temper tonight, but Stour was like a human burr. He burrowed under your defenses, then clung and rubbed till he drove you mad. Most provoking of all, he hadn't even given her the satisfaction of being a rigid authoritarian. Instead, he quoted Pitt at her, the British statesman most sympathetic to American grievances before the revolution.

She shifted in her seat, acutely aware of how quiet the room had become. She would have to eat humble pie—retaliation would only hamper her cause—but she would resent every bitter bite. Stour was wrong about his manners. He had the polish of a gentleman, she couldn't deny that, but under the surface, where it really counted, lurked the instincts of a cad.

She forced a pleasant expression onto her face. *Help me get the words out without choking*, she thought to the entities. *Make Stour receptive. A little guilt wouldn't hurt him, either.* "Please accept my apologies," she said stiffly. "I'm afraid I interpreted your words as an insult to me and my country, but an admirer of William Pitt would hardly have intended them that way. In any event, it was wrong of me to have responded in such a personal fashion. That was no way to repay you for allowing me into your home and inviting me to dine.''

Luke suppressed a smile. Susannah Stone looked as if she had swallowed a rancid lemon. The sense of triumph he felt was utterly unprecedented. Like any sane man, he preferred winning to losing, but he had never before derived any pleasure from besting a female. It was the natural order of things, and thus only to be expected.

Still, he was dealing with an unusual woman. No matter how thoroughly she had retreated, her surrender had been reluctant in the extreme, and he wanted to make sure his victory stuck. "You're correct on all counts. Your apology was long overdue. Your actions, both tonight and for the past few weeks, have been intrusive and disrespectful. If you persist in such behavior, you won't be admitted here again, much less invited to stay. And you did misinterpret my comment just now. It wasn't an insult, but an objective observation. I find many things to admire in your country, but a support for excellence isn't among them. You Americans extol the taste and good sense of the common man to such a high degree that one would think that a lack of breeding and an inferior education were attributes all of us should strive for.''

Sukey's resentment flared, then blazed out of control. She squared her shoulders, wondering where the blasted entities were when she really needed them. ''Perhaps Americans and Englishmen have different notions of what constitutes good breeding, then. Where I come from, a gentleman doesn't deliberately humiliate a woman, and he doesn't provoke her into losing her temper, either. When he receives an apology, he doesn't belabor the point with a lecture, but accepts it graciously.''

Stour sat motionless, stoically holding his wine. Sukey had learned by now that the angrier he was, the colder he became, and his eyes were as frosty as a Sierra winter. She didn't care. *Someone* had to set the man straight. ''As for education, we Americans were founding schools back in the 1600s—and unlike the English ones, those schools were for all of our children, not just the rich and privileged. That's something you're only just getting around to in your country. In fact, Taipan, if you truly believed in universal public education, you never would have removed your daughter from my school. You would agree that all children, even one as young as Ellie, have a hunger for knowledge, and you would feed that hunger. Instead, you keep her locked away in this house, intellectually starving to death.''

Luke set down his glass, but only because if he had continued to hold it, he might have gripped it so hard that it shattered. In his thirty-odd years, no female had dared speak to him that way.

As he straightened, his gaze swept the room, reminding him of the presence of his three assistants. He longed to order the chit out of his sight, but couldn't; it would make him look like an impotent fool, incapable of controlling what transpired in his own home. God knew he was beginning to feel like one.

He sought the girl's eyes, outwardly glacial but inwardly seething. Every other female he knew would have been quaking and contrite after such an outrageous display of temper, but Miss Stone, while tense, appeared totally unrepentant. She was wise to remain a spinster, he decided, because given her continual misconduct, few husbands would have resisted the urge to take a frequent hand to her bottom.

And then she met his gaze, and it happened once again. He abruptly caught fire. He remembered her words in the hall and had a sudden vision of Tyson Stone flinging her over his shoulder, marching her upstairs, and tossing her on her bed. Stone, as her brother, would have stalked back out, slamming the door behind him, but Luke pictured himself staying . . . pinning her under his body . . . touching and kissing her until she was clinging to him and pleading for release . . . pleasuring her with a swift, fierce passion that left her reeling and submissive.

She looked away. Heat rose up his neck, and he quickly did the same. He had never made love in anger; he had never even felt the urge. He had never seen courting as a game, with conquest as the ultimate goal. He was rational and civilized, wasn't he? So why would he desire a girl who insulted and defied him? Why would he want to dominate her in the most primitive way imaginable? He felt humiliated, perturbed, and very bewildered.

Those were hardly emotions he enjoyed, but at least they were less disturbing than rage or lust. For a trained scientist and a seasoned campaigner, he realized, he had been singularly stupid. He had played to Miss Stone's strengths—her persistence, brazenness, and glibness—but to succeed in battle, you had to exploit your enemy's weaknesses.

He had noted two this evening. She had such an inflated notion of her own consequence that presumed slights brought on fits of temper, and she was uneasy around males, especially around him. He lazily got up, then glanced around the room. His assistants were riveted but uneasy. In his two weeks here, he had never revealed his feelings so clearly. If the men had learned anything in those two weeks, it was that he would never let conduct such as Miss Stone's pass.

As for the lady herself, her back was straight, her chin was high, and her mouth was tight with disapproval, but her cheeks were also flushed, and her hands were clamped together in her lap, twisting nervously.

He smiled wryly. "You gentlemen know Miss Stone better than I do. Tell me, is she always this difficult?"

A sigh of relief whispered through the library. "Not at all," Shaw replied. "She's generally the most agreeable of females, Stour. To keep her that way, all you have to do is give her what she wants, and since what she wants is invariably reasonable, that's an easy and delightful task."

Her expression softened. "Thank you, Mr. Shaw. That was very gallant of you."

Luke ignored her. "Invariably? Then she's never unreasonable? Always right? Perfect, in short?"

"I've never claimed to be perfect, but I do listen to opposing arguments." Her chin rose a fraction higher. "Unlike you, Taipan."

Once again, he pretended not to hear. "Douglas? Kilearn? Give me your thoughts. What sort of woman am I dealing with?"

Kai-wing Douglas permitted himself a slight smile. "A beautiful and intelligent one, Lord Stour. If you wish further information, I suggest you consult Mr. McClure. He knows her far better than we do."

Luke shook his head. "*Too* much better, I'm afraid. He spoke of her at length during our voyage, but in terms an older brother might use. While McClure's comments were probably germane to the social sphere, Miss Stone came here to discuss a professional concern. You've described her attributes as a friend, gentlemen, but I was interested in her qualities as a teacher. One looks for prudence in an educator. Decorum. Rectitude.''

"If those are the traits you find most important, Ellie and William will be stifled and very unhappy,'' she stated. "A teacher should be knowledgeable. Enthusiastic. Creative. Fond of children.''

It wasn't a bad list, Luke thought, but he continued to ignore her. "Kilearn? You're a good judge of character. Do you believe she possesses those qualities?''

Kilearn looked confused. "Uh, which set, Lord Stour?''

"I wasn't aware that more than one was under discussion,'' Luke said mildly.

Miss Stone's eyes narrowed. "I refuse to be treated as if I'm not present, Taipan. If you have concerns about my qualifications as a teacher, you should address them directly to me, not to three gentlemen who have never set foot in my classroom.''

He finally looked at her, visibly astonished. "You mean you would give yourself anything less than a glowing recommendation?''

The question left her gaping in outrage, but not for long. Before he could savor the success of his squelch, she said curtly, "If you're asking whether my opinion of my proficiency as a teacher is as high as your opinion of your ability as a taipan, then the answer is no. I'm not nearly that arrogant. Unlike you, I know I make mistakes.''

He stiffened at the insult, but kept his temper in check and smiled indulgently. After all, if you grabbed a tigress by the tail, you had to expect to get clawed. "Confidence isn't the same as arrogance. I don't bother displaying false modesty about my accomplishments. They're exceptional and everyone knows it.

From what I've seen of you, you're no more diffident than I am. On the contrary, you're prone to exaggerate. So if *you* don't consider yourself exceptional—"

"I didn't say that. And I don't exaggerate."

"—what rating would you give yourself? As a teacher, that is, not as a wine expert—though you're correct about not exaggerating, at least in regard to that particular claim. You didn't. You simply lied."

She glared at him. "Fibbed a little, and only because you were so blasted mulish about talking to me that you left me no choice. The fact is, my students love coming to my school. They love learning. Every single one is educationally advanced for her years. But I wouldn't expect you to take *my* word for it, Taipan. Why don't you talk to their parents? They'll confirm every statement I've made."

Luke didn't care to reply to that suggestion, at least not in front of his subordinates. The topic was too personal. He walked to the sideboard, inwardly grimacing. On the other hand, there were no secrets in this colony, especially in regard to him, and it was pointless to pretend otherwise.

"I've heard as much of their opinions as I care to. You appear to have forgotten why I withdrew my daughter in the first place." He picked up a corkscrew, then continued crisply, "Let's have a final round of tasting before we dine, gentlemen. I would like to give our producer an estimate of what amount of each sherry we'll likely order. Miss Stone? If you would join me? I've some additional questions for you, but I can ask them while we sample the wine."

Sukey warily crossed the room. Stour was up to something, but what? Retaliation for how sharply she had spoken? She winced at the unruliness of her tongue. She knew she had a temper—it was her worst fault—but nobody had ever spurred it the way Stour had. He possessed an uncommon talent for getting under her skin.

And she under his, she acknowledged, though it didn't take much to set a man off when he was that tyrannical and self-important. Indeed, she had seldom seen a gentleman so incensed, so why hadn't he summoned a servant to eject her? Or even tossed her over his shoulder as Ty so often had and done the job himself?

And that burning look he had given her . . . She flushed as she joined him at the sideboard, where he was calmly uncorking wine. It must have been the spell, she thought. It had sliced through his fury and distracted him from exploding.

But even if it had saved her, she decided, she would have to reverse it. He might be straitlaced, and normally too refined to make advances to an innocent female, but there was no telling how he might act if the entities got him in thrall. Even worse, there was no telling how she might respond.

True, she disliked him, but he was inordinately handsome and undeniably brilliant. When he'd bantered with his children in the foyer, she had felt an unnerving tug of attraction. As careful as she was around men, her defenses weren't impregnable. If the past was any guide, deep down, she was too passionate for her own good. If Stour sought to charm her rather than command her . . .

But he wouldn't, she suddenly realized. Cajolery was alien to his nature. Instead, he would try to control her by mocking her views and ordering her about, and she would have no difficulty resisting *that*. The entities' exertions were likely the only thing keeping him civil, so it would be best to leave the spell in place.

She stood silently by his side as he finished with the wine. "Miss Stone, if you would help me—" Their eyes met, then held. "With some, uh, some pedagogical research. In the cataloguer's office. If you gentlemen would excuse us . . ."

He turned away, looking disoriented. The dratted entities were at it again, she realized, prodding him into God only knew what. "We'll be back . . . in a short while," he finished slowly. "In the meantime, please help yourselves to more sherry, and, uh, continue with your tasting. Miss Stone? If you would come this way?"

Sukey followed him across the room, resisting the urge to wipe her palms down the sides of her dress. When Jeremy was taipan, she had used this library often, for work as well as for pleasure. The cataloguer's office was at the far end, through a small door. It was quiet and private, the perfect place to peruse the list of holdings—or to conduct an intimate conversation—but it wasn't so much a room as a closet. The desk, the chair, and the card files took up almost all the available space. To be sequestered there with Stour, practically rubbing up against him . . .

She gave a disgusted shake of her head. The man was a gentleman, and her friends were only twenty feet away. He had given her the perfect opening to talk about Ellie, and only a fool wouldn't take advantage of it. And he admired Pitt, so his mind might be more open about education than she had assumed.

Then again, the entities were in a devilish mood tonight. They were making Stour react in ways that were foreign to his nature. She glanced at him—tall, imposing, and coldly handsome—and an uneasy quiver snaked down her spine.

Chapter 4

Luke lit the lamp in the cataloguer's office, quashing the urge to pull a handkerchief out of his pocket and swipe it across his brow. Disaster had struck from nowhere, and he couldn't fathom how. He'd had Miss Stone exactly where he had wanted, in such a high state of pique that her poise had been destroyed, and had planned to conduct a crushing interrogation next—to intimidate her with his odious male presence and defeat her with the force of his logic. But instead some idiocy about pedagogical research had spouted from his mouth. And he had directed her into this dim and intimate office.

He closed the door to ensure privacy, reminding himself he was a scientist, and thus skilled at analyzing human behavior, even his own. The fact was, at least three times tonight, something had sent him reeling out of control. He had said and done things he hadn't intended, always to the benefit of Miss Stone. On some primitive and irrational level, he was so powerfully attracted to the girl that his judgment and behavior had been affected.

Even now, he could feel her eyes on his back, setting his nerves on edge. He was sure of very little just then, but he knew better than to meet her stare. If there was any saving grace to this situation, it was that these bizarre lapses seemed to occur only when he was regarding her very intently. Once he looked away, he was able to collect himself. Had he believed in magic, he might have assumed she could bewitch him with the force of her gaze.

As a scientist, however, he knew that prolonged celibacy was likely the cause of his spells. He needed a mistress, that was all, a soft and submissive creature who would delight in his company and see to his needs. He decided to attend to the matter as soon as he had a few spare hours.

In the meantime, he had Miss Stone to contend with, and she hadn't a tractable bone in her body. If he was to rid himself of her nagging, he would have to keep his eyes to himself and his temper under control, because otherwise, he might do something even stupider than ushering her into a room so tiny he could barely take a step without bumping into her. That prattle about pedagogy . . . He grimaced in disgust. If he couldn't back it up with a plausible explanation, he was going to look like a demented dolt.

He turned around, thinking furiously. McClure had once mentioned that he envied Luke this library, which contained books in nearly a dozen languages and was one of the finest in Asia. Given McClure's friendship with Jeremy Burns, it was logical to assume that he and his family had used it at will. And since his family included Miss Stone . . .

He took a quick, safe look at her. She was standing with her back to the endmost cabinet of file cards, her body at rigid attention and her jaw locked tight. For whatever reason—her dislike of men or of him personally—she was as uneasy as he was.

"I understand from Mr. McClure that you're familiar with the holdings here," he remarked. "I assume we own books about education, both practical and theoretical. If there are titles you particularly admire, please pull out the cards and leave them on the desk."

Several seconds passed before she replied. "Are you telling me you're willing to read the books?"

"Yes, when I have the time." And so he would, because he always kept his word, but his inspection would be as cursory as he could make it. "I'll have the librarian retrieve the volumes the next time he comes in."

"That would be on Wednesday," she said. "Normally, Father Alvares works here only that one day, but he would fetch the books tomorrow morning if you asked him to. Just send him down a note."

She knew more about the workings of this house than Luke did. He had met Alvares only once, when he had enrolled his son in the priest's school. The building was inside the Burns complex, next to the cottage Alvares shared with his grown niece.

He swallowed his annoyance at being told what to do. "I'll instruct Tung to see to it, Miss Stone."

"And you'll keep an open mind? Reconsider your decision about Ellie in light of the ideas the books present?"

Her use of the name "Ellie" was beginning to grate on him. She should refer to his daughter as Lady Eleanor. He didn't correct her, though, because an argument would have ensued. And one little slip—one inadvertent glare—could make his passions ignite, obliterating his common sense.

"Naturally," he replied evenly. "As you might have heard, I was a teacher myself once, at Oxford. Though you've imputed more faults to me than I could possibly enumerate, I've never claimed to be omniscient. I do understand that tutoring young men may be different from instructing little girls, so I propose to educate myself about the subject." He forced a smile. "With your guidance, of course."

Sukey nodded, then sidled to the initial cabinet of cards. Stour was good at disguising his emotions, but she was learning to see beneath the facade. Under his calm tone and bland smile, he was edgy and irritated.

To her relief, he strolled to the desk, so that instead of looming almost atop her, he was several yards away. She opened the first drawer of cards and began to thumb through them, though she suspected it was a waste of her time.

After all, Stour never would have come in here if the entities hadn't prodded him into it, and then to offer to review his position from out of nowhere, after weeks of rigid refusals . . . His change of heart had been much too sudden. Either he was lying baldly or his mind was still addled, and in neither case would he read the books. As matters stood now, he would never return Ellie to her school.

As she pulled out the cards she wanted, she could feel him standing behind her, radiating displeasure and impatience. Unnerved, she wanted nothing so much as to finish the job and flee, but she hadn't come this far only to scurry away like a mouse. The least she could do was stick to her original plan and try to reason with him.

"In my years as a teacher, I've found that people tend to underestimate the capabilities of young children," she began, riffling through the G's. "Even girls as young as five or six are able to do more than sing, draw, and play games, Taipan. Even more important, they're eager to. They're like dry little sponges, ready to sop up knowledge about the world. I know from my own experience that they can start to read, to write, and to solve simple mathematical problems by that age. I've discussed geography and history with them, and I've taught them a surprising amount of Latin. I've even demonstrated some of the basics of science by means of nature walks and elementary experiments.''

She removed another card, then glanced over her shoulder to learn whether the mention of science might have engendered any enthusiasm in her listener. It hadn't; he was leaning against the desk with his arms folded across his chest and a blank expression on his face. Frustrated by his machinelike demeanor, she turned on her heel, walked to the desk, and dropped the group of cards beside the lamp.

He didn't move, not a whit. She found it disturbing to have him so close—her pulses were throbbing with a disconcerting mixture of anxiety and sensual awareness—but she held her ground. "I find it difficult to speak to someone when nothing comes back the other way. If you're as openminded as you claim—"

"I try to be. I *am* listening, Miss Stone."

Luke stared into the middle distance. It was bad enough that he was trapped in this stifling room, he thought, forced to endure Miss Stone's pronouncements, but to be castigated for failing to reply . . . What did she expect him to do, question her like a disciple at the feet of a master? The idea was ludicrous.

She muttered something to herself, then turned away. Relief mingled with his irritation. His manhood had stirred the instant she had glanced at him, so that he'd had to fight off the urge to touch her as she had stood within reach. It was safer to have her back at the files.

Unfortunately, she resumed her lecture with renewed fervor, plucking out cards all the while. He shifted position, seeking to ease the discomfort of his aching erection, but it didn't help. He stared at the floor, and instead of viewing wood, he saw the gentle flare of a hip, the curve of a naked buttock, the arch of a back in the act of making love . . . He cursed under his breath. Procuring a mistress moved higher on his list of priorities.

Her yammering washed over him like an interminable succession of waves. And then the bubbling enthusiasm in her voice broke through his annoyance, capturing and holding him, and he found himself attending to her words.

". . . and it was the most amazing discovery. Everyone so sure she was slow, even her parents, when she was only hard of hearing! So I spoke loudly into her ear whenever I taught her, and I learned I had a little marvel on my hands." She laughed in pure delight. "My poor voice. I was hoarse at the end of each week, but within a year, I'd caught her up to the others. It was my most thrilling experience as a teacher. I was able to save that child, to give her back her life. It was humbling. It's not often that we're given the opportunity to do the Lord's work."

She pulled out a card, then closed the final drawer and turned around. "And your daughter . . . She's the brightest little girl I've ever instructed. She has a grand future ahead of her. She could be anything—a physician, an attorney, even a scientist like yourself. Surely you can see why I have to have her back. She's a darling child, and during our month together, I grew extremely attached to her, but it's her intelligence and creativity that drove me here tonight. She's like an exquisite bud, Lord Stour. I have the skill to give her the challenge and stimulation she needs to burst into full bloom, but if she's stuck here all day with Mei-mei . . . The girl is very sweet, but Ellie will wither under her care.''

Luke stood motionless, his eyes on Miss Stone's chin because he didn't dare look any higher. He was filled with such mixed emotions that, for one of the few times in his life, he was at a loss for words. He had enjoyed hearing his child praised in such glowing terms, but Eleanor was his daughter, not his son, and society frowned upon women who lived the lives of men. Labeled them eccentrics or freaks. Gossiped about them and snubbed them.

Having endured a bellyful of such treatment for his own lack of conformity, he wasn't about to expose his cherished daughter to anything similar. Eleanor would be happiest as a wife and mother. If she needed a creative outlet, she could write or paint, the way Penny did.

He pondered the subject further. Never in history had women excelled at pursuits such as medicine or science. Obviously they lacked the capacity for it. Their abilities, such as they were, lay in other directions. When one came right down to it, the notion of a female Lister or Newton was outlandish. Absolute rubbish.

What mattered most of all, though, was that Eleanor was *his* flesh and blood, not Susannah Stone's. *He* would rear her and mold her. *He* would determine her future. He picked up the cards by the lamp, then held out his hand. ''If I might see the others . . . ?''

Sukey stared at Stour's outstretched fingers with a mixture of bewilderment and dismay. He had appeared to take an interest in her words. Indeed, she could have sworn he was pleased by the notion of his posterity achieving great things. But instead of the favorable response she had anticipated, he had delivered a request so cold that she might never have spoken at all.

She opened her mouth to object, remembered how stubborn he was, and realized it could take days before he saw reason. Besides, he was so prickly, one never knew what might set him off, and she *had* pressed him rather vigorously just now. It couldn't hurt to butter him up a little. Use his title now and then and confess to her sins.

She closed the distance between them and handed him the cards. "I know I intruded on your evening, Lord Stour. Though I was prompted by my concern for your daughter, perhaps I was overly bold. If I've interfered with your plans, I apologize. I hope I haven't annoyed you beyond redemption. It was gracious of you to hear me out and generous of you to offer to do some reading."

"For once, Miss Stone, we're in complete agreement." He flipped through the cards, too quickly to do more than scan the entries. "The demands on my time have been extremely heavy of late, and I don't expect relief any time soon. You've recommended eleven books, which is far too many for me to review. Select the three you most wish me to inspect, and I'll endeavor to give you my decision by Christmas."

"By Christmas?" she repeated unhappily. It was only November 10. "But Lord Stour—"

"By Christmas, Miss Stone. That's the best I can do."

"But children forget so quickly, and by January—"

"And learn again just as rapidly." He handed back the cards. "The subject is closed."

Not to Sukey, it wasn't. Stour's dictum was as unfeeling as it was unreasonable. "And what about Ellie's wishes? Tung told me about her tantrums. If you deny her, she'll be restless and unhappy, and—"

"My daughter's emotions are my concern, not

yours, madam," he said icily, "and her name is Lady Eleanor."

Sukey had heard that tone before, out in the hallway. Stour was enraged. She should have held her tongue, she supposed, but there was something about the way he had stood there, barking interruptions while refusing her even the courtesy of a direct look, that had spurred her on.

Still seething, she began to look through the cards. She eliminated five titles, then started again. Stour, meanwhile, was staring at his toes, so coldly it was a wonder they didn't succumb to frostbite.

It wasn't until Sukey was down to four books, debating which was the least important, that she realized how odd his behavior was. A glare from Stour was enough to collapse the stiffest of spines, and he knew it. It didn't make sense that he would relinquish such a potent weapon for the sake of a mere snub.

She nibbled her lip, reviewing the evening's events. Now that she thought of it, he had been much more vulnerable to the entities' prodding—and to her own wishes—when they had met each other's eyes. He must have noticed it, too. While he couldn't possibly have understood the reason for his own weakness, he must have resolved to avoid the trigger.

Her heart began to race. Did she dare deliberately entice him to look at her? She, who never even flirted? Who despised playing the fragile female?

She straightened. Dammit, where was her blasted gumption? The entities had opened a path to victory, and she had to take it. A child's future was at stake.

She swallowed hard and reminded herself that nothing could happen to her with her friends outside. "Lord Stour?" She mimicked the soft, husky voice she had heard other women use when they wanted something from a man who desired them. "I seem to have a problem here."

His only response was a low grunt that she interpreted as an order to proceed.

She injected a scolding pout into her voice. "It's hard to confide in a man who won't even look at you, Taipan. Is there something displeasing about my form? Repugnant about my face?"

Luke shifted his weight. He knew what the girl was doing—trying to cajole him into meeting her eyes. If he had ever doubted that she knew the power she could wield, he no longer did. He raised his chin and stared at her, his jaw clenched and his eyes shuttered. He hated the loss of control he immediately experienced, but she had issued a challenge only a coward would have refused.

Despite his best effort to prevent it, a wave of desire slashed through him. He stepped forward, but she quickly retreated. He wanted to keep going—to trap her against the files, to trail his fingers down her body, to slip his tongue between her lips and taste her mouth—but he ruthlessly suppressed the urge. He wasn't going to lose this battle again.

"I'm not interested . . ." he began, and then stopped. His hands curled into fists at his sides. For the fourth time that evening, he felt muddled. Feverish. Overwhelmed.

Sukey had the sense she was looking at a man who was tottering at the edge of a pit, trying desperately not to fall in. "Send your daughter back to my school," she said rapidly, "and I promise to protect her. Nobody will hurt her feelings or even speak about the past. She'll be busy and happy. I give you my word."

"I don't . . . Perhaps . . ." The request made sense,

Luke thought, but for some reason, he found himself resisting it. Confused, he closed his eyes and felt his head begin to clear.

Intense anger surged through him. Back in his youth, he had had his fill of being a puppet. First his father, then his mother, then his father-in-law . . . Now, nobody pulled his strings. Only fools even tried.

He opened his eyes. This girl was no fool, yet *she* had tried, and come perilously close to succeeding. How? His abstinence couldn't explain it. He had gone without a woman before, for even longer periods. He had *wanted* a woman before, even more profoundly. And yet never had he proven so vulnerable to feminine wiles.

Then the answer finally came, and his fury gave way to amazement. It was the scientist in him, he supposed, forever analyzing things, forever enthralled by new knowledge. He was dealing with an accomplished magician, it seemed. She needed to learn just how dangerous her quarry could be.

Beginning to enjoy himself, he gave her a stony look and removed the cards from her hand. Visibly unnerved, she backed further away, wincing when she bumped into the files.

"I believe I'll add a book about hypnotic trances to the list," he said dryly. "When I have the time, we can practice together. A trick like yours would be an invaluable business tool." He glanced through the cards. "Hmm. Four books. Do you have a problem with simple counting, Miss Stone?"

Sukey cleared her throat, which was suddenly so dry she would have drunk anything to moisten it, even Stour's wretched sherry. Him and his blasted mockery . . . She should have known he would prove too willful to control. And now that he knew she had deliberately tried to manipulate him, he was hell-bent on revenge.

"Uh, no," she croaked. "It's just—I couldn't seem to get it down to three."

"More books will require more time." He smiled coolly. "You're the teacher. I've told you my rate of reading. Why don't you tell *me* exactly when I'll finish?"

"When you'll—? Oh. I see." He had posed her a mathematical problem. She concentrated on calculating the answer. If he could read three books by Christmas, which was—twenty plus twenty-five—forty-five days away, divided by three equalled fifteen days each, times four books came to sixty days in all . . . "On, uh, on January ninth, but—"

"Yes. Precisely."

"But the new term will have begun, Lord Stour. Couldn't you just—" She cut herself off. Why waste her breath? He wasn't going to bend.

"Couldn't I what, Miss Stone? Skip judiciously, perhaps? Give you an answer by the first of the year?" He paused. "I suppose I might be willing to do that."

She licked her lips, wondering what price he would exact. "Uh, I would be very grateful."

The sight of her tongue had the usual effect on Luke, but he was resigned to it by now. She was lovely and sensuous, and a man didn't have to be spellbound to notice it. Still, he was curious about what was real and what was only induced.

He strolled over to her. "I do have a question before we go. It's very clear that you're not interested in my attentions. In fact, you seem to be afraid of me. Isn't that so?"

She blushed. "I don't—of course not. You're a gentleman. You're Alex's friend. You would never do anything improper."

"Not normally, but every time you mesmerize me to try to control me, you complicate the issue by making me desire you. Why, Miss Stone? Given your dislike of me, that would seem to be self-defeating."

She pressed herself against the files. "You're standing too close. I want you to move away."

Ignoring her, he tucked a finger under her chin, stared straight at her, and felt his passions ignite. For once, he didn't try to repress them, but let her see exactly how much he wanted her. It was the act of a cad, he supposed, but he needed to show her that further interference—further insolence—would simply not be tolerated. "You haven't answered my question, Miss Stone."

Sukey had seen that same unbridled look during the assault, and it frightened her. She went from crimson to ashen in seconds. "It's because—because I don't seem to be able to help it. I can't do one without the other."

"Then might I suggest that, in future, you don't do either one?"

She took a quick, unsteady breath. "I won't."

"Good." Stour released her and backed away. "You look tired, Miss Stone. Perhaps you should go home."

Sukey was more than willing. She was less uneasy now that Stour had removed his hand, but his company was as objectionable as ever. Besides, she would accomplish nothing more tonight. "Yes. You're probably right."

"About my daughter . . . If I decide to let you visit, you'll receive a note stating the date and time. See that you follow it exactly. If you mention your school, you'll never be asked here again. Is that clear?"

"Yes." Did he think her a dunce?

"Otherwise, you're not to enter this house again, or even to write to me. Is *that* clear?"

She felt a stir of resentment. It was bad enough to have fallen so short of her goal, but to be bullied this way . . . "Abundantly, my lord," she said crisply.

"I thought we'd established that sarcasm doesn't become you." Stour opened the door and snuffed the lamp. "And here I was feeling guilty about denying you access to this library, which I gather you were accustomed to using whenever you pleased. Of course, it's possible I could be persuaded to reverse my decision, given the proper sort of request."

Not only bullied, Sukey thought irately, but taunted about her defeat. He wanted meekness from her, abject servility, but he wasn't going to get it. If she needed books, she would have Alvares fetch them.

Luke took her arm, carefully masking the amusement he felt. Miss Stone seemed incensed enough to explode, but she didn't dare. She had too much to lose by offending him. "Too stubborn to ask nicely, hmm?"

She glared at him. "A gentleman wouldn't require me to plead. He would offer freely."

He finally grinned. "Obviously you're wrong, my dear, because my manners are flawless. Allow me to escort you to the door."

Sukey quashed the urge to snap that she would find her own way out and let him lead her along. Back in the library, he tugged on the bell to summon a servant, then informed his underlings that Miss Stone was weary after a long week at school and had decided not to stay.

Stour instructed a servant to have her carriage brought around. They started down the hall, entering the foyer to find Jade Douglas coming down the stairs.

At twenty-eight, she was the middle Douglas sibling, two years younger than Kai-wing and four years older than Pearl.

Like Sukey, Jade owned her own business, a shop where she sold the cosmetic and medical potions she manufactured. Sukey wasn't as close to Jade as to Pearl and Kai—Jade was more reserved than her siblings and, ironically, less comfortable around foreigners—but she still felt a certain bond. They were both independent-minded females in a world ruled by men.

"I felt the need to walk," she explained to Stour, "so I decided to pay a visit to my cousin Mei-mei. I hope that was all right."

He released Sukey and smiled gently at Jade. "Of course, Miss Douglas. As I've told you, you're always welcome here, as are your two fine sons."

Sukey was relieved that some small trace of gallantry flowed in the man's veins. Jade had suffered a terrible betrayal at the hands of Jeremy Burns, and it showed in her drawn face and the increasing looseness of her clothing. According to Alex, Jeremy's wife had hated Hong Kong from the moment they had first arrived here. After two years, she had returned to England with their children, enrolling their son at Eton. Far from being heartbroken, Jeremy had lost little time in seducing the exotic and beautiful Jade Douglas, then seventeen, and setting her up in a house about a mile away. Such liaisons were common in Hong Kong; the Chinese community didn't fault the women who engaged in them. Jade had been Jeremy's mistress ever since, bearing him two boys, now nine and six.

Then Mrs. Burns had died, and Jade had begun pressing for marriage. She hadn't wanted to end up like her mother, who had given her heart to an English colonial official, only to be abandoned when a long-sought appointment to India had come through. But for the next three years, Jeremy had put Jade off. First he had reminded her he was in mourning, then he had claimed their marriage would prevent his daughter's betrothal to an English viscount, and then he had insisted it would adversely affect his business at a time when he could least afford it.

Finally, however, Jeremy had run out of excuses. With Stour set to replace him as taipan, he had promised to make Jade his wife as soon as he was relieved of his duties. Instead, within days of Stour's arrival, he had left for a tour of China, to say good-bye to his friends. But before his departure, he had given Jade the deed to her house and set up trust funds for his sons under the control of their uncle Kai-wing.

Those were hardly the actions of a man who intended to return and take her to England, and she knew it. Her concoctions were in such high demand that she could have looked after herself even without Jeremy's financial assistance, but money wasn't the issue. Emotion was. She had loved him, and he had abandoned her.

Sukey looked at her, saw the dark circles under her eyes, and wanted to embrace her, to comfort her. Instead, fearing the gesture might be unwelcome, she murmured, "I was just waiting for my carriage. It's getting late. You must be tired. Why don't I give you a ride home?"

Jade was quick to accept, and as soon as the women had taken their leave, Sukey found out why. Not even Jeremy's perfidy could kill Jade's spirit and curiosity. She knew from Pearl why Sukey had come tonight, and wanted to learn what had transpired.

Sukey directed the coachman to drive around Happy Valley while she told her story. She omitted any mention of witchcraft—not even Pearl knew of her activities—but made no secret of her feelings. "If you want my opinion, the man has a mean streak," she finished. "He wanted to defeat me, Jade. To humble me. He's arrogant and conceited. Thinks he knows everything."

Jade looked amused. "Then it is good that he also wanted to bed you, Sukey. Otherwise, he would not have listened at all. Will he woo you, do you think?"

She burst out laughing. "Good Lord, no. I told you, we dislike each other. We can only stay civil for a minute or two at a time. Anyway, you know how I feel about marriage."

"Yes. You have been wiser than I." Jade's smile faded. "I envy you your decision to remain free. Were it not for my beloved sons, I would wish I had never met Jeremy Burns. I might let another man into my bed, but never into my heart. I care only for my family now."

"But you're still so young. If you met someone wonderful, someone like Kai-wing, then—"

"There are no men like Kai." Jade sighed. "No unmarried ones, in any event. Neither for you nor for me."

But she was wrong, Sukey thought. Somewhere on this planet, there was a man she was destined to love. After tonight, however, she was in no hurry to meet him. Between Stour and Jeremy Burns, she was out of charity with the entire male sex.

Chapter 5

Luke set down the thick ledger he had been studying and wearily rubbed his eyes. In September, after a long and steady decline, income had finally increased, then risen again in October. But the figures still weren't where they should be, and the question was why.

He had been searching for the answer for over two months now, from the day he had arrived in the East. He had pored over bills, invoices, and statements, tightening procedures and looking for irregularities. He had prowled through warehouses, examining shipments and searching for theft. He had talked to more producers and merchants than he cared to recall, both in Hong Kong and throughout China.

What he had found, on the face of it, was a run of astonishingly bad luck. Either the company couldn't get enough merchandise to sell, or prices suddenly dropped, or losses from damage and piracy increased, or cumshaw—the bribes they paid to local officials—shot up. He had never encountered this sort of misfortune before except during worldwide depressions, and since in one fashion or other he had been involved in commerce since the age of sixteen, he certainly should have. He didn't trust the anomaly.

So, like Jeremy Burns, he had concluded that the cause was fraud, not bad joss. Not mismanagement. Some individual—or more likely, some group, given the range of the hong's losses—was stealing from him. But he could find no patterns. He could locate no discrepancies.

True, the decline finally had stopped, but even if his profits began to soar, he still would want to punish those responsible for his losses. Unfortunately, he hadn't been able to track them. He didn't know how to trap them. He hated to admit it, but he was edging toward the same decision Jeremy had made, that he would need the help of an expert.

He locked the ledger inside his desk. According to Tung, Hong Kong was already whispering that the hong had problems. If a detective began nosing around, the talk would grow more pointed, leading to such a lack of confidence that the firm might fail. He decided to work on the matter for another week, and then, if he made no progress, call in McClure.

He let himself out of the building, refused a servant's offer of a sedan chair, and started up the hill to Number One House, a distance of seven blocks. It was the custom here for the great taipans to entertain their partners and griffins each evening, since so many of the men were bachelors, but Luke had declined to follow suit. Hong Kong had labeled him a churlish skinflint, but he didn't care. If he hadn't seen his children after work, he would barely have seen them at all. He invited his associates to dine twice a week now, and considered it an unpleasant necessity.

Tonight, a Tuesday, wasn't one of his evenings to play host, something for which he was profoundly grateful. The day had been hellishly long. So when he walked into the house and heard a feminine voice, his jaw clenched. He was certain Miss Stone had returned.

The girl was impossible, he thought, her impertinence exceeded only by her lack of common sense. The previous Thursday, at her relentless behest, Alex McClure had hunted him down at the Hong Kong Club to ask him how his reading was going. Having been generous enough to invite her to visit his children three times in under two weeks, he was outraged by her lack of gratitude. He had sent a stern message in return: If she nagged him again, even through Alex, she wouldn't be invited back. Alex had been amused by the whole business, but Luke certainly wasn't.

He stalked into the parlor ready to toss her out, then halted and blinked. His older sister and his brother's widow were doing the talking, not Susannah Stone. Breaking into a smile, he continued across the room. "Penny! Victoria! You can't imagine how pleased I am to see you. What are you doing here? When did you arrive?"

Both women stood to be kissed. "Visiting you," Penny said, "and late this afternoon, but we were told you were working. Believe me, we knew better than to interrupt."

"I'm impressed by how well I've trained you. I trust you've been properly taken care of?"

"And then some. Lexie is here, too. She's upstairs, playing with Eleanor and William. And Victoria's maid, Alice, of course. We've been fed, unpacked, and thoroughly spoiled, thanks to your very estimable majordomo. Tell me, Luke, do you sit and gossip with the man? Because he seemed to know all about us."

Luke laughed. "I'm sorry to shock you, but I talk to Tung as often as I can, albeit not about my family.

Very little goes on in this colony that he doesn't hear about.''

"Ah! Then he's an informant.''

"Among other things. As for his knowledge of you and Victoria, I assume it came from the children.'' Luke's expression sobered, and he took Victoria's hands in both of his. She was so small and delicate that he always felt huge beside her. "I'm dreadfully sorry about little Arthur, my dear. I wish I had been there to comfort you.''

She gazed back at him, her blue eyes misting over, her blond hair a little untidy, and he caught his breath at how beautiful she was. Tragedy and pain had erased the hard, ambitious edges from her face, and she looked haunted now. Poignantly fragile.

"But you were,'' she said in her whispery voice. "I had your wonderful wire, Luke. It was the sweetest message I received.'' Her lips trembled. "It's been awful in Kent. Day after day, seeing the places they loved, passing by their graves . . . And after a while, I couldn't bear it anymore.'' She sniffled. "I had to get away, or—or go mad.''

Luke was about to tell her he would do his best to cheer her when she burst into tears and threw her arms around his waist. Stricken by her sobbing, he pulled her close and stroked her hair. He was so filled with pity and tenderness that a lump formed in his throat. He couldn't imagine anything worse than losing one's child.

She wasn't only overwrought, but also exhausted—on the verge of a cold, Penny informed him. He soothed away her tears, then insisted she get some rest. He and Penny walked her to her room and handed her over to Alice. The maid was old and feeble, but so loyal she would have followed Victoria into the depths of Hades—which, in Luke's opinion, was a fair description of Hong Kong.

They continued to the next floor. His mother's namesake, Victoria's daughter Alexandra—Lexie to the family—was playing tag with her two cousins while Mei-mei chased after them, trying frantically to corral them. The game came to an abrupt halt when William barreled around a corner, crashed into his father, and wound up prostrate on the floor.

Luke assured himself that his son was unharmed, then lined the children up and delivered a stern lecture about how disobedience and the lack of self-discipline would ruin their lives. Heads hung low, they apologized and slunk away. He and Penny followed, his sister holding back laughter.

"Hypocrite," she whispered. "We were ten times worse and you know it."

"Speak for yourself."

"I stand corrected. The rest of us were, not you. And we weren't ruined at all. We turned out splendid."

His eyes twinkled. "Granted, but I'm the most perfect of the lot, which proves my point. Besides, we had a dragon for a nanny, and Mei-mei is a sacrificial lamb. The children would make haggis out of her if I didn't keep them in line."

He herded them into the schoolroom and read them a story, a nightly ritual, then left Mei-mei to get them washed and into their nightclothes. As always, he would return in half an hour, to discuss the day's events and tuck them into bed.

A few minutes later, down in the parlor, he and Penny sat down over a bottle of sherry to catch up on each other's lives. Unlike Miss Stone, his sister had impeccable taste. She selected the driest blend.

"I've read your wires to Hugh," she said, referring to their younger brother, a canon at Canterbury Cathedral, "so I know how busy you've been, and how frustrated you are by your lack of progress. I'm sorry to descend on you, but—"

"Don't be. It's been an interminable three months. It's wonderful to see you."

"To see us, yes, but I'm afraid we'll be staying for longer than you would like. Victoria's had a difficult time since little Arthur's death. She's been depressed and very agitated. She got it into her head that she needed to get away, and nothing short of imprisonment could have stopped her. She was in no fit state to look after herself, much less take care of Lexie, and God knows Alice couldn't do it. She didn't particularly want company, but I insisted on going along. I thought I could investigate the local plants."

Luke yawned and stretched, feeling relaxed for the first time in months. He had been small for his age as a child, and more interested in study than in pranks and sports—a disappointment to his athletic father, an enigma to his vivacious mother, and a favorite victim of the boys who were bigger and stronger. Only Penny, with her love of botany, had understood him, encouraged him, and argued for his right to live his life as he chose.

He had stopped needing that sort of support about the time his growth finally had spurted, but old habits died hard. Penny was still the protective older sister, and he had given up telling her not to be. He was intensely loyal to all the members of his family, but Penny was the one he loved best. She was the only one who knew the full truth about his marriage and his wife's death, the only one he trusted completely.

"But why did Victoria choose Hong Kong?" he

asked. "Why not go someplace more interesting and civilized?"

"I don't know." She sighed. "I tried to talk her out of it, Luke. I told her you wouldn't have time to squire us to parties or show us the sights, but she insisted on Hong Kong, and that was that."

"Parties? Sights?" He snorted derisively. "There are precious few of either here. Europe or even America would have been better. Could nobody talk some sense into her? Not her parents? Not Mother? Not even Roger Albright?"

Penny shook her head. "No, and heaven knows they tried. Sir Roger isn't happy about this at all. He's afraid she'll take sick or suffer a nervous collapse. He asked her to postpone the trip until he could accompany her—he needed to go to France on some business for the Foreign Office—but she refused. So here we are. Truly, I thought he might refuse the assignment and travel with us to Hong Kong, but I'm sure he'll be here soon. He's more besotted with her than ever."

Luke nodded absently, his mind a step ahead. "If she was worried about the future . . . Hugh did receive my instructions about that, didn't he? He did assure her I would always take care of her?"

"Of course. He's performed magnificently in your absence. He's enjoying his duties immensely. The dean grumbled that his activities at Stour Hall were taking him away from his work at the cathedral, but Hugh made a sizable donation in your name, and that took care of that." She sipped her sherry. "As for Victoria, she doesn't seem ready to move yet, but—"

"Move? Good Lord, Penny, it hasn't been even three months. She can stay in any of my homes for as long as she likes."

"I'm sure she knows that, Luke," Penny said soothingly, "just as she knows what a generous allowance she'll receive, and what a fine house you'll lease her. If she has fears about the future, they're obviously wholly irrational, but I doubt that's why she's come. I imagine she was desperate for distraction from her grief, and she convinced herself she would find it in Hong Kong."

She was mistaken, then. "Believe me, Penny, the chief activities in this miserable village are gossip and commerce. Victoria will be bored to tears."

His sister murmured she had feared as much. "I was thinking we might visit China. They say it's a fascinating country."

"And so it is, but the accommodations are primitive. Sickness is rife. The officials are dangerously capricious. It's no place for an unaccompanied female. I couldn't possibly allow you to go there."

"You couldn't, eh?" Penny slanted him a cool look. "And what about my work? How am I supposed to find and paint the medicinal herbs the Chinese use if I don't travel there?"

That was just what he needed, Luke thought. Another female challenging and badgering him. "I can introduce you to a woman who's an expert in that area. She manufactures various tonics using herbs from local suppliers."

"But I need to see them in the wild," Penny said with exaggerated patience. "A garden simply won't do."

"Then you can investigate Hong Kong Island and Kowloon. Surely the plants grow here, and Jade can tell you where." He lazed back on the sofa. "You'll enjoy meeting her, Penny. She's beautiful, intelligent, and very independent, a demimondaine of sorts. My comprador's sister, and Jeremy Burns's former mistress. Sound intriguing?''

"Very. Has she expressed any interest in replacing Mr. Burns with his successor?''

Luke laughed at his sister's sly tone. "No, but even if she had, I haven't had time for a mistress."

"You had time in England. You'll work yourself into the grave at the rate you're going."

"All right, then, I have had time, but I prefer to spend it at my club. Women are too demanding. About Victoria—"

"About my herbs," Penny said firmly, "if I can't find them in the colony, I intend to look in China. And I expect your help, runt. You know the area and I don't. If you have time for male diversions, you have time to arrange a tour."

Luke took the childhood nickname in good grace, but only because it was Penny, and only because they were alone. "I suppose you'll hie off by yourself if I refuse," he muttered.

"You suppose correctly. After all, I've traveled all over the world without your permission, and I've coped as well as any male."

She had a point. Penny was the opposite of Victoria, tall and strong, with dark hair and eyes. For a female, she was exceptionally capable, and besides, the colleagues he had met during his recent visit could see to her safety and comfort. "Very well. I'll arrange it, but Victoria will have to remain behind."

Penny frowned. "But you could be stuck with her for weeks. She'll grow bored and restless and drive you mad."

Luke knew that perfectly well. "What choice do I have? Even healthy, Victoria lacks the temperament and constitution for arduous travel, and given her current condition . . ."

"Hmm. I suppose you're right." Penny swirled her wine, pursing her lips as she stared idly at the glass. "I know. Your friend McClure—might his wife be willing to entertain her?"

Luke had met Mrs. McClure twice now, when she and Alex had come to dine. She was intelligent and lively, and when she had looked him in the eye, he had seen compassion and trust in her gaze. "Probably, if I throw myself on her mercy." But complications would ensue if Penny left Hong Kong. "You and Victoria should probably move out of the main house. There's a vacant cottage on the other side of the garden where you can stay. It isn't large, but it's comfortable and charming."

Penny regarded him quizzically. "Move out? But why?"

"You've been here for hours already, Pen. Surely you've heard. I was Victoria's lover for years—just think, incest and adultery, all in one blow. In fact, I fathered her children under my sterile brother's nose, which is why they're fair like me rather than dark like Arthur."

"My, but you were busy in England. I'm amazed you had any energy left for business." Penny slid closer and put a consoling hand on his wrist. "No wonder you hate it here, Luke. In London they only whispered such filth, but in Hong Kong they obviously shout it to the world. Who told you about the gossip? Your majordomo?"

"No. He's far too discreet to repeat something so vicious. Alex McClure did. Like me, McClure believes ignorance to be folly. He feels that it's best that I know what I'm up against."

"And Arthur's accident? Kate's suicide?" Penny's voice was low and bitter. "They were actually murder, I suppose."

"Of course. In fact, my lust for power and position was so great, I even disposed of my own son."

"Little Arthur, you mean?" Her face contorted in outrage. "People can't actually believe that. My God, you were on a steamer in the middle of the ocean at the time!"

Luke squeezed her hand. It was good to have her here. Good to be reminded of her love and faith. "Since when does logic have anything to do with gossip? Some of them probably believe it, though McClure is doing whatever he can to stop the talk. For most people here, scandal is simply an amusing pastime, while the remainder view character assassination as just another business method."

"That's despicable." Penny jerked up from the couch and started pacing. "I won't leave you. It would only make things worse. At least if I stay . . . Only an idiot would think you would make love to your mistress with your sister in the next room."

On the contrary, they would say Penny knew and didn't care. A wave of queasiness roiled through him. Or they would believe that something sickeningly perverse was going on. It was better to have her gone. "They'll talk in any event, but I can count on the servants to gossip about what they see. If Victoria is in the cottage, they'll expect me to spend my nights there. They'll look for the usual signs—sneaking back and forth, a disordered bed—but they won't find them." He wasn't going to admit that they might not report the truth. "That should quell the rumors."

Penny grunted and kept pacing. Luke checked his watch. It was time to return upstairs, but he couldn't leave yet, not when his sister was so upset. "Stop fretting, Pen. I've dealt with worse, you know. I'll be fine."

She came to an abrupt halt in front of him. "Will you? You've been viciously attacked. You're disheartened by your lack of progress. The tension all but oozes out of you. I almost wish you were less pleased to see me, because part of your joy is relief that I'm here to confide in. And only two months have passed. What will you be like in six, Luke? Or in twelve?"

Luke had never lied to Penny in his life and didn't intend to start. "Truly, Pen, I can take whatever Hong Kong dishes out, but I'm concerned about my children, and it's made me—anxious and somewhat short-tempered. I haven't had a problem with William. He's in a class with boys his own age, and the headmaster is very strict. He doesn't permit talking during lessons, and the play periods are structured and well-supervised. But Eleanor's school was a permissive sort of place, with girls of all ages together, probably jabbering up a storm, and Eleanor heard gossip. It distressed her, so I had to remove her. You know how much I want them here, but if I can't protect them, I'll have to send them back to England with you and Victoria."

Penny dropped back onto the sofa, looking thoughtful now. "Eleanor's teacher . . . Was her name Miss Stone?"

"Yes." The very mention of the woman made Luke scowl. "What about her?"

"Oh, my. You do dislike her. Eleanor said that you did, but I thought she must be wrong, since you allow her to visit. Eleanor went on and on about her—how smart she is, and how pretty, and how many things she knew. So what did she do to offend you? Surely it was more than her lenience, or the gossip she permitted at her school.''

"Yes. Surely it was." Luke checked his watch again. The children would be waiting, but they would probably forgive the delay if he extended their bedtime by half an hour. "She's presumptuous. Haughty. Conceited. She respects nothing—not paternal authority, not social position, not intellectual superiority. And if that isn't enough . . ." He lowered his voice. "She'll do anything to get her way. The chit had the effrontery to hypnotize me.''

Penny gaped at him. "To do what?''

"You heard me.''

"Yes. I did. But I didn't believe my ears." Her lips twitched. "For heaven's sake, Luke, you can't be mesmerized against your will. As a scientist, surely you know that.''

Glowering, he recounted Miss Stone's offenses in scathing detail, ignoring the frequent flashes of amusement he divined in his sister's eyes. Blood might be thicker than water, but gender was obviously thicker than either.

When he finally finished his story, he fixed her with a moody stare. "You're on her side. You women all stick together.''

"On the contrary, she sounds outrageous. Only a saint would permit her in his home." Penny ruffled his hair, something she knew he despised. "And since you're anything but a saint, there's more here than meets the eye. I can't wait to meet the woman.''

Victoria was crying again. Luke gathered her into his arms, cradled her against his chest, and petted her as if she were William or Eleanor. This was the fourth night in a row he had paid her a visit, and the fourth night in a row she had soaked his coat. On each occasion, he had managed to calm her, but her serenity never lasted.

A sense of deep helplessness had begun to mingle with the pity he felt. Like Sir Roger Albright, he was worried about the consequences to her health. Both she and Lexie were suffering from miserable colds, and he had often observed that one's emotional state could affect one's recuperation. If she couldn't pull herself together, bronchitis or even pneumonia might result.

He massaged her neck, very gently, guiltily aware that her boredom was making things worse. Penny had left with Jade on a tour of Hong Kong Island, while Alice, though healthy, was a tedious companion. If it hadn't been for his nightly visits, she would have had no one to amuse her at all.

Fortunately, Mrs. McClure had promised to show her the sights as soon as she recovered, and he would allow Lexie to spend her days with Eleanor the moment the child stopped hacking. But until then, Victoria would be stuck in this cottage with Lexie, and she wasn't accustomed either to confinement or to her daughter's constant presence. As a result, she was even more agitated and depressed in Hong Kong than in Kent.

Her breakdown was briefer this time, which Luke took as a positive sign. Looking embarrassed, she withdrew to tidy up. She seemed composed when she returned, but her cheeks were a ghostly bluish-white and the circles under her eyes were darker than ever.

She sat down beside him, absently smoothing her hair. "I look awful. Puffy where I'm not gaunt. I hate having you see me this way."

Objectively, she was right, but her pain and vulnerability had melted Luke's heart, so that he thought her as lovely as ever. "Nonsense," he said. "Nothing could make you less than beautiful. Besides, within a few days, your cold will be gone, and you'll be as good as new." He took her hand in both of his. "And if it's not, I'll summon a physician. I know you dislike them, but I'm concerned about your mental state, not just your physical one."

"I know. You're sweet to worry." She sighed and rested her head on his shoulder, her eyelids fluttering down. The heat of her body warmed his chest, and the scent of her perfume invaded his nostrils. "Sometimes I think I married the wrong brother."

He had to school himself not to stiffen—to remind himself that her words hadn't been meant to wound, and that her closeness was only a cry for comfort. In any event, she had made her choice years ago, and they would both have to live with it. "If you mean that I'm still here while he's gone, then perhaps you did. But otherwise . . ." He patted her hand in a brotherly way. "He gave you the sort of life you wanted, Vicki. The grand houses, the wonderful parties, the amusement and adventure . . . And you loved him. He was fun and I wasn't. Popular, dashing, and full of life. Besides, he was the heir—"

"But that's not why I chose him. I did love you, Luke. Just—not as much as Arthur. But now . . ." She stroked his cheek and looked into his eyes. "You have qualities he lacked. You're prudent. Stable. Responsible. I'm older and wiser now. I appreciate those attributes more."

Luke felt as if the collar around his neck had tightened. The qualities she had described were those one would value in a friend, and thus entirely proper to praise. Indeed, had a mistress described him in such dull terms, he would have been disappointed. But Victoria wasn't regarding him as one would a friend. Quite the opposite.

He looked away, searching for the right thing to say. He had been alone with her on many occasions, especially after his brother's death, but nothing like this had ever happened before. If she wanted any man, it was Albright. Anyone who watched them together could see the affection they shared. Surely, then, he was mistaken about what he thought he was seeing.

"Thank you," he finally replied. "If you truly believe that, then you know—"

"I do. And I'm grateful." She slid her hand into his hair and pressed her lips to his cheek.

It was a sisterly kiss—at least, Luke devoutly hoped it was. Except that her hand lingered in his hair, and her mouth remained only inches from his cheek. A warning bell went off. "Uh, Victoria . . ."

"Mmm." She pecked him again, on the jaw this time, then slid her mouth toward his own. He grasped her shoulders to ease her away, but she had already started to kiss him. On the mouth. With her lips parted. With her body arched against his.

For a moment, he froze. She was a beautiful, desirable woman, and he could feel her full, firm breasts through the dressing gown she wore, rubbing against his chest. Her mouth was wildly seductive on his, her tongue teasing and tasting him, her teeth gently nibbling his lip. He didn't intend it, but his hands somehow tightened on her shoulders, and his mouth opened hungrily under hers.

Then, abruptly, he came to his senses, and the fiery kiss he'd been on the verge of bestowing turned into a harmless brush against her forehead. Taking a deep breath, he lifted her up, carried her to a chair, and gently set her down. Then, forcing his chaotic emotions under control, he returned to the sofa. For a moment, he thought he saw something tense and calculating in her eyes, but he decided he must have been wrong. She had been through a great deal, that was all. She was simply lonely and confused.

"There. That's safer, I think." He managed a rueful smile. "I do apologize, Victoria. I've been far too— familiar. What happened was entirely my fault."

"That's very chivalrous of you, but both of us know it's not true. I wanted to kiss you, so I did. What's more, you wanted to kiss me back." She returned his smile, her face suddenly alight with mischief. "Why don't you? Haven't you always wondered what it would be like? I know I have."

She didn't mean kissing, which they had done in abundance once. She meant making love, and the answer was yes, he had. But that had been a long time ago, when he had loved her. When she was newly married to his brother, and he had lost his virginity to his first mistress and learned what sexual pleasure was all about.

He didn't reply directly, just reminded her that she was his brother's widow, and in the eyes of the law, still his sister. "We've known each other for far too many years for me to be dishonest with you," he added, and then lied gallantly. "I've never stopped caring for you, and if our laws were different, I might have courted you after Arthur's death. But as matters stand . . ." He sighed, doing his best to look bereft.

"I know. We can never marry. But that doesn't mean we can't . . ." She lowered her eyes. She seemed younger suddenly, and terribly unsure of herself. "You know. Enjoy each other. I would like that, Luke. Wouldn't you?"

"I would refuse to let myself," he said firmly. "It's

illicit, Victoria. I'm flattered you would want to, but the guilt we would feel . . ." He stood. Given her irrational state, it was better not to be alone with her. "I really should leave—"

"No. Please don't." She worried her bottom lip, and he realized she was trembling. "It's just . . . I loved Arthur dearly, you know I did, but his war wound . . . Our, uh, our marriage in that area . . . I don't want to shock you, but the women in my set discuss the most intimate matters—"

"Victoria, this really isn't appropriate—"

"You know how gossip spreads, and after you left England, your mistress went on and on to her friends about what she would miss most—"

"Vicki, for God's sake—"

"—and she said no man she'd ever had could give her as much—"

There was a knock on the door, right in the middle of the word "pleasure." Never had an interruption been more welcome. Luke didn't care *how* complimentary Clarissa had been; he didn't want to hear the details from Victoria. To his relief, he opened the door to find Tung outside, holding an envelope in his hand.

The majordomo bowed. "This arrive by messenger, Lord Stour. I think I should find you. Look important."

Luke took the letter. The outside was marked with his name and the words "Confidential. Open at once." Since Tung didn't read English, Luke wondered how he had known to bring it around.

He frowned. "It came just now? Who brought it?"

"I don't see. Someone knock, then leave letter and run away. A half hour, maybe." Tung's face was bland. "Ten minutes after you leave to visit countess,

Taipan. You gone a very long time. I think I better not wait.''

In other words, Luke had been here for so long that gossip would have erupted if he had remained any longer. "I see. Thank you for coming to find me." It appeared that the McClures weren't his only friends in this colony.

Chapter 6

S ukey smiled impishly, then announced she was in despair over the whole male sex. "Just look, ladies." She made a sweeping motion with her hand over the orchestra section of the City Hall Theatre, which was visible below the balcony where she and her companions were seated. "There are five men to every woman in this colony, yet the audience is two-thirds female. And I'll wager that most of the men were dragged here by their wives and will be snoring by intermission. Men have no refinement. How am I going to find one worth marrying?"

"Culture isn't everything," Melanie said with a laugh. Her husband, Alex, was among the philistines who had begged off, mumbling that he preferred gambling at the Hong Kong Club to the prancing of Italian dancers. Tolerant of his male foibles, she had gotten up a party of women to join her in the McClures' box.

Pearl Douglas had come along, but not Jade, who was touring the island with Stour's elder sister, Lady Penelope Wyndham. So had Maria Alvares, a gentle young woman who had arrived in Hong Kong in July to keep house for her uncle and teach at his school. The final member of the party, a last-minute addition, was Melanie's friend Martha Gibb, the wife of a taipan with a suspiciously unreliable back.

"In fact, I can't wait until you fall in love," Melanie continued. "When you're mooning around in a daze, saying that he heats your blood and curls your toes—"

"Melanie, really!" Sukey whispered, nodding furtively at the innocent Maria.

"—babbling about how you've met your soul mate, insisting he's the most wonderful creature on earth, I'll remind you of this conversation."

Pearl looked amused. "But Melanie, Sukey says nobody broke more engagements than you did, or was more reluctant to wed, even after you first met Alex."

"And even after you fell in love with him," Sukey reminded her.

"Well, of course not," Melanie said blithely. "No man is perfect to begin with. We have to train them before they're fit to marry. Alex is a paragon now— other than the fact that he prefers billiards to ballet— and I'm the happiest of women. Marriage is a marvelous institution."

"Lord, spare me the sermons of converts." Grinning, Sukey turned to Mrs. Gibb. "I'm pleased you were able to join us. I do so enjoy teaching your little Caroline. Tell me, do you concur with Melanie's view of marriage?"

"For the most part I do, despite Mr. Gibb's duplicity. It's astonishing, but his back never acts up before a horse race or a party, only before concerts and such." Her eyes twinkled. "He's not very convincing, I'm afraid. Even the children know when he's dissembling."

"Ah, but children see more than we give them credit for, especially when they're as bright as your daughter. Speaking of which, I've been concerned about her health. She's normally one of my most attentive pupils, but twice this week, she's fallen asleep at school. Has she been sick lately, or stayed up past her bedtime, or slept poorly at night?''

Mrs. Gibb started to shake her head, then reconsidered. ''Now that you mention it, her amah reported a problem with waking her up. It isn't every morning, only once or twice a week, and in the afternoons she's always as sprightly as ever, so I wasn't worried. But if she's nodding off in class . . .'' Mrs. Gibb's brow furrowed. ''Do you think it's serious? Should we summon a physician?''

''I wish I knew,'' Sukey answered. ''You see, Caroline isn't the only one who's fallen asleep lately, but if there's a contagion going around, it's a very peculiar one. The girls don't sneeze or cough, or complain of any pain, or perspire unduly, or show any other signs of disease. They simply drop off at their desks, as if they haven't gotten enough sleep the night before. I first noticed the problem a month ago, and truly, I don't know what to make of it.''

''I doubt the condition is infectious,'' Mrs. Gibb said, ''or, if it is, it's probably only slightly so. After all, my Charlie is right as rain. As active as ever, Miss Stone.''

Pearl Douglas leaned forward a little. ''You mustn't worry so, Sukey. As I've told you, these outbreaks are common in Hong Kong, and usually harmless. The symptoms vary—an itchy rash, a mild irritability, or the sort of drowsiness that has affected our girls. The problem always appears suddenly, strikes at random, and finally vanishes. Truly, as long as brief naps in your office put our students to rights, I see no reason for alarm.''

Pearl had logic on her side, Sukey knew that, but when it came to her pupils, logic flew out the window. She had a troubling mystery on her hands, and she wouldn't be content until she had discovered the cause.

She grimaced in frustration. Lord knew her first theory had come a cropper. If her girls were tired, it wasn't because they were eavesdropping on their parents' gossip about Stour. As far as she could tell, they had lost interest in the topic weeks ago. Besides, they were an honest bunch, and they had denied even staying up late.

"This illness—or syndrome—it seems harmless *now*," she said, "but suppose it proves dangerous in the end?" A new avenue of inquiry occurred to her, and she looked at Maria. "The boys at your school . . . Have they experienced anything similar of late?"

Maria hesitated before replying. "As you know, my uncle is very strict. His lectures are lengthy and serious, so it is not unusual for boys to fall asleep. Still, I do not believe he has imposed any more punishments for that infraction in November than in September or October."

Sukey was appalled. "You mean he considers being tired an infraction? He punishes the boys for exhaustion?"

"For failing to pay attention," Maria corrected. "The first time a boy transgresses, he must memorize and recite Bible verses. The second time, he cleans out the privies. After that . . ." A shadow crossed her face. "He is paddled. Ten strokes, then five more each time. My uncle says boys need firm discipline. There is rarely a third infraction."

Given the price the boys paid, Sukey could believe it. No matter how bored or fatigued they were, they wouldn't daydream or fall asleep, not if they could help it. But Hong Kong Latin was a large school with many classes, and Alvares couldn't be everywhere at once. "You work a good deal with the youngest boys, don't you, Maria? Has any of them ever nodded off? Charlie Gibb, for example, or Melanie's son Wyatt?"

The final warning bell sounded. Maria turned away. "I have noticed nothing unusual. I believe the performance is about to begin."

Sukey remembered the discomfort on Maria's face when she had spoken of the beatings. "We still have a few minutes." She put her hand on the younger woman's arm. "Tell us what you've seen. It won't go any farther."

Maria glanced at Mrs. Gibb, visibly uneasy now. "Most men are stern with their sons. Is this true of your husband, ma'am?"

"I suppose so. He's harder on Charlie than on Caroline, certainly. But as I told you, my son has never . . ." Her voice trailed off, and her face grew slightly flushed. "You mean it's not only Caroline who's been ill? It's Charlie, as well?"

Maria turned toward the stage. "Not at all, Mrs. Gibb."

"But I won't tell my husband, Miss Alvares." Mrs. Gibb pulled out her fan. "I wouldn't let my son be punished for something he can't control."

Maria sighed, then softly confessed that her experience had been the same as Sukey's. Her uncle spent the first hour of each day with the youngest boys, she explained, and then turned the group over to her. On several occasions, she had no sooner entered their classroom than Charlie had dozed off. "I believe he is able to stay awake with my uncle because he knows he will be punished if he does not. Perhaps he gets up promptly each morning for the same reason. In any event, I let him rest, and he soon recovers. He doesn't seem ill, only sleepy. I have not said anything to my uncle. Charlie is a diligent boy. He keeps up with his work.''

"Are any others affected?" Sukey asked.

"Only Lord Stour's son. There were three offenses. There hasn't been a fourth."

So William had been flogged. The boy hadn't told Sukey, so she doubted he had told his father. She wanted to march up to Stour with the truth, then ask him whether he approved of his son being abused, but she knew he would bar her from his home if she interfered. "Because he waits to fall asleep until after your uncle leaves the room. He knows you won't report him."

"Yes," Maria admitted.

Mrs. Gibb looked more agitated than ever. "Oh, dear. The boys are friends. Charlie and Lord Stour's son, that is." She fanned herself vigorously, continuing in a hushed voice, "The gossip about his father . . . Mr. McClure assured us it was nonsense, and my husband said he didn't give a fig what other people did, if Charlie wanted to play there, he could. But I was just thinking . . . Do you suppose there's a connection? That Caroline could have infected Charlie, and Charlie could have infected William?"

Before venturing an opinion, Sukey reviewed her roster of students. In addition to Caroline, two of the affected girls, both the daughters of taipans, had brothers at Hong Kong Latin. But when she asked Maria if they had displayed any symptoms, Maria said no.

"And Stour's daughter?" Sukey asked Pearl. "She's always been lively during my visits, but I go there in the afternoons. How about the mornings? Has your cousin mentioned any problems?"

Pearl smiled. "Only the opposite. I'm afraid Mei-mei has difficulty keeping up with her."

Deeply puzzled, Sukey said to Mrs. Gibb, "It sounds as if the syndrome is only mildly contagious, or not contagious at all, just as you originally suggested. Certainly it's striking at random, as Pearl said, even within the same households. So no, there's no reason to think Charlie gave it to William."

A pianist started to play, and the curtain slowly went up. A couple appeared on stage, then began a slow pas de deux. Sukey regarded them distractedly. Something was afflicting her girls, but what? An organism in the air or water? A pestilence carried by insects? Would it remain as harmless as it currently appeared to be?

Too agitated to remain and watch, she slipped out of her chair and went for a walk in the corridor.

Luke absently stroked the front of his neck as he slipped inside the storeroom where the spare lanterns were kept. If his increasingly sore throat was any guide, either his cold had worsened, or he had caught Victoria's, as well. He checked his watch. It was a quarter before eleven, almost time to leave. The letter had been very precise.

If he was curious about the losses at Burns, it had read, he should go to the north godown at midnight and enter through the east door, leaving it ajar behind him. He was given a lengthy series of instructions next, telling him to navigate various aisles in the precise order given, then wait at the finish until his informant arrived. In return for a sizable sum of money, he would be furnished with the information he sought.

He had no idea who had written the letter, and only two tangible clues. The first was the printing, which he had compared to letters written by his underlings

and colleagues. Nothing had matched, but he hadn't
expected it to. The writing was awkward. Tentative.
Stiff. Luke assumed he was looking at a copy, not at
the original . . . that to protect himself, the informant
had paid someone who was illiterate in the Roman
alphabet, and thus couldn't comprehend his message,
to duplicate it stroke by stroke.

Since he was in Hong Kong, the copier was likely
Chinese. Unfortunately, every European in the colony
had Chinese servants. Indeed, even if he supposed that
the scribe was a petty criminal rather than an innocent
pawn, the group of suspects wouldn't be narrowed to
those with shadowy connections. Everyone knew
where to find men of questionable character—at the
gambling dens, the brothels, the docks . . .

As for the second clue, the amount of money he had
been told to bring, that too was of little help. True,
only someone knowledgeable about commerce would
have known how much cash a taipan would keep on
hand, but only someone knowledgeable about commerce could have been the informant in the first place.
Since an honest man who had stumbled across information wouldn't have demanded payment, Luke assumed the informant was a participant in the scheme,
a thief who had fallen out with his nefarious comrades.

He fetched down a lantern, adjusted the bank notes
he had tucked into his coat, and secured his revolver
more firmly in his waistband. Then he let himself out
of the storeroom, exiting the house through the trades-
men's door. The north warehouse was a ten-minute
walk away.

If he was heading into a trap—if his informant
planned to kill him or rob him—the fellow would
likely arrive early, then lie in wait. Luke had allowed
for a full hour's head start, but he suspected twenty

minutes would have been long enough. The degenerate mind, he had found, was inclined toward impatience.

The night was a dark one, lit only by a clouded half moon and the lamps in various houses, but he knew the compound well and was able to make his way through the garden and down to the shore without the use of his lantern. People were visiting and talking in the flats of the Chinese quarter a few blocks from the warehouse, but the area around the docks was deserted. As usual on a Saturday night, no work was going on, and the questionable amusements the seamen favored were all to the south, in Happy Valley, and to the west, in the seedy areas of Victoria.

He let himself into the building next door and stationed himself by a window, a vantage point that afforded a view of both entrances to the godown. As far as he could see, everything was dark and quiet.

The warehouse, the company's largest, was an old brick hulk, its north/south aisles labeled with letters and its east/west ones labeled with numbers. Crates and other containers were stacked every which way, creating blockages, so that the interior resembled a giant maze. Windows ringed the building below the roofline, letting in sunlight during the daytime hours. Gaslights along the interior walls provided additional light when needed, but in Luke's experience, the workers seldom bothered with them.

He repeatedly scanned his surroundings, and soon noticed that the windows of the godown weren't pitch black, as they should have been, but a fraction lighter. Someone must have entered with a lamp. The intruder wasn't near a wall, however, because if he had been, the windows closest to the light would have been brighter than the others, and they were all the same. He was evidently somewhere in the middle, his lamp barely illuminating the perimeter. Of course, in a warehouse that large, the middle was a sizable area.

As Luke continued to observe, he realized that the intensity of light in the windows wasn't changing. The intruder wasn't moving about, as someone working would, but remaining stationary. He was almost certainly the informant, then, lying in wait.

So much for his theory about the impatience of the criminal mind, Luke thought. But if the fellow was poised to attack, at least it wouldn't be within seconds of when he first walked in. The intruder was too far from the door to strike rapidly.

Every now and then Luke glanced up the hill at Number One House. He couldn't see his watch in the darkness, so he had instructed Tung to place a lamp in an attic window and extinguish it just before midnight, as a signal. The time dragged—he felt as if two hours had passed, not under one—and he finally groped for a chair, dragged it to the window, and sat down. The air had turned raw and dank, unusual weather for a Hong Kong autumn, so that even within the protection of this building, he felt chilled and uncomfortable.

Shivering, he massaged his throat, then pinched his nostrils together to ward off a sneeze. Finally, the attic light went out. He struck a match and ignited his lantern, slipped out the door, and warily crossed to the godown.

The east entrance was locked, just as it should have been. The intruder had either broken in through the west or used a key. But even if he owned a key, that didn't prove that he worked here. Hong Kong was such a larcenous place that a sufficient bribe could buy a man almost anything, including keys to locked warehouses and floor plans of the merchandise inside. Luke paid his people well, but that was no guarantee of loyalty in this wretched colony.

Following the instructions in the letter, he let himself inside and left the door ajar. He took a quick look around, but saw no one. Then, with his back against the wall for protection, he reviewed the directions he had been given. According to his calculations, they would take him to K-11.

He committed the first eight steps to memory, but, his orders to the contrary, he had more sense than to adhere exactly to the circuitous route he had been given. He started forward, one hand poised on his pistol and the other holding the lantern aloft. He planned to vary the route slightly, taking a roughly parallel course, and to watch both his back and the area above his head while he did so.

His light cast eerie shadows on the cartons and crates, and his footfalls reverberated unnervingly off the floor and walls. He listened for other sounds—someone following or approaching—but heard nothing. Given the mazelike quality of this place, he wasn't surprised when dead ends intervened, but he always managed to work around them. He began to hope that the encounter would prove exactly what his correspondent had promised, a meeting to exchange money for information.

He completed the first half of his journey, then memorized the remaining steps. They took him to every part of the godown, gradually bringing him nearer to K-11. He was in row L, he estimated, probably a few aisles beyond 11, when he noticed that the intersection ahead of him was slightly brighter than the area he had just come from. He assumed he was closing in on the intruder, or at least on the intruder's lantern. And then he heard a noise from somewhere in front of him. It wasn't the sound of walking, he realized, but of someone shuffling around in a limited area.

His senses sharpened. Bracing to defend himself, he warily rounded a corner . . . and spotted the intruder. The fellow was directly ahead of him, about four aisles away. He was hidden in the shadows, so Luke crept closer. Since the man's head was down—he appeared to be studying a book of some sort—Luke couldn't see his face. With his dark hair and average build, he could have been almost anyone.

Despite Luke's prudence, his subject straightened and looked around. "Who's there?" he asked. He sounded surprised someone had come. That wasn't the way Luke imagined his informant would react.

Luke couldn't place the voice, but the accent was English. He was about to identify himself and demand the intruder's name when he heard something behind him . . . the ominous whisper of slippered feet, rapidly and stealthily advancing. Cursing his own stupidity— why hadn't he realized there could be two men involved?—he set down his lantern. His hand closed around his revolver, but he was too late. As he pulled out his weapon, he heard a loud report. Then a cloth closed over his face from behind, and the sharp smell of chloroform filled his nostrils.

The world wavered and spun, then abruptly blackened. As if in slow motion, he felt himself fall. He heard a second explosion, and then a third, but he couldn't have said whether the sounds emanated from outside, or from the whirling confusion of his own mind.

He awoke feeling muzzy and nauseated, with such a throbbing pain above his left temple that a minute passed before he could make himself move. Grimacing, he finally sat up. His revolver, which was wedged between his hand and his body, clattered to the floor. As he retrieved it, a wave of queasiness assailed him, and, unable to quell it, he turned to the side and retched. Shivering, he wiped his mouth, then tucked the gun back into his waistband.

His mind was operating at a torpid rate of speed, but he remembered that he had come here to meet an informant. That he had heard something behind him. Fallen to the floor.

His lantern was still sitting beside him, burning steadily. He looked around, but saw and heard nothing. He was evidently alone again. He suddenly remembered his bank notes, and felt inside his coat. They were undisturbed. But why lure him here and attack him, if not to rob him? He hadn't even been harmed, not in any serious way.

He woozily stood, taking the lantern with him. He was about to leave, when out of the corner of his eye, he noticed a dark shape on the floor about fifty feet ahead of him. That was when he recalled that a man had been standing in the area—that he had spoken only moments before the attack. Luke wove forward, ignoring his pain and dizziness, afraid that the shape was a human body.

It was. The fellow was lying inert on his side. Luke's heart rate soared, and he broke into a trot. Though his head was pounding insanely and his stomach was turning over, his mind had cleared completely. When he saw a puddle of red on the floor, touching the man's head, he remembered the loud reports he had heard and realized what they had been. Gunshots. Someone had killed this fellow—or rather, had tried to. The man was breathing, he realized in relief, but too quickly. Too noisily.

Luke knelt by the victim's shoulder and held the lamp to his face. It was Robert Kilearn, and he was badly wounded. The right side of his hair was so matted with blood that Luke couldn't tell how deep the bullet had gone, and the opposite side of his coat was just as bloody, indicating there was a second bullet in his shoulder.

Luke was in no fit state to carry out Kilearn by himself, not without stumbling and endangering the man, so he struggled to his feet to go for help. He had taken only a few steps when he heard a loud halloo. The speaker sounded Chinese, so Luke prayed the man would understand him. "Over here!" he called. "Somewhere near J-15." He kept yelling, trying to lead the man to his voice.

Some two hours later, Tung opened the door to Number One House and admitted the Hong Kong superintendent of police, Captain W. M. Deane, showing him into the parlor where Luke was sitting and sipping broth. Kilearn was in a bedroom a flight up, sleeping peacefully. An inch this way or that, the doctor had said, and the damage might have been fatal, but Kilearn had been lucky. He was seriously concussed, but his wounds were superficial.

As for Luke, the only physical reminder of his adventure was the bump he had sustained when his head had hit the ground. It throbbed like mad, but his sore throat and queasy stomach were far more bothersome. Indeed, he was so miserable that, when Deane proved relentless to the point of impertinence, he lacked the energy to feel anything beyond mild impatience.

No previous earl of Stour had ever been examined like a common thief, he was sure of it, but then, no previous earl of Stour had ever been in trade, or been labeled everything from a supercilious snob to a homicidal maniac. Deane was one of the first of the Hong Kong cadets, British university men who had entered the consular service and received extensive training in the Chinese language. He was said to be honest and capable, a rare combination in a policeman, so Luke was inclined to put up with him. Besides, from the moment his employees had heard gunshots and rushed to the warehouse to investigate, there had been no keeping tonight's incident a secret.

He finished his account, which Deane had interrupted time and again with questions, then pointed to the table in front of the sofa. "And as I told you, that's the revolver I was holding when I came around."

"You say it was in your hand, Lord Stour. You placed it back in your trousers, but you didn't look at it until you returned to the house. And that's when you discovered that it wasn't your weapon at all. That you'd never seen it before. You had looked around the godown when you regained consciousness, but so far as you can recall, your own revolver was nowhere in sight."

"That's correct, Captain. I would have picked it up if I had seen it. I would have realized I was holding someone else's gun."

"Quite right. Let's have a look at it, shall we?" Deane walked over, picked the gun up, and checked the chambers. "You said you heard three reports—"

"But my employees heard four. I must have passed out before the final one."

"Hmm. Four chambers are empty. It appears to be the weapon used in the attack." He set it back down. "The chloroformed rag you mentioned . . . It was gone, as well."

"Yes. My attacker obviously took it with him."

"But he didn't take your bank notes. You still have them in your pocket. If I might see them . . . ?"

Luke pulled them out of his coat and tossed them onto the table. Deane inspected them, obviously startled by the amount involved. "The letter you say you received . . . You had it with you in the warehouse, but it was missing when you came around?"

"Yes."

"And nobody else saw it?"

"No, only the envelope it arrived in. As I told you, Tung brought it down to my sister-in-law's cottage, but naturally he didn't open it. And even if he had, he doesn't read English and couldn't have understood the contents."

Deane sat down again. "But there was a delay of half an hour between the time it was left and the time you received it. And you were gone all that time. Visiting your ill sister-in-law, you said. But you admit she departed the room on several occasions."

In other words, Luke thought, he could have left the envelope himself, presumably to deflect suspicion if he were spotted carrying out the latest of his murderous schemes. "Captain Deane, if I had manufactured a letter to explain my presence in the warehouse so late at night, I would hardly have decided it should mysteriously disappear."

"Unless there was in fact no letter inside, sir."

Luke stiffened. Under normal circumstances, he would have dressed the man down for his insolence, but in his present condition, he couldn't summon the strength. "Ask anyone who knows me. They'll tell you that if I were going to concoct a story to prove my innocence, I would be thorough about it. I would fabricate a letter as well as an envelope, and keep both to display."

"And besides, you had no reason to harm Kilearn. You didn't, for example, learn that he was responsible for the losses Burns had suffered, and decide to take vengeance."

Luke's temper finally boiled over. "Look here, Deane, if I wanted to take vengeance against a man for stealing from me, I wouldn't kill him. I would ruin him. Put him in debtors' prison." He fixed the officer with a hard stare. "Make his life a living hell. And I'm no more charitable toward men who insult me than I am toward those who cheat me."

Deane didn't even blink. "I see, sir," he said in his bland policeman's tone. "And your own theory about the crime? Have you had time to formulate one?"

"It's pointless to speculate," Luke snapped. "When Kilearn's head clears, he'll be able to tell us more."

"And if he dies?"

It was possible, of course. Though the bullets hadn't been fatal, Kilearn might develop an infection that was. "Then I would suggest he was lured there, just as I was. That the person who shot him intended to kill him, and attacked me in order to frame me for the murder."

"That would be the same man who sent you the letter. Who knew you were carrying money enough to support him for years. Who rendered you unconscious and unable to identify him. Yet he didn't bother to rob you. That's extremely odd, Lord Stour. How would you explain it?"

Luke glowered at him. "It's not my business to explain it. It's yours. If you're going to level accusations, you had damned well better be prepared to back them up."

Once again, Deane wasn't at all intimidated, but there was no reason he should be. He was popular in this colony and Luke wasn't. His skills were desperately needed here, while Luke was only another taipan. He had the full support of the governor, while Luke had only MacDonnell's suspicions.

"It wasn't my intention to accuse you," Deane replied. "I was merely trying to get to the bottom of this. Let me remind you that I have only your word that you were rendered unconscious. Very little time elapsed between the moment the shots were fired and the moment your employees arrived at the warehouse, yet you were perfectly lucid when you were discovered."

Luke quashed the urge to dismiss the man. While he would likely obey, he would only return later with the same impudent questions. "My attacker knew how much chloroform to use. He knew I would have no witnesses. He knew there were people only two blocks away, and that the sound of gunshots would bring them to investigate. And he knew that, by not taking the bank notes, he would make me look guilty. The person who did this wanted both Kilearn and myself removed. Uncover the motives involved, Deane, and you'll find your criminal."

"That's exactly what I plan to do," the policeman said, and looked at Luke in a way that told him he would be watched carefully from that point on. Luke had the sense that every decision he had made since his arrival, no matter how reasonable—to keep to himself, to ignore the attacks on his character, even to protect his daughter from the taunts of other children—was about to come back to haunt him.

Chapter 7

⌒⌒∽◯◯∽⌒⌒

Melanie ushered Sukey into her bedroom and firmly closed the door. "If my seam hadn't unraveled, I would have had to dream up some other minor catastrophe, just to get you alone," she said. "The tension between you and Stour is so thick I'm afraid armed conflict will break out. Why won't the man look at you? And why won't you look at him?"

Sukey shifted uneasily. While Melanie never complained about her magic, she wasn't enthused about it, either. "You're imagining things, Mel. We said hello to each other, didn't we? We even exchanged a few sentences about the lessons I've been doing with Ellie."

"I didn't say you hadn't." Melanie removed a sewing box from her dressing table, then took out a needle and thread. "Here. Use these. And I stand corrected. You did look at each other, just once, when you attempted to joke with him about the tiff you broke up on Tuesday between his daughter and his niece. As I recall, he didn't laugh. In fact, I suspect he was about to lecture you about how it was Mei-mei's place to discipline the children and not yours. But instead, he got a fiery gleam in his eyes, as if he wanted to haul

114

you to the nearest bed and make love to you, and then excused himself in the most abrupt fashion imaginable and stalked away.''

Flushing, Sukey settled onto the floor. As usual, Stour had blamed her for the whole business, blithely ignoring the fact that while she had slipped and looked at him, he had looked right back. "It's the aftereffects of the attack, I expect. That knock on the head must have muddled his mind.''

"Humph. What nonsense. The attack was a full week ago. He's perfectly fine now. Besides, he doesn't stare at anyone else that way. What in the name of heaven is going on between you two?''

"Nothing,'' Sukey insisted. She burrowed beneath Melanie's gown, turning the skirt inside out to reach the unraveled seam. "We don't like each other, that's all.''

Melanie rolled her eyes. "I had gathered that. After all, you've grumbled no end about what an ogre he is to have withdrawn his daughter from your school, and it didn't escape my notice that he doesn't include you when he invites me and Alex to dinner. Really, Sukey, I wish you hadn't nagged him so much. He was so put out that Alex had to twist his arm to get him to come tonight.''

The men had conversed on Wednesday, Sukey knew, when Stour had summoned Alex to Number One House to discuss the losses at Burns. For all his stubbornness, the man had possessed sense enough to know that when a problem turned violent, as it had on Saturday night, it was time to call in an expert. Alex was now investigating both the losses and the attack at the godown. "My, he does hold a grudge, doesn't he? I haven't pestered him for weeks now.'' She began stitching. "So how did Alex rope him in?''

"By promising you would be on your best behavior, for one thing. You will be, won't you?"

Sukey made a face. Alex had lectured her about the topic for a full ten minutes. "Didn't I say I would? Really, Mel, I'm not the hermit here. From what I'm told, the only place Stour goes other than his office and his sister-in-law's cottage is the Hong Kong Club, and even there, the only men he converses with are Alex, Hugh Gibb, and his colleagues from Burns."

"Which is a large part of his problem." Melanie frowned at Sukey's ministrations. "Those stitches are awfully uneven."

She squinted. "Hmm. You're right." She started to get up. "Why don't I fetch my reading glasses—"

"Oh, no, you don't." Melanie pushed her back down. "If I let you leave, I'll never get you back. Now where was I?"

Sukey returned to work, gloomy about her prospects for escape. Melanie was as tenacious as a bloodhound when she wanted information. "Stour's lack of sociability."

"Oh, yes. As I've told Alex, Stour should be friendlier. Get out more. Let people get to know him. Truly, Sukey, he isn't cold at all, not deep down, and certainly he's ethical and loyal. The more I see of him, the better I like him."

"There's no accounting for taste." On the other hand, Sukey thought, nothing ventured, nothing gained. "Speaking of taste, your chef was telling me about the new turkey dish he's preparing for dinner, and—"

"You're wasting your time. I won't be distracted." Melanie paused. "Most people agree with your opinion, I do realize that. After all, no sooner did Kilearn revive than he told Captain Deane that he'd gone to the warehouse Saturday night because he was bothered by a discrepancy in the inventory and wanted to check one of the shipments. So Stour didn't lure Kilearn out with an anonymous message, and he couldn't have followed him, either—he was with Lady Stour when Kilearn left home. The attacker couldn't have planned to kill Kilearn and frame Stour for the murder, because Kilearn went to the warehouse on the spur of the moment. If only he had seen something more than shadowy figures before he was shot . . . But he didn't. So despite Deane's repeated questioning of everyone involved, we've got a mystery on our hands. But the people in this colony persist in saying it was a dastardly murder plot on Stour's part, and do you know why?''

Sukey provided the answer Melanie expected. ''Because it makes for better gossip. Because the less people know about a man, and the less they like him, the more inclined they are to make up stories about him.'' She finished repairing the seam and snapped the thread. ''I won't say he deserves the accusation—nobody would—but he does have quite a history, Mel. Besides, he looks down his nose at almost everyone in Hong Kong and makes no secret of his contempt for the place. I know the people here started it, but his reaction is only making things worse.''

''Which is why I suggested tonight's dinner party— to help him win everyone over. But without the attack, I doubt he would have agreed to come.'' Melanie stroked Sukey's hair. ''Especially given your intolerable presence, my love. Which reminds me—you never answered my question. Why did he look at you that way?''

Sukey pursed her lips in chagrin. So much for her

attempts at obfuscation. "I suppose you're going to badger me until I confess."

"Yes. And don't bother to fib. You don't have even half my talent for it."

"It's a sad state of affairs when an honest nature is a liability," Sukey grumbled, "but very well, I'll tell you." She put away the needle and thread, then joined Melanie on the bed. "I put a spell on the wretched man."

Melanie buried her face in her hands and shook her head, very slowly. "Dear God. I should have known." She peeked between her fingers. "All right. Let's get it over with. What did you do wrong *this* time?"

"What makes you think I did something wrong?"

"Because you always do. I swear to you, you're the most inept witch on the planet." She dropped her hands, looking resigned now. "I can guess what you were after. You wanted his daughter back. Frankly, it seems like a simple enough request, so how you managed to botch it so badly—"

"It wasn't *my* fault. The entities were in a mischievous mood that night." Sukey recounted the unfortunate effects of the spell and described Stour's subsequent behavior. "So I would have gotten nowhere without the entities, and maybe that's why they took the tack they did. In any event, Stour thinks I can hypnotize him just by looking at him—that I cast some sort of erotic spell whenever I do." She folded her arms across her chest and frowned in vexation. "Let me tell you, Mellie, it's very unnerving. Every time he looks at me, he wants to . . ." She hesitated. "You referred to it as making love, but surely that's the wrong term. He dislikes me, so I doubt any tender feelings would be involved. He just—he has these urges, and as much as they appall him, he's desperate to relieve them. I'm not a person to him, only an object he believes he wants.''

"What you're talking about . . . A man wanting to use you . . ." Melanie's eyes softened with concern. "It reminds me of what happened in Ohio. And you say it only unnerves you? It doesn't frighten you half to death?''

"It did at first," Sukey admitted, "but now that I've thought it over . . . Stour is very willful. He would never give in to his lust, and even if he did, the moment he stopped looking at me, he would stop wanting me.''

"And suppose you're wrong? Suppose there's more to this than the spell? If he slips . . . I'm sure he would try to control himself, but passion can be a powerful force, even stronger than dislike. It would torment you to have to defend yourself, even if it were only verbal. We can't have him craving you that way." Melanie shook out her skirts, then added reflectively, "Unless you want him to, that is. He's devilishly handsome, and if he's meant to be your husband . . . Remember that letter I had from Emily Randall, Alex's cousin's wife?''

"Yes. But even if she praised Stour to the skies, it wouldn't matter. I wouldn't have him on a plate.''

"Even if you knew that his former mistress can't stop talking about how much she misses him and how generous he was in bed? And out of bed, too, come to think of it. They say she has some lovely jewels. So knowing you wouldn't have to be afraid of him that way—that he would be patient and kind—does he begin to interest you?''

"Only the way a snake does," Sukey retorted, but it wasn't entirely true. Intelligence and complexity *always* interested her, even in a cad like Stour. "Anyway, he might have been nice to Clarissa St. Simon, but he's been obnoxious to me. He's not my future husband. He's nothing like Sarah described." Except in one way. He was a devoted—if misguided—father. "Well, almost nothing."

Melanie reluctantly conceded the point. If Stour had been generous to Mrs. St. Simon, she admitted, it was probably because she had catered to his every whim. "Which is all he probably wants from a wife or mistress. You could never put up with an attitude like that in a man, not even for long enough to reform him, so you'll have to remove the spell."

That was easier said than done, Sukey thought glumly. "Frankly, I'm not sure I can. The entities might not be the brightest stars in the zodiac, but they do have minds of their own. Suppose Stour came tonight only because they pushed him into it? I need them, Mellie. His newfound sociability is a step in the right direction. If he and Hong Kong accept each other, he'll return his daughter to my school."

Melanie stood, then asked wearily, "And if you make some progress on that score? Will your dimwitted friends stop their infernal meddling?"

Sukey was horrified by Melanie's bluntness. "For heaven's sake, Melanie, be careful how you put things. They might be listening."

"Because if they won't, you'll have to go elsewhere when I give parties for Stour. You're not the only one with something at stake here. Stour is Alex's friend, and Alex wants to help him. But when he looks at you, the air fills with tension, and whatever progress we've made is instantly reversed."

The rebuke brought Sukey up short. Until that moment, she hadn't realized how selfish she was being. "I'm sorry. I didn't stop to consider . . . Of course, your first loyalty would be to Alex." As hers should be. The McClures were practically family. "I don't know why I feel so involved in all this. With his daughter, I mean. It's irrational. After all, how long could I have her as a student? A year? Two years? About tonight—"

"Could it be the entities?"

"Pushing *me*, you mean? Uh, no. The spell I cast would only have affected Stour." Except that she wasn't exactly a crack witch. Her throat tightened. Lord, she'd made a hash of things. "The party will go more smoothly without me. I'll have dinner in my room. Would you tell everyone I have a headache?"

Melanie draped her arm around Sukey's shoulders. "I'll do no such thing. Come now, don't be so upset. If progress is what's needed, tonight is the perfect time to make it. Lexie is dying to attend your school, isn't that right?"

Sukey nodded. According to Ellie, Lady Stour was the type of mother who saw her offspring only to say good morning and good night, so Lexie's constant presence in Hong Kong had irritated her beyond endurance. The moment Lexie was well, she had begun to deposit the girl at Number One House to spend the day with Ellie. But the two had spatted so much that Stour had limited his niece's visits to the afternoons.

Lady Stour had found the subsequent mornings and evenings a great trial. She wanted to send Lexie to school, but Lexie was afraid to go without Ellie. Jade had reported that Lady Stour had been grumbling about Stour's intransigence to Penny since the moment Penny and Jade had returned from their tour of the island on Thursday.

"You think I should try to make friends with Lady

Stour," Sukey said. "That she could prove a valuable ally."

Melanie nodded. "But be subtle. Keep out of Stour's way. You can't let him realize what you're up to. You know how he feels about your campaign."

"Yes." Sukey managed a smile, but it was a tense one. "When he gets angry with me, he doesn't know whether to strangle me or try to seduce me."

The women returned downstairs to find they were in luck. The earl was on the veranda with his host and the governor, engrossed in conversation. The party was rather quiet at first, but grew livelier after Stour's sister and sister-in-law arrived with Patrick Shaw. The women had expressed a wish to see the "authentic" Hong Kong that day—the bustling Chinese bazaar in Taipingshan—and Shaw had volunteered to take them. By all accounts, he had proven a splendid escort.

Of course, the man was an accomplished Don Juan. No sooner had Lady Stour gotten over her cold on Monday than he had managed to meet her "by chance" in the gardens behind Number One House. She had liked him—most women did—and since his relationship to Stour made him family of a sort, Stour had permitted him to squire her to several dinner parties that week.

Sukey lost little time in introducing herself, finding that Lady Stour and her sister-in-law knew all about her from the children. Ellie had even mentioned the gossip at Sukey's school and its role in her departure. Lady Penelope, who asked to be called Penny, quizzed Sukey about her work, while Lady Stour, who didn't ask to be called Victoria, allowed that schools were a marvelous invention and Lexie should surely attend one. Sukey didn't discourage her, but she was careful not to agree too ardently.

Then Stour came in and headed toward his family, and her nerves promptly unraveled. Fortunately, Jade Douglas and her brother had arrived by then, and they were always willing company. She smiled in the direction of Stour's head, mumbled something about having a question for Jade, and fled.

The siblings had settled on the sofa to talk, so Sukey approached them and begged to be rescued. Kai was soon telling her about his newest business venture, which involved manufacturing Jade's products in large enough quantities for export overseas. Sukey thought the idea a brilliant one and said so, and Kai beamed and teased her about backing up her warm praise with cold, hard cash.

Jade immediately chided him for flirting, which he had been, but Sukey hadn't minded a bit. Of all the bachelors in Hong Kong, Kai was the one with whom she felt most comfortable. He liked and respected women, perhaps because of his sisters, and treated her with gentle courtesy.

And then disaster struck. Sukey was talking about California, telling Kai it would be a good market for his products, when Maria Alvares walked in with her uncle. Patrick Shaw gazed at Maria and smiled. Maria shyly smiled back. Father Alvares, thank God, was greeting Governor MacDonnell and didn't notice the exchange. Melanie's face, meanwhile, had taken on an expression of abject horror.

Jade groaned softly, then leaned close to her brother. "I thought Alvares was ill. You said he had sent his regrets this morning for himself and Maria."

Sukey confirmed it. In fact, she told her friends, it wasn't until Alvares had canceled that Melanie had thought to invite Stour's top assistants. She'd had more than enough room, and she'd hoped their presence would relax him. Robert Kilearn was still recuperating and had reluctantly declined, but Patrick Shaw, like Kai-wing, had accepted.

"He must have recovered and changed his mind," Kai murmured. "And McClure is always such a generous host, he obviously felt it unnecessary to send a note." He took Sukey's arm. "Come, Susannah. We should speak to Shaw."

Kai had never called her by her first name before, much less taken her arm, but Sukey didn't have time to analyze his behavior, or to worry about Jade's disapproving frown over his attentions to a woman who wasn't Chinese. As they strode across the room, Sukey caught Melanie's eye and silently indicated that she and Kai would keep Shaw in line. Lord knew somebody had to, because if Shaw made advances to Maria or even kept looking at her that way, Alvares would charge him like an enraged bull.

The two men had first come to blows back in September. Unbeknownst to Alvares, Shaw had been pursuing Maria ardently. She was too innocent to understand that courting was only a game to him, so when he had sworn eternal devotion, she had believed him. She had fallen hard—and then her uncle had found out.

Father Alvares was volatile and puritanical, always raging against sexual excess, and Shaw had long been one of his favorite targets. His lack of chastity was vile, the priest had said, and his claim that he was a gentleman because he never deflowered virgins was depraved. But to steal kisses from a girl behind her guardian's back . . . He deserved the deepest circle of hell for that transgression.

Since Shaw was nothing if not practical, he had ended the affair at once. His desertion had left Maria hurt and confused, but she had recovered quickly and was soon laughing at her own foolishness. Alvares, however, had been less forgiving. Given how incensed he was, the gentlemen of Hong Kong had decided that he and Shaw should never be invited to the same affair, at least not until his temper had cooled.

Sukey and Kai intercepted their quarry, then hustled him to the side door. "Miss Stone needs some air," Kai said. "She would like you to join us in the garden."

"Ah, Miss Stone, if only that were true." Grinning, Shaw looked over her head at Maria. "You know, I had forgotten how lovely she is. Why did I stop seeing her?"

Sukey wanted to pummel him. "Because her uncle would have killed you if you hadn't, you idiot. For heaven's sake, leave the girl alone. Stick to Lady Stour. She has the experience to handle you."

He laughed at that. "Are you mad, Miss Stone? I'm not afraid of Alvares—I'm a much better shot—but Stour would have my head if I trifled with his precious sister-in-law." He allowed himself to be hurried along. "But very well. If you're worried about Maria, I won't renew our acquaintance. I'll be leaving now, though in all fairness, the good father is the one who should go. It isn't at all the thing to uncancel a cancellation." He kissed Sukey's hand. "Good evening, ma'am. I'll miss your delightful company tonight."

Shaw opened the door, then hesitated. "By the way, he was reading one of your books on Monday. It was while he was recuperating from the attack. He summoned me to Number One House to give me some instructions, and he was so engrossed when I first walked in, he didn't even notice I was there. With a little luck, I believe you can win the day. I'll keep my fingers crossed for you.''

He slipped out the door into the garden, and Sukey couldn't help but smile. Time and again, just when she lost all patience with the man, he did something thoughtful, and regained her good opinion.

As the highest-ranking male among the company, Luke was seated on his hostess's right at dinner, across from Governor MacDonnell. The two were spinning amusing tales about life in Hong Kong, but the discussion that truly interested him was taking place at the opposite end of the table. To his chagrin, Penny and Victoria had developed a sudden and profound interest in education for females and were quizzing Miss Stone on the subject. Since they were sitting at the far end while Miss Stone was smack in the middle, that involved the social solecism of talking over the heads of those between, but even that hadn't stopped them. They simply had dragged their entire half of the table into the conversation.

Miss Stone, he noticed, was conveying her opinions more cautiously than usual and kept sneaking anxious glances at him. McClure had assured him the girl would behave, and Luke began to believe his friend must have threatened her with the torments of hell in order to accomplish it. She was so miserably ill-at-ease that she reached for her wineglass continually and quaffed rather than sipped, especially after the conversation went from the general to the specific. From the philosophy of her school to how Eleanor and Lexie could benefit from attending.

McClure, alas, had excellent servants. The level of the wine in one's glass no sooner diminished than they increased it, so he doubted Miss Stone realized how much she was drinking. Concerned and a little guilty, he waited for a break in the conversation, then caught the eye of his comprador, who was sitting on her right. "Douglas, pass me Miss Stone's wineglass, would you?"

"Of course, Lord Stour." Poker-faced, Douglas picked it up and sent it down the table.

Miss Stone's head jerked around. After an early breach, she had avoided his gaze, but now she regarded him with ferocious indignation. He felt the usual surge of desire, but for once, he wasn't annoyed. Her eyes were too feverish with drink to hold her accountable for her actions.

"How remarkable," she said. "My late father appears to have come back in the highhanded guise of an English earl."

Every voice stilled. The denizens of Hong Kong relished a good quarrel, and it was obvious whose side they were about to take. Luke resented their hostility, but he also knew that McClure had been right. He couldn't rejuvenate Burns and Company with the whole colony set against him. He would have to swallow his distaste and exert himself to get along with these people.

"Since I've evidently driven you to drink," he said with a rueful smile, "I felt an obligation to stop you. You've had considerably more than your usual half a glass, Miss Stone, and I fear it's my fault. If I've made you uneasy, I'm sorry. Rest assured that I don't expect you to censor your conversation on my account."

Sukey was so astonished that her jaw all but plummeted open. She had been discussing Ellie's schooling, something Stour had ordered her not to do. In the past, far from regretting his ability to make her nervous, he had coolly exploited it. So why had he apologized?

It had to be the entities, she decided. They had out-done themselves tonight, dominating him completely. In the normal course of events, she never would have pressed the advantage—she had promised to behave— but as Stour had surmised, she was a little tipsy by now.

Normally, she wasn't much of a drinker. Ever since the assault in Ohio, she had been far too frightened of losing control. This evening, however, knowing she was safe in her own home, feeling unbearably tense as she had sat at the table with Stour, she had exceeded her limit.

So while her brain told her to smile politely and thank him for his concern, she couldn't make her mouth obey. "You don't? In that case, I hear you've been doing some reading about education. What did you think of the books I recommended? Have they changed your opinion about sending your daughter to my school?"

Luke picked up his wineglass. He had indeed skimmed the books, mostly because he'd felt too ill to concentrate on anything deeper and too bored to do nothing at all. He had found them enlightening, but still, his daughter's schooling was nobody's concern but his own, and nobody with a shred of manners would have raised the subject. Especially after she had been warned not to.

He glanced around the table. The McClures were visibly anxious, but the others were watching him with amused interest, even his traitor of a sister. Miss Stone deserved a harsh rebuke, but these people would think him a bullying hypocrite if he delivered one. After all, he had just accepted responsibility for her intoxicated state, which was what had loosened her tongue in the first place.

"The books were informative and well-argued," he finally replied. "I'm persuaded that children, even very young ones, do benefit from attending school, given a suitable program. But that doesn't imply that starting them later rather than sooner has to hamper them. Individual circumstances vary. Compensations can be made. In my daughter's case, I believe it's wisest to keep her at home."

Miss Stone appeared surprised—even excited. "Compensations? If that's the direction of your thoughts—"

But whatever she was about to say was lost when Victoria interrupted. "But Luke, there isn't only Eleanor to consider. There's Lexie, as well. As I've told you, she's dying to study at Miss Stone's academy, but she's afraid to go there without someone she knows." She smiled sweetly, as if to beg his indulgence for pursuing such a sensitive topic. "You know how much Eleanor wants to attend. Please say you'll reconsider. After all, situations do change. What harm can there be in giving the school another try?"

Luke took a healthy draught of wine, cursing females and their insufferable missions, wondering what a man had to do to get a little peace in this life. In fact, Victoria was proving even more troublesome than Miss Stone. Not only had she taken to nagging him about Lexie, she had developed an obsessive desire for his company. God knew why, but she had fixed on him as the one man who could provide the distraction she so desperately craved.

The problem was her grief and anxiety, he understood that, but that didn't make it any less embarrassing. Red-faced, he had explained that his alleged sexual prowess had consisted of nothing more creative than ascertaining what Clarissa had enjoyed, then do-

ing it, but it hadn't helped. Victoria had gotten it into
her head that bells would peal and stars would explode, and that was that. He had eluded her thus far,
but the hell of it was, at times, he was tempted to do
the opposite, and morality be damned.

He set down his glass. She had chosen her turf well.
There wasn't a person at this table who didn't agree
with her views. If he refused her, it would be yet another strike against him, making it more difficult to
win these people over.

He was about to reply that this was a family matter
that should be discussed at home when Miss Stone
weighed in, so firmly that even Victoria didn't interrupt. Ellie and Lexie were two different children, Miss
Stone said, and their different situations shouldn't affect each other.

"If Lexie is afraid to come to school without knowing anyone, we can arrange for her to visit some of
the girls in their homes," she continued. "When she's
comfortable, she can attend classes. As for Ellie, as
much as I would like to instruct her, as a teacher I've
found that the best education in the world isn't as important to a child as a loving and devoted parent.
While Lord Stour and I have frequently disagreed, I
know he has her best interests at heart. I have to defer
to that, Lady Stour. We all do."

She looked him straight in the eye. The flash of
impersonal lust he felt was joined by something gen-
tler and deeper. At this point, he supposed, respect and
support—from any quarter at all—were only too welcome. "Perhaps you would allow me to design an individual course of study for her. Something more
challenging and structured than the work we've done
so far. I know you're extremely busy, but perhaps you
could find a few minutes each day to help her. Watch

her write her letters and numbers, and so forth.''

He was so accustomed to impertinence from the woman that his first instinct was to refuse. The suggestion, however, was a sound one. She had presented it with the proper respect. If he permitted Ellie to stay up thirty minutes longer each evening . . . ''It's a possibility,'' he said. ''Give some thought to the specifics, then present me with a detailed plan.''

Her whole face lit up, and he realized with a start that it was the first time she had smiled at him and meant it. ''Would after dinner be too soon?''

Once again, he felt a jolt of surprise. Far from preferring to avoid her, he was content to converse. The difference, he supposed, was this. When it came to what was best for his child, only one opinion mattered. His. In the past, Miss Stone had refused to accept that. Now she finally did.

''After dinner would be fine,'' he said.

Chapter 8

Exactly a week later, at midnight, Sukey drew her circle, purified her implements, and began to chant. The candle that burned on her altar was red with a core of black, the colors of reversal. She had anointed it with bat's blood oil, the herb for breaking hexes. The message on her vellum was so simple that not even the densest of the entities could fail to interpret it correctly. "Remove the spell on Luke Wyndham, the earl of Stour," she had written.

After tangling with the man repeatedly, she was relieved to be canceling the blasted charm, but she was exultant, as well. Despite some unnerving twists and turns, she had succeeded brilliantly. Ellie was back at her school.

The previous Saturday, as she and Stour were concluding their conversation, he had quietly remarked that he wondered how fair he was being to his daughter. Lexie would have the company of other children all day, he had said, while Eleanor would be stuck at home with Mei-mei. She was bound to be jealous and resentful, perhaps not unreasonably so.

In response, Sukey had murmured that she was sure he would do what was best, but in truth, she was secretly elated. Stour had proved surprisingly reasonable about Ellie's course of study, something she attributed to her magic. His qualms about leaving the girl with Mei-mei likely had the same roots. Still, she had learned not to take him for granted. On Monday, she had sent a messenger to Number One House with the first month of lessons, asking him to make whatever revisions he wished.

In reply, she had received a note that was as gratifying as it was terse: "Miss Stone—An excellent job. My compliments. I shall begin at once. Stour."

In the meantime, Lexie had played with two of Sukey's students and asked to begin classes. The attack had prompted Stour to take some extra precautions, especially with his family, so he had sent the girl in the company of a male servant on Tuesday and Wednesday. On Thursday, however, Stour himself had shown up, with Ellie as well as Lexie in tow. He had decided to enroll her, he had announced.

Stour being Stour, he hadn't explained why, but Alex had later told Sukey that when things had gone well with Lexie, he had decided to give the school another chance. His daughter's attendance would please the people of Hong Kong, but first and foremost, he wanted the girl to be happy.

Sukey had harbored only one real worry about having Ellie attend, that she and her cousin would squabble. When the reverse had proved true, she had asked suspiciously whether their spatting had been an act, and Ellie had giggled and confessed. Thanks to their bickering, she'd said, Papa hadn't wanted them around, so in the end, they had gotten their way. As always, Sukey was amazed by the inventiveness of the juvenile mind.

All in all, the week had gone splendidly. The cousins seemed happy and no further gossip had erupted. True, two of the girls had fallen asleep at their desks, but Pearl had taken them into Sukey's office, and within an hour, both had revived completely.

Now, as Sukey beckoned to the entities, she felt such intense joy and fulfillment, such sharp excitement and soaring triumph, that her call resembled a chant of jubilation. The entities manifested quickly, arriving with such a great torrent of energy that she wondered if more than the usual number were present. They relished human emotion, so perhaps they wished to share in the feelings she was experiencing so strongly.

She continued to chant, describing her victory, praising them for their help, and explaining why her influence over Stour should be ended. The best witches knew exactly what sort of a response they were evoking, but Sukey could detect only a tone or a mood, never specific thoughts. She hoped they would be pleased and relaxed tonight—and above all, in a compliant frame of mind.

At first nothing came through, and then, to her confusion, resistance. So she started anew, explaining and praising, but the resistance increased instead of diminished. Beginning to panic, she breathed deeply to calm herself, then picked up Nepenthe. The entities enjoyed the sound of purring, so she scratched him until he obliged. She hoped it would make them more compliant.

Then, for the third time, she asked them to cancel the spell. To her horror, their resistance gave way to impatience. Anger. Resentment. She fought down her fears. Negative human emotions would make them flee, and she needed to make them understand.

But they were the ones who made her understand. For the first time in her life, a verbal message came through. It wasn't in the form of words, but somehow, she knew exactly what the entities were thinking.

They weren't unwilling to reverse the spell. It was just that Stour would have to take the lead in asking. Until he did, they would influence him however they pleased.

This time, she couldn't contain her panic. To meet their demand, Stour would have to stand within her circle, purified and naked, and do precisely what she said when she said to. Even more appalling, before he could lead any rituals, she would have to initiate him into the craft. Install him as a head witch. Join him in the Great Rite.

"But that's impossible!" she wailed. "You know I can't do the things I would have to do. All that—that touching and kissing...And even if I could, he wouldn't go along. He doesn't believe in you."

Then convince him to, they thought, and abruptly vanished.

She gave them a couple of days to reconsider, and then, on Wednesday night, she tried again. She had no other choice. The thought of initiating Stour made her queasy with mortification, but then, it would have been pointless even to suggest it. He was a scientist. If she'd told him she was dabbling in magic, he would have thought her an eccentric at best, a lunatic at worst, and removed his daughter from her care.

She had pleaded a headache that evening, so she was alone except for the children, the other adults having gone to Number One House to dine. Afterward, Alex and Stour would be meeting with Kilearn, Douglas, and Shaw to discuss the losses at Burns, while Pearl visited with Mei-mei, and Melanie conferred with Lady Stour and Lady Penny. At the McClures' suggestion, Stour had agreed to host a grand party on the final weekend of the year at his retreat on Victoria Peak, and the women were arranging the details.

It was a bold social gambit, but the earl was entertaining more often these days, and the McClures felt he had made progress enough with the people of Hong Kong that the party would be a success. According to Alex, he disliked such events himself, but had gone along out of a concern for Lady Stour, who adored them. He hoped the planning involved would divert her from her grief and lift her spirits.

Certainly the setting would be splendid. Argyll Castle, named for the county from which the Burns family hailed, had been Jeremy's favorite spot on the island. He had held parties up there the year round, not just during the summer, when the heat at sea level was often intolerable. Hong Kong was of the opinion that the castle was as fine a home as any on the Peak, so an invitation to spend the weekend was generally a coveted commodity. Certainly Sukey looked forward to going. She was on civil terms with Stour now, so she assumed she would be included.

At the moment, however, the only matter on her mind was the spell she was about to cast. The night was serene and balmy, the perfect conditions for magic. Her chanting, when she finally began it, was inspired. But despite her best efforts, the entities ignored her. To her disappointment and alarm, not even a spark of energy came through. She was still awake and fretting at one in the morning, when the family finally returned from Number One House.

Inevitably, then, she was tired and a little short the next day, and to make matters worse, Pearl woke up hot and shivery, though she insisted on coming to school. When the girls proved unusually unruly that

morning, Sukey thought resignedly that it must be true
about bad luck running in threes.

Or in fours, she thought thirty minutes into the session. She had no sooner ordered an exhausted Pearl to
go home to bed than Ellie yawned and drooped. That
was all she needed, Sukey thought. Stour was protective of his child to begin with, and if he learned she
had taken ill . . . He wouldn't care that numerous other
children had succumbed to this same ailment. He
would blame Sukey.

She hurried into the secondary room, where the girls
were working on a writing assignment, and summoned
her star pupil into the primary room to give a spelling
test to the older girls while the little ones drew pictures. Then she led Ellie down the hall to her office
and settled her on the sofa. Pearl always gave the girls
tea, a special restorative brew that Sukey often drank
herself when she felt tense or tired. It was on the tart
side, but had a minty flavor she found pleasant and
invigorating.

She fixed a pot—she kept a kettle of water sim-
mering on the stove—and then, as the tonic brewed,
she questioned Ellie about her activities. She had gone
to bed at the usual hour, the girl reported, and had
slept soundly all night.

Sukey poured the tea, added honey, and joined Ellie
on the sofa. "I think you'll like this. It's one of Jade's
brews. She makes wonderful tonics."

"I know." Ellie yawned, obediently sipping the tea
as Sukey held the cup to her lips. "She visits all the
time, Miss Stone. We like her boys. They play stupid
games with William, like throwing cricket balls . . .
into wastebaskets." The girl blinked, yawning again.
"Jade has tonics . . . for everything. She gave me one
for colds . . . and I didn't catch Aunt Victoria's."

"And how did it taste?" Sukey asked, trying to keep the girl awake.

"It was sweet." Ellie took another few sips. "That's . . . her secret. Her tonics . . . taste good. So you always . . . want more."

Somehow Sukey got the tea down Ellie's throat before she nodded off. Pearl always stayed in the office while the girls napped, so Sukey decided to do the same. First, however, she dashed into the primary room, collected the spelling tests, and instructed her substitute to read the class a story.

Back in her office, she corrected the tests and recorded the grades, then took out a book on Oriental art she'd been meaning to review. But she had barely begun the task when Ellie stirred.

She looked up, startled. Not more than fifteen minutes had gone by. "I didn't expect you to waken . . ." Her voice trailed off. The girl was sitting bolt upright, staring into space.

She hurried to the sofa and put a gentle hand on the child's shoulder. "Ellie? Are you all right?"

The girl answered in an eerily flat tone. "I've told you, it's too soon to speculate."

"Too soon to speculate about what?" Sukey asked in confusion, surprised Ellie knew a word that long. "What are you talking about?"

"It's my money, Alex," Ellie said in the same unearthly monotone. "If I want you to speculate, you will bloody well speculate. Now out with it."

Bloody? Sukey was in shock now. The girl didn't use language like that. Her father would have lectured her until she cringed.

"If you insist. I plan to watch Kilearn. He keeps the books. Control the money, and you control the business. And he was in the warehouse that night. We can't assume he told Deane the truth about why. I'll poke around Taipingshan, Luke. See what I can find out.''

A slight pause. ''And Shaw?''

Another pause. ''You said Sir Roger Albright told you he had his eye on the main chance. I've learned that there's bad blood between the two. The incident happened six years ago, while I was visiting America. Albright was in the Royal Navy at the time. His sister came to see him in Hong Kong, and Shaw seduced her. Left her and broke her heart. But even if Albright has an ax to grind, he may be right about Shaw. On four occasions during the past two years, Stratton and Adams made a large profit on consignments Burns was offered first, then declined. Jeremy Burns made those decisions, but Shaw was the one who provided the background information.''

Sukey realized she was listening to a conversation between Stour and Alex, memorized and parroted back verbatim. Given the length and content of the discussion, that was astonishing in itself, but even more incredible, the girl had repeated words she couldn't possibly have understood. Many of them—''incident,'' ''seduced,'' ''consignments,'' and so forth—had come out somewhat garbled, but Sukey had deciphered them from the context.

''But I've read the supporting documents,'' Ellie continued, speaking Stour's part now. ''Telegrams and letters from merchants and shopkeepers. Are you saying they were forged?''

The girl hesitated for a second. These brief delays seemed to mark the end of one speech and the beginning of the next. ''Perhaps, but people can also be paid to make false statements. Tex Stratton made a bundle on those consignments. He could afford the bribes. I plan to go to Canton on Friday, to question the men involved.''

There was another pause. Stour again: ''Penny sails there in the morning. Her blasted plants again. I've been forbidden to object, but I want her protected. If you could get away earlier . . . Go along with her . . .''

Alex: ''Of course. I would be delighted to look after your sister. Take her wherever she wants to go.''

Stour: ''I'm grateful, Alex. That's one less thing I'll have to worry about. And Douglas? Am I to distrust him, as well?''

Alex: ''Kai-wing makes no secret of his ambitions. He would like to control his own hong someday. But he'll pursue his goal honestly, Luke. He won't cheat you.''

The girl continued in the same vein, repeating the conversation in an expressionless voice. The men had discussed the incident in the warehouse next, reviewing Alex's continuing investigation as well as Deane's. And then Sukey heard her own name mentioned, and her pulses jumped. Stour had remarked that he was sorry she'd been unable to come that night, and Alex had replied that Stour wasn't sorry at all, that she irritated him even more than Victoria at her most restless and demanding, and that he was far more relaxed when she wasn't present.

''That's true,'' Stour had answered, ''but when I clash with Susannah, at least it's not a boring—''

And with that, Ellie fell dead asleep. It was as if her brain could contain only so many words and had reached its limit. She awoke fifteen minutes later, seemingly in perfect health, with no memory of talking in her sleep.

*   *   *

That evening, describing the incident to Melanie, Sukey admitted she was at a loss to explain the cause. "At first, I assumed the parroting was part of the sleeping syndrome. That it happened whenever a child took ill. But then I recalled that both Stour's son and Gibb's had fallen asleep at school. And both of us know that Maria didn't mention any talking."

"Which she likely would have, if it had taken place," Melanie said thoughtfully. "Do you believe this was an isolated incident, then? That Ellie happened to sleepwalk and heard the two men talking, and that their conversation was somehow imprinted on her mind? And that, this morning, she began babbling by chance in her sleep?"

"It's possible," Sukey conceded. "The human mind is very complicated. But the girl seemed to be under a powerful hypnotic spell. I doubt even the most brilliant mesmerist could induce such a state, so I suspect it was the work of an extraordinarily psychic witch."

"Oh, Lord, not witchcraft again." Melanie wearily rubbed the bridge of her nose. "But is it possible? A witch might be skilled enough to make the entities understand what she wanted and convince them to try to do it, but the feat would involve enormous mental control over the child and an amount of memorization that rivals a one-act play. It defies logic, Sukey."

"Don't you think I know that? I wouldn't have believed it, either, if I hadn't seen it with my own eyes. Yet it did occur. I'm afraid we're dealing with something evil rather than benign." In truth, Sukey confessed, she knew almost nothing about the darker side of magic, which was controlled by entities who were mean-spirited or even downright fiendish. She had always avoided the creatures, who could be extremely dangerous.

"Which is what worries me most of all," she continued in a hushed voice. "Suppose Pearl is involved?" Her assistant was still in bed, suffering from fever and chills. "She's the one who always stays with the girls, and she would have done so again today, if she hadn't taken ill. And the tea she always gives them is formulated by her sister."

"But Pearl is never present when the *boys* nod off," Melanie pointed out. "Besides, you and I drink that tea all the time, and it's never made us talk in our sleep." She thought for a minute. "Let's approach this from another direction. What motive could the perpetrator have? What's to be gained from the information the girls impart?"

"Blackmail material," Sukey suggested. "Business intelligence."

"But neither sister is suspiciously rich, and neither has ever mentioned any unusual investments."

Nor had Kai, Sukey remarked. On the contrary, he preferred to put his money into ventures of his own creation. "Lord, this is frustrating. We're going around in circles. Maybe Pearl is right and the ailment is just another peculiar Oriental syndrome, with the talking a bizarre part of it. Does your clairvoyance tell you anything? Whether Stour is still in danger, for example?"

Melanie shook her head. She could sense danger only to herself and those close to her, and Stour, while a good friend, wasn't close enough yet, she said. "I just wish Alex were in town, so we could ask his advice."

But he was in Canton, and would likely be gone for another week. Kwangtung wasn't the only province

Penny had decided to explore. She was set on visiting Fukien, as well, and Alex had agreed to accompany her, even though it meant delaying the family's Christmas celebration by several days.

In the end, a week proved too long for Sukey to wait. She began to investigate on her own, learning from Maria that none of her dozing boys had prattled in his sleep, and from Pearl that the reverse was the case with the girls. Two in addition to Ellie had sat up and babbled, but Pearl hadn't thought it important enough to mention. English wasn't her native tongue, she pointed out. When someone spoke it flatly and quickly, as the two girls had, she found it almost impossible to comprehend. So she had ignored the chatter, and in fifteen or twenty minutes, it had stopped.

As for the tea, Jade said with a laugh that it had never produced such remarkable symptoms in *her*, then explained that her potions could be unpredictable. They worked differently on different people depending on what they had eaten or done that day, and even on the individual's unique yin and yang. The tea's restorative value was undeniable, but if Sukey was worried about its effect on her students, she should refrain from offering it.

And there the matter would have rested, but for two disturbing coincidences. Lying sleepless in bed Friday night, Sukey suddenly realized that every child affected had been the son or daughter of a taipan. If they sleepwalked, the conversations they stood to overhear in their fathers' parlors would be far more significant commercially than the average discussion. Even more suspicious, the outbreak had begun when Stour had arrived in China, becoming more marked after he had settled in Hong Kong.

Only one conclusion was possible. Whatever was

going on in this colony, it involved commerce in general and Stour in particular. The fact that he had been mysteriously attacked only confirmed the theory. After all, he had a natural enemy here, the man who had stolen from Burns. His success at slowing the losses must have prompted the fellow to intensify his hostile activity.

At best, Sukey thought worriedly, Stour's enemy wanted only to bleed the hong dry, but more likely, he wanted Stour destroyed, and wouldn't rest until the deed was done. She couldn't ignore something like that. Alex, like Melanie, deemed him a friend—such an intimate one, she now knew, that they called each other by their given names in private.

It was her duty to warn him, she realized, but the prospect made her teeth ache with anxiety. The man considered her a trial to begin with, and the attacks involved the sort of supernatural phenomenon that a rationalist like the earl would deny existed. She would more confidently have cautioned a grizzly.

She continued to toss and turn. On the other hand, Stour had invited her to Argyll Castle, and when he had spoken of her to Alex, he had referred to her as Susannah. Surely, she thought, both the invitation and the use of her Christian name indicated some softening on his part.

And besides, however much she exasperated him, at least he didn't find her boring.

Chapter 9

Luke now knew that there was something even more taxing than having Susannah Stone as an adversary, and that was having her as a friend. With flawless timing, she had arrived at his home as he was walking up the drive, apologized profusely for disturbing him, and announced she had something important to discuss. And then their eyes had met, and it was the same damned thing as before. But whatever she was doing, she obviously didn't want to. She had flushed too deeply for the trick to be deliberate, and looked away too quickly.

Naturally, he had invited her inside. Eleanor was safely in her clutches now, so he assumed she hadn't come here to nag him. Besides, she had seemed so distressed by whatever was on her mind that he'd felt it his duty to reassure her. So he had ordered her some refreshments, sat her on the sofa, and listened to her story.

And what had his indulgence earned him? Thirty straight minutes of the most ridiculous drivel he had ever endured. An endless, utterly pointless half hour.

It just went to show that intelligence, which he had learned she possessed in abundance, had nothing to do with common sense. Even for a female, she had an outlandish imagination. She somehow had leaped from the fact that a handful of children, among them his daughter, had dozed off in school and babbled in their sleep, to some wild theory about a master mesmerist, a plot to bankrupt him, and a conspiracy to send him to his doom.

His tolerance had given way to annoyance, and then to a pressing urge to escape. It wasn't only that she had wasted his time, but that he couldn't sit close to her without being intensely aware of her, and pent-up desire wasn't a feeling he enjoyed. Though she was dressed primly, in a gray skirt and jacket and a high-necked white blouse, his attention kept wandering in the most improper directions. He was vastly relieved when she finished her account, and he could thank her and send her on her way.

But when he opened his mouth to do so, he felt such a rush of shame that he instantly changed his mind. True, she had the imagination of a third-rate novelist, but her intentions were those of a guardian angel. Her voice had been husky and earnest, as if she were desperate to be believed. Her hands were clenched together in her lap, a sign that she was extremely anxious. In his entire life, only two people had fretted about him that way, his mistress at Oxford and his sister Penny. He was touched.

So instead of dismissing her, he gave her knotted fists a gentle pat and told her she was worried over nothing. To his chagrin, he felt the touch everywhere, from his palms to his loins. "I promise I'll continue to be careful," he added. "I've made enemies before, and I've always outwitted them. If the fellow wanted me dead, he would have shot me in the godown. And don't forget, I have Alex in my corner now."

Sukey's throat was so dry from tension that she grabbed her tea, holding it with an unsteady hand as she gulped it down. Stour made her miserably uneasy, sitting so close beside her, listening so coolly to what she said. He hadn't accepted a word of it, she was sure of it, but then, how could you expect a man to believe himself in mortal danger if you cravenly omitted to mention the source of that danger? Her story must have seemed like nothing so much as a series of odd coincidences and bizarre goings-on.

She put down her cup. He would think her addled if she raised the subject of witchcraft, which was why she had sought to avoid it. Yet she possessed information he lacked, and it was her duty to convey it. That meant she would have to convince him she spoke the truth, but heaven only knew how.

She cleared her throat. "There's one thing I haven't told you yet. This particular enemy . . . The means he employs . . ." She hesitated. *Go on*, she thought. *Just say it and get it over with.* "The trance I observed in your daughter was extremely powerful, Lord Stour. I don't believe you comprehend how precisely she repeated your conversation with Alex."

A flash of annoyance crossed his face. "When I agree to listen to someone, I assure you I pay attention. You said *verbatim*. I do understand the meaning of the word. You also said Eleanor repeated only a portion of my conversation, which would explain how she managed to retain it."

"I'm terribly sorry. I didn't mean to imply that you hadn't listened." He was going to be difficult, Sukey saw, but that was only to be expected. "It's just—it was a very substantial portion. A huge amount of memorization was required. I told you the trance appeared induced rather than spontaneous, but I failed to mention that no mere mesmerist could have effected such a state." She paused, then continued more forcefully, "To my knowledge, only one sort of person could, someone who was in touch with the darkest of supernatural forces. So when you speak of being careful . . . Physical caution won't be enough. The attack could be subtle and diabolical. You'll have to take more active precautions."

She peeked at him to assess his reaction. She was anticipating even greater irritation, but unless she missed her guess, he was trying desperately not to smile. "I'll consider what you've told me," he said, using the tone one might adopt with an agitated child. "I'm grateful for the warning. I know you've had a difficult week, what with Miss Douglas being ill. I can see how tired and upset you are, so I want you to go home, get some rest, and put this out of your mind."

Sukey silently translated the statement. *You're as crazy as a loon, my dear, but you've obviously been working too hard, so I won't hold it against you*. He wasn't only indulging her; he was patronizing her, as well. Even acid ridicule would have been less humiliating. Indeed, he wouldn't have treated a male that way, only a simpleminded female who was too overset to know what she was about.

Her temper sparked, and she squared her shoulders. "Believe me, Lord Stour, this isn't a figment of my imagination. I happen to have studied such matters at length—"

"You mean witchcraft," he interrupted, and the laughter in his voice was only too obvious now. "That *is* what we're talking about, isn't it? You believe someone has cast a spell on these children and turned them into an army of—of miniature automatons, sleep-marching stealthily through the night, spying on me at their master's behest.''

Now *that* was ridicule. She raised her chin. ''Dramatically put, but yes, that's exactly what I believe. They're all the offspring of taipans. The confidential information they could be expected to overhear might prove extremely helpful to someone who was trying to destroy you.''

''Indeed it might, but unfortunately for your theory, witches don't exist.'' He paused, visibly forcing his amusement under control. ''This syndrome you've witnessed is obviously exactly what you surmised in the first place, an unusual Oriental ailment. And since it seems to be entirely harmless, there's no reason for concern. I want you to forget the whole thing.''

''Harmless to the children, but not to you,'' Sukey insisted. ''If you'll remember, you were brutally attacked two weeks ago. Your firm has suffered serious losses. I don't know how those things tie into the syndrome—''

''Because they don't. You're seeing conspiracies where only coincidences exist.'' He covered her hand for a moment, then continued gently, ''You're very intelligent, my dear, I do recognize that, but you tend to become . . . rather obsessed with things. Living in the Orient has obviously exposed you to certain . . . mystical ideas. You lack the background to analyze them objectively, so you've taken them far too seriously. But I'm a scientist. I've studied the natural world at length. And I can assure you that there's no reliable evidence whatsoever for the existence of a supernatural phenomenon such as witchcraft.''

Sukey told herself the man must stand in front of a mirror and practice being condescending, he was that good at it. ''Living in the Orient has nothing to do with it. Witchcraft works. I studied it in California, and—''

''And how do you *know* it works? Because you've observed witches flying around San Francisco on broomsticks?''

''Of course not. That's a ridiculous stereotype. But black magic is real, and if you have any prudence—''

''Black magic? Oh, well, that's something else entirely, isn't it!'' He grinned at her. ''Then you've seen them cavorting naked with demons amid sulfurous smoke. Witnessed them turning men into beasts, raising up storms, and drinking the blood of sacrificed infants.''

''Not that, either,'' she said coolly, ''although the aura they create is undoubtedly extremely negative. And kindly stop interrupting me.''

''Gladly, if you'll stop spouting nonsense.'' He gave a gruff shake of his head. ''Believe me, Miss Stone, I'm trying to be patient here—I know you have good intentions—but if someone is harming me, it isn't with charms and spells. Magic doesn't exist. Hexes don't work.''

That was it. Sukey had heard enough. She grasped Stour by the shoulders and glared at him. ''You don't think so? Then look at me. Ask yourself what you feel. And then ask yourself why you feel it.''

Luke stared back at her. Her fingers were digging into his shoulders, sending erotic shock waves through his system, and her body was so close, the heat seemed to burn through his clothing. He wanted nothing so much as to pull her into his arms and end the torment he felt, and if she thought witchcraft was the reason, she belonged in Bedlam.

''You know damned well what I feel,'' he muttered.

"Spells have nothing to do with it. It's the way you look at me."

Sukey dropped her hands but continued to glare. "So you still believe I mesmerize you. That I'm putting you into some sort of . . . some sort of erotic stupor."

"I know you are. Sometimes . . . there can be a powerful sort of chemistry between a man and a woman, and when their eyes meet—" Luke looked down, feeling short of breath. "Something happens. It's like a bolt of lightning slices through you, and you can't think straight, the ache is so intense. You saw it the first night we met—the effect you were having—and you took full advantage of it. And now, even though you would prefer to end it, you can't. It's nature. Biology. Neither of us can control it. But magic has nothing to do with it."

"And this—this *thing* you insist happens . . ." Her tone was withering. "Has it ever happened to *you* before?"

"No." Luke had thought himself immune. It was daunting to learn he was fallible. And oddly reassuring, too.

She abruptly turned away, staring out the window into the garden. He gazed at her back—the delicate bones of her spine, the indignant thrust of her shoulders, the wild cascade of her auburn hair—and wanted to groan.

"And what do you suppose would happen if you kissed me?" she demanded. "This feeling you say you have . . . Would it diminish or grow more intense?"

Luke thought that had to be the most preposterous question a woman had ever asked him. "I can't answer that—not without talking in terms no gentleman would use to a lady."

"Then I'll answer it for you. You believe you would want me more. That you would wish to keep going, and not stop until—" He saw her swallow hard. "Well, you know."

She had that part right. His member was already swollen and stiff. "Yes. Precisely."

Sukey took a deep breath, then slowly turned around. Stour had denied the existence of magic, so she would have to show him it was real. "You're wrong. It won't happen that way at all. The fact is, I wanted your daughter back in my school, and you wouldn't listen, so I cast a spell on you to make you—"

"You did *what*?" He looked incredulous.

"You heard me. I thought it would be easy and quick. But they don't always do things the way you want them to—"

"They?" he repeated, beginning to smile now. "Are we talking about creatures in the astral plane, Miss Stone?"

"Yes, Lord Stour, we are, if one defines the astral plane as a higher dimension, beyond the normal reach of our human senses. That's science, not superstition, although I'm not at liberty to tell you where my knowledge comes from."

"Ah, yes. Blood oaths and all that. The rituals are a great secret." He chuckled. "And you say there were no orgies or miracles involved? How disappointing for you."

"You can mock me as much as you like, but it won't change the fact that you don't know nearly as much as you think you do. These creatures—these entities—do exist. I wanted them to push you into sending Ellie back to my school, but instead, they gave me this—this power we just spoke of. They obviously realized—"

The chuckle turned to a great gust of laughter. "You mean I'm bewitched? Well, that certainly would explain it. Why I'm so susceptible to you, that is."

She pursed her lips. "Look here, Stour, how am I supposed to finish if you keep interrupting me?"

"My apologies, Miss Stone. Truly, I'm completely riveted. I won't say a word. Pray continue."

Sukey told herself he wouldn't be laughing when she was through with him. "The entities have a twisted sense of humor. They've evidently observed that human males . . ." She paused, momentarily tongue-tied by embarrassment. "That is, sometimes, they, uh, men that is, they can be led by their . . . their animal passions. But the entities are far from omnipotent, and when someone is as . . . as willful as you are . . . They can control you only when our eyes meet. So the desire you think you feel . . . It isn't real. You have to be looking at me. If you want proof of that . . ." A hot flush rose up her neck. She didn't want to do this—she was sure she would find it unpleasant—but she didn't see what choice she had. "Then close your eyes and kiss me. You'll find that I'm right."

He was silent for several seconds. Finally he asked solemnly, "Am I allowed to speak yet?"

She scowled at him. He was enjoying this, damn him, enjoying her discomfort. She wanted to dash her tea into his miserable male lap. "Yes, although I fail to see why you would want to. You're a scientist, aren't you? So perform the blasted experiment."

If there was anything Luke disliked, it was being ordered about, but in this particular case . . . It didn't matter that Miss Stone's claims were utter claptrap. She obviously believed them to be true, and God knew he was willing to show her they weren't. More than willing. The blood was pounding in his ears. His manhood was throbbing violently. And whether he looked at her or not made no difference at all to how he felt.

He took a firm grip on his passions. "You want me to make love to you? Right here? Right now?"

She edged away from him. "Not make love to me. Conduct a scientific experiment. After you finish, we can analyze your reaction."

Luke hadn't forgotten how wary she was around men. Indeed, she looked so reluctant now, so uneasy, that he wondered if she had ever allowed a man to touch her. "Let's define our terms. There are different types of kisses, and in order for the experiment to be valid, the kiss would have to be . . ." He struggled to come up with a description that wouldn't offend her.

"Romantic," she finished. "With tongues and all that." She stared into her lap, blushing fiercely, but there was nothing bashful about what followed. "California isn't England, Stour. Females aren't pure little vessels that are kept untouched until they marry. I've been kissed by half a dozen men. I do know what we're talking about."

"Half a dozen? Really?" He smiled at his own folly. And here he'd been worried about shocking her with his vile male appetites! "Well, hell, Susannah, you've certainly got me beat."

She looked at him sharply. "I didn't say you could call me that."

She was erecting a barrier, trying to keep him at a distance, but he wasn't about to permit it. He deliberately moved closer. While she didn't retreat, she lowered her eyes, and her whole body tensed.

"I couldn't kiss a woman whom I thought of as *Miss* Somebody." He twined a lock of her hair around his finger. It was silky and soft. He wondered how it would smell. "So you're a woman of the world, are you? In that case, why are you so nervous, my dear?''

"You have that effect on people,'' she muttered. "Surely you've noticed.''

"But there's no reason that I should have it on you. We're friends now.'' He trailed his fingers to the back of her neck and gently massaged her nape. "Despite everything you've said about how I'll react, are you worried I'll lose control? That you'll have to fight me off?''

"Of course not. I told you, you won't even enjoy it that much.'' She sounded a little breathless. "Why are you fiddling with my neck? That has nothing to do with kissing.'' She pushed away his hand. "So? Are you going to do it or aren't you?''

If she wasn't fearful, Luke thought, she was probably repelled. He had traveled that road before, and he wasn't taking it again, not even in the interests of science. "I think not. I would never force myself on a woman who found my attentions . . . distasteful.''

But Sukey found them anything but. On a primal level, Stour heated her blood. He was the last man she should have desired—he was arrogant, condescending, and closed-minded—yet she did. It was unnerving. Appalling.

"For heaven's sake, look in a mirror,'' she mumbled. "If you bothered to be the least bit charming, you could have any woman you wanted. The issue isn't whether I'll enjoy it or not. It's whether you will.'' She licked her lips. "Now will you please just get on with it?''

Luke sucked in his breath. The sight of her tongue made him picture it on his body—everywhere on his body, stroking and tasting him. "Sometimes, what we want and what we think we should want are two different things," he said evenly. "Is that your problem, Susannah?"

She finally met his eyes. "Do you know something, Stour? If you had been around in the days of Socrates, he wouldn't have needed to drink hemlock to end his life. He could have had you analyze him to death."

Luke took that as a yes. He had made sport of her ideas, and she was insulted. Naturally, she didn't want him to touch her. Yet.

"The point of caressing you"—he massaged her nape again, very gently—"is to relax you. You aren't responsible for biology, my dear. Your body has a will of its own, so stop fighting it. After all, it's only a harmless kiss."

She didn't answer, just sat there looking irritable and uneasy. Smiling to himself, he massaged her neck and shoulders and fondled her hair. He could see her mounting excitement in her quickened breathing, but she sat motionless, outwardly ignoring him, resisting what she felt.

Years ago, he had learned to take his time with a woman, but this was something more. Not just sensual stimulation, but erotic persuasion. In the past, the notion had never appealed to him—why pursue a reluctant female when willing ones were available?—but with Susannah, it was intensely exciting. An intoxicating challenge. The barrier she had erected was crumbling, and there was passion on the other side. Passion for him. And he wanted to unleash it.

Leaning closer, he lifted a strand of auburn hair to his face and breathed in the fragrance. "You smell delicious. Like sandalwood and lemon." He trailed his fingers down the sleeve of her jacket. "Let me take this off you, Susannah. I want to touch you."

In Sukey's opinion, Stour had done quite enough

touching already, tender and very seductive touching that had made her desperate to escape. She was miserably uncomfortable with the way he was making her feel—hot and breathless with arousal, queasy with anxiety. But unless she stayed, she would never prove her point.

"I don't see why you need to," she said. "I'm as relaxed now as I'll ever be. You should be kissing me, not—not tugging at my hair, mauling my back, and trying to remove my clothing."

"Did I tug and maul? I'm sorry, my dear. I'll try to be less clumsy." He touched the collar of her coat. "As for this . . . I'm doing the kissing, not you. I would appreciate a little leeway in how I go about it." He began to unfasten the buttons. "My experience may not be as vast as yours, but I've been told I have a reasonable amount of skill at this sort of thing. You're not relaxed at all, not yet, but if you give me half a chance, you will be. I promise you, the kiss won't be too hideously objectionable."

He was amused, blast him. He knew precisely what he was doing, and precisely how he was making her feel. Too late, she recalled Lady Randall's letter about his talent in bed, and realized she should have expected him to take this tack. But a man who was imperious and impatient in every other area of his life had no right at all to be a sensitive lover.

He eased off her jacket and tossed it aside. His fingers didn't touch her breasts, didn't even come close, but she felt as if they had. Her flesh grew hot and her nipples puckered, and she didn't like the sensation at all. She liked it even less when he unbuttoned a sleeve of her blouse, pushed up the fabric, and brought her hand to his mouth.

She shuddered when he nuzzled her palm. Every

nerve in her body seemed to fire, radiating out from her hand in the most alarming way. If this was biology, she had no earthly use for it. And then he ran his lips up her bare arm, kissing his way from the inside of her wrist to the crook of her elbow, and her chest grew tight with the effort to breathe. His lips were warm and soft, but very firm. She wondered how they would feel on her mouth.

The thought was so unnerving that she yanked away her arm. "That's enough, Stour. Leeway would be the Pearl River. You're taking the Pacific Ocean. The experiment involves kissing, not seduction."

He stood. Removed his jacket. Sat back down beside her, his thigh pressed against her own. "I wasn't trying to seduce you. I just meant—to interest you a little more. That's why I suggested we define the nature of our encounter. In order for the experiment to be valid, I would have to enjoy the kiss—or at least, I would have to have some prospect of doing so. But if you don't respond, that prospect won't exist."

She couldn't just permit him to kiss her? She had to want it or else he wouldn't? "That's absurd," she mumbled.

"I don't agree. I don't believe in taking. Even if it's only a kiss, it's much too close to rape." He put his arm around her and fondled a lock of her hair. "Of course, you *were* growing interested. That's why you stopped me. Your body was sending a message your mind was afraid to accept. Shall we continue on my terms, or forget the whole thing?"

She regarded him suspiciously, saw desire flame in his eyes, and hastily looked away. "You'll observe your reaction objectively? And then you'll stop and report what you felt?"

"Of course. That *is* the point of the kiss."

Every other man Sukey knew would have believed his pleasure was the point. Even for a scientist, Stour was a paragon of logic and detachment. She was obviously worried over nothing.

"Oh, all right," she said, a little put out that he was so much calmer than she was. "Do whatever you want—within reason. I'll even try to like it. Just don't expect me to moan and pant the way your mistress did, that's all."

"My God, not you, too," he grumbled. "Everyone in the world must have heard what she said. We might as well have made love on the stage at Covent Garden."

He sounded so peeved that she almost laughed. But then he curled his fingers into her hair, eased back her head, and lowered his lips, and Clarissa St. Simon went straight from her mind. His mouth was gentle but ardent, planting kisses on her throat and neck, and she responded with a heat and intensity that made her reel. It was as if they had never stopped to talk. There was the searing, shattering heat. The fear in the pit of her stomach. The feeling that she couldn't breathe, that she needed to run, that she was dying for the taste of his mouth.

He dropped kisses up the length of her jaw, nuzzled her ear, and nipped the lobe. A shock of excitement tore through her at the hint of pain, especially between her legs. Confused and appalled—she shouldn't have enjoyed something like that—she took a quick, panicky breath. "Stour, I don't think—"

"Hush, Susannah. I'm sorry. I'll slow down." He eased away from her, then slipped his hands into her hair and massaged her scalp.

It felt wonderful from the first moment. Bewitchingly pleasurable. Hypnotically soothing. He had marvelous fingers, strong but exquisitely gentle, and he knew exactly how to use them. The massage went on and on, as if he had all the time in the world. She finally allowed her eyes to droop shut, turned slightly, and nestled against his chest.

He nuzzled her closed lids. "So you like that, hmm?"

She was floating halfway between wakefulness and sleep, her fear submerged deep inside her. "Yes. It's lovely."

He kept going. She yawned and snuggled closer. "I'm so tired, Luke. It's been such a long week."

"I know, darling. Mine, too." He tucked a finger under her chin to lift it, then kissed her temple, her cheekbone, the bridge of her nose, and finally the dimple below her mouth.

Her lethargy vanished instantly. She knew what would come next. Her heart was pounding wildly even before he took her in his arms and sucked gently on her bottom lip, but this time, the excitement that flooded her senses swamped every other emotion—her doubt, her uneasiness, even her fear. After all, she thought hazily, it *was* only a kiss, and she had agreed to try to enjoy it. She parted her lips and slid her arms around his waist. His body was warm. Muscular. Powerful.

He nibbled and sucked, toying with her mouth, making her want more than he was giving. Her arms tightened around his waist, and she began to taste him, touching his lips, then hesitantly seeking his tongue. He tasted her back, meeting her tongue and then withdrawing, deliberately teasing her until she was clinging to him, dizzy with heat, breathless with longing. Somehow her hands found their way under his shirt.

She explored his bare skin, pressing herself against him, nipping at his retreating mouth.

He groaned softly and cupped her chin. They stared at each other for a long moment. "I don't think I've ever wanted to kiss a woman as much as I want to kiss you right now," he said. "And you're telling me that once I start, I won't want to continue?"

She shivered. "Not as much as you think you will."

He released her and grabbed a couple of cushions. Tossed them into a corner. Gently pushed her down. "By God, I'm going to enjoy this."

The next moment he was pressing her against the pillows, his chest flush against her breasts, teasing her again. He meant the victory, not the kiss, but she didn't care. She was too aroused to object. And then he slipped his tongue between her lips, and nothing else existed.

He was gentle at first, coaxing and sweet, just barely taking what she offered, and it made her frenzied with frustration. She dug her nails into his back and thrust her tongue into his mouth, demanding more. He quickly provided it, with a probing, dominating kiss that went on and on, exploring and conquering until her bones felt like jelly and she was shaking violently. He cupped her breast and found the tautened nipple beneath her corset, and she was wholly unable to stop him. Or unable to make herself want to, which amounted to the same thing. He kneaded the nipple until she moaned. If anything, she wanted him to be rougher. More commanding. More insistent.

Then, abruptly, he jerked away. By the time her head cleared and she pulled herself up, he had crossed to the window and was staring outside, still breathing hard as he shoved his shirt back into his trousers. She straightened her blouse, then ran her hands through her hair, trying to smooth it into some semblance of order.

She was still trembling, but not from passion. For seven years, she had barely let a man near her . . . and now this. She had sworn she would never again lose control, yet she had ceded it. Willingly. Eagerly. And to Stour, of all people. He had done exactly as he'd wished, and she had welcomed it. Would have permitted even more. It was horrifying. Mortifying. What could have possessed her?

He finally turned, giving her a slow smile. "Well, Susannah? Did it feel as if I wanted to stop? Even a little?"

"No." She lowered her eyes, too embarrassed to keep looking at him. "But you did. You could. It proves my point."

Luke cursed under his breath. After what had just happened, he couldn't believe Susannah was still holding on to her crack-brained notions. "I told you, there *is* no spell. There's no such thing as witchcraft. I stopped because I'm a gentleman, although God knows you've accused me often enough of being the opposite."

He started forward. In all his life, he had never experienced such hunger. He was still dizzy from it, still on the verge of exploding. The way Susannah kissed . . . The feel of her nails on his back . . .

The men who had preceded him—that lucky six— had taught her well. She was irresistible. Demandingly passionate one moment, sweetly submissive the next. And even if she was mulish and unruly—even if she would bring as much discord as pleasure into his life— he couldn't let her go. For as long as he was in Hong Kong, he wanted her in his bed.

He sat down beside her, wanting nothing so much as to carry her to his room and strip off her clothes.

"A gentleman asks, Susannah. He doesn't just take, no matter how eagerly a woman offers. So I'm asking."

Sukey's whole body grew stiff and cold. She wasn't naive enough to believe Stour was proposing marriage. In 1871, this was what happened when you forgot yourself, when you let yourself go. You were considered a trollop and treated as such. "You want me to go to bed with you. To become your mistress."

Luke heard the ice in her voice—the awful hurt—and grimaced. So much for his claim to be a gentleman. He had handled this about as gracelessly as one could. "Susannah . . . Please forgive me for insulting you. I'm not myself right now. I look at you, sit with you, touch you, and all I can think about is making love to you." He took her hand, which was clammy and limp. "You're lovely, passionate, and spirited. I don't want you as a mistress, not if the term implies you're some sort of kept woman, at my beck and call. Both of us know the notion doesn't fit you at all. You have your own life, just as I do. We're both very busy. But we could give each other pleasure. Make each other happy. That's all I was suggesting."

As propositions went, it wasn't a bad one, Sukey thought, but it also indicated a total blindness about the qualities she longed for a man to admire. "What you mean is, you want me to spend a discreet hour in your bed whenever you can find the time. No, thank you, Stour. I'm not interested in that sort of connection."

"That's not what I mean at all." He stroked the back of her hand. "Before, when you were cuddled against my chest, before I even kissed you, you called me Luke. I liked the way that sounded. I liked the way you felt in my arms. I want to spend as much time with you as I can, not just making love to you, but talking and laughing.''

"But what on earth would we find to talk about?" Sukey was more offended than wounded now. "You find me ignorant and irrational. Exasperating and silly. Someday, I'll meet the man I'm destined to marry, and he won't babble about my spirit and passion. He'll value me for my intelligence, my knowledge, and my judgment.'' She reached for her jacket. "I have to go now. I think it would be best—''

"Wait a moment, Susannah. Please.'' Luke was beginning to think he had made a horrible mistake here. A woman with any experience didn't talk about marrying her soul mate. Yet the way she had clawed at him and kissed him . . . A virgin that reckless didn't remain a virgin for long, either.

Confused, he kept hold of her wrist to prevent her from leaving. "Those six men you mentioned . . . The ones you've kissed . . . How many were your lovers?"

She tugged away her hand. "That's none of your damned business.''

If the answer had been none, she would have said so. Indeed, she would have slapped his face the moment he had asked her to share his bed. Quite clearly, she was telling him she didn't care to discuss the subject with a man she had refused. "I'm sorry. Under the circumstances, you're completely right.''

She stood, shrugging into her jacket. "What circumstances? Your previous lovers are none of my business, either. The rule would hold true even if you had asked me to be your wife rather than your mistress.''

He was on his feet by then, putting on his coat. He didn't agree—a man had a right to know if his betrothed was chaste—but he wasn't inclined to argue. Susannah had drawn more than enough blood already.

He offered her his arm, then said in his best host's voice, "Thank you for coming. Believe me, I do appreciate your concern. I'll walk you to your carriage."

"That won't be necessary. I'll see myself out." She started toward the door, then stopped. Sighed. Turned. "Just be careful, all right? Whether you accept it or not, you *are* in danger." Another pause. She stared at his chest. "It, uh, it might be best if we pretend this visit never occurred. You know how the people here gossip, and if Alex caught wind of it . . . If he learned you had asked me to—well, you know. The thing is, he's known me since I was a girl, Stour, and he's very—protective of me."

Which implied there was something to protect, Luke thought, and felt more bewildered than ever. "Of course, Susannah. Whatever you wish."

"Miss Stone," she said, and strode from the room.

Chapter 10

Luke entered his home on Wednesday, glanced into the ballroom, and stifled a groan. What had begun as a quiet dinner for Alex and Penny, a belated Christmas celebration following their return from China, had evolved into utter bedlam. He shouldn't have given Victoria free rein in planning the party, he thought. In truth, he never should have agreed to it in the first place.

Lord knew he hadn't been eager—the less he saw of Susannah Stone, the more tranquil his life would be—but after a month of Victoria's company, he would have done almost anything to get her out of his hair. Arranging parties improved her mood, but even more to the point, he had hoped the increased activity would distract her from her insane fixation about the two of them becoming lovers.

Unfortunately, it hadn't, but then nothing in this benighted colony ever turned out the way one planned. Complications always arose, in this case, the arrival on Sunday of Sir Roger Albright. Just as Penny had predicted, he had come in pursuit of Victoria.

He hadn't argued when she had refused to return to London, but simply had made himself at home in

Number One House. Victoria had promptly declared that tonight's dinner should be preceded by a reception, so that Albright's friends from his naval days could welcome him back to Hong Kong. Inevitably, the word had gotten around, and now half the city seemed to be enjoying Luke's food and wine.

He walked into the ballroom to greet his guests. Given everything else that had gone wrong of late, it was probably inevitable that almost the first person he should encounter would be Miss Stone. As usual, she was dressed demurely, in a long-sleeved gray and burgundy gown, but it clung to her from the high neckline to the dropped waist. Looking at her, he remembered the way her body had strained against his as they had kissed, and how her nipple had hardened under his exploring fingers. Her hair was up for once, not spilling all over her shoulders, but the knot on top had loosened a bit, and a few tendrils had escaped. She looked prim and tousled and sensual, all at the same time.

She smiled when she noticed him approaching, but she also turned a deep shade of pink. If he had ever doubted he had made a mistake on Saturday, he no longer did. She was too uneasy to be the siren he had taken her for. Still, he was only human, and he couldn't help thinking about getting her alone somewhere, then kissing and touching her until that buried passion of hers blazed back up to the surface and exploded in his arms.

He shook the hand she held out, his gaze skittering to her throat, his mind on how exquisitely responsive she had been—on the warm, soft feel of her flesh against his lips. "Happy Christmas, Miss Stone." His throat was so hoarse with desire, he was forced to clear it. "I'm pleased you could come. You look lovely in that dress. Is it new?"

"Uh, yes. Thank you. It was a present from Melanie. It was kind of you to include me." As usual, she avoided his eyes, focusing on his mouth instead. The feel of her gaze on his lips made him ache to kiss her. "Lord Stour? Could I have my hand back?"

"Oh. I'm sorry." He hadn't realized he was holding it. Suddenly, the last thing he wanted was to escape. He released her, then moved closer. "About what I said last Saturday . . ."

"I should never have bothered you. There was never any chance—" She looked at the floor, biting her lip. "That is, I wasted your time. I'm sorry I disturbed you."

She still did, more than she knew. "I wasn't talking about our initial discussion. I was referring to my assumption about—about your previous friendships. To the inexcusable suggestion I made."

"It wasn't inexcusable at all. Under the circumstances, it was perfectly natural." She took an awkward step backward. "Please, forget it ever happened. I have."

Her hands were clenched together, which told him she hadn't forgotten at all. Indeed, she seemed distressed by his very presence. "I can't, not unless you allow me to apologize. Not unless you're able to forgive me."

"I told you, there's nothing to forgive." Her voice grew low and agitated. "I was the one who started it. I *wasn't* the one who stopped. What happened was entirely my fault." She took a quick breath, then continued hurriedly, "The only thing I find offensive is your self-reproach. Suppose I had been exactly what you'd thought? You wouldn't see a need to apologize.

You have one standard for virgins and another for—
for more experienced women.''

He was puzzled by the disapproval in her tone.
''Naturally I do. Society does. A man can't ask a virgin to sacrifice her virtue, but if a woman has already
done so—''

Her chin shot up. ''And do you suppose that women
compromise themselves on their own? Of course not.
Men are always delighted to help them along. So much
for your alleged social rules.''

He quashed the urge to reply in the same sharp vein.
''Just because some men are less than gentlemen, Susannah, that doesn't make society's standards any less
proper or valid.''

''Oh, no. Of course not. But then, you men make
those standards, and you suit your own convenience in
applying them. You could have a dozen Mrs. St. Si-
mons in your past, and nobody would fault you for it,
but you believed my—my so-called friendships had
utterly ruined me.''

That was when Luke remembered the articles he had
read by Sarah Maravich Stone, the hellion who was
married to Susannah's brother. She insisted females
should lead the same sorts of lives as males did—
receive the same type of education, have the same
civic duties, work in the same jobs, belong to the same
clubs. She even railed against the different sexual standards for men and women, calling them absurd and
unjust.

He said crisply, ''You've been influenced by your
brother's wife, that's obvious, but you should analyze
her arguments more carefully before you accept them.
You'll find that her views about men and women don't
hold up to scientific scrutiny. We have different abilities. Different emotional responses. Different biolog-

ical roles.'' He bowed stiffly. ''Enjoy the party, Miss Stone. I'll see you at dinner. If you would excuse me..."

She nodded curtly. "Of course, Lord Stour."

Scowling, he made his escape. For the next thirty or forty minutes, he greeted his guests, none of whom caused him one-tenth the aggravation that Susannah just had. He had been mad to consider a closer relationship with the woman. She would have turned him into a glassy-eyed wreck who muttered to himself like a deranged professor.

Finally, his duties as a host fulfilled, he retreated to a corner with a cup of tea. Hong Kong was a maelstrom of vendettas and resentments, but Victoria, oblivious to the undercurrents, had invited everyone who wished to attend. He kept watch over the throng, hoping the evening would conclude without warfare breaking out.

He was helping himself to something to eat when the first potential crisis arose: Patrick Shaw was elbowing his way toward Maria Alvares. Maria's uncle was only a few yards away, talking to Sir Roger Albright and Captain Deane, and if he noticed...

But, no. It wasn't Maria whom Shaw was pursuing, but Susannah, who was standing nearby. She was speaking with Kai-wing Douglas, smiling in a way she had never once smiled at Luke. In fact, Father Alvares never even saw Shaw pass by. Both he and Deane had been here in the middle sixties, when Albright had served here, and the three were engrossed in an animated conversation.

Albright finally said something that made the policeman laugh, then clapped him on the shoulder and walked away. A tall, rather slender fellow, he had sandy hair, eyes the same blue as Victoria's, and a ready smile. Indeed, his manner was so open and engaging that he was stopped and greeted repeatedly as he crossed the room.

He finally reached Luke's side and held out a glass of sherry. "To dull the pain," he said. "Believe me, Stour, I'm sorry about the commotion. I tried to keep Victoria in line, but you know how she is when she gets an idea into her head. And ever since she lost little Arthur . . ."

"Yes." She had been more impulsive than ever. Luke set down his plate. "There's no need to apologize. She's happy you're in Hong Kong. She enjoyed organizing the party. That's all that matters."

Albright grimaced. "That and getting her back to England, not that I'm having any luck. I've told her that running won't help her to recover, but she denies that's what she's doing. I'm at my wit's end with the situation."

"Don't give up," Luke urged. "She's headstrong, but she does love you. I'm sure she'll listen to you eventually." At least, he prayed that she would.

The two men gazed at her. She was talking to Tex Stratton, the American taipan who had bested Jeremy Burns on so many occasions. "The black pearls were an inspiration," Albright remarked. "They look beautiful against her skin. Still, I'll be glad when she's out of mourning."

Luke had given Victoria a necklace and earrings for Christmas, while Albright, whose means were more modest, had bought her presents in India and Macao. Among them was the silk stole she now wore.

"Yes. So will I. About the pearls . . ." Albright had never witnessed Victoria's pursuit of him—she was always discreet around others—but Luke still felt guilty about her behavior, as if he somehow had provoked it. Besides, he had sensed that Albright was a little jealous of him—of his money, his title, and his importance in Victoria's life. He wanted to make it clear that the gift hadn't been improperly personal. "She seemed concerned about her future. I wanted to reassure her she would be treated as she always has, as a cherished member of my family."

"But her circumstances have changed." Albright lowered his voice. "I know you controlled the purse strings even when Arthur was alive, but surely they'll be tied more tightly now. After all, she's no longer the earl's mother. She can't expect to be maintained in the same lavish style."

The comment was exceptionally frank, but if anyone had the right to be candid, Albright did. "Victoria is my brother's widow and the mother of my niece. It's true that I expect her to economize, but I assure you I'll be more than generous. As for Lexie, I'm her guardian. She'll be treated exactly as my children are." He paused. "Victoria can be impetuous and extravagant, both of us know that, but I expect you'll rein her in after you marry. And far more effectively than my brother did, too."

Albright smiled at the notion. "I intend to, but for God's sake, don't tell her so. She'll never have me if you do." He sipped his wine, then nodded at Captain Deane. "In case you hadn't noticed, my old friend has been prowling around your ballroom, questioning people about the incident with Kilearn. Looking for evidence you were involved, I expect. If I were you, I believe I would take offense."

Luke *had* noticed, but if Deane could solve the case, he didn't care a whit if the man abused his hospitality. "I can't afford to," he drawled. "You know Hong Kong, Albright. The people are forever feuding. I'm counting on Deane to prevent bloodshed.''

Albright chuckled, saying Luke had a point. Even for Hong Kong, this was a contentious collection of guests. Later, as Luke continued to observe, he realized that the losses at Burns, and Alex's investigation of the cause, had increased the tension still more. Alex had been discreet about his activities, but as always, nothing remained secret in this colony for long.

Watching Shaw and Kilearn, Luke decided at least one was likely a thief. They had gotten along tolerably well in the past, but they were ignoring each other tonight. The innocent man might have been snubbing the guilty one, he thought, or they might have been partners in crime who had turned on each other under the pressure of possible exposure.

Then there was Tex Stratton, whose strapping dimensions were exceeded only by the size of his thirst. Toward the end of the party, he marched over to Alex, stuck his ruddy nose in Alex's face, and began to upbraid him. Alex later confirmed that Stratton was furious with him for investigating his business dealings, and finally had gotten drunk enough to say so.

''He was livid I had questioned his integrity, which suggests to me that he probably has none,'' Alex said. ''The ironic thing is, I couldn't find any proof of my theory, at least not yet. I've gotten some promising leads, but I'll have to go back to China to follow them up.''

Alex had returned only that afternoon. They had stuck to small talk at the party, agreeing that business could wait until later. ''Where in China?'' Luke asked now, his curiosity getting the better of him. ''What sorts of leads?''

''Amoy. Ningpo. Shanghai. I received hints in Canton that bribes had been offered to help other hongs at Burns's expense, but I couldn't learn who had paid them, much less who had received them—public officials or merchants or both. No one would do more than hint. But my contacts up the coast are better. My written report contains the details. We can go through it after dinner.''

''Assuming we ever sit down,'' Luke said. The meal should have started half an hour ago, but the party was still going strong. ''Tell me, Alex, having fed and watered these people so munificently tonight, do I still have to entertain them this weekend?''

''I'm afraid so. Everyone's looking forward to it, especially the women in my family.''

One of whom was Susannah. Luke sighed heavily. ''And now? If I throw them all out, will I undo the gains I've made?''

Alex laughed. ''Yes, which is why *I'll* do it.''

If Kai-wing Douglas wasn't the finest man in Hong Kong, Sukey thought, he ran Alex McClure a close second. They had been discussing his newest business venture when he had suddenly smiled, then remarked that he should probably leave Jade's tea off the list of exports, seeing as it had produced such odd effects. Sukey had replied that she didn't know whether it was the tea or not, but something had obviously caused her girls problems. It had seemed the most logical thing in the world to imitate the way Ellie had spoken and repeat the things she had said. After all, Kai was the comprador of Burns, and as such, had a strong interest in the hong's success. Besides, Alex trusted him completely.

Somehow, one thing had led to another, and she had found herself pouring out her problems—telling Kai of her clashes with Stour, of the spell she had cast on behalf of Ellie, and of her inability to reverse it and end its unnerving effects. In the process, they had moved from the ballroom to the hallway, and then, when the need for discretion increased, into the cataloguer's office off the library.

In early November, the room had felt tiny and stifling, but now it merely seemed cozy. Unlike Stour, Kai didn't bully her, mock her, or embarrass her. He didn't consider females an inferior form of life. And she didn't feel as if she were baking in the summer heat when he took her arm or leaned close to her body.

"So give me your opinion," she finally said. "Could supernatural forces be at work on my girls, or am I being overly imaginative to think so? And if it's the former, what should I do about it?"

"Given the extraordinary incidents you have described, I believe it is extremely likely," Kai replied. "After all, Burns has many rivals, and not all of them are honorable. It would not be the first time in Hong Kong that someone has employed magic to gain an advantage. As to what you should do . . ." He pondered the matter for several moments. "There is no point approaching Lord Stour again. He is a prisoner of his background, Susannah. If his science cannot explain something, he will reject it out of hand. I will seek to learn the identity of the hong's enemy, but even if I am unsuccessful, a spell can still be cast to negate his influence."

Sukey could have hugged him, she was so grateful. "Thank you, Kai. That's exactly what needs to be done." Then she recalled what such a course entailed, and shuddered slightly. "But black magic can be dangerous, can't it? Are you sure the sorcerer you have in mind is powerful enough—"

She stopped and cocked her head. Someone was in

the library, calling her name. She opened the door and peeked outside. Melanie and Jade were standing in the central reading area, looking decidedly cross.

She waved to them. "I'm in here, talking to Kai."

Melanie rolled her eyes. "You can chat some other time. Alex got rid of the crowd ten minutes ago, and everyone is in the dining room, waiting to eat."

"We'll be finished in a moment." Sukey closed the door and turned back to Kai. "About the magician you plan to approach. . . . They say it's harder to destroy black magic than to create it. Does he really have the ability to defeat it?"

"The ability, yes, but nothing is certain in such matters. His success will depend on the nature of the original spell and the power of the sorcerer." Kai took her arm. "As you have pointed out, we could be dealing with ominous forces. I know you are eager to remove the charm you cast on Stour, but I want you to leave the task to my magician. You have conceded that your skills are . . . somewhat limited, and I'm afraid of what might happen if you risk yourself again."

Sukey's eyes teared up. Other than her brother and Alex, no man had ever worried about her that way. No man had ever treated her so gently. "I promise, Kai. Thank you for caring." She smiled tremulously. "Even if your magician is unsuccessful, you have no idea how grateful I am that you listened and believed me."

She linked her arm through his, and he drew her closer. "I find you easy to care about, Susannah. You have an honest soul and a warm heart."

They strolled out of the office arm in arm. Sukey wondered if she had been blind all these months—if Kai could be the man she would marry. Until now, she had thought of him simply as a friend, but if anyone understood how prejudice felt and would support the work she was destined to do, it was Kai. And he could pursue his commercial interests as easily in America as in Hong Kong.

They entered the library to find Melanie and Jade standing with their arms folded across their chests, looking no more cheerful than before. "I searched for you everywhere," Jade said to Kai. "The boys expected me almost an hour ago. If I had known you would disappear this way, I would have found myself another ride home."

"I'm sorry, but the matter was an important one." He released Sukey, then kissed her hand. "Good night. We will talk again on Friday." He took Jade's arm. "Come along now. And stop pouting. The boys will be fine."

Sukey watched him escort Jade from the room, then grumbled to Melanie, "I'll bet she wouldn't be half so put out if I were Chinese. Ever since Jeremy left, she's got this bee in her bonnet—"

"Don't count on it," Melanie interrupted. "She has a right to be annoyed. For heaven's sake, Sukey, it's almost nine o'clock, and Jade wasn't the only one you inconvenienced. If Stour schedules dinner for eight, the least you can do is show up in the dining room by eight-thirty."

Sukey flushed. True, the man was impossible, a closed-minded, imperious grump, but as God was her witness, she had never deliberately provoked him. She didn't know why they couldn't talk without arguing. Why everything she said and did, no matter how good her intentions, kept turning out wrong. Why her body caught fire whenever he looked at her, which made her so uncomfortable and resentful that she wound up hissing and spitting like a cornered cat. She was beginning to think she was as hexed as he was.

"I'm sorry," she said miserably. "I lost track of the time, Mellie. I wish you had begun without me."

"Stour has better manners than that. Frankly, he's in a foul mood. Not only was his home just invaded by a mob; he's had to head off two different quarrels tonight. First Tex Stratton drank too much and accused James Whittall of trying to destroy his firm, and then Father Alvares spotted Patrick Shaw with a group that included Maria, grabbed him by the scruff of his neck, and all but dragged him from the room. Rumor has it that you and Stour crossed swords earlier this evening. I don't care whose fault it was, Sukey—I don't want it repeated. The man has endured as much aggravation tonight as he can bear."

In other words, Sukey thought, she wasn't to say a word at dinner beyond "How true, Lord Stour," "You're right, Lord Stour," and "Would you kindly pass the salt and pepper." She nodded, wishing she could plead a headache and go home.

Chapter 11

Argyll Castle was perched nearly a thousand feet above sea level, along the bridle path between Victoria and the reservoir at Pok Fu Lam. The building faced west toward the China Sea, Lantau Island, and what Luke had been told were spectacular sunsets. He arrived there with his family in time for lunch, then spent the next several hours strolling through the gardens and hiking along the trails. He soon saw why Jeremy had loved the place. It was scenic, isolated, and tranquil. A man could relax and think.

By four o'clock, a steady stream of guests had begun to arrive. Reluctant to give up the peace he had found, Luke assigned Victoria and Penny the task of greeting them and retreated to the back veranda. A series of terraced gardens lay below, and beyond them, a children's playground. In addition to some shrubbery and the usual play gear—two swings, a slide, and a teeter-totter—it contained life-size characters from books, a winding stone wall to walk on, and in the very center, a large Chinese pine.

As he gazed at the area contentedly, he heard a loud whoop from somewhere in front of him. He searched for the source, and caught a glimpse of crimson and gold in the tree—the silk of a Chinese costume, he thought. He squinted, and spotted the small blond head of his daughter. Unless he missed his guess, Lexie was up there, too, along with an adult whom he presumed to be Mei-mei.

He trotted toward the trunk. A high-pitched squeal erupted, then a cry of warning: "Attack! Attack from the castle! To arms, men!" It was his son, he realized with a smile.

Up in the tree, Sukey jerked around at William's shriek and saw Stour charging forward. She grimaced, steeling herself to be rebuked for leading the children into frivolous pursuits and endangering their very lives. But then she discerned the expression on his face, which was one of carefree amusement, and she relaxed.

He came to an abrupt halt at the base of the trunk. "I'm the monarch here," he said with a glower. "Get off my land, you lowly peasants."

William scrambled along a branch. "You are evil, king! We shall fight you to the death!" The boy pulled off a pine cone, and then, before Sukey realized what he meant to do, hurled it downward.

His aim was perfect. The cone collided with Stour's skull, then bounced away. He started, yelped, and rubbed his head. "Rebel scum!" he roared. "Whoever attacked me will pay dearly."

A moment later his coat was off, and he was clambering up the tree. The children giggled in delight, William grabbing another pine cone. Sukey crawled onto his branch and held out her hand. "Oh, no, you don't. One was enough. Give me that, young man."

Grinning, William relinquished his weapon. Sukey sat herself on the branch, her legs swinging freely, and pulled him onto her lap. Stour had reached their level by then and was eyeing them coldly, standing on one branch while holding another for support.

"What a pitiful little army," he said with a sneer. "I shall crush your pathetic revolt. I'll have a confession now, treasonous scum. Who attacked me?"

Nobody said a word. Stour's gaze settled on Sukey, who could hardly believe this playful, easy creature was the same man who had brooded through dinner two nights before.

He glared at her ferociously, but she didn't miss the twinkling warmth behind the look. "Aha!" he spat. "I see incriminating evidence in your leader's hand. You'll pay a heavy price, traitor."

Lexie's eyes widened. "Are you really going to punish her, Uncle Luke?"

"Of course he will," Ellie informed her cousin. "He's a cruel tyrant. That's what they do. Torture people and hang them."

"That riffraff is correct," Stour said. "An attack on the person of the monarch is a capital offense."

"That means hanging or a firing squad," Sukey explained to the children. But given the way Stour was gazing at her, he obviously preferred torture to execution—the sort of torture he had employed a week ago, when he had teased her into a state of dazed arousal.

William finally spoke up. "But I am the guilty one, king. Leave our leader alone. You must punish me."

"Hah! A likely tale. It is nothing but deluded loyalty and misplaced chivalry." But true all the same, Luke knew. He had seen William in the tree, puffed up with triumph, only moments after the cone had found its target. But Susannah was more fun to accuse.

She was clothed in the Chinese fashion, in loose trousers under a filmy, slender top that reached below her thighs, and wore her hair in a long braid with a crimson scarf tied around the end. All in all, she looked delectable, especially the ample part of her that was in contact with the tree. He envied his son his place on her lap.

"It is useless to try to protect the traitorous wench," he said. "She will hang in the public square. But you, miserable scum, may plead for your life. You are only a lad, and I am not without mercy."

His daughter regarded him sternly. "Yes, you are, Papa. You're ruthless and hateful, remember?" She pulled off a pine cone. "You'll have to kill us all, unless we can kill you first."

Giggling, she sent the cone flying, but it missed him by several feet. He grinned at Susannah, unable to resist an opportunity to needle her. "It was a mistake to mount an attack with so many females, wench. They are weak. Inept with their weapons. They couldn't kill a tyrant from five feet away."

Sukey didn't think; she just reacted, flicking the cone she was holding straight at Stour's manhood. His leg shot up to stop it, but not quickly enough. It hit him square in the crotch, then bounced harmlessly away.

He was so startled, so flabbergasted, that she dissolved into laughter, and watching her, knowing where the cone had landed, so did the children. "Maybe we couldn't kill one," she drawled, "but we could surely unman him."

"Unman him?" William repeated. "What does that mean?"

"Never mind," Stour muttered, then gave her a fierce look. "You have sealed your fate, traitor. Before, I might have spared you if you had begged me hard enough, but not after such a dastardly assault. You will die a slow and painful death."

He started toward her. William scrambled off her lap. "Retreat!" he shrieked. "Run for your lives, men!"

Squealing, the children descended. Susannah followed, calmly cautioning them to take their time and watch their footing. She would make an excellent mother, Luke thought, assuming some man was brave enough—or foolhardy enough—to take her on.

He waited until they were almost to the ground, then climbed down. They were fleeing by then, the children dashing toward the castle while Susannah trotted protectively behind them. He grabbed his coat and gave chase, but there was only one person he wanted to catch.

When he reached her, he put his hands on her waist and stopped abruptly. She stumbled, tumbling backward, and he lost his balance and toppled to the ground. She wound up atop him, her back to his chest, gasping for air. He had once wondered what Chinese women wore under their clothing, and, holding her, he learned the answer. Very little.

She struggled to gain her freedom, and he reacted as any man would when his manhood was ground against an alluring female bottom. His grip tightened, and he arched his hips. Immediately appalled at himself, he abruptly sat up and lifted her off his lap. She was breathless and flushed, but she made no further attempt to escape.

He glanced toward the castle. The children were on the next terrace up, staring in fascination. "Go into the house and find Mei-mei," he said. "I need to have a word with Miss Stone."

Eleanor chewed on her lip. "Are you angry with

her, Papa? What are you going to say to her?"

"Of course I'm not angry. I simply want to thank her for taking such good care of you."

William made a face. "*I* think you want to kiss her. Yuck."

William, of course, was right. "No, just speak to her." He made a sweeping motion with his hand. "Go on, you three. Scoot."

They giggled and went. Luke ached to pull the scarf off Susannah's braid, then run his fingers through her hair to unknot it, but somehow kept his hands to himself and his voice composed. "I didn't realize you had arrived. Did you come with Melanie and Alex? I haven't seen them yet."

Sukey licked her lips. She knew Stour was aroused—she had felt him moving beneath her, tumid with lust—and wondered how he could sound so calm. Not only was her heart in her throat and her body on fire; more unnerving still, her mind wasn't resisting in the least. The blasted man had charmed her senseless.

"They're probably not here yet," she murmured. "I came early, so I could have some time with the children." She had seen them only once during winter break, for a few minutes before Wednesday's party. "I've missed them during the past week."

The trio was on the veranda now, watching avidly. Luke decided it was pointless to order them inside. They would only have hidden behind a window and continued to observe. "Maybe I *should* punish you," he said teasingly. "I don't recall your asking my permission to take them up that tree."

Sukey felt more breathless than ever. Stour was the last man she would have expected to flirt. She was astonished he even knew how. "I couldn't. You disappeared." She raised her chin a fraction. "Anyway,

I thought you were going to thank me for taking such good care of them."

He chuckled. "True enough. You were wonderful with them, Susannah. Children need to be protected, but they also need to be challenged. You do both. In future, if you want to visit, don't feel you need to wait for an invitation."

It was the best compliment Stour could have paid her. She thanked him, then shyly smiled back. "This is nice. Having a normal conversation, I mean. It's much more pleasant than arguing at parties or ignoring each other over dinner, don't you think?"

"Yes." Luke stood and helped her to her feet. He wanted to tell her it wasn't as nice as making love to her on the sofa, but he had more sense. He couldn't have her as a mistress, so if he wanted to take her to bed, marrying her was the only option. And that, of course, was out of the question.

Argyll Castle contained eighteen bedrooms in a central structure and two small wings, and by six that evening, not a single bed was free. In addition to Luke and his family, those present included the McClures and their children, the Douglas sisters, and Miss Stone. Four taipans had accepted, among them Tex Stratton, who had apologized for his behavior on Wednesday and promised not to repeat it. And various colonial officials were here, including Captain Deane, whom Luke had invited only because Alex had insisted he would look guilty if he didn't.

Finally, he had included his top assistants, but since Alvares and his niece had accepted, and the good father was more important to his success here than Shaw, Luke had asked his cousin to plead a previous engagement and decline. Shaw had done so, but he also had pointed out that *he* wasn't the one who kept quarreling. Since there was some truth to the complaint, Luke had been tempted to reverse himself, but the presence of Albright had stopped him. He wasn't supposed to know about the bad blood between Shaw and Albright, but he did, and he wasn't enough of a gambler to tempt fate by having *two* smoldering feuds under his roof.

Since the castle was extremely isolated, and primitive compared to Number One House, Luke had brought along an army of servants under the direction of the formidable Tung. They saw to it that the rooms were spotless, the twenty-five guests were pampered, and the food was fresh and savory. Luke wasn't looking forward to the weekend ahead, but by the time dinner was over, he decided it might not be as intolerable as he had feared.

He never had curried favor in his life, but Alex insisted it was necessary, so after the meal, he shepherded everyone into the main drawing room and went to work. Fortunately, the denizens of this colony were snobbish enough to be impressed by an English peer, even an allegedly murderous one, and a man didn't move among the aristocracy for thirty-odd years without accumulating a host of good stories. Some were about his mother, a grande dame who could have intimidated a herd of thundering bison, others were about Oxford, which often resembled some bizarre foreign land, and the remainder were about society in general.

Much to his surprise, he was soon enjoying himself immensely. His audience hung on every word and laughed in all the right places. It was oddly seductive, this business of being liked. Then again, his servants were as attentive as McClure's, so that everyone was drinking freely, and not only tea and coffee. Under the circumstances, even a simpleton would have been deemed a brilliant monologist.

Perhaps it was the port, perhaps the exercise, but around ten o'clock, Luke was suddenly assailed by such a strong wave of fatigue that his mind began to cloud and his tongue grew thick. He was in the middle of a story at the time, a racy tale about his mother's friend Lavinia and her lover. Somehow, he stumbled through to the end, describing how his mother had kept Lavinia's brutal husband from discovering her in flagrante delicto one day.

It was much too early to retire, but he was in no fit state to go on. "I apologize," he murmured with a yawn. "My hike this afternoon must have tired me out. Perhaps one of the ladies would play for us."

A collective groan arose. "But you can't stop there," Lady MacDonnell insisted. "Surely Lord Linison suspected something. After all, your mother had enticed him into the woods and induced him to chase her toward the trap. By all logic, she should have tumbled inside before he did. So what happened next?"

Luke had left Linison in a deep pit built to catch poachers. He yawned again. "Did I mention that the bottom was covered . . . with a thick, fetid muck? He got, uh, stuck. They had to lasso him . . . like a steer and pull him out. Lavinia's lover was long gone by then. Linison's servants scrubbed him for hours . . . but it was hopeless." Yet another yawn. "Bath after bath, and he stank for days. Mother said his stench matched his character."

Everyone laughed, but his guests were still unsatisfied. "But wasn't Linison angry?" Mrs. Gibb asked. "Surely the grand passion your mother had feigned was never consummated, so he must have realized it was a ruse.''

"Actually, he didn't. The trap was an old one. Made to take the weight . . . of a large animal. And Mother . . . is less than eight stones, so she ran right over it. My father arrived home and demanded to know . . . what Linison had been doing in the woods with his wife. And the bounder . . . blamed Mother. Said she was try-ing . . . to seduce him.''

"Which Papa chose to take offense at," Penny con-tinued with a grin. "Of course, he knew very well what Mama had been up to. He came within inches of challenging Linison to a duel over her honor, but Papa was a crack shot, so Linison apologized, took respon-sibility, and swore never to go near her again.''

"But what about Lavinia and her lover?" Sukey asked. She had thoroughly enjoyed the tale, but like Stour, she was wilting rapidly. There must have been something about the fresh air on this peak . . . "Did Linison find out? He didn't beat her again, did he, Penny?''

"Only once. Then Mother spirited her out of her house and hid her in Papa's hunting lodge, and by the time she was well enough to leave . . . Luke was only nineteen that summer, but he had disposed of Linison very handily.''

The choice of the word "disposed" triggered sur-prised murmurs and startled looks, but Stour remained blissfully unaware of them. His eyes were closed, and he was snoring gently.

Penny was visibly puzzled at first, but her lips soon tightened in anger. "What in the name of heaven is wrong with you people? How can you accept a man's hospitality and think what you're thinking? As a child, he used to go around releasing mice from the traps and setting them free in the fields, so he would hardly harm any higher form of life.'' Her expression said she wasn't sure those in the company qualified as such.

She walked to Stour's chair and nudged him. "Luke. Wake up. These people want to know how you handled Linison.''

He grunted, then opened his eyes. "Oh. Please excuse me, everyone. I didn't mean to nod off. What was the question again, Pen?"

"Tell them about Linison. What happened with Lavinia and Ian.''

Luke had been having a vivid dream full of bizarre and erotic images. He gave his head a confused and rapid shake, then asked thickly, "You mean with his investments?''

"Yes. Tell them how you got rid of him.''

He hesitated. People had been smiling when he had fallen asleep, but the room seemed to be filled with tension now. Since napping was hardly a major social infraction, he assumed Penny must have told everyone about the final, brutal beating Lavinia had suffered.

He decided to keep his explanation brief, to avoid distressing people further. "Linison was a gambler. Proud of it, too. But his investments put him at risk, and I, uh, maximized that risk. His position was precarious to begin with, and I saw to it . . . that I was the one holding the noose around his neck.'' The rest, he assumed, would be obvious.

"And what exactly did you blackmail him into doing?'' Deane inquired.

Luke arched an eyebrow at the policeman. "Blackmail, Captain? I wouldn't call it that. Linison was persuaded . . . to listen to reason, nothing more.'' But only after Luke had tightened the noose viciously. "Lavinia wanted her own house. Her own life. He agreed.''

"Lavinia and Ian were discreet, so society looked the other way," Penny added. "Linison died a few years later, and Lavinia and Ian married eventually. Mama took full credit for the happy ending." She smiled at her brother. "You're falling asleep again, Luke. Why don't you do us all a favor, spare us your snoring, and go up to bed?"

Luke pulled himself to his feet, apologized for his early departure, and told everyone to enjoy the rest of the evening. Then he dragged himself to the taipan's quarters on the second floor and stumbled into the bathroom. He seldom had felt so woozy and suspected that he wasn't merely tired, but ill again. Only with the greatest force of will did he managed to wash, strip, and slip under the covers before he collapsed.

Down in the drawing room, Sir Roger Albright took over where Luke had left off, spinning tales from his days in the navy. Listening to him, Sukey grew increasingly restless. Kai-wing Douglas had arrived with Jade only minutes before dinner, so she hadn't yet had a chance to ask him how their project was proceeding. She was dying to get him alone.

Afraid her fatigue would get the better of her before they could talk, she caught his eye and gave him a speaking look. Then, the moment Albright finished his latest story, she stood, smothering a yawn. "I believe I need some air. Please excuse me, everyone."

She slipped out to the veranda and walked to the railing. As she had hoped, Kai joined her within minutes. "I gather you want a report on my progress," he said quietly. "I am tempted not to tell you. Some would say the less you know, the safer you will be."

Spare me from overly protective males, Sukey thought with a sigh. "It's too late for that, Kai. I'm already involved. Casting spells, cautioning Stour, insisting that something is afflicting my girls . . .'' She gazed at the sea, her hands resting on the railing. ''I know things, and that makes me an enemy to the people I want to stop. If they perceive me as a threat, they'll attack me, whether or not you tell me what you've arranged.''

Kai covered her hand with his own. ''I admire many things about you, Susannah, not the least of which is your logic. You are right, so I will tell you what you wish to know. The sorcerer I spoke of has agreed to help us. He is a man of honor and power. But he has not yet acted, because the time is not yet auspicious for casting a spell.''

Some nights were better than others for magic. The Chinese excelled at the art of selecting optimum dates. ''Then when?'' Sukey asked.

''In eight days more. A week from Saturday.'' Kai's grip tightened possessively. ''I am afraid I bring news of a disappointment. The sorcerer will not be able to reverse your spell. He says that if the spirits have told you that *you* must do it, they will not change their minds. But he assures me that if the forces you evoked were benign, you will not be harmed. Still, I hope you will be careful.''

Sukey promised she would, thinking she would try again next Saturday, since it was such a favorable night. She knew Stour wouldn't cooperate, not that she was brave enough to ask him, but perhaps the entities would finally be in a mood to listen.

She and Kai stood at the railing for several minutes longer, trading impressions of the guests at the party. Only rarely had Sukey felt in such perfect sympathy with a man. And then she shivered, feeling cold even in the long-sleeved gown she wore, and Kai insisted they should go inside.

The heat of the drawing room was soporific after the crisp night air, and she was soon fighting to stay awake. She would have liked to remain downstairs—everyone had grown jolly and lively—but finally conceded defeat and excused herself. She was sharing a room with Maria, but doubted her friend would disturb her when she came to bed. Indeed, she was so bone-tired that the party could have been moved into the hall outside her door and she probably wouldn't have roused.

Luke was walking through a wild and fantastic world in which nothing made sense, yet everything seemed perfectly logical. He was standing in a country lane in Kent, yet he was surrounded by the imposing buildings of the City. A herd of animals came strolling the other way. A giraffe next to a lion. An antelope with a tiger. A unicorn with a naked woman on its back. It was Susannah, he realized. She waved to him, and he waved back.

He stirred, rousing just enough to recognize how irrational the dream had been, then fell back asleep. He entered a jungle next, and realized he was naked and alone. The colors were beautiful, orange trees and green and silver flowers, and when he came upon a lake, the water was yellow. His yacht was sailing placidly in the middle. The next thing he knew, he was standing on board. A woman took his hand—Susannah again—and led him to a huge, circular bed, right there on the deck. She bound his wrists to the headboard, then ran her hands down his body, slowly and erotically.

He awakened again, trembling and panting, and

threw off the covers. He was hot, sweaty, and desperate for something to drink. Moonlight filtered in through the curtained window, illuminating the teapot and cup on the table beside his bed. The tea was tepid, but it quenched his thirst.

The dreams continued. Each time, the images in his mind seemed logical until he awoke, and then he realized how bizarre they had been. He felt a woman touch him, then tie a scarf around his eyes to blindfold him. He tried to move, but couldn't. He felt her soft, silky hair as she dropped kisses on his face. Smelled the sandalwood and lemon scent of her soap as she nuzzled his neck and chest.

Her lips flicked over his nipples. He moaned softly. "Susannah? What are you—?"

"Yes," she whispered. "Shh."

Her mouth moved lower. He decided he must be dreaming, because the Susannah he had come to know would never have nibbled her way to his belly as this seductress was doing. She stroked his turgid member with her tongue, then took him in her hands and fondled him. He wanted to grasp her head, to ease it back to his groin, to thrust himself in her mouth, but he couldn't. His body was shaking violently, but he had no control over its movements. He didn't like that. It made him feel helpless and confused.

She continued to arouse him, licking and nibbling his shaft. He stopped questioning, stopped fighting, and let her do as she pleased. If this was a dream, he thought hazily, it was splendid, and he damned well meant to enjoy it.

Her mouth closed over his member and began to suck. He couldn't respond, not actively, but it didn't matter. She was taking him higher and higher, pulling him closer and closer to the edge. Her mouth grew erotically rough, working him faster and harder, and he abruptly exploded.

She withdrew before he was finished, but it didn't matter. The world was spinning. Blackness was closing in. He was in another place, suddenly, a deep cave with water flowing down the walls that somehow felt as hot as a desert.

The next time he awoke, the room was a little brighter. The sun hadn't yet risen, but it would shortly. His mind was still befogged, but he knew he had dreamed vividly the night before. Images kept flashing into his mind only to skitter out of reach, to be lost forever.

Yawning, he rolled over—and saw a naked woman in his bed. Susannah. She was sprawled on her back, the covers reaching only to her waist. Beside her on the pillow lay the scarf she had used to blindfold him—the same one she had tied around her braid the day before. He sucked in his breath. Her chest was delightfully freckled, and her breasts were white, firm, and full, crowned by pale pink nipples. She truly was lovely, and the skill she had displayed with that soft, pouty mouth of hers . . . At least one thing last night hadn't been a dream.

A week ago, she had refused his request for a liaison, but something had changed her mind. Their encounter in the tree, perhaps. She wasn't innocent at all, it seemed, but simply particular. A man had to charm her. Win her favor. He hadn't done so with *this* in mind, but Lord knew he wasn't about to turn it down.

Her surrender, and the spectacular way she had announced it, seemed as unreal as last night's dreams, but he was in no condition to question it. She had given him heart-stopping pleasure, but received nothing in return. He stroked her breasts and nuzzled her neck. He wanted her hot and frantic before she even woke up. Then, when she was moaning in his arms and straining against his body, he would bury himself deep inside her and take her to the stars.

Chapter 12

Melanie awoke with a jerk and bolted up in bed. The fear had come as it always did, completely without warning, but never before had it roused her out of a sound sleep. She shook Alex, who was dozing beside her. He opened his eyes and regarded her groggily, squinting in the predawn light.

"Something is horribly wrong," she said. "The danger—the air is throbbing with it." She began to tremble uncontrollably. "If we don't do something soon—"

"Easy, love. Everything will be all right." Yawning, he pulled himself up and took her in his arms. She clung to him, calmed by his warmth and strength. "Try to concentrate," he murmured. "Can you sense the source? Identify the person in danger?"

She closed her eyes and opened her mind. Her presentiments were so alarming that only in recent years had she trained herself to allow them inside. "It's very close. Within this house. Near this room." She felt for additional details, and received a stab of naked, primal terror. "Oh, God, Alex, she's so frightened. So helpless." She shuddered violently. "Whatever is happening—"

"Who is? One of the children? Sukey? Pearl? One of your friends?"

"I can't . . ." Melanie hesitated. The fear was rational and orderly. Adult, not juvenile. "It's not a child." The victim felt a sense of violation. A resurfacing of old and terrifying memories. The aura was very intense, which meant the woman was especially close to her. When she added everything up . . . "I think it's Sukey, Alex. That she's being attacked. What I sense—I'm afraid she's reliving the rape."

Alex released her and strode to the door. She grabbed her dressing gown from the wardrobe and hurried after him. He glanced over his shoulder as he stepped into the hall. "Which room—"

"In the east hallway. The second from the right." Melanie had known this house where the Stours hadn't, so she had assigned the rooms. "But Alex—"

She wanted to tell him the danger seemed closer than the apartment where Sukey was quartered, but he was already charging to the opposite side of the floor. Only seconds later, he opened Sukey's door. Then he turned around, shaking his head. Melanie caught up to him and looked inside. Pearl was sleeping soundly, but Sukey's bed, while disarrayed, was empty.

Now that the first flush of panic had passed, the only thing on Melanie's mind was protecting her friend. She closed the door with grim determination. "Follow me. When I come to the right room, I'll feel it."

She walked rapidly to the next door down, paused for a moment, and turned into the north corridor. As she proceeded, the aura of danger grew steadily more intense. By the time she reached the far corner, she was pale and queasy. The hallway beyond, the west one, was the corridor from which they had begun. She had the awful feeling she was closing in on the taipan's suite, which was in the very center. She and Alex had been sleeping only two rooms away, but on the other side of the suite from the spot where they were now standing.

Below her, in the foyer, she heard footfalls and muttering in Chinese. The servants were up and about. A door inched open—Victoria's door, at the opposite end of the west hall. Sir Roger Albright peeked out, caught sight of them, and smiled sheepishly. Melanie wanted to wait for the sake of discretion, but the terror was too intense to permit delay. She hurried to the next door down.

At first, Sukey thought she was dreaming. She had slept restlessly that night, experiencing lurid sexual visions that had awakened her over and over, leaving her shaken, exhausted, and so thirsty she had reached repeatedly for the tea by her bed. Then, as her head began to clear, she realized this was no nightmare. She was in a strange room, with no idea how she had gotten there—indeed, with no inkling of where "there" even was.

She attempted to look around, but could barely move her head or focus her eyes. The room was a dim blur. She knew only that she was naked, and that someone was touching her. Rubbing his palm over her breasts and kneading nipples that were hard with fear. Putting his mouth on her belly and running his fingers along her thighs.

She wanted to flee, but could only tremble. She tried to cry out, but could only whimper. It was even worse than the assault in Ohio. Back then, she had been able to resist, but now, her only responses were involuntary—the terrified slamming of her heart, the panicky rush of her breathing, and the impotent tears in her eyes. Her attacker wasn't hurting her, only degrading her, but it was still unspeakably horrible.

He raised his head, and she got a glimpse of broad shoulders, a muscular back, and blond hair. Terrified or not, she realized at once that only two men at the castle had hair that color, Albright and Stour. Then it struck her that Albright was much slighter than her assailant, and confusion mingled with her fear. She didn't understand why Stour would do this to her. She had thought they were becoming friends. Was there some fatal flaw in her makeup, that men she had trusted kept attacking her this way?

He eased his hand between her legs, then bent his head to her belly. As his mouth moved lower, she was flooded by shame and outrage. The place he was kissing—it was only inches from being indecent. His hand trailed higher, closer to the juncture of her legs. With every ounce of her will, she fought to defend herself, but it was useless. She managed to twitch and moan a bit, but that was all.

Her panic intensified, and she grew weak and dizzy. She knew about the things men did to women—she had badgered Sarah into explaining—and she didn't want them done to her.

But they would be, as many of them as Stour wished. He nuzzled her hipbone, then kissed his way down its length. His fingers found the entrance to her womanhood and lightly brushed it, then moved higher, to the most sensitive spot of all. It was the center of a woman's pleasure—she knew that—but she felt only shock and humiliation when he touched her there. Gagging, she managed to turn her head to the side, and retched.

Then the door flew open. Alex burst in. He strode toward the bed, demanding in a low, furious voice,

"What in bloody hell do you think you're doing?"

Stour jerked upright, but Alex was already grabbing him by the hair. He hurled Stour backward, slamming him into the headboard. The room spun and darkened. As if from a great distance, Sukey heard Melanie talking, saying something about going back to sleep, that she and Alex would handle things. A stream of rapid Cantonese followed, then the sound of a door being closed.

Within seconds, Melanie was sitting beside her, holding out a dressing gown. Sukey's vision returned, and the room gradually stopped weaving. She regarded her friend through relieved but tearful eyes. The power she had been under was finally fading. She could move enough to slip into the gown, and when she tried to speak, a thick, "I'm . . . all right, Mellie," came out.

Stour, meanwhile, was rubbing his head and trying to catch his breath. "Look, Alex, I know what you're thinking, but you're wrong." He pulled the bedclothes over his body. "She's been here most of the night. She came of her own free will. I was simply—"

"Raping her. Look at her, you bastard. She's ashen. Her face is stained with tears. Nobody could think she wanted this. I ought to kill you."

Stour hadn't looked at Sukey during the assault, not even a passing glance, but now he finally did. She met his eyes for long enough to observe that he was flushed and grim, and then, mortified by the liberties he had taken, she turned away. "I don't care how she seems right now," he mumbled. "Perhaps she doesn't want you to know it, but things happened exactly the way I said."

"Never in a million years," Alex replied angrily. "She was assaulted once before. She would never risk it again."

"Dammit, McClure, there was no assault. No risk. She came here in the middle of the night and woke me up. I spoke her name and she answered. I smelled the scent she always wears." He grabbed a crimson scarf—her scarf—and held it up. "She was wearing this in her hair yesterday afternoon. She used it to blindfold me last night. And let me tell you, she was damned good at what came next."

"That's ridiculous," Melanie snapped. "She's terrified of all that. Anyway, she wouldn't even know what to do with a man. She's a virgin, for God's sake."

"With a mouth that skillful? I doubt it." Stour balled up the scarf, then flung it away. "And just now . . . She was enjoying every moment. Trembling and moaning—"

"No." Sukey shook her head in frantic denial. "I . . . wasn't. It was . . . awful."

"You didn't think it was so awful last week, when you couldn't stop kissing me." He glowered at her. "Anyway, if it was so bloody repugnant, why didn't you say something? Or push me away when I—"

He stopped abruptly, turning dead white. "Dear God. I just remembered . . . In the middle of the night, when you—when the act I referred to took place, I couldn't move." He ran a hand through his hair, and she realized he was shaking. "Are you telling me *you* couldn't, either, just now? And the way you were speaking . . . The moans I heard . . . They were from fear, not pleasure? You couldn't talk to tell me to stop?"

Sukey nodded, frightened in a whole new way. If Stour was telling the truth about his actions, then she had made a powerful enemy in this colony, just as she had feared. And last night, the man had struck at her ruthlessly.

"I was having the most disturbing dreams . . . and I awoke after one of them . . . and I was in your bed, and you were touching me," she said. "I don't know who you were with . . . in the middle of the night, but it wasn't me."

Stour closed his eyes and gulped for air. When he opened them again, he looked dazed—with shock or guilt, she wasn't sure which. "The dreams . . . I had them, too. They were intensely erotic. Illogical and disorienting, but that's no excuse for my behavior. I'm sorrier than I can say, Susannah. Whoever the woman was . . . I never would have touched you if I had realized—"

"I know. It's all right." And it truly was. When she thought of the intimacies he had inflicted, she wanted to dive under the covers, but she wasn't angry any longer. Given the circumstances, she could hardly blame him for the assumption he had made.

"But the scarf," he mumbled. "The scent . . . I was meant to think she was you. Why?"

"Because after the way she made love to you, most men would respond exactly as you did . . . when you woke up and saw me in your bed. That problem with my girls . . . I've asked too many questions. Played detective, spouted my theories, arranged to fight back with magic . . . The man who mesmerized them . . . Whatever he's after, I've gotten in his way. He wanted me raped . . . or at least badly frightened. He was warning me to mind my own business."

Stour rummaged through the bedding. After a minute, he held up a hair—a long, straight, black one. "She was Chinese, probably. A whore, I assume, instructed to convince me she was you." His lips tightened in revulsion. There was no prejudice in the man, so Sukey assumed he was repulsed to have been pleasured by a type of female he had always avoided. Until that moment, it had never occurred to her that men could feel violated in the same way as women did.

Alex pulled a chair over to the bed and dropped into it. Sukey had seldom seen him look so somber. "Luke, about what I said and did . . . Mellie sensed Sukey was in danger, and when I saw you touching her . . . The conclusion I reached was unforgivable. Knowing you as I do, I should have realized you would never assault her. That there was an acceptable explanation for your behavior. I apologize."

Stour was staring into the middle distance, seemingly a million miles away. "Uh, right, Alex. I would have done the same thing in your place." He absently massaged his head, then winced. "But not as effectively, probably."

"Some ice might help. I'll see to it in a minute." Alex looked from Sukey to Luke and back again. "I gather you two are—better acquainted than I was told. I know how you value your independence, Sukey, but I promised Ty I would look after you, and if a previous encounter contributed to the misunderstanding here this morning, I would be remiss—"

"It did," Sukey said hastily. That was all she needed—a discussion of her bungled magic and its effect on Stour. Alex was even more dubious about her experiments than Melanie. "I would prefer not to discuss it."

But Melanie, drat her, was one step ahead of her. "Oh, Lord. Our discussion about the way Stour looks at you . . . Last Saturday, when you went to see him, you didn't tell him about the spell and try to prove—"

"I'm afraid I did. Now can we drop the subject?"

The answer was no. Alex demanded the facts, and while Sukey might have persuaded Melanie to hold her tongue, Luke seemed to believe that confession was good for the soul.

He was a master of euphemism, Sukey had to give him that, but the details he relayed, however tactfully put, left no doubt as to what had occurred. Most humiliating of all, he concluded by declaring that he had behaved like a fool as well as a villain. "I should have known she was a babe in the woods, Alex. No woman with any experience would attribute our mutual attraction to something as absurd as magic. But I allowed myself to believe otherwise because I was aching to take her to bed."

The remark was more than Sukey could abide. "Why don't you try asking yourself *why* you wanted to bed me? Take a good look at me, Stour. I'm far from irresistible. The entities have only made you believe that I am."

Luke gazed at her. She looked delectable—tousled and vulnerable, her lids seductively heavy, her mouth pouty with vexation. "Very well, Susannah. I'm studying you." He smiled slightly. "And I beg to differ."

Alex straightened, appearing amused for the first time all morning. "I know you're a skeptic, Luke, but she has a point. The events of the past few hours strongly suggest enchantment. As for the spell Sukey cast, it's possible it went awry in exactly the way she claims. Believe me, it wouldn't be her first disaster. As witches go, she leaves a lot to be desired."

If Luke hadn't known he was wide awake, he would have thought himself beset by another vision. Indeed, this whole morning had resembled a nightmare. He had been used in a way that angered and sickened him. He had abused and frightened a woman who was innocent and kind, however much she could try a man's patience. And now, his only real friend in Hong Kong, a fellow he had believed to be rational, intelligent, and shrewd, was sitting there talking about magic as if it actually existed.

He couldn't keep his jaw from dropping open. "What happens to people after they move to this colony? Are they infected by illogic? Engulfed by superstition? Enchantment exists only in fairy tales. I don't pretend to understand everything that's happened to me of late, but—"

"You don't understand even the smallest part of it," Susannah informed him with a sniff. "As I told you before, your knowledge of the physical world is extremely limited. There are dimensions—"

"Unlike yours. You know things other people don't, even a scientist with twice your experience and education."

"As a matter of fact, I do, Lord Stour, and you do *not* have twice my education."

He didn't bother to hide his exasperation. "At least twice, Miss Stone, but I'd almost forgotten—you're not at liberty to disclose the origin of your so-called facts. I must say, that's very convenient for you."

Alex was the one who replied. "Hardly, since it makes it impossible to provide you with a scientific explanation. I understand how hard it must be to accept what we say on faith, but I'm asking you to do so. Remember, humans can't perceive light waves directly, either, yet they *are* real, and so is magic. By all indications, somebody used it against you and Sukey last night. Both of you were fatigued and retired early. You both had unusual dreams, and you both were affected by paralysis." He leaned forward, then continued soberly, "I should have seen this coming,

Luke. I doubt you were chosen at random. Like Sukey, I believe there's a connection between the syndrome she's observed in her girls and the problems you've experienced at Burns. You have a common enemy, and whoever he is, he wanted Sukey attacked and frightened, and he wanted you accused and vilified.''

"Yes. Just as with Kilearn," Luke murmured. But even if he conceded he had been a target in this incident, manipulated by an outside force, he would never believe that force had been witchcraft. "We were probably drugged. It's a damned sight more logical an explanation than magic.''

Susannah gave him an irked look. "Naturally you would think so. It's beside the point that no herb on earth has all the effects—''

"And you, of course, know every property of every herb ever grown. Very well, Professor Stone. Perhaps more than one was employed.''

"Oh, I see. We were dosed with a whole *raft* of drugs. And how, pray tell, were they administered without our knowledge?''

"If your taste for food is as refined as your taste for sherry, it wouldn't be difficult at all," Luke retorted.

"For God's sake, you two, stop baiting each other," Melanie said impatiently. "Drugs or a spell—it makes no difference. We have a much more immediate problem on our hands than who was trying to harm you, or why, or what means he employed to influence you. Socially, you've been placed in an impossible situation. You've been compromised beyond redemption.'' She lowered her eyes, grimacing. "I should have sensed something was wrong long before this morning. I'm sorry, Sukey.''

Luke flushed, knowing he had behaved badly. Thanks to his temper, Melanie was wan with distress—on the edge of hysteria, in fact. Like all women, she was quick to perceive problems but blind to obvious solutions. "Don't worry," he murmured. "Nobody will even know Susannah was here. Alex and I will figure out a way to sneak her back to her room."

But Alex shook his head. "I'm afraid it's too late for that. Albright saw you two together. So did half a dozen servants. You were both naked, and you appeared to be making love. By Monday, no matter what we do, the story will be all over Hong Kong."

Sukey could hear the gossip now. It was bad enough to be reminded that Stour had seen almost every inch of her, but to realize that others would know it, too . . . She turned scarlet. "Why can't we just tell people the truth? Explain what was done to us? Tell them we were innocent victims?"

Melanie put a consoling arm around her shoulders. "And how many do you think would believe you?"

"But when we find the man responsible—"

"You mean, *if* we find him," Alex said. "We might not be able to. Or it could take months. And in the meantime . . ." He sighed heavily. "You're a teacher, Sukey. People expect your morals to be above reproach. At worst, you'll be branded a trollop, but even if you're only labeled the naive victim of a depraved seducer, your reputation has been damaged irreparably. Melanie and I have considerable social power, but under the circumstances, I doubt it will be great enough to protect you. Most people will snub you. For every father who supports you, three or four will withdraw their daughters from your school."

Alex was right, Luke thought. Susannah would be ruined. She would have to close her school and depart Hong Kong, or suffer continual social rejection. "But what if she were clearly blameless?" he asked slowly.

"I could have stolen into her room in the middle of the night and carried her in here. Subjected her to attentions she tried to refuse—"

"But you didn't," she interrupted, "at least, not knowingly, and I'm not going to allow you to claim that you did. It would be bad enough if they thought you had tried to seduce me—they would cut you dead or even run you out of town—but if they believed it was attempted rape—"

"I don't recall asking your permission, Miss Stone. I got you into this, and I'll bloody well get you out. How I choose to do that—"

"—will not be by confessing to something that will destroy your life. I warn you, Stour—if you lie about this, I'll contradict you."

Luke glared at her, furious all over again. After all, he was hardly without guilt. He *had* made love to her, and he should have known better. "So I'll be whipped and shunned. I'll survive it. I've lived through worse."

Sukey glared back at him. He was a true gentleman, she couldn't deny it, but did he think she had no courage? No integrity? "I refuse to sacrifice an innocent man to save my own skin. Besides, what about your children? Would you give them a pariah for a father? Turn them into social outcasts?"

Luke paled a little, realizing he was trapped. He could either protect Susannah or rear his children, but not both. Thank God he had a family to back him up. "I'll do whatever is best for them. I always have. You're not to distress yourself with any problems my decisions may create."

She rolled her eyes. "If you were any more patronizing, you could give lessons to the emperor himself. I won't let you rescue me, Stour, and that's final."

She would have been far less trouble, Luke thought

irritably, had she been like most of the other women he knew. Dependent. Submissive. In need of a man's protection. Instead, she was willful and generous, which suggested a very different course of action. Despite the mess he was in, he smiled at the notion. "Then would you care to rescue me? Portray yourself as a wanton seductress who broke into my room and ruthlessly had your way with me?"

She blushed but held his gaze. "Nobody would believe it, but even if they did, they wouldn't excuse you. You would be labeled an unmanly weakling and ridiculed soundly. My sister-in-law says our patriarchal society—"

"Yes, Susannah, I've read what she says, but we're not going to debate it right now." Luke looked at Alex. "So we're depraved libertines. Social pariahs. Hong Kong will condemn us and shun us."

Alex hesitated, then reluctantly confirmed it. "Without quicker proof of your innocence than I can hope to obtain, yes. You should probably go home. And if your sins follow you . . . Well, vast oceans have a way of diluting even the greatest scandals."

Luke retorted that he had come here for a purpose and damned well meant to accomplish it. Sukey insisted that no matter how much suffering she endured, she would rather defend herself and fight for her school than flee into the night like a thief.

"But to what end?" Alex asked wearily. "Naturally, Mellie and I will stand by both of you if you decide to stay, but you can't run a school—or a hong—with most of the colony set against you. Your position is hopeless."

A glum silence settled on the room, all of them retreating into their private regrets. A long minute passed. And then, frowning thoughtfully, Melanie asked Alex, "Suppose they were to marry?" She pondered the idea, her expression brightening. "It could work, you know. After all, all the world adores a lover, so if they were to claim they were madly in love and had planned to marry—confess they had drunk too freely, then lost control of themselves and anticipated their vows . . . Once the ceremony took place, people would quickly forgive them, don't you think? You could track down the villain and obtain proof of their innocence, and as soon as you produced it . . ." She snapped her fingers, triumphant now. "They could proclaim the truth. Admit the marriage was a fiction. Have it dissolved."

"And if I never unmask the villain?" Alex asked.

Melanie beamed at him. "You will, darling. You're a brilliant detective."

Sukey had no less faith in Alex than Melanie did, but that wasn't the point. "It's a clever plan, Mellie, but I can't possibly marry him, not even temporarily. He's the wrong one, and both of us know it. He has almost none of the qualities listed. You've admitted as much yourself."

"But I told you—it would only be a fiction."

"Even if that's so, there was nothing about a previous marriage in what she said, not even a marriage of convenience."

"You're talking as if she told us everything. She didn't. That was very clear."

Luke looked from one woman to the other, scowling. He didn't know what they were talking about, only that he was vastly offended. "Tell me, Miss Stone, exactly what qualities am I supposed to lack?"

"Never mind," Sukey muttered. "It doesn't matter."

But it did to Luke, though he didn't stop to ask

himself why. "And who told you about them? What was the source of her information?"

Sukey inched warily toward the side of the bed. Stour was on the verge of losing his temper again, and she didn't want to push him over the edge. "I'm not at liberty—"

"Oh, for God's sake, don't start that again!" Luke exploded. The only source he could think of was utterly absurd, but when one was dealing with a female who believed herself a witch, what could one expect? "You've visited a fortune teller, I suppose. She gave you some ridiculous drivel about the man you would marry, and you took it as the gospel truth."

She thrust up her chin in a way he had come to recognize only too well. "No, Lord Stour, but I do have a clear idea of what my future will be like, and it won't include you."

"I should hope not," he said acidly. "If the marriage were real, you would turn me into a babbling wreck within days. But it won't be. Nothing will have to change. We won't have to converse. We'll barely see each other."

"But she would have to move into Number One House and act as your hostess," Melanie pointed out. "You would have to keep up appearances until Alex could sort things out."

Alex nodded. "Mellie is right. And given the intensity of your alleged passion, that would require a certain level of—of feigned affection between the two of you. Evidence of marital bliss."

"I believe he's referring to fiery looks and barely contained lust," Melanie explained helpfully.

"Not to mention a disordered bed, I suppose," Luke muttered.

"Precisely," Alex agreed. "So what do you think?

Is the plan feasible? Could you carry it out?''

Sukey thought they had all gone mad. ''Could he—
Are you— If you think for one moment—'' She
crossed her arms in front of her chest. ''But I won't.
I simply won't.''

Luke's lips twitched. He could carry it out just fine,
if only for the pleasure of provoking the sort of sput-
tering outrage he had just been privileged to witness.
''It's a sound approach. Not only does it circumvent
our opponent's effort to get us out of his way; it buys
us time to identify him and defeat him. With luck, I'll
be able to finish my work here and leave, with only
some minor inconvenience. Of course, he's obviously
very dangerous. We'll have to be extremely careful.''

''I always am,'' Alex said.

''And don't overlook the protection of my clairvoyance,'' Melanie added.

Sukey shook her head in violent rejection. ''Would
the three of you just stop? Marriage is more than a
minor inconvenience. I told you, Mellie, he's the
wrong one. I won't go along with this.''

''Do you have a better idea?'' Melanie asked gently.

Sukey admitted she didn't. ''But even if you're right
and the marriage wouldn't count, it simply won't do.
It feels—threatening, somehow. It makes me uneasy.
I suppose it's the spell I cast.'' She thought about her
behavior the previous Saturday and bit her lip. ''It
could make Stour—unpredictable.''

Luke looked at the ceiling, praying for patience.
''Fine, Susannah. Let's assume there really is a spell,
and that it's turned me into a savage beast. If it worries
you so much, why don't you simply remove it?''

She glared at him. ''Don't you think I've tried? I
couldn't. Alex told you—I'm only a middling witch.''

''A considerable understatement,'' Alex drawled.

She ignored that. "So now I'm stuck with it, at least for the time being, and it could make you do things—"

"—that I normally wouldn't." Luke had heard all this before, and he didn't much care for it. "Such as rape you. That is what you're saying, isn't it, Susannah?"

Sukey gazed into her lap, horribly embarrassed now. "No. I know you would never do that."

Luke remembered the way she had kissed him on Saturday, and he finally understood. "Oh, I see. I'm a sorry specimen of my sex and you won't have me even as a pretense, but there's still this damnable attraction between the two of us, and you're terrified you'll give in to it if I exert myself to seduce you."

"Yes. The spell I cast—"

"—can be resisted. I've done so repeatedly, remember?" When you were in a madhouse, Luke thought, you had to play by the inmates' rules. "Suppose I promise to control my baser passions, Susannah? To be a perfect gentleman? Would that relieve your mind?" He gazed at her until she met his eyes, then smiled coolly. "Remember, my dear, I'm a rational man. To consummate the marriage would be both deranged and self-destructive. Believe me, if I'm tempted to slip, the mere thought of tying myself to a hellion like you would stop me in my tracks. But even if it didn't, surely you would come to your senses before you gave yourself to an arrogant, pompous, overbearing, insufferable, patronizing—"

"Yes. Surely I would." But Sukey had seen the other side of Stour—the side that could charm and tease—and that was the man she feared. She supposed she would have to go along with the marriage—it seemed the only way out—but in a week, when the conditions were auspicious for magic, she was going to draw another circle and cast another spell. And this time, she wasn't going to fail.

Chapter 13

By Sunday evening, Sukey's nerves were so frayed that she pleaded exhaustion and went to bed early, just to avoid the annual New Year's Eve festivities at the McClures—and the company of her alleged beloved. For two days now, she had smiled adoringly, gazed admiringly, and blushed modestly, and she was thoroughly sick of it. Stour, meanwhile, had enjoyed himself immensely, especially when it came to giving her orders.

As he had been quick to point out, if Hong Kong knew only one thing about him, it was that he expected obedience from those beneath him. He would hardly tolerate defiance in his future wife, so either she displayed a convincing level of deference, or people would know they were shamming.

Sukey considered herself Stour's equal, not his inferior, but society was less enlightened. Knowing that, she had swallowed her principles and gone along, but only because she had never dreamed he would take such full advantage of it. "Come sit with me, Susannah." "That's enough wine, my dear." "Women shouldn't involve themselves in commerce, Susannah." "We wouldn't want to bore our guests with politics."

Had she been English, she probably would have lowered her eyes each time and murmured a chastened, "Yes, my lord," but that was where she drew the line. If she looked away, it was only to hide her indignation, and she would have choked on her own bile before she "my lorded" him. The suitor she had liked best, Kai-wing Douglas, never would have dictated to her that way. Indeed, though Kai was disappointed by her betrothal, he had been as gracious as a man could be.

And that made it all the more galling that she should feel nothing for him save fondness while hungering for Stour in the most ardent way. Incensed or not, whenever she sat with him, took his arm, or merely gazed at him, she would remember the way he had kissed and caressed her on Saturday morning, and blush. She began to wonder how she would have reacted had she been aroused rather than frightened that day, the way she had been the first time he had made love to her. She didn't dare get him alone to protest his tyranny—God knows what it would have led to—so she was trapped. And he knew it, blast him.

But as intolerable as the weekend was, Monday was even worse. The morning began with a call on Bishop Burdon, who had heard of her misadventures and wanted to be sure Stour hadn't violated her—that she was entering into the marriage freely. She assured him she was, feeling lower than a worm to have to lie to a member of the clergy. In response, Stour smiled and took her hand, then fondled it till she trembled. He was the Anglican here, not she, yet he had no compunction whatever about acting the role of the moonstruck lover.

Watching them, Burdon chuckled and agreed to the

marriage—on Thursday, the fourth, "to give you a few days to grow accustomed to becoming a wife, my dear." The men smiled knowingly as they settled the details. Sukey was relieved to finally escape.

A round of calls came next, visits to the New Year's parties given by the governor and the great taipans. The year before, she had accompanied the McClures on this annual pilgrimage, and she had bantered, debated, and overeaten—and had herself a whopping good time.

This year, however, Stour was her sole companion, and whenever she was less than ridiculously proper, he gave her a cool, sharp look that made her feel like a small dog on a short leash. Even more distressing, Kai seemed more wounded than ever, barely responding to the eager attentions of Sophie Hotung, though she clearly adored him. The beautiful daughter of a prominent Eurasian family, she had returned from a year in Europe only the week before.

Sukey's emotions rose higher by the hour, combining into a confusing tumult of resentment, guilt, and arousal. By the time Stour handed her into his carriage to travel to Number One House for the final reception of the day, she had taken as much as she could bear. She squared her shoulders and glared at him. "I want a word with you, Stour."

Luke sat down beside her, then closed the door. He could see she was cross, but he couldn't imagine why. From his point of view, the day had been a great success—Burdon accommodating, the entertainment diverting, and the colony delighted about their wedding. As for Susannah, he was proud of her. She had been lively and charming, and if he had been forced to rein her in now and then, that was only to be expected. A female didn't learn to be a countess, even a temporary one, without some gentle instruction.

He smiled at her, thinking an authentic marriage might not be as disagreeable as he had supposed. "Is something the matter, my dear?"

She responded with such a litany of complaints and accusations that within thirty seconds, he stopped listening and simply watched her, which was far more agreeable an occupation. Even when she was standing across a room, he was keenly aware of her, and when she was sitting beside him or he was holding her hand . . . He wasn't supposed to tempt her, he knew that, but it was delightfully dim in this carriage, and her closeness was making him ache.

In the end, he couldn't stop himself from raising his hand, capturing a lock of her hair, and twining it around his finger. He decided to kiss it, and bent closer.

She flinched, stiffened, and stopped in mid-tirade. "Just what do you think you're doing?"

There was no point lying. "Caressing you. I can't seem to help it." He nuzzled her hair, then kissed her neck. An image blazed into his mind—he was relieving her of her virtue, right here in the carriage. Lord knew he was up to the task—explosively so. "Did I mention how beautiful you look today? I've lost count of the times I've wanted to kiss you."

Sukey took a quick, sharp breath, then grabbed Stour's lapels and held him away from her, shrinking backward into the seat in panic. Only seconds before, she had been furious, but he told her she was beautiful in that husky way he had, and she melted. A brief touch of his hand, a fleeting brush of his lips, and her chest tightened and her throat closed up. It was impossible. Unacceptable. There had to be another way.

He straightened, gazing at her soberly. "No, my dear?"

"No," she said, but she was dizzy and short of breath.

Luke struggled mightily to comply, but it was damned difficult when a woman he desired this sharply was clutching his coat and regarding him through eyes that were smoky with passion. Once again, what she wanted and what she thought she wanted were two different things. And he was human enough to long to teach her the difference.

Still, he hesitated. He could see she was distressed. Lovemaking frightened her, and with good reason. But then he thought about how she had responded when he had coaxed her—how the fear had faded and desire had taken over—and in the end, he couldn't resist the challenge. The blood was roaring in his ears and his manhood was pounding violently, but somehow, he managed to go slowly—to cup her chin, to brush his lips across her mouth, to gently taste her lips.

Sukey shuddered and fought for air. She knew she should push Stour away, or at least pull her mouth from his lips, but she couldn't seem to do it. He was teasing her to death, sucking and nibbling and proffering playful kisses, and the hunger he evoked was growing so fast, she felt she would burst if it weren't assuaged.

Moaning, she put her arms around his neck and closed her eyes. Within seconds, she was nuzzling him back, offering him the sweetness of her mouth, blindly seeking his tongue, but he refused to deepen the kiss. Her arms tightened in frustration. "All right, damn you. Yes." He nipped her, and she shivered. "God, Luke, please . . ."

"That's right, love. Don't be afraid. Take what you want."

Something inside her snapped. She thrust her hands into his hair, nipped him sharply, and kissed him fiercely and deeply. Sanity disappeared, and she entered a world of driving need. If she could have devoured him, consumed him, she would have.

She leaned over him, pushing him backward until he was pinned against the door, his body warm and hard beneath hers. He put his arms around her and gently steadied her while she dug her nails into his shoulders and quietly went mad. And then he abruptly took control, tasting her with hot, slow, dominating thrusts of his tongue, and the madness grew more intense. She surrendered completely, willing to give him whatever he wished. But it was passion he wanted, not submission. He withdrew and teased her again, and the kiss became a mutual ravishment.

By the time he eased away, she had long ago ceased to think. "It's probably too dark for people to see us," he said hoarsely, "but we've been sitting in front of Number One House for several minutes now, and there's quite a crowd outside—"

"Oh, God." Her mind restarted with a jerk, spewing out frantic and mortified thoughts. "This shouldn't have happened, but it did, and it will again. I can't possibly marry you. It won't work." She struggled to sit up. "I'll ruin my life if I do—"

"Easy, darling. Just calm down."

"—because I can see how it would be. We would— you know—do this again, only do *everything*—"

"Make love, you mean."

"Yes. And then I would be stuck with you forever, and you're not the right one. The past three days are proof of it, Stour. You've been insufferable. Con-

stantly watching me, judging me, finding fault with
me . . . If you correct me even one more time—''

"Hmm. Yes. So you told me before." Unlike her,
Sukey realized, Stour was perfectly composed. "Everything will be fine, Susannah. Believe me, I'm truly
sorry. I promised not to tempt you, and I broke my
word."

She calmed a little. At least he realized who was at
fault here. "Yes. You did." She glanced out the window, then winced. "There are so many people out
there."

"They were waiting for our arrival, I imagine." He
sighed. "It was the spell, my dear. We can't have you
tethered to the wrong husband, so we'll have to get it
removed as soon as we can."

She heard amusement in his voice and squinted at
him suspiciously. "If you're making fun of me
again—''

"Only a little. I believe I'm entitled." He grinned
at her. "I've seldom been vilified so thoroughly, my
love, especially for doing my duty—in this case,
teaching my future countess how to behave—but since
you interrupted your lecture to kiss me more passionately than any woman ever has in my life, I don't have
the heart to punish you."

She didn't know whether to be annoyed by his teasing or terrified he actually meant it. "I'm not your
love. And I'm your future countess in name only."

"Naturally, Miss Stone."

"I won't be abused, no matter what I may say or
do. Husbands and wives should be equals."

"Really? You're willing to elevate me to your exalted level?"

A man—she thought it was Tex Stratton—asked
whether they ever planned to leave the carriage, and a

great gust of laughter rose up. She flushed, dreading the next five minutes. "I'm serious, Stour. You're not to correct me again. And you're not to tempt me, either."

He sobered. "I'll correct you if you step over the line—"

"Dammit, I am not an unruly puppy, to be scolded and glowered at—"

"But perhaps I can move the line. Give you a little more leeway." He straightened his coat. "You're an American, after all. People will make allowances. As for tempting you . . . I won't kiss you again, Susannah, I promise. Not until Thursday morning, in any event."

At their wedding, he meant. People would expect it then. "All right. You can kiss me *there*. But not after that. And no fondling or nuzzling me, either."

"Of course not," he agreed.

He was as good as his word. He didn't charm, he didn't tempt, and he didn't correct, but then, Sukey was so anxious about the wedding she didn't have the spirit to misbehave. Hong Kong was well and truly foxed, and since it was obvious what she and Luke had been up to in the carriage, the ribald remarks started the moment she entered Number One House and never let up.

The teasing was trying enough, but contending with Luke's relations was even worse. They knew the circumstances behind the marriage; Luke had told them the very first morning and ordered them to exhibit delight. Sukey had seen them repeatedly that day, Victoria paying calls with Albright while Penny tagged along with Jade, and they had playacted impressively. Indeed, Penny, who had never been less than friendly, had grown positively chummy.

Of course, right from the start, whenever Luke had been especially imperious, Penny had sought Sukey's eye and made a comical face. She had insisted that Sukey was exactly what he needed if he were to be dragged into the modern era, but Sukey had politely declined the honor. And Penny had accepted her decision—until tonight.

Now, thanks to Sukey's abandon in the carriage, Penny was convinced she was fighting her true feelings and would make Luke a wonderful wife. The confirmed spinster had turned into a champion of wedded bliss—other people's bliss. Sukey thought if she heard even one word more about Luke's merits, she would cover her ears and run screaming into the night.

But Penny's matchmaking was a minor irritation compared to Victoria's contempt. Penny assured Sukey that Victoria was being short with everyone—that she was in a pet because this was the hong's party, not Stour's, and he had barred her from any official role. But even if that were so, Sukey received special treatment. Victoria had stomached her when she was a mouthy American peasant, but a creature who would smooch a man virtually in public was beyond the pale. Her years in English society had taught her the art of snubbing—a barbed word here, a pointed look there—and she practiced it with deadly precision.

In the end, feeling frazzled and overwhelmed, Sukey fled to the one place she was sure to be welcomed—the schoolroom, where the children, still on winter break, were awake and drawing pictures. And that led to the most painful encounter of all, because they believed the betrothal was real. They thought they would have a new mother or aunt—one couldn't entrust big secrets to little ears—and they were thrilled. She played games with them for the next hour, allowing herself to pretend they were right. And then Melanie came upstairs to fetch her, and when she kissed them good night, she felt as if someone had reached into her chest and squeezed her heart.

By the following afternoon, she had decided she couldn't go through with the marriage. She didn't care what price she would have to pay for her alleged sins; though she was willing to deceive Hong Kong and even to risk upending her life, she refused to hurt the children any more than they already would be. The carriage was at the Burns complex, fetching Alex home, but the moment he returned, she planned to travel to Luke's office and inform him of her decision.

In fact, however, she never got out the door. She had no sooner mentioned her intention than Alex was shaking his head. As he had worked at the hong that morning, he reported, Jeremy Burns had strolled in, fresh off the steamer from Shanghai. He had carried a fat ledger under his arm, the property of a retired merchant in that city whom he had encountered in a saloon one evening.

The two had gotten to drinking and talking, and the merchant had suffered an attack of conscience. Back at his house, he had given Jeremy the ledger he was now holding and suggested he should compare it to the inventories maintained by Patrick Shaw. If *he* were Jeremy, the merchant had said, he would sit Shaw down and have a long conversation.

The records had been fetched and the comparison carried out. Luke and his men had found that, on numerous occasions, a rival had undersold Burns even though Shaw's inventories showed that the hong had sufficient stock, acquired cheaply enough, to lower its price and compete. But the conversation with Shaw had had to wait. Nobody had seen him since Friday.

Until Jeremy's arrival, Luke had assumed Shaw was elsewhere on the island, still pouting about his exclusion from Argyll Castle, but the ledger—and Alex's discoveries in China—had made his absence more ominous. Alex put out feelers to find him, and the men continued to pore through records. A pattern slowly emerged. Surprisingly often, a merchant who had been a steady customer for some specific commodity had taken his business elsewhere. And Burns, in turn, had been stuck with surplus inventory.

More than anyone else, Shaw knew what was coming in and going out. Luke believed he had told Burns's rivals what price to charge to undersell the hong, particularly when there was a glut of some product on the market. More than likely, he also had furnished Jeremy with erroneous information on which to make important decisions. He would have been well-paid for such services. But with Alex continuing to investigate, he must have realized his days here were numbered. The only question was: Had he helped himself to a final financial windfall before he had fled?

Luke and an army of griffins were taking inventory right now, seeking the answer to that question. When all was said and done, Shaw's treachery would probably account for only a part of the hong's losses, but Luke was still in an abominable temper. It was bad enough that his late wife's cousin had betrayed him, but he had watched the man for over three months without spotting it, and was cursing himself for a pigeon. Alex advised Sukey to avoid him until he had come to terms with the situation.

She agreed. With the wedding still two days off, she could afford to wait. And it was well that she did, because Luke's mood did improve. Nothing was found to be missing save Shaw, and according to the note she received from Alex the next morning, he probably would be found before long. The police wanted to question him, and had joined Alex's agents in the search.

Within minutes, she was on her way to the Burns complex to break her engagement. She found Luke in his private office with Alex and a group of griffins. They were gathered around a table piled high with ledgers, trying to determine the scope of Shaw's double dealing. He smiled and kissed her hand, then settled her into a chair and poured her a cup of tea. Obviously he had expected her. She wasn't surprised. He and Alex were intimate friends, so naturally Alex had warned him of her intentions.

She was making small talk with the griffins, wondering how soon she could politely ask to talk to Luke alone, when a clerk entered the office to report that Captain Deane was outside and wished to speak to Lord Stour. Luke told the fellow to show Deane in, then said to Alex, "Perhaps Shaw turned up. With any luck, they have him in custody now."

"In a manner of speaking, we do," Deane said, striding into the room, a leather satchel in his hand. "Good morning, Miss Stone. Gentlemen. In fact, his body was found early this morning in Taipingshan, Lord Stour. He was murdered."

A general gasp arose, then a low, shocked buzz. Sukey didn't say a word—she had much too large a lump in her throat. Shaw had always been kind to her, and he had often made her laugh. All in all, she had found it impossible to dislike him. But he had also been a cad and a cheat, and obviously it had caught up with him.

Deane continued matter-of-factly, "He was shot

twice, in the back of the head and between the shoulder blades. The apparent murder weapon was found beside his body. A coat of arms is engraved on the grip.'' He pulled a gun out of his satchel and placed it on the table. ''Would this be the pistol you claimed was missing, Lord Stour?''

The room grew utterly silent. Every eye swung to Luke, who had turned into pure, hard ice. He glanced at the weapon. ''Obviously, it would, Captain Deane.''

''In that case, I would like to speak to you in private.''

The griffins hastened to comply, exchanging uneasy glances as they hurried from the office—not that they wouldn't listen from behind the door. Alex, however, paid no outward attention. ''When did Shaw die?'' he asked Deane.

''With the weather turning so cold, it's difficult to say. Most likely Monday night. Possibly a day sooner or later.'' Deane retrieved the revolver, then turned to Sukey. ''If you would excuse us, ma'am . . . ?''

Sukey didn't budge. Unless she missed her guess, Luke was about to be accused of murder—again!— but Deane hadn't asked Alex to leave, only her. It was yet another example of how women were disparaged. She had a far greater right to be here than Alex did. After all, she was Luke's betrothed, while Alex was only his friend.

''I believe I'll stay.'' She sat rigidly in her chair, giving Deane the coldest look she could muster. The man had been at Argyll Castle, for pity's sake. Gun or no gun, if he had paid even minimal attention, he would have realized that an honorable man like Luke was incapable of violence. ''Go on, Captain. Please state your business.''

Luke walked to her chair and held out his hand. He

was smiling, but there was no mistaking the tension in his body. "Come, Susannah. I'll get you settled outside."

She took his hand, squeezed it gently, and released it. "I belong right here. I suggest we continue."

Luke shifted his weight. He had told Susannah to leave to spare her what threatened to be an unpleasant scene, but even more to the point, he expected to be obeyed. A man had to begin as he meant to go on, even in a marriage of convenience. And whether she liked it or not, there *would* be a marriage tomorrow morning. It was the only way to salvage their reputations and allow them to attain their goals.

On the other hand, he thought, she had dug in her heels, and a recalcitrant Susannah Stone wasn't a creature to be taken lightly. If he wanted her gone, he would have to lift her out of the chair and carry her out bodily. He wasn't prepared to do that, not when she had looked at Deane as if she wanted to scratch out his eyes. And not after the tender way she had squeezed his own hand.

Watching her now, he could hardly fail to understand how fiercely she believed in his innocence. She had depths he was only beginning to discover. Strength. Loyalty. Resolve. A man wanted those qualities in a wife. The prospect of a permanent marriage grew more appealing by the day.

He put his hands on the arms of her chair and bent close to her. "All right, tigress, you win," he whispered. "But I expect you to hold your tongue, hmm?"

Sukey flushed and nodded. She had seen heat in Luke's eyes, which unnerved her, but also respect, which she liked very much. "She'll stay," he said to Deane. "So will McClure. I assume you want me to account for my whereabouts for the past three days. I was either at parties where a great many people saw me or here in this office, where the same was equally true.''

''And at night?''

''I was at home in Number One House.''

''Alone in your bedroom,'' Deane said, ''which raises the possibility that your gun was never missing at all. Perhaps you fired it at Kilearn, then realized he would live—and that you were about to be discovered inside the godown. You went home, where you fetched a second weapon and removed four bullets in order to pass it off as the gun employed against Kilearn. By the time I arrived, you had hidden your own revolver away. Then you realized Shaw had betrayed you, and you tracked him down and killed him with it. That way, you could claim you didn't have it, that the murderer had left it by the body to pin Shaw's death on you. It would be an excellent way to divert suspicion.''

''Or to implicate me, which is what it appears to have done.'' Luke's tone was mild, but his eyes were frigid with anger. ''Tell me, Deane, why would I attack Kilearn? After all, Shaw was the swindler.''

''At the time, you might have thought Kilearn was the guilty party,'' Deane replied. ''Or perhaps you mistook one man for the other. They do resemble each other.''

Alex spoke up, in far less measured a manner than Luke had just employed. ''We'll put aside the fact that your accusation is pure drivel. The fact is, Shaw had no shortage of enemies in this colony. He trifled with Father Alvares's niece. He seduced Sir Roger Albright's sister. He took bribes from any number of taipans, Tex Stratton almost certainly among them, and one of them might have decided to remove him. He might have had partners here at Burns who wanted to silence him, Kilearn for one. They've been at odds recently. Even Jeremy Burns had reason to hate him. Not only did his crimes cost the hong money; they caused Jeremy to suffer the indignity of being removed as taipan. So why focus on Stour?''

Deane raised his eyebrows. ''Why, the gun, of course, Mr. McClure. It belongs to Stour. Murder, moreover, invariably has an element of passion connected to it, and Stour had reason to be furious with Shaw *right now*. The other grievances you've named were either old and stale, or presented no immediate threat. The one exception is Mr. Burns, but he wasn't yet in Hong Kong when Shaw probably died. Finally, Lord Stour was alone every night, all night long. It would have been easy for him to slip out unnoticed and commit the crime.''

Sukey had the feeling that no matter what Luke said in his own defense, Deane would find a way to negate it. Luke was new here, only tentatively accepted by the inhabitants, and tainted by a string of past deaths. Deane obviously had taken those facts—particularly the last of them, she suspected—and added them to details he considered incriminating. And Luke had become his prime suspect.

She shifted in her seat, picturing an arrest, a scandal, a trial . . . Men had been convicted on less, so there might even be a hanging. But even if Luke was acquitted, he would be put through hell, and he didn't deserve that. After all, he was a man with courage enough, honor enough, to confess to a rape he hadn't attempted, simply because he had felt it his duty as a gentleman.

She stood, drawing herself to her full height. Deane's accusations were outrageous. Heinously unjust. Nothing but persecution. Luke had been ready to sacrifice everything to protect her, and she could do no less for him.

"I'm sorry, Luke. I know you'll disapprove of my course of action, but I can't let this nonsense continue." She thrust up her chin and fixed her gaze on Deane. "You were at Argyll Castle, Captain. You know what happened there, and I confess it was no aberration. I can't bear to be alone, and my betrothed indulges me. Do I make myself clear?"

Deane looked dubious. "If you're claiming you were sharing his bed—"

"Precisely."

"Every single night, Miss Stone?"

"Every single night, Captain Deane, both at the Castle and in Happy Valley."

"But of course, nobody saw you at Number One House."

She snorted. "Don't be absurd. I may be clever, but I'm not *that* clever. Alex drove me back and forth to Number One House and sneaked me in and out through the back. He didn't tell you that because he wanted to protect my somewhat stained reputation, but it's true nonetheless." She paused. "Isn't that right, Alex?"

"I'm afraid it is," Alex said with a sigh. "You know females, Deane. They're weak. Slaves to their own emotions. Susannah has no willpower at all when it comes to the man she loves. She insisted I take her to his side, and he instructed me to oblige her. He said she would nag him to death if I didn't."

Deane's lips twisted in disbelief. "But you were the only witness, Mr. McClure. And you just happen to be Stour's closest friend in Hong Kong."

Sukey feared Alex would say yes, but fortunately, he was too busy trying to keep a straight face to reply right away. "Of course not," she said quickly. "Lord Stour and I were extremely discreet, but you know Tung, Captain Deane. Nothing goes on in this colony that he doesn't take note of, especially when it occurs under his own nose. He saw me there on two occasions that I know of. You can ask him yourself." But not today. It was his day off, and she knew all his haunts in Taipingshan. She would get to him long before Deane did.

"Oh, I will," the policeman said.

Alex collected himself. "While you're asking questions, perhaps you should talk to the other suspects. I certainly plan to do so."

"I'm sure you do, McClure."

"And, of course, you'll remind them they're not to leave the colony until you conclude your investigation."

"I know how to do my job, McClure. I don't need instruction from the likes of you."

"I didn't mean to imply that you did," Alex replied, but of course, that was precisely what he had meant.

Luke crossed the room and stood by the door. He was taking her alibi-making surprisingly well, Sukey thought. Indeed, she was amazed he hadn't interrupted, seeing as she had just turned him into a henpecked fornicator.

He rested his hand on the doorknob. "Naturally, Deane, I would appreciate your discretion. I know I should have refused Miss Stone's entreaties, but it's difficult to deny a woman when one is passionately in love with her." He opened the door. "If I can be of further assistance . . ."

"I'm certain you can. I'll be back." Deane's mouth was a grim slash. He bowed curtly, then took his leave.

Luke flicked the door shut, regarding his future wife

with a wicked twinkle in his eye. She was a marvel—dauntless, resourceful, and utterly steadfast. "Thank you, my dear. That was very charitable of you, seeing as how you'll have to go through with the marriage now."

Sukey hadn't stopped to analyze the consequences of her actions—she simply had plunged ahead—but Luke was right. She couldn't claim to be wantonly in love with him, then refuse to marry him. His alibi would go up in smoke. No wonder he had allowed her to rescue him. Marriage was precisely what he wanted.

She bit her lip, more troubled than ever. "Is there no way out? I'm worried about the children, Luke. They're so excited. They'll be so hurt when it all ends. Suppose they never get over it?"

Luke had never imagined *that* was Susannah's motive. He had assumed it was her willful nature—her dislike of even the gentlest male discipline—or her fear of her own desires. But he should have known better. She adored the children. And she wasn't the sort who made a promise, then broke it without very good reason.

"I'm afraid we're stuck," he said, "but don't fret, my dear. The children will understand. I'll explain everything." In about fifty years, he told himself. His tigress needed taming, that was abundantly clear, but in every other way he could think of, she suited him very well.

Chapter 14

It was over, Sukey thought. She was married. Burdon had intoned some phrases she barely had heard, she had made promises she wouldn't have to keep, and she and Luke had exchanged a brief, almost chaste kiss. She had walked from the cathedral with a straight back and a frozen smile.

A wedding breakfast at Number One House had followed. She had feared it never would end—most of Hong Kong had come to wish them well—but their guests had finally departed, followed by a haughty Victoria Stour, a delighted Lady Penny and Roger Albright, and three very excited children. Now Sukey was sitting with the McClures and her newly minted husband in the taipan's private salon, presiding over tea. They had decisions to make, strategies to devise.

Melanie helped herself to a biscuit, then remarked with a smile, "I believe you've turned the corner here, Luke. I eavesdropped shamelessly today. Everyone was talking about Shaw, speculating about who had killed him. You'll be pleased to learn that except in the opinion of Captain Deane, you were well down on the list of suspects."

Luke was aware of that. He had eavesdropped a bit

himself. "The consensus being, I'm so stinking rich by now, I wouldn't have exerted myself to murder yet another relation simply because he had cost me a little money." He cleared his throat, which was dry and scratchy again. "Isn't that how it went?"

"Actually, I believe it was your irrefutable alibi," Alex said. "Tung's efficiency never ceases to amaze me. A word here and there, and suddenly the whole colony knew about Sukey's nocturnal visits."

"Including your staff," Sukey added to Luke. "Tung's got most of them convinced they actually saw me here."

Melanie affected shock. "Such debauchery. It's lucky the two of you are held to be so madly and helplessly in love. You probably would have been stoned otherwise."

"I doubt it. Hong Kong has enjoyed clucking at us too much. If even one more person tells me it's a good thing we're safely married . . ." Sukey's voice trailed off, drowned out by Luke's hacking. She removed a tin of tablets from her purse and dropped a pair into a cup of tea. "I'm concerned about that cough, Luke. I imagine it's the strain you've been under. These will help. You're to take them four times a day. I'll see that you don't forget." She stirred the mixture briskly and handed him the cup. "So why is Deane so determined to convict you? He's usually so logical. Did you offend him in some way? Behave even more arrogantly than usual the night Kilearn was shot?"

Luke decided that if the price of being fussed over was tolerating a little cheek, he was willing. "Hardly. I was too tired to be arrogant." He sipped the tea. "But sons of men in trade who attended the University of London and live on modest salaries have been known to resent sons of peers who attended Oxford and control enormous sums of wealth.''

"Really?" A devilish gleam entered Sukey's eyes. "How extraordinary. Money is one thing, but to be envious of a second-rate college like Christ Church and an antiquated system like the nobility . . . You English certainly are peculiar.''

That was too much cheek entirely. Luke thoroughly enjoyed it. He edged closer to Susannah on the sofa and looked her up and down in a lazy, probing way. "Have a care, Lady Stour. If you continue to call attention to your tongue, I'm likely to remember that teasing me isn't its chief talent.'' She turned bright pink and moved the other way, which he enjoyed even more. "So tell me, Melanie, if I'm not the leading suspect except in the eyes of Deane, who is? Alvares? Kilearn?''

Laughing, Melanie nodded. "And Jeremy Burns. Everyone noticed how he danced attendance on Jade this morning—''

"Ah, yes.'' Luke had watched them with interest. "He spent the day with her and the boys yesterday, you know. But so far as I can see, his campaign to win her back isn't succeeding.''

"Even so, people are saying he never intended to desert her. That by the time you arrived here, he had learned about Shaw, and having lost face as well as money, resolved to kill him. He didn't confide in Jade because he was afraid she would slip and expose him. So when he went to China to say good-bye to his friends, he planned all along to sneak back into Hong Kong, commit the murder, and leave again. And now he's returned publicly to patch things up with the woman he loves.''

"And I thought Deane's theory was convoluted,''

Sukey said. She kept her eyes on her friends, having realized that to tease her husband was to play with fire. It aroused his passions, which made him ponder whether she might give him pleasure enough in bed to compensate for her many faults. "Personally, I believe Jeremy missed Jade terribly and realized how much he loved her. He knew that without his family, not even a knighthood and a seat in Parliament would make him happy. So he came back for her and their sons."

Alex labeled her a hopeless romantic. In truth, he explained, Jeremy had returned for only one reason, to show Luke the ledger. But when he had visited Jade the day before, his old feelings had resurfaced, and he had decided he wanted her back. "He told me he intends to resume where he left off—no marriage, only a liaison. He wants to keep his options open, and he's sure Jade loves him enough to agree."

Melanie's eyes narrowed. "The snake. I'd like to shake him until his rattles fall off. Can't you talk some sense into him, Alex? And some honor?"

"Hmm. Let's see. I'm supposed to learn who bewitched this pair and why, but we've all agreed that first, I should find Luke's attacker and Shaw's killer, and clear Luke's name. And now, presumably in my spare time, you've assigned me to get Jeremy married off." He paused. "Is there anything else you would like me to do? End the opium trade? Depose the tsar? Locate the source of the Nile?"

Melanie tossed her hair in the timeless manner of irked wives everywhere. "If you don't want to interfere, why don't you just say so?"

"Very well. I don't. Jeremy has children and grandchildren in England. A life of great privilege awaits him there, but not if he arrives with a Chinese family in tow. If he marries Jade, he'll have to remain in

Hong Kong or settle in Australia in order to live in peace. And even so, there are bound to be slights. He has a difficult decision to make—but it's *his* decision, not mine.''

Sukey looked at Luke, her resolve to tread carefully instantly forgotten. Males thought about only two things—their own comfort and convenience. "I suppose you agree with that. You probably sympathize with the man.''

A distinct chill invaded Luke's eyes, the kind that made her regret she had spoken. "Don't compare me to Jeremy Burns, Susannah. I was never unfaithful to my wife. My mistresses agreed with me from the start that we would never marry. I've tolerated a great deal from you, but you're not to question my honor. Is that clear?''

Heat rose up her neck at his dictatorial tone. He had cause for complaint, she recognized that, but so did she, blast him. "I apologize, Stour. I would never impugn your honor or your courage. But you refuse to grant me the same consideration. You treat me as a lesser form of life—''

"Not now, Susannah.''

"—like a child or a dimwit, and judge me against a standard that's not only archaic, but monstrously unjust. I will not be—''

"I said that's enough, madam!" Luke roared.

"—interrupted, bullied, or corrected. Or thundered at, damn you. Is *that* clear?''

They glared at each other. Alex sighed heavily. "They're going to kill each other, Mellie. I swear to God they are. I thought this marriage was a good idea, but—''

He looked at the door. Someone was rapping firmly. Luke jerked out of his seat to answer it, sure they had been overheard and utterly furious about it. The place was crawling with servants, his family was still about, and his bride persisted in shrieking like a bloody fishwife. He had never laid a hand on a woman in his life and didn't intend to start, but as God was his witness, Susannah was pushing him to the very limit.

To his relief, he found Tung outside—one of the few men he trusted with his secrets. A large package was cradled in the majordomo's arms. "From steamer, Taipan. Boat just come in. Captain send seaman to house. He say deliver right now."

Luke took the carton. To his bewilderment, it was addressed to the Earl and Countess of Stour at Number One House in Hong Kong. Even more puzzling, the sender was someone in Rome, Italy—an "S.M.," according to the legend on the package.

He thanked Tung and turned away, but the majordomo wasn't yet ready to be dismissed. "One thing more, Taipan. You want wife who obey. Excuse me, but very foolish. If she obey you yesterday—no help at all. Besides, no chance. She do as she please, always." He smiled broadly, and Luke realized it was the first time he had seen Tung look amused. "But she excellent woman. You listen more, she like you better. Fall in love. Then she obey, maybe."

Luke was too incredulous to take offense. Had his majordomo really just given him marital advice? "Not bloody likely," he muttered. He closed the door, carried the package inside, and set it on the table in front of the sofa. "From a friend of yours, Susannah?"

Sukey didn't know which dismayed her more, Luke's icy tone or the carton itself. "S.M." could only be Shelby March, but if the future was trying to catch up with her, she had no desire to meet it halfway. "Never mind that now. We were talking about the way you treat me. I can't possibly live with you—''

"In other words, yes, and for some reason, you're not eager to see what's inside. As for how I treat you, we'll discuss it later, in private." He tore off the wrapping. A card fluttered out. He read it aloud: "Dear Sukey and Luke—Life sure is interesting, isn't it? These are for Luke. I heard he's going to need them. The sooner you get it over with, Suke, the better. Love, Shel."

Luke opened the box. Inside, nestled in red satin, he found a knife with a black horn handle, a wooden wand, a chalice, a censer, a long length of braided red cord, and a pentagram charm on a silver chain. He set them on the table, as intrigued now as he was bewildered.

"These are witches' tools," he said to Susannah. He had read about them when he was studying the Inquisition. "Who is Shel? Why did he send them? And how could he have known weeks ago that we would marry when we didn't even know it ourselves?"

Sukey's heart felt as if it were exploding in her chest. She knew what Shelby was telling her—initiate Luke and nullify the spell—but she simply couldn't. There had to be a mistake. History couldn't possibly have developed this way. "Uh, Shelby March. The March is a stage name. She's—you've heard me talk about my sister-in-law Sarah . . ."

"Far too often. I know who Miss March is, though I had forgotten she was Sarah's sister. If you're anyone at all, you don't let her perform in London without attending. I've heard her twice. The beauty of her voice . . . The way she reaches an audience . . . She's extraordinary."

"Yes." He didn't know the half of it. Shelby was

of course Sarah's daughter, not her sister, but the two had traveled back to the past from different years in the future, resulting in such a small difference in their ages—thirteen years—that representing themselves as sisters was far more plausible. Shelby's mental powers, present at birth and honed through extensive training during her youth, defied nineteenth-century comprehension. She could perceive people's thoughts, speak to them with her mind over vast distances, and influence their beliefs and actions without their knowing it. When she sang, she changed her listeners—and history—just slightly for the better.

Sukey twisted her hands together in her lap. Luke was staring at her, waiting for the answers to his questions, but how did she explain what she wasn't supposed to discuss? "She, uh, she has a sort of clairvoyance—like Melanie's, only stronger. You've noticed it yourself—the way she affects an audience. And, uh, she gets the most uncanny premonitions—"

"You mean *she's* the fortune teller you consulted?"

"Not exactly. She just—she had a presentiment about my future, and she passed it along." It was a flagrant lie. As far as Sukey had been told, Sarah and Shelby had checked her biography while in the future to see if she would wed, and whom. But the timing of this gift—and its contents—indicated Shelby had studied her life more thoroughly than she had admitted. She played by her own set of rules, so perhaps she had even read Sukey's diary. "The man I told you about— my future husband—Shelby described him to me. And she's never wrong."

The scientist in Luke said nobody could possess the prescience Susannah had described, but then, nobody should have been able to affect an audience as Shelby March did. He didn't know *what* to believe. "Go on, my dear. I gather your Prince Charming has any number of sterling qualities. Do enumerate them for me."

Luke was still in a temper, Sukey thought, but it would pass, just as it always did. Then something would ignite his passions and he would start desiring her again. She shivered, knowing she would never feel safe until he was as eager for the marriage to end as she was. But if she couldn't tell him the truth . . .

Then again, Shelby wouldn't have sent the tools— or the note—if she had expected total silence. Sukey would have to be careful about what she revealed, that was all. "He'll be strong but tender," she began. "You *are* strong, but if there's tenderness and indulgence in you, you've never bestowed it on me. He'll be honorable and patient. You have honor enough for ten men, but you aren't at all patient. Your temper is icy rather than hot, but it's excessive all the same. He'll be a wonderful father. You do qualify on that score. And he'll be smart but not arrogant. I admit you're extremely intelligent, but you're also the most arrogant male I've ever met." She took a deep breath. "So there you have it. Only four of seven. It's just as I said. We can't possibly remain married. You're the wrong man."

Melanie arched an eyebrow at her. "Aren't you forgetting something, Sukey?"

"I don't think it's necessary—"

"But it's a point in his favor. It's only fair."

She raised her chin. "Fine. She said he'll be fantastic in bed. Rumor has it you are, Luke, but it's not something I care to verify through personal experience."

"Hmm. Five of eight," Alex said teasingly. "Perhaps as many as seven, because he's tender and patient with his children and almost saintly with his late brother's wife. It's close to a perfect score. But the arrogance is a definite stumbling block, Luke. Sukey is right, there.''

Luke managed a smile, but in truth, he felt like a Spanish bull, bleeding from a dozen different stabs of the picador's lances. He was accustomed to Susannah's tirades, but this was something different—a cool recitation of his failings. It didn't matter whether the accusations were fair or not; she believed they were, and it stung. Somehow, she had stolen her way into a select company: He cared what she thought. She had the power to hurt him.

He kept his tone light. ''In that case, it would appear that I am indeed, as Susannah insists, the wrong man, not that I can recall expressing an interest in being the right one.'' He glanced at the implements on the table. ''About these tools . . . They're personal possessions, to be used when casting spells, isn't that correct, my dear?''

Sukey nodded. The Luke she had come to know was never this breezy, which meant there were feelings he was trying to conceal. Not anger—he grew frigid when annoyed. Pain, perhaps. She probably had wounded him. She cursed her tongue, and the anxiety that had made it so intemperate.

''But before one can cast a spell,'' he continued, ''one has to be initiated into the craft. Isn't that true?''

She nodded again, then murmured, ''For someone who denies the existence of magic, you know an awful lot about it.''

''I'm exceptionally well-read. I'm also aware that the process begins with periods of reflection and instruction—a year and a day each. In other words, I can't use these tools for over two years, yet Miss March sent them now. Why? In fact, why did she send them at all? What sort of spell does she mean me to cast?''

Sukey hesitated. The man had a brilliant mind. His logic was flawless. She considered evasion, then rejected the idea. If she didn't enlighten him, Melanie or Alex surely would. ''A spell of reversal,'' she mumbled.

''Reversal of what?''

''Your own enchantment. The entities—''

''Ah, yes. The creatures in the astral plane who have turned me into a prisoner of induced lust.'' He grinned at her. Nothing seemed to restore his good humor like making sport of her, she thought irritably. ''Tell me, my dear, are they present right now?''

''I have no idea. I can only sense them when I'm performing my magic.'' She folded her arms across her chest. ''Do you want me to answer your questions or don't you?''

He did. He even refrained from interrupting while she explained about the entities' intransigence in canceling the spell and their insistence that he take the lead in ending it. ''As for the waiting periods,'' she finished, ''they obviously mean them to be omitted. They want a third-degree initiation. That was very clear. But even if you're willing, I won't do it.''

''Ah. Third degree. No wonder you didn't request my cooperation.'' He lazed back on the sofa, chuckling. ''I don't know that I am—willing, that is—but I must admit, it's an interesting ritual. I'm sure I would find it—stimulating.''

She wanted to bury her face—her very hot face— in her hands and never look up. ''You know what it involves?'' she choked out.

Luke did. Nudity. Blindfolds. Binding and ritual scourging. Kissing the most private parts of the initiate's body. And in the end, the Great Rite, sexual union. Even if performed in token rather than in true, it was disturbingly suggestive.

His throat tightened and his loins began to burn. Suddenly, the prospect wasn't amusing at all. "I told you, I'm exceptionally well-read," he said in a slightly strangled tone. "I know the ritual is, uh, somewhat erotic. I suppose you're afraid of where it could lead. But you also believe the entities are influencing me to desire you beyond my ability to resist, and you fear that just as much."

He sipped his tea to moisten his throat. His earlier words to the contrary, he intended the marriage to stand. It wasn't only that he wanted Susannah badly—after all, he wasn't the sort to be ruled by his male member—but that she would make an excellent mother and wife. He made a silent wager with himself. Before the month was out, she would be purged of her outlandish notions and molded into the woman he wanted. She was stubborn, but her will was no match for his own.

Before he could change her ways, however, he would have to nullify the spell—or rather, he would have to perform whatever acts she demanded, since magic was arrant nonsense. Otherwise, she would refuse to believe that any affection he exhibited, any passion he displayed, any feelings he professed, were real rather than artificial.

"We have to be dispassionate about this," he said. "The spell unnerves you, Susannah. It makes you fear me. I never thought I would offer to take part in a magical rite, but we could be living together for months. If we're to do so without constant friction, the spell will have to go." He picked up the knife and ran his fingers over the hilt. "If Miss March is as prescient as you claim, she must have sent me these tools because she divined you would initiate me. And she did say 'the sooner, the better.' I suggest we get it done with tonight.''

Sukey shook her head. He was right in every way, but she didn't care. She couldn't do it. ''No.''

She looked so frightened and vulnerable that Luke wanted to take her in his arms and soothe her. Instead, he covered her hand, which was clammy and shaking, and then gently squeezed it. ''You have nothing to fear, my dear. I'll be helpless. Blindfolded and bound. Even if I were burning to, uh, to tempt you, I would be physically unable to.''

She stared straight ahead. ''We would have to finish with the Great Rite. You would be untied by then.''

''Performed in token,'' he pointed out. ''A knife plunged into a glass of wine. Then we can reverse the spell. You've assured me I'll no longer desire you afterward.''

She still believed that, but she couldn't take the chance she was wrong. ''No.''

He sighed. ''I've always controlled myself, even when you failed to, and I promise I always will. Still, if it would reassure you, you can leave me bound until the rite is finished and the spell is nullified.''

''But sooner or later I would have to free you, and the touching and kissing during the initiation—'' She knew what such things did to a man. She pulled away her hand. ''No. We're legally married. You could make love to me with a clear conscience, and I have this unfathomable weakness where you're concerned . . . I might not stop you, and then I would have to divorce you. There would be a scandal that could affect the work I plan to do. I can't risk that.''

Luke was growing increasingly uncomfortable. Alex

and Melanie were dear friends, but this was no conversation for a husband and wife to be having in front of others. "Please pack up Susannah's implements and send them over," he said. "If there's anything else she uses in her magic—an altar, perhaps, or her cat—send that as well." He stood, and the others immediately followed suit. "Perhaps you would join us for dinner tomorrow evening. We have a great deal more to discuss."

Alex accepted the invitation, told Luke he would continue with his investigation, and escorted Melanie from the room. Luke took Susannah's arm. "Come. Let's walk in the garden."

Sukey nodded. Luke did nothing without a reason, so if he wished to go outside, he obviously had more than a stroll in mind—a discussion so sensitive, she assumed, that privacy was utterly essential. But no matter what arguments he made, she wasn't going to change her mind.

Chapter 15

L uke removed his coat and draped it over Susannah's shoulders, then opened the French doors into the garden. They walked down a deserted path to a wooden bench and sat down. Never in a hundred years had he pictured himself saying what he was about to say, but then, never in a hundred years had he expected to remarry.

"For as long as I can recall, all I ever wanted was to be a scientist," he began. "My brother Arthur entered the navy when he was fourteen, just as all the men in our family had, but I refused to do the same. In my heart, my life began only after I went up to Oxford."

"You loved it there," Sukey murmured. She didn't know why Luke was telling her about his past, but she was content to listen. For all that he frustrated and exasperated her, she had never failed to find him intriguing.

"Yes." He smiled distantly, as if recollecting those early days. "Unlike most there, I attended to my studies. My favorite professor was a geologist named Pemberton. Victoria was his daughter—fifteen to my seventeen when we first met. I fell in love with her, but I wanted to be a fellow, and fellows are required to be celibate. I decided to delay our marriage until I was ready to leave Oxford—after three or four years as a don. I planned to remain in town after that, set up my own laboratory, and support us by writing and lecturing, but I also had a modest private income. One of my schoolmasters had left me a small bequest when I was sixteen, and I had invested it well.''

"So you excelled at business even as a boy."

"Yes. My father noticed. He took to relying on my guidance, but I always disliked the analysis I was required to do in order to advise him wisely. Business wasn't pure and elegant like science, but tedious and prosaic. Making money didn't excite me the way making discoveries did.'' He paused. ''Three years later, I decided to introduce Victoria to my parents. Arthur was twenty-eight at the time, and our father had decided he should leave the navy and take up his responsibilities at home. The family had gathered at Stour Hall to welcome him back to England. Everyone loved him, Susannah. He was a dashing figure, like a young god—tall and handsome, a hero of the Indian Mutiny and the Opium War in China, a superb sportsman, a wonderful raconteur—''

"And the heir to a prosperous earldom." Sukey saw no point in professing ignorance about what had followed. "Victoria threw you over. She married Arthur. Alex mentioned it before you arrived here." She felt a heaviness in her chest. She didn't care *how* exceptional Arthur had been; an honorable man didn't betray his own brother. "Frankly, judging from the past couple of months, you had a narrow escape. Victoria may be a great beauty, but her character leaves a lot to be desired. She's snobbish, selfish, and extravagant. She wouldn't have made you happy."

Luke didn't reply for several moments. Then he said gruffly, "She's a member of your family now, Susannah. You're not to speak of her that way."

Sukey was framing a biting retort when she noticed Luke's eyes. When he was angry, they grew cold, but they were suspiciously bland now. "Humph. You're a fraud, Lord Stour. You happen to agree with me. And I'll tell you something else. You're talking about your past because you want me to understand what shaped you. I don't know what your ultimate purpose is, but I do know this. Deep down, you're pleased I said you were too good for her."

Luke fought down a smile. He enjoyed it when Susannah charged to his defense, but still, she had far too loose a tongue. "I'm your husband now. For as long as this marriage lasts, you'll do as I say."

She rolled her eyes. "If you want servility, Stour, why don't you get yourself a dog?"

He was tempted to pull her onto his lap and tame her with a kiss, but instead, he laughed and gave up the fight. All in all, he was content with her. For all her complaints about his behavior, she had never failed to support him when it counted. In his thirty-odd years, he had trusted only one female without reservation: his sister, Penny. Susannah was a hellion, but somehow, without his quite noticing it, she had become the second.

He hadn't intended to tell her about walking into the barn and finding Victoria and Arthur in each other's arms, but the story tumbled out. Despite the pair's stammered apologies, he wasn't fool enough to marry a woman who wanted another man, so he had stepped aside. The two had wed that Christmas. His father had died a few months later, and Arthur had taken control of the Wyndham assets.

"I returned to Oxford, as an undergraduate and then a don, to study the relation of fossils to evolution. Like most of my colleagues, I ignored the rule about chastity and took a mistress, a widow in her thirties who ran a small inn in the town." He felt himself flush. "I was completely green in those days, Susannah. Clumsy and ignorant about—about intimate matters. Jane decided I needed, uh, instruction in the art of pleasing a woman."

He noticed his bride had colored as well. "I realize I'm speaking of things a gentleman shouldn't discuss with his wife, but—"

"But I'm not really your wife." Sukey didn't want him to stop. She was fascinated by this glimpse into his youth. He was so confident now, it was hard to picture him as awkward and callow. "Anyway, we've already established that you have your reasons for confiding in me. I confess I'm intensely curious as to what they are."

"All in good time," he murmured, and proceeded to recount how his mother had visited him at Oxford three years after his father's death to inform him of a horrifying discovery: Arthur had pulled money out of sound investments to indulge his taste for yachts, gambling, and high living. Then, trying to recoup, he had speculated rashly and lost even more. The family accounts were so depleted that the estate in Kent had begun to suffer. Arthur would turn her into a penny-pinching dowager, she had complained. Penny would have to suspend her work, Hugh would be forced to leave Oxford, and Diana, the youngest, would be lucky to have any dowry at all. Luke had to rebuild the family fortune, and there was only one way to get the stake he would need to accomplish that: marry an heiress.

Sukey remembered that story, as well. "I know.

You married Kate MacKenzie. When her father developed a bad heart, you took over MacKenzie and Burns rather than watch the firm fail. And you paid a high social price for it.'' She shifted uneasily. Luke's behavior was a tender subject; and having wounded him once today by speaking too bluntly, she didn't wish to do so again. "Jeremy said you were your own worst enemy. That the more people disapproved, the colder and more imperious you became." She rested a hand on his arm, regarding him with sober concern. "Knowing you as I do, I don't doubt there's some truth to Jeremy's assertion, but I don't pretend to understand the English aristocracy, either. This is the nineteenth century, not the twelfth. Commerce is the source of wealth, not land. In America, you would be admired for your success, not snubbed for dirtying your hands. Were you arrogant out of resentment, or was it a matter of intimidating people? Making sure they didn't dare to cross you?"

"A little of both," Luke admitted. He wondered if Susannah realized how tenderly she was touching him . . . how earnestly she was gazing at him. She cared for him more than she knew, he thought.

He slid his arm from her grasp, draped it along the back of the bench, and let his fingers trail onto her shoulder. She tensed slightly, but she didn't move away. "But I'm the son of a peer. The system works to my benefit, and I would be a hypocrite not to acknowledge it. I do believe in advancement based upon merit, but men with sufficient gifts can win scholarships and raise themselves up. I have no quarrel with the status quo."

She looked at him out of the corner of her eye.

He affected a long-suffering sigh. "That's right, my

dear. Only men, not women, and your cherished America is little better.''

Her chin went up. "I beg to differ. I earned a degree from Oberlin. If I lived in Wyoming Territory, I would be able to vote. I admit we have a ways to go, but I'm going to work to get us there as quickly as possible.''

Not from an estate in Kent, she wasn't, but he let the statement pass. Instead, he began talking about Kate, a subject so wrenching, he knew he would find it impossible to talk at all unless he took the story one step at a time.

He started with the courtship, explaining that Kate had resisted the marriage. Her mother had died after a string of miscarriages when Kate was only ten, and she had grown increasingly close to her father. As his hostess, she had enjoyed an unusual amount of freedom and hadn't wished to relinquish it.

But she was MacKenzie's only child and he had wanted a male heir. Luke was exactly the man to sire one, an educated, intelligent gentleman with a talent for business. He would sit on Burns's board, adding status and acumen. And if Arthur, childless after four years and rumored to be sterile due to a war wound, should fail to father a son, so much the better. In the end, Kate had done as she was told.

"It never occurred to me that we wouldn't be content. I would have my science, and Kate was obedient and well-bred. She ran my home to perfection and charmed people by listening to them attentively. Society accepted her at once. But she was oddly self-contained. There was a barrier I couldn't penetrate.''

Luke stared into the garden, struggling over what to say next. It was an insult to his new wife to keep harking back to his old mistress, but unless he did . . . "With Jane—there was teasing and laughter, Susannah. We would talk for hours. I was certain I could have that with Kate, too, if I tried hard enough. Jane had, uh, educated me at length, and I thought I could reach Kate if—'' He stopped. That was impossibly crude. ''That is, Jane had explained that if a woman was—'' He grimaced. That was no good, either. ''What I'm trying to say is, if a man is gentle and patient—''

''I see,'' Sukey said. She liked Luke this way— embarrassed, flustered, and thoroughly human. In truth, she was flustered herself, but not nearly as much as he.

''You do?'' He looked as if he wanted to dive under the bench and never come out. ''Uh, what, precisely?''

She blushed, her eyes sparkling with amusement. ''Coward. But very well, if you're too embarrassed to say it, then I shall. Although I must point out that for all your difficulty in speaking of such matters, you don't have the slightest bit of trouble with the actual deeds. Remember, I've been exposed to your methods of persuasion.'' With a dismaying amount of susceptibility, she thought, and took a shaky breath. ''You believed if you gave Kate pleasure, she would emerge from her shell. Grow eager for your company and content with the marriage. Fall in love with you. Become more like Jane.'' She sobered abruptly, suddenly recalling the tragic end to this tale. ''But you didn't succeed. You were never able to break through her reserve.''

''No. No matter how much time I took, she never found any enjoyment in—in our lovemaking. And of course, there were two children in two years. The births were hard ones. She grew more and more reluctant. More and more withdrawn.'' He looked down, adding hoarsely, ''I didn't bother her often, but whenever I did, she would lie there like a stone. I felt like a rapist whenever I touched her.''

That was when Sukey remembered the first time Luke had kissed her—how grim he had been at the thought that he might repel her. She understood now why he had brought her outside. "You want me to know I can trust you. That you can't endure how you would feel afterward, if I weren't eager. That if I initiate you, nothing will happen unless I invite it.''

Susannah had gotten the gist of things so quickly that Luke was tempted to say yes and have done with it. But she would never comprehend how determined he was unless she knew the full truth. "I'm not that noble. There's more. If there weren't, I would probably seduce you without a qualm.''

Sukey thought about Kate's death—that plunge off a cliff—and her stomach turned over. Kate must have been a suicide. Luke must feel he had driven her to it. She asked him to go on, quietly bleeding for him.

By the time his son, William, had been born, he continued, England was mired in depression, putting MacKenzie under tremendous pressure to keep his firm from failing. The stress had been too much for him. He had developed severe angina, and Luke had been forced to spend more and more of his time on Burns's affairs. Kate, meanwhile, had devoted herself to her father, spending most of her days by his side. And then, one afternoon, needing to speak to MacKenzie about an urgent business matter, Luke had dropped by his house without warning.

"You've heard me speak about London society.'' His voice was a pained rasp. "You know how debauched it can be. Kate and her father . . . I thought I was beyond shock, but nothing could have prepared me for what I saw them doing when I . . . when I walked into my father-in-law's bedroom.''

He stood, running his hand through his hair. He was so ashen and unsteady that Sukey's heart began to hammer with horror. Whatever he had seen had seared his soul.

"That night at the castle . . . The, uh, the sexual act the whore performed . . . The way she used her mouth . . .'' His jaw tightened. He was breathing very hard.

"Dear God. Kate wasn't—'' Sukey was too appalled and sickened to go on. Then she squared her shoulders. If Luke needed to speak of this, she would damned well help him to do so. "She was doing that to her father. You must have wanted to kill them both.''

He simply stood there, saying nothing, looking ravaged. She got to her feet and gently embraced him. He resisted for a moment, remaining stiff in her arms, then shuddered and pulled her close. They held each other for a long minute. Finally, easing away, he linked her arm loosely through his and began to walk, slowly and silently. She wondered if he had decided not to reply.

In fact, however, Luke was steeling himself to continue. He knew the telling would be agonizing. Yet when he finally managed to go on, he found that Susannah helped him immeasurably. For a virgin—for any female confronted by such depravity—she was astonishingly composed. He could sense her shock, but she listened quietly, encouraged him when he faltered, and even filled in phrases when the words refused to come.

He had sent Kate downstairs, then informed MacKenzie that he would never again permit her to visit. A violent argument had ensued. Far from displaying guilt, his father-in-law had insisted they shared higher, purer love than any marriage, and that society was petty and narrow to condemn it. The activity obviously had started when Kate was a helpless child, but MacKenzie claimed she was an eager participant. The quarrel had ended only when he had developed such severe chest pains that a physician had to be summoned.

Luke had considered him a monster, and Kate his innocent victim, but later, when Luke tried to question her, to explain that he wanted to protect her, she went dead white and refused to discuss the matter. And they never did. In the end, with MacKenzie mortally ill, he bowed to her wish to visit daily, but never again did he leave the two alone. Instead, he confided in his sister Penny, who made it her business to accompany Kate everywhere. MacKenzie's fatal heart attack came eight months later.

Kate was grief-stricken at first, but gradually seemed to recover. That summer, she took the children to the MacKenzies' summer house on the shore in Folkestone, and Luke soon joined her. He hadn't touched her since discovering her in MacKenzie's bedroom, but after an unusually happy week together, he decided a resumption of a normal marriage might be possible.

"I was wrong," he said tightly. "I tried to please her, but it was the same as it always was. She simply lay there, silently enduring it. And the next day, when she was out with the children . . ." He swallowed hard. "Anne—our nanny—she was with them. She said Kate lost her footing and fell, and it was ruled an accident. But later, going through Kate's belongings, I found her diary. She had kept it since the death of her mother. It was all there—her father's abuse, her fear as he demanded more and more, her confusion about whether it was right . . . But he'd told her it was beau-

tiful and natural, the greatest love a father and a daugh
ter could share. He was all she had, and she loved him
and believed him. It was only . . . only after I found
them together and she saw my horror that she began
to question what he had said. And she grew so guilty,
so miserable, that in the end . . ." He shook his head,
too drained and guilty to go on.

"She couldn't bear it. She jumped."

He nodded.

Sukey had never seen a man look so numb. "Are
you positive, Luke? Do you know it for a fact from
Anne?"

He nodded again. "I kept pressing her. I had to
know the truth. She had no choice but to tell me."

Sukey slipped her arm around his waist and rested
her head on his shoulder, trying to bring him back to
life with the warmth of a human touch. "It wasn't your
fault. She was horrifically scarred. Hellishly troubled.
But she didn't show it, so how could you have
known?"

"She was so stoic. I should have recognized
something was wrong. Questioned her sooner. Found
a way to help." He pulled away, then stood rigid, his
arms at his sides and his feet sightly apart. "And God
help me, I never should have made love to her in
Folkestone. I should have left her alone after William
was born—taken a mistress—but my principles
wouldn't allow it. Neither would my pride. I was sure
I could make her want me, and in the end, my priggishness and conceit drove her to her death as surely
as her father did."

"But Luke . . ." Sukey faltered. How did she alle-
viate raw agony? The words in her mind seemed pu-
erile and insipid.

Luke dropped onto a bench, resting his elbows on

is knees and his head in his hands. "I want you, Susannah—God knows I do—but I would stab myself in the heart before I would take you. Because if I coaxed you into it—if you didn't choose it freely, and you regretted it later on—it would be Kate all over again, and I couldn't live with that." He finally looked up, his eyes hooded and his body shaking with tension. "I don't believe there's a spell—I suppose you realize that—but you do, and that's all I care about. It's standing between us, and I want it gone. After what I've told you—given the hell I've put myself through to tell it—I'm sure you understand why."

She sat down beside him, feeling anguished and confused. He gave her credit for more perception than she possessed. "Because you want me to be sure your feelings are real?"

He didn't look at her. "Obviously. You'll be afraid to give yourself, otherwise."

"But . . . but Luke . . . A marriage needs more than desire. You think I'm unruly and impudent. I irritate you no end. We disagree about almost everything."

"Everything and nothing." He took her hand in both of us, staring at it as he held it in his lap. "Where it counts—our respect for each other's honor, loyalty, and courage—we agree completely. As for the rest of it . . . You're young and inexperienced, Susannah. You have a lot to learn, but I'll teach you. In time, you'll settle down."

In other words, he would correct her radical beliefs and eradicate her irrational notions. An hour ago, she would have bristled, but she had heard too much and ached for him too deeply to take offense.

She studied him. He was so somber and intent. She wondered if she had moved him in any way. Roused something deeper than desire. After all, there *were* things about her he admired.

Her eyes slid away, and she asked very softly, "Are you telling me you think you could love me?"

Luke wondered why women had to ask that question. A few improvements, and Susannah would make him an excellent wife. He would be a kind and faithful husband. Surely that was all that mattered.

"Twice in my life, I thought I was in love," he finally replied, "with Victoria and then with Kate, but each time, after it ended, I went on with my life with only a slightly bruised heart. So either I didn't love them, or I'm incapable of the emotion." He paused. "I realize the assault still distresses you, but unlike Kate, you desire me ardently. When you're ready, you'll come to me. In the meantime, I won't pursue you or even tempt you. I'm sure we can give each other pleasure. I know you'll be good to my children. There's no reason we shouldn't be happy."

His speech, while sincere, was nothing if not coldly logical. She listened and bled, but she didn't know why. After all, if Luke wasn't the man she was destined to love, why should she care that his decision was based on reason and lust? But he couldn't be, she told herself. He was too arrogant, too closed-minded. Besides, he was an English earl whose future was an ocean away from hers. "So the answer is no," she said.

He sighed. "The answer is, I have no idea."

Many times over the years, she had wanted to ask Shelby and Sarah about her future, but never more than now. Deep down, she knew why Shelby had sent the tools. Tonight, she realized, she would obviously sit down and write in her diary about Shelby's actions. Shelby had likely read that entry during her final visit to the future, but even if she hadn't, she was a telepath. A little mental eavesdropping, and she would know exactly what was going on here. In any event, something had made her decide to send the tools, and if they were here, they must have been used.

But to what effect? Had Luke lost interest in her because he was the wrong man? Or had she begun to love him because he was the right one? Was it possible that, very soon now, he would start changing into the paragon she had been told to expect?

She longed to contact Shelby and demand the truth, but there was no point even in trying. While Shelby would have heard her mental call—she remained open to those she loved while blocking all others—she wouldn't have answered Sukey's questions. And there wasn't only the problem of changing the future for the worse, but of damaging Shelby's mind. Except with her mother, Shelby always did the contacting, so she wouldn't be mentally overburdened at a dangerous time. She called Sukey every week or two, but in six long years, she had never revealed anything significant.

There was only one way to learn about the future, Sukey thought with a shiver of fear. She would have to trust Luke and reverse the spell.

Chapter 16

~~~ᗺᗺ~~~

Luke entered his bedroom, locked the door, and crossed to the entrance into the taipan's private study. Until six that evening, the chamber had housed his most cherished possessions—his favorite scientific books, artifacts, and instruments. Now it contained the implements of magic, including his witch of a wife. The change seemed to symbolize the differences between them.

The aroma of incense drifted in under the closed door. He knew what lay beyond. Susannah had given him a short book to read and told him to prepare himself according to its instructions, then join her at midnight. He had fasted all evening except for some medicinal tea, then bathed in saltwater, donned a dressing gown, and attempted to meditate. It had been rough going, though, since he knew she would be dressed just as he was when she greeted him. And when he thought about what would happen next . . .

The clock began to chime. He opened the door, struggling against the rising sexual excitement in his blood. He might as well have resisted a tidal wave. His member was like an electric eel, charged and ready to strike. Then he saw Susannah, standing in the center of a circle drawn in flour in a room lit by candles, cupping a chalice in her hands, and it was all he could do to breathe. Her hair flowed wildly over her shoulders, and the curves of her body were plainly visible beneath her white silk robe.

Her face was pale, her nipples erect, and her eyes, bright but glazed. He closed the door, his desire diminishing in the face of her fear. She raised the chalice to her lips, her hands trembling, and quaffed the contents without a pause. Then she set the cup down.

Two sets of witches' tools rested atop her altar, one on each side of the white rose in the center. Numerous candles sat behind, four burning and two unlit, along with two bottles of sherry. Her Siamese cat Nepenthe dozed beneath.

According to her book, she would have completed her preliminary rituals by now. He walked to the edge of the circle, feeling uneasy as he drew to a halt. He was about to be shackled, scourged, and sexually tormented, and he didn't look forward to the experience. "Are you—" The words were a husky croak. He coughed and tried again. "Are you ready for me yet? These creatures you believe you can summon—"

"Are here in force." She frowned, annoyed by his skepticism. If nothing else, irritating her did wonders for her anxiety. "And by the time we're done, you'll feel them as strongly as I do." She picked up a white scarf and a long length of braided red cord. "Turn around, please."

Luke obeyed. Susannah was tall for a woman, but she still had to stretch upward to blindfold him, and her breasts brushed against his back as she secured the scarf around his eyes. The ache in his loins returned with a rush.

"Now remove your gown," she said crisply.

He did so, then placed his hands behind his back. She bound his wrists securely, and then, taking care to avoid his privates, twined the rope around his body and tied it behind his nape. Her hands came down on his naked shoulders next, turning him around, and fire shot through him. He wondered how in the world he was going to complete this ritual without spilling his seed like a green schoolboy.

Several seconds passed. He could picture her removing her robe . . . fetching her knife . . . positioning herself in the center of the circle and holding the implement out. Finally she spoke. "It would be better to rush on my blade and perish than to make the attempt with fear in your heart."

He uttered the required response. "I accept the challenge with perfect love and trust." He started forward, feeling foolish and dishonest to be taking part in this ritual but determined to see it through. If it would convince her the spell didn't exist . . .

"You agree to be purified and to learn?" she asked. "You accept the suffering you will have to endure?"

"Yes." He continued until he felt the tip of her blade against his chest. No test she inflicted could possibly be as uncomfortable as the desire searing his gut.

Sukey set down her knife and stepped backward. She had seen naked men many times, on canvas and in marble. She had even viewed a few in the flesh, when she and her friends in Nevada City had come upon some local boys frolicking in Deer Creek. But none of them had prepared her for the sight of her sky-clad husband.

Maybe it was the three goblets of sherry she had consumed—too much wine entirely for the requirements of magical rites, but her courage had evaporated by the time she had begun—but she was more fascinated than frightened. Luke was lean but muscular, with a light covering of hair on his arms and legs but very little on his chest—all in all, the most splendid specimen she had seen. His male member was imposing, its demeanor as impressive as its size, but she didn't feel threatened by it. He was helpless—blinded and trussed like a roast—and besides, she had come to trust him.

She raised her hands to his shoulders and stood on tiptoe, then glanced downward. As soon as she leaned forward to greet him . . . Flustered, she backed away.

He shifted his weight. Waited a few seconds. Cleared his throat. "Uh, aren't you supposed to welcome me with a kiss?"

She pursed her lips. He might be intriguing to look at, but she had no desire to experience him any more directly. "Yes. But the way you stick out . . . You're in the way, Luke. Can't you do something to . . . to deflate yourself?"

He burst out laughing. "No, Susannah, I can't. That particular reaction is beyond my control. But seeing as how you'll have to do far more than feel me against your belly before we're through, I should think you would welcome the opportunity to accustom yourself to my male quirks."

He had a point, but he didn't have to sound so damnably amused about it. "Oh, very well. I'll proceed. But you're not to make sport of my lack of experience."

"I'm not?" Grinning, he flexed his muscles to test his bonds. "But so little else is left to me, my dear."

Scowling, she returned her hands to his shoulders, but her frown turned to a smirk when she recalled the next step in this ritual. He was laughing now, but very shortly . . . She was so absorbed in plotting her revenge that she didn't even flinch when his manhood nudged her flesh. Her kiss was warm and lingering, her thoughts a million miles away.

He stiffened briefly, then opened his mouth and stepped closer. His tongue slid between her lips, his chest grazing her breasts as his manhood probed at her belly. She was startled at first, then overwhelmed by sensation. The warm, hard feel of his member, the power of his muscled chest, the demanding thrusts of his tongue . . . Desire surged through her, making her flush and tremble.

Shuddering, she kissed him back, sucking at his tongue and pressing her tautened nipples against his chest. Pleasure mingled with yearning—sharp, desperate, and mounting recklessly. Nepenthe yowled. Intense energy flared in the room. The entities approved, she realized hazily. They were drinking in the passion in this chamber, the eruption of human emotion.

Her awareness of their enjoyment—the reality of their presence—brought her up short, and she jerked away. "You weren't supposed to do that," she grumbled.

He smiled, wholly unrepentant. "You weren't supposed to kiss me so enthusiastically."

She was still reeling from the taste of his mouth, the feel of his flesh. "But you said you wouldn't tempt me—"

"I'm only human, Susannah. Still, if you hadn't stopped, I would have." He sobered, his voice dropping to the sort of husky rasp that always sent chills down her spine. "By the way, my dear, how much wine have you drunk this evening?"

Too much, she thought in disgust, and turned on her heel. The sudden movement made her dizzy. She filled a chalice with sherry—her blend, not his—and carried it over. "Here, Stour. Bottoms up." She held the cup to his lips and poured a healthy swig down his throat.

As she had expected, he gulped, sputtered, and backed away. "God, that stuff is foul. You're to give me the blend I prefer."

She grinned in triumph. "No. You agreed to suffer in order to learn—"

"I thought you meant the scourging I'll have to endure. You're supposed to initiate me, madam, not torture me."

Amusement filled the air—the entities again, pleased by the sharp interplay of emotions in the room. "You didn't mind the taste of it in my mouth," she pointed out.

"That's different. If you offer it *that* way, I'll take as much as you like. But I won't drink it. I positively refuse."

"You'll do as you're told. I'm in charge here, and I've decided that drinking it will teach you some qualities you need to learn. Obedience. Forbearance."

Luke was hard-pressed not to smile. In truth, he was blessing the wretched sherry, which had transformed his anxious and wary bride into a brazen siren. He never had imagined that being physically helpless, sexually frustrated, and intolerably defied could be so outrageously erotic.

Contriving to look grim, he opened his mouth. She gave him the stuff slowly, making him taste every hideous drop. And to add insult to injury, when he suggested he should receive a reward of some sort for cooperating, she replied that the submission he had learned should be reward enough.

He sighed. "If you ask me, this ritual contains far too much servility and suffering." His heart began to race. Without being told to, he dropped to his knees and leaned forward. "I forbid you to enjoy flogging me as much as you enjoyed forcing down the sherry, Susannah."

"I won't enjoy it at all," she said in a strained voice.

Her reluctance pleased him, but it also increased his unease. By the time she delivered the first blow, a good half minute had passed. He flinched at the contact, but her scourge was made of knotted silk cords, and her strokes were very light. As her book had instructed, he focused on the slight stinging sensation she inflicted, trying to transport his mind to a higher, more profound plane, but at first, the hint of pain was more erotic than hypnotic. Then, as the flogging slowly continued, he grew drowsy and disoriented. He suddenly had the sense that he and Susannah weren't alone here, that something was watching and judging them.

"That's the forty strokes," she finally murmured, and put a gentle hand on his head. "Are you all right, Luke?"

"Yes." He took a deep breath. "It was—interesting. For a moment, I felt an odd sort of energy. An otherworldly presence."

"Ah," she said.

If she thought she was turning him into a believer, she was wrong. "Very clearly, the scourging put me into a state where my mind began to play tricks on me."

"Where your perceptions were expanded," she corrected.

He didn't bother to argue. This would be over soon enough, and then the absence of any change would force her to admit that magic was nothing but bunkum. He followed her around the circle as she presented him to creatures who didn't exist, administered a nonsensical oath, and chanted some mumbo-jumbo about divine spirits and the forces of nature. It was tedious in the extreme. But the five-fold kiss would come next, and when he pictured her mouth on his body, his besieged manhood, so buffeted by his changing fortunes, sprang to life again. At the rate he was going, he would be a lunatic by the time this was over.

He heard the sound of wine being poured. It wasn't a part of the ritual, so obviously it had a more prosaic use. "Tell me, my dear, would your entities approve of your getting courage out of a bottle?"

"They don't seem to mind."

He didn't know whether to be amused or concerned. "But you know how low your tolerance is. Any more wine, and you could pass out before we finish."

To Sukey, oblivion sounded like a fine idea. "If I want to drink, I'll drink." She downed the sherry, then grabbed a jar of oil and returned to Luke's side.

Unfortunately, the wine did nothing for her frazzled nerves. Though muzzier than ever, she could hardly help noticing the condition of his member, and dreaded the coming encounter. She hastily slathered oil on his legs, arms, and chest, her hands trembling the entire time. And then she stepped behind him, and looked at his exposed back.

It was still pink from her lash. She felt a rush of guilt. The scourging wouldn't have hurt him, she knew that, and it had served an important purpose in expanding his mind, but still, she had hated inflicting it.

Her touch gentled as she worked the oil into his scourged flesh. He moaned softly, then sighed and slackened. "That's nice. Very soothing. Thank you, Susannah."

"Uh-huh." She continued to massage him. This

anointing business wasn't so bad after all, she decided. He was smooth and firm. He rippled in the nicest way. He was pleasing to rub and stroke.

She settled onto the floor. "Blessed be your feet, that walk along the path," she said, and kissed each in turn. She licked her lips. He was salty from his bath.

She lifted her eyes, but only a fraction. There was no sense dwelling on what lay ahead. "Blessed be your knees, that kneel within the circle." She kissed the right one, and he twitched. He did the same when she pecked the left. "Ah. So you're ticklish, are you?"

"In a few places," he admitted warily.

She trailed a pair of exploratory fingers up and down his legs, and he laughed and backed away. "Behave yourself, my dear. I won't be trussed forever, you know."

"But I've learned how to defeat you." She sat back on her heels, grinning. "If I were you, I would think twice before I gave me any more orders."

He smiled wolfishly. "Then I'm yours to command. It's hell, being kissed all over my body, but you've taught me the value of submission. Abuse me however you please."

She glanced upward, at her next target, and flushed. He was so enlarged. So solid. So—so *male*. Suddenly, this wasn't humorous at all. Staring at the floor, she made herself go on. "Blessed is your phallus, without which we would not be."

A long minute dragged by. He wasn't really her husband, she thought. She shouldn't touch him that way. But the ritual was magical, not sexual, wasn't it? There was no shame in it. Except that he was very aroused. He had enjoyed it—was eager for the next step. She wasn't, but she couldn't deny feeling twinges of excitement now and then. Surely that was dangerous.

"Perhaps you could just kiss me in the general area," he suggested.

She shook her head. "No. It has to be your member."

"Then don't think about it, Susannah. Just do it."

"But I don't want to," she said.

Luke was dying by inches, desperate for the feel of Susannah's mouth, yet in such an agony of frustration that any resolution at all was better than standing and waiting. "Suppose you didn't look? Just, uh, closed your eyes and—and sort of felt your way home?"

Sukey hesitated, thinking it over. "That might be easier." She closed her eyes and reached out her hand, biting her lip in concentration. "Yes. This will definitely help."

Luke felt her fingers on his thighs and swallowed a groan. Him and his blasted promises. How was he supposed to endure this and not make love to her tonight? He could plunge himself in ice and he still wouldn't sleep a wink.

Her fingers moved higher, awkward with inexperience and clumsy with drink. She prodded and patted, and it was hell. And then her thumb jabbed into his testicle, which was hell of a much different sort. He stiffened and sucked in his breath.

Sukey's eyes flew open at the sound of Luke's gasp. She paled. He was doubled over and shriveled up. "Oh, my God. Did I cripple it?"

A minute passed before he straightened. "It's, uh, you hit a sensitive spot."

Why hadn't she been more careful? Shelby had taught her to defend herself, so she knew men were horribly vulnerable there. He was probably suffering acutely. "Would it help if I stroked you? Soothed you? The way I did with your back?"

He shifted his weight. "Uh, yes. It might."

She cupped him, desperate to make amends. These particular male parts weren't daunting at all, she decided, but rather nice. Warm and fuzzy. In fact, none of him was alarming at the moment. His member remained limp and reduced.

As she tenderly massaged him, however, he began to stiffen and expand. She watched curiously as he returned to his former size. "Is it better now?"

"A little." But Luke was in worse pain than ever—dizzying, exquisite pain. His wife had a natural talent for this sort of thing. Indeed, he was going mad with the need to thrust himself against her hand, to seek his release, but he didn't dare. Any movement in that direction might frighten or repel her. It was just as well that he was bound and helpless, he thought.

Sukey's fingers wandered to Luke's shaft. If she had to kiss him, she decided, she should probably touch him first. Get used to the way he felt. She held him in one hand and stroked him with the other. He was soft yet smooth. Firm and hot. Downright fascinating, in fact. "Is the pain gone yet, Luke? I didn't do you any lasting harm, did I?"

"No, Susie." He sounded breathless. "But the way you're touching me . . . It's a little too pleasurable to let you continue. Do you think we could move things along?"

Susie. Nobody had ever called her that before. She liked it. She bent her head to his member and pecked it, then felt a yearning to do more. So her mouth lingered. She nuzzled him, and then, wondering how he would taste, stroked him with her tongue. He was salty. Musky. He groaned and writhed against her. She felt daring and very powerful. It was amazing, really.

A few kisses and caresses, and a man with thrice her strength came utterly unhinged.

Her lips moved higher. She was beginning to enjoy herself now. It was exciting to be able to affect Luke this way. Her body seemed to be charged with energy, the air around her was pulsating madly, and Nepenthe was yowling loudly. "Blessed is your breast, formed in beauty and strength," she murmured, and nuzzled her way to his chest.

She rose, twining her arms around his neck and pressing herself to his body. His flesh felt lovely against hers—solid and very warm. "Blessed are your lips, which utter the ancient chants." She planted kisses around his mouth, which was open now, desperately seeking her out. She nipped him, and felt him tremble. She was shaking a bit herself. Smiling, she pecked him on the lips, then withdrew to his chin.

He pulled his mouth away, panting. "That's enough, Susannah. What you're doing—it isn't fair. I know I promised to control myself, but I didn't expect to be teased half to death."

She slowly backed away. The room had begun to reel. Her thoughts were a jumble of confusion and guilt. "I'm sorry. I didn't mean to." She hadn't noticed it before, but her heart was pounding wildly. "It just . . . happened. I don't know why."

He took a deep breath. "You've had far too much to drink. It isn't conducive to common sense."

"No. Of course not. But Luke—" There was more. It was throbbing all about her. "The energy . . . The aura of excitement . . . Surely you feel it."

"Obviously," he muttered.

"Not within *us*. Within the room. The entities. Can't you sense them responding to us? Enjoying our emotions? They've entranced us. They're spurring us on."

After all he had endured tonight, Luke was in no mood to listen to any more claptrap about imaginary creatures. "In the first place, they don't exist—"

"If you would open that analytic mind of yours—"

"And even if they did, you should be more honest than to blame them—or the sherry—for what happened. You want me, my dear. And sooner or later you're going to give in and take me."

Sukey put her hands on her hips and glared at him. "I've never denied desiring you. But the entities did charge things up. Even the cat felt it. Why do you think he howled?"

"For God's sake, Susannah, he's a Siamese. They always—"

"Not Nepenthe. He's quiet for his breed. I should have realized what was happening—guarded against it—but it won't happen again. Very soon now, the spell will be gone and you'll stop wanting me. You'll be as eager to end the marriage as I am."

His jaw tightened in exasperation. "And if I still desire you? Will you admit there was no spell? Stop jabbering about magic and entities?"

"You won't," Sukey said, but it was the sherry talking, not the voice of reason. In truth, she was afraid Luke's male appetites would more than compensate for the nullified spell. And if they did, she would be right back where she had started, with no solution in sight.

Chapter 17

S ukey finished the initiation, measuring Luke with a cord, presenting him with his tools, and reminding him to do good and not harm. Normally, she would have freed him at that point, and when she failed to do so, she felt a buzz of annoyance. The entities disapproved of his helplessness. She ignored them, striding to the altar and filling her chalice with sherry, then plunging his knife into her wine.

The anger that greeted this action was so intense that she cringed. In the ten years she had dabbled in magic, the entities had never been so forceful—or so clear about their demands. She shook her head in panicky refusal. "No. You can't ask that of me. He's not really my husband. I won't do it."

Luke cursed softly. As a scientist, he understood that the human mind could convince itself of whatever it wished, but Susannah was behaving like a madwoman. If she hadn't been as drunk as a sailor, he would have feared for their future happiness. "I suppose they're talking to you. And you don't like what they're saying."

"Not talking, exactly." She sounded distracted as

well as unnerved. "It's—it's like with Shelby. I just know—" She stopped abruptly.

"Like *what* with Shelby?" If she told him the girl was really an entity, he was stopping this here and now and summoning a physician.

"I can't explain, Luke. I'm sorry."

His temper began to simmer. "Another of your many secrets, I presume?"

"You—you wouldn't understand. The point is, they want the rite performed in true, and—" She stopped again. "Oh. Not precisely in true, but—" Her tone grew strangled. "It's, uh, the pleasure they're after. They don't seem to care—Not just pleasure? Oh, dear Lord."

Luke's patience wore thinner than ever. "Kindly stop babbling, Susannah. There *are* no entities. The thoughts in your mind come from your own imagination. Let's just do what you secretly want to and get this nonsense behind us."

Sukey was too distressed to take offense. "You're wrong. They're real. And they say . . . They want someone to be, uh, sated. But you can't do it to me, not all trussed up that way, not that you would succeed. Because you're the wrong man. Your mind is as closed as ever, that's obvious. So I wouldn't, uh, you know. Be able to finish." She was sure she must be crimson and was grateful Luke couldn't see her. "To be honest, I don't even know what finishing actually is, but I'm sure I would recognize it if I felt it. Anyway, it can't be me, so it will have to be you."

Luke's loins began to burn. If she meant what he thought she did . . . "You believe you'll have to bring me to fulfillment in order to satisfy these creatures' wishes?"

"Not wishes," she mumbled. "Demands. Otherwise, they'll go away. The spell will remain in place.''

"I see.'' His mood improved rapidly. He wanted to smile at his good fortune, but when one stood at the gates to paradise, one didn't risk offending the angel in charge by making sport of her. Still, he wasn't averse to taking full advantage of her innocence. "I'm extremely uncomfortable in this state, my dear. No matter how vigorously you stimulate me, I'll never be able to reach, uh, the required condition unless I'm completely free.''

She refused, saying she wouldn't feel safe with him unbound. He insisted, reminding her of his promise and claiming that freedom was necessary to his pleasure, although sight, he admitted, was not. They negotiated. Five minutes later he was flat on his back with a leg of the heavy altar between his arms and only his wrists still bound. But he had stiffened and clenched his muscles as she shackled him, so there was more slack in the rope than she realized.

After all, he reasoned, she wasn't like Kate. She was passionate and very responsive. If he was creative about this—if he aroused her sufficiently—surely he would be able to give her her first climax. Then she would have to admit that he wasn't the wrong man, after all.

"I'm much better at pleasing than at being pleased,'' he remarked, lying through his teeth. "I require a great amount of attention and manipulation. You'll have to—''

"But . . . that's impossible. That is, throughout the entire ritual, you seemed so—so very heated. Most of the time, your manhood—''

"And so I was.'' She might be innocent, he thought, but she wasn't stupid. "But there's a difference between being aroused and being sated, my dear. I confess the latter is somewhat difficult for me, and my imprisonment will make it considerably harder. If I'm to achieve it, you'll have to follow my instructions to the letter.''

Sukey worried her lip. She knew she had no choice but to do as Luke ordered, but she couldn't see how she was going to manage it. It didn't matter that nothing he would ask would be anything she hadn't yet done. She had been in the throes of madness earlier, but now she felt dismayingly sane.

''I'm stiff from being bound, so why don't you give me a massage first? You can start with my legs.'' He broke into a grin. ''But kindly avoid my knees, Susie. If you tickle me, I fear you'll have to work twice as hard to get me heated enough to sate.''

Her anxiety subsided a little. When he joked that way and called her Susie, she found herself wanting to please him. He asked her to work his muscles hard, and since her hands were strong, it was easy to oblige.

He quickly relaxed. To her surprise, the touching was as pleasant as before. Quite stirring, in fact.

She moved to his arms and then his shoulders, eliciting such fervent moans of pleasure that she feared his contentment might diminish his arousal. But to her relief, when she inspected his manhood—which she did several times more, purely to check her progress, of course—it was straining skyward.

He sighed deeply when she finished. ''That was lovely, Susie. I look forward to returning the favor. Now straddle me. Sit on my stomach with your legs gripping my sides.''

Her anxiety returned with a vengeance. ''But Luke . . . If I do that, my flesh will be—well, you know.''

''Yes. Fully open to me. I'll need to feel you, my

dear. Picture your female parts. It won't work, otherwise."

"Oh," she croaked, and gingerly mounted him. She felt horribly vulnerable this way. She looked over her shoulder at his rigid member. If she moved backward even a little . . .

"Now lean forward. You can brace yourself on my shoulders if you like. I'll need to kiss your breasts very thoroughly. The pleasure won't come unless I do." He smiled again. "You can choose which one to offer first."

She hesitated, remembering her excitement of two weeks before, when he had fondled her through her clothing. And that hadn't even been close to *thoroughly*. But obviously it was necessary, so she steeled herself and did as he wished.

He kissed and tasted her, and it was just as she had feared. A wave of heat rippled through her. Then he found her nipple and took it in his mouth, and she closed her eyes and fought for air. He suckled it slowly and gently, and it hardened and swelled. The heat seemed to settle between her legs. It sharpened her desire and dulled her common sense. Unable to help herself, she arched her back and pressed herself closer, writhing in tempo with his sucking mouth.

His pace increased. Her heart was drumming so hard now, her whole body seemed to be pounding. And then he pulled away his head, and she shuddered and dug her nails into his shoulders. She didn't want him to stop.

"Now the other breast, Susie. I feel an urge to be slightly rougher." He lifted his head and nuzzled wherever he could reach. "It excites me to use my teeth on a woman, but I might hurt you a little if I do. Do you think you'll be able to bear it?"

His teeth? A thrill of alarm shot through her. "Uh, I'll try." She proffered her breast, tensing as he took it in his mouth, but he used it as gently as the first one, merely tasting and suckling her. This time, however, her arousal rose faster and higher. It left her whimpering, feeling a desperate need to move against him in the most primal way. Appalled, she resisted it.

Then the sucking grew harder. He began to nibble and nip, but the pain was inseparable from the pleasure. She moaned and gave in to her hunger, rocking back and forth on his stomach, rubbing herself against his rippling flesh.

But once again, he turned his head and called a halt. "That was, uh . . ." He swallowed. He was breathing as fast as she, she noticed, and was covered with a film of sweat. "Nice. Highly effective. I'm ready to enjoy your mouth. Stretch out beside me. You'll probably find it most comfortable if you hook your leg over my stomach and put your hands on my shoulders."

She was still dazed and full of longing. Barely able to reason. In truth, she didn't want to withdraw, just resume what they had been doing. But it was her job to sate him, and he knew better than she how to achieve that. She obeyed.

His suggestion didn't work. She was soon wriggling around atop him, seeking a more serviceable position. Only when she was half covering him, her breasts flush against his chest, could she reach his mouth without straining. Touching him had come easier than ever, she realized in chagrin, but then, giving her breasts to his mouth was surely a more intimate act than draping herself on his body.

"Now tease me with kisses." He used that husky voice again, the one she found so completely irresistible. "And, uh, it excites me when you claw me, so you can use your nails however you like." He paused. "Torment me, Susie. Make me desperate for you. Don't give me your tongue until I beg you for it."

His words left her hot and dizzy. Before, with the sherry, he hadn't really submitted. He had only pretended to. But now, if she was skillful enough, he truly would, and the thought of driving him to a state of such frenzied need both frightened and inflamed her.

She hesitantly nuzzled his lips. He didn't respond, but lay motionless beneath her, so she repeated what had heated him so violently before, kissing him on the corners of his mouth, then directly above and below. He grunted and moved his head, seeking her lips. Though she was eager by now to offer them, she moved them to his ear. As she sucked on the lobe and probed the canal with her tongue, it struck her that he might beg her before he was desperate, either by design or by mistake. She would have no way of knowing if he were truly ready. And if he wasn't, the sating would take longer than ever, if it even happened at all.

She nipped his ear, using her teeth in the same way as he had, and felt his breathing quicken and his heart begin to roar. Teasing aroused him, that was clear. He was already intensely excited. But given his admitted problem, the more frustrated he was when she finally kissed him, the likelier he would be to reach his goal. She pleasured his other ear, and he writhed against her, using his body to caress her nipples. They tingled and ached. Her womanhood began to throb. The desire to kiss him nearly overwhelmed her, but she had no intention of giving in to it. She nuzzled his eyes, kissed the dimple in his chin, and sucked at his lower lip.

Luke, meanwhile, was working frantically at the rope around his wrists, afraid he would explode before he could free himself. He was making progress, but the bonds were tighter than he had supposed. Between the way they chafed and the hard edges of the mahogany leg, he was in considerable pain. It distracted and cooled him, but not nearly enough.

Susannah was too provocative. Too responsive. Her massage alone would have unraveled a lesser man. As for suckling her, he had expected her to enjoy it—that was the whole point—but not to squirm and moan that way. Not to rub herself against him, so that he could feel her wetness and smell her scent. And, naturally, he had anticipated that teasing him might excite her, but he hadn't expected her to be quite so passionate— or so stunningly skillful at it. She had learned too well and too fast.

He felt her tongue tracing the outline of his upper lip and knew it would have to stop. He needed a respite. He would order her to do something less arousing, he decided, such as rub his feet. That way, she wouldn't notice what was happening under the altar.

"That's enough." To his disgust, he was panting and trembling like a boy in his teens. "It isn't working. You'll have to try something different."

"It isn't?" She sounded amused. "I'm sorry, Luke. It's all my fault. You asked me to be ruthless, and I let you down."

She licked at the line between his lips, and when he moved his head, moved along with him. "Come, Luke. Open your mouth. Let me tempt you with my tongue." She actually giggled. "Remember, I'm new at this teasing game. The least you can do is give me another chance to excite you."

He tugged at the blasted bonds. "Don't, Susie . . ."

Her tongue slipped between his lips. He groaned and gave up the fight, but the torture only grew worse. The shallow penetration she offered was more frustrating than none at all. He stretched up, probing with his tongue, trying to take her mouth, but she slowly withdrew. And then he remembered he was supposed to beg.

It came amazingly easy. "Please, Susie. Let me kiss you properly."

Her leg moved off his body, sliding boldly over his suffering member. "That's asking, Luke, not pleading. But perhaps if I could spur you a little higher . . ." She took his manhood in her hand and massaged the tip with her thumb, very lightly. "I've been told men like this. Is it true?"

"God, yes." His seed was leaking out. She rubbed it into his straining shaft. "Dammit, Susie, if you don't stop that, I'll . . ." He yanked at the rope viciously.

Her mouth took his in a slow, deep kiss, then retreated. "You'll what?" She gently raked him, using her nails in a way he had never imagined she would discover, and he began to shake. "My, but you're stubborn. Beg me, Luke."

He tried to hold on, but she was nibbling his lips and toying with his member, and it was utterly impossible. He was going to lose this contest. Plead with her to finish him off. And then his right hand finally slipped free, followed immediately by his left one.

The next instant, Sukey found herself tumbling onto her back. She instinctively snapped her legs together, but Luke used his thigh to open them, then settled himself fully between them to part them still wider. A stab of panic slashed through her—it was like the rape—except that it wasn't, not at all. It was Luke, and he wouldn't break his word. He might tempt her— was surely about to do so—but he wouldn't take her, and he would never, ever force her.

His tongue plunged into her mouth for a savagely

passionate kiss while his manhood stroked her feminine core with gentle insistence. It was like being flung into an erotic maelstrom. The shattering excitement she experienced was far beyond anything she had believed existed.

A driving need for something she couldn't identify took her in thrall. She put her arms around his waist and kissed him back, clinging to him as she arched into his thrusts. The energy in the room was immense. Nepenthe mewled, a sound he had never before made.

Luke held her hips and stroked her harder, then whispered into her mouth, "Wrap your legs around me, love."

She wanted to, but even half mad with longing, she knew it was horribly dangerous. "But Luke . . ."

"Just do it, Susie. Now."

She shuddered and obeyed. When he used that commanding tone, it was impossible not to. He moved lower, coming closer to the entrance to her womb, and the pleasure was too great to object. She thrashed mindlessly beneath him, seeking more.

Luke probed at Susannah's womanly passage, felt a rush of triumph when her legs tightened around his hips, and pushed himself a little ways inside her. He knew it carried a risk—with his seed seeping out, he could give her a child—but he didn't care. He wasn't going to take her virginity tonight—he had made a promise, and she was in no fit state to release him from it—but she would offer herself very soon. It was inevitable. She needed to understand that.

Sukey convulsively pushed back, barely able to think by now, knowing only that Luke could have her if he asked, that she lacked the will to deny him her body or anything else. But instead of taking her, he stroked her again, and then, when she was sure she would shatter from the pleasure, resumed his gentle probing. It moved her backward from the place she wanted to be, and she dug her nails into his back in frustration. "Please, Luke, if you don't do something to end this . . .''

"Easy, love. Just trust me. Let yourself enjoy it."

So she did, even the teasing, until her need grew so great that she splintered apart. The pleasure went on and on, in stunning, almost painful waves, until she could barely endure to be touched. She was drained and shaken when it was over. Luke jerked upward, and she felt something hot and wet on her flesh. He had spilled his seed onto her belly.

The next instant, her eyes filled with tears. She sniffled noisily. How could she have permitted this? Dear God, how could she have kissed him and touched him as she had? Teased him that way? Allowed him to get so close? Her flow was very regular, and it was the wrong time in her cycle to conceive a child, but still, she must have been insane.

He rolled onto his back, then yanked off his blindfold and pulled her into his arms. She resisted at first, but he insisted on having her where he wished, and he was so gentle and warm that she surrendered and slackened against his chest.

He stroked her hair. "Please don't cry. Everything will be all right."

Meaning, she supposed, that he expected her to obey his every command just because he had sated her. Vexed with him, she stopped sniveling. "I won't stay married to you, Luke."

He nuzzled her temple, chuckling. "No? Did my lovemaking disappoint you so much, my love?"

He knew it hadn't, damn him. "There's more to

marriage than sexual pleasure. And I'm not your love."

"But I thought only your future husband could give you the ultimate—"

"I was obviously mistaken about that. Given your closed mind and backward views, you can't possibly be the right man."

"You have an unfortunate habit of changing the rules in the middle of the game, but we'll see." Smiling, he trailed a finger down her body in a way that was as possessive as it was sensual. "You're more beautiful than ever, you know. Being sated obviously brings out the best in you."

She supposed she should be mortally embarrassed, but after all that had happened, it was ridiculous to blush because he was seeing her naked, or teasing her about succumbing to his talents, or even touching her wherever he pleased. "You did live up to your billing, I'll give you that," she said tartly. She considered his playful tone—his boastful words—and felt a twinge of suspicion. He was much too self-satisfied for this to have occurred without his having planned it. "You don't have a problem at all, do you? All that stimulation you demanded . . . It was simply a clever way to tempt me, wasn't it?"

"But the entities insisted—"

"Humph. Don't give me that. You don't believe in them. I'll wager you were restraining yourself the entire time. You deliberately set out to sate me. You weren't going to take your release unless you could give me mine first."

"Guilty as charged." He sat up, taking her with him. "In time, you'll come to appreciate my self-control, Susie. And now, I believe I have some magic to perform. I noticed there were two unlit candles on your altar. Am I to execute a second charm in addition to the spell of reversal?''

He never missed a thing, she thought crossly. In fact, she had hedged her bets, preparing a brown image candle to banish the affections of a lover—his, in case he felt any for her—as well as the red and black taper of reversal.

He listened attentively as she told him what to do, then executed her instructions with a confidence she envied. Compliance and satisfaction pulsed through the room. The entities were exceptionally pleased. As soon as they withdrew, she remarked that, surely, he must finally have felt their presence. But as always, he shrugged and shook his head.

They shared some cake and wine, dissolved the circle, and returned to the bedroom. She wanted to inquire whether he still desired her, but lacked the courage. Instead, she went meekly into the bathroom to wash, then crossed to her dresser while he did the same, pulling out a nightdress and nervously slipping it on.

Unlike her, he remained naked after he emerged. ''I suppose I'm to sleep in your bed,'' she murmured.

''You suppose right.'' He lifted her into his arms, carried her over, and playfully tossed her down.

They got under the covers and extinguished the lights. Nepenthe jumped onto the bed, settling in his usual spot by her feet. She waited for Luke to object, but he merely yawned and remarked, ''I can honestly say that I've never spent a more interesting day.''

Sukey had, the first time she had met Sarah and Shelby, but this came in a close second. ''Oh,'' she said.

He rolled over. Cupped her face. Nuzzled her lips until she moaned and parted them, then kissed her deeply and at length. Naturally, she kissed him back. She always did.

"Lord, but you're sweet," he said. "In case you were wondering, I want you more than ever, knowing how much pleasure we'll give each other whenever we make love."

"I told you, what happened tonight won't be repeated—"

"You're right. Next time, I'll have your maidenhead, wife, and freely given."

"You won't."

"Ah. Then you admit there *will* be a next time?"

"No," she said, but he only chuckled.

Chapter 18

Sukey awakened the next morning to the aroma of hot chocolate. Luke had ordered breakfast sent up. Since he couldn't take her on a wedding trip, he announced, he had decided to do the next best thing and keep her company here in Hong Kong.

She jerked upright. He was still sorting through records at work, trying to determine which of his losses to attribute to Patrick Shaw, and she knew he was eager to complete the task. With Deane forbidding him to leave the city, she had assumed he would depart for the office at the crack of dawn. She had expected some solitude today, some time to regain her bearings, but instead, she wound up sitting only inches away from him, sharing an intimate meal. It was almost as unnerving as initiating him as a witch. Broad daylight made everything seem so much starker.

If he shared her discomfort, it didn't show. He seemed relaxed and cheerful, threatening to keep her there in bed, pleasuring her over and over until she wearied of fighting and gave herself completely. She feared she might do exactly that if he pressed the issue, but obviously he was only teasing. Indeed, when she

289

suggested they should spend the day with the children, he quickly agreed.

By ten, they were seated in his carriage, traveling westward into Victoria. At the children's behest, they stopped at the McClures first, so the youngsters could invite the family to join them. Alex was out, busy questioning murder suspects, but Melanie and her brood were happy to go along. Melanie ordered a picnic lunch, then listened to Sukey grumble about her wedding night while Luke and the children engaged in horseplay nearby.

William soon decided he was hungry, but Sukey had come prepared. She pulled a tin of chocolates out of her purse, and was immediately surrounded by six little outstretched hands.

Melanie watched the scene with a bemused look on her face. "It reminds me of Shelby's prediction. The part about rearing six children."

Sukey hushed her and nodded toward Luke, but he was already looking their way. "Miss March had a vision of you with six children?"

"Never mind," Sukey said. "It doesn't concern you."

"But if I have to father them—"

"You don't."

Melanie rolled her eyes. "Of course he does." She handed the tin to her oldest, Wyatt, and told him to take the children outside and divvy up the spoils. They raced away, and she continued, "After last night, how can you doubt it? For seven years, you wouldn't let a man near you, yet you allowed Luke to—"

"Mellie, I told you about that in confidence," Sukey wailed.

"Well, he *was* there. He knows what took place. Surely it must have occurred to you that if he weren't the right man, you never would have permitted him to make love to you. You would have been far too frightened.''

''But the entities left me no choice. Anyway, the fact that I've come to trust him has nothing to do with—''

''Actually, *she* did most of the lovemaking,'' Luke interrupted, ''and with remarkable enthusiasm, too. After all, I was bound until the last few minutes. But I promise you, Melanie, once I was free, I tried mightily to please her.'' He grinned broadly. ''Did she happen to mention whether I had succeeded?''

Sukey had taken as much as she planned to. ''Oh, stop strutting, Stour. I have a weakness for you, I've acknowledged that repeatedly, but that doesn't make you my future husband. You're not at all what Shelby described, and that's that. I refuse to discuss the subject further.''

''If you insist, my dear, but six children . . . !'' His eyebrows knitted together. ''Even if we subtract William and Eleanor, I still have a herculean task ahead of me. If you weren't so skillful at stimulating me, I would worry about my ability to accomplish it.''

Sukey glowered at him and threw her purse at his chest, causing the contents to scatter all over the floor. Fortunately, their picnic arrived as she was gathering everything up, and they were able to get on their way. They traveled on foot, a pair of servants trailing behind with their possessions. With so many curious little ears nearby, there could be no more talk of last night.

They visited the museum in City Hall, then strolled to the Cricket Ground to dine. At least twice while they ate, Luke glanced around, something he had done numerous times that morning. A little puzzled, Sukey finally asked whether they were being followed.

"I don't know," he said. "I haven't seen anyone, but I can't shake the sensation that someone is watching. I've felt it on and off for days now."

But nobody else could sense it, not even Melanie, whose clairvoyance would have warned her of any danger. Still, she and Sukey decided to keep their eyes and ears open from that point on.

Their next stop was Taipingshan, a warren of narrow streets and colorful Chinese shops, most of them tiny and all of them crammed with goods. William and Annie were yawning by then, so they were installed in hired sedan chairs to catnap while the company browsed. The children received toys and trinkets, Sukey bought materials for her students' art projects, and Melanie selected some silks. As for Luke, late that afternoon, he led them into a jewelry store and purchased a suite of gold set with emerald-colored jade, "to match your eyes," he informed Sukey.

She didn't argue about accepting the gift, but she didn't intend to keep it after they had parted, either. *If* they parted, she thought in confusion. For a male, Luke had been amazingly patient about their shopping. He was wonderful with the children, balancing firm discipline with teasing good humor. And when he smiled at her or took her arm . . .

The servants were laden with packages now, and even the adults had begun to tire. They started home along Queen's Road, still checking for pursuers, still seeing nothing. And then they came to Pedder Street, where Jade's shop was located, and decided they couldn't spend the day in Victoria without stopping in to say hello.

Jade kept free samples of her newest creations by the door—today, various types of spiced cookies—and the children lingered to taste them. Jade herself was nowhere in sight, but Jeremy was ringing up a sale behind the counter. His customer soon departed, and he smiled broadly. "You see before you a beaten man, my friends. It isn't enough that I've consented to marry the woman. Here I am, a great taipan, and she's turned me into a mere clerk."

Jade emerged from the factory behind the salesroom carrying a tray of small bottles. "Watching the shop for an hour because my girl has taken ill and I have orders to mix is not being a clerk, Jeremy. And I have not yet consented to marry *you*."

"She will," he said to Luke. "She's just punishing me for dragging my heels, not that I don't deserve it."

Melanie regarded him sternly. "Yes. You do. What finally brought you to your senses?"

"I realized why I'd been traveling around China all these months. Not just to say good-bye to my friends, but to avoid leaving for good." He gazed at Jade with a tenderness impossible to miss. "Sometimes we don't value what we have until we lose it. I was a fool ever to leave you, but I know you still love me, just as I love you. Now that I've returned, I aim to win you back." He drew himself to his full height as he turned back to Luke. "I plan to remain in Hong Kong, where our sons will have the opportunity to become great men. Perhaps even taipans of Burns one day—if the controlling partner doesn't veto that possibility."

There was a time when Luke might have done exactly that, but men like Tung and Kai-wing Douglas had taught him better. "My only concern is a man's talent, and the color of his skin has nothing to do with that. If your sons inherit their father's skill in business, naturally they'll be in line to become partners and even taipans."

"Their father's skill?" Sukey gestured around the

shop, which was one of the largest in Taipingshan. "And what about their mother's, Luke?"

He regarded Susannah warily. They had spent a delightful day together, and he didn't wish to jeopardize the progress he had made by quarreling about women's alleged rights. "Well, that too, of course."

"But if Jeremy and Jade have a daughter—"

"She can follow in her mother's footsteps, my dear."

"But not her father's?"

He sighed. "This is hardly the time or place to discuss the subject. We should be going now—"

"According to you, there's never a time or place. You won't recognize that females can do everything males do. If you believe I could ever accept such an opinion—"

"Males have wider abilities, Susannah. That's a matter of fact, not opinion, but if you're so keen to debate the topic—"

"With an arrogant, bullheaded philistine like you? What would be the point?"

Enough, Luke thought, was enough. He took Susannah's arm and growled into her ear, "Mind your tongue, madam. Your disrespect would be intolerable even if my children weren't present, but they are, and I won't have them hearing you insult me."

Sukey pulled away from him. In fact, the children were absorbed in tasting sweets, paying no attention whatsoever to the adults across the room. Thrusting up her chin, she marched over to Jade. "Remember how you once told me you envied me my freedom? Well, right now, I envy you yours. Being a mistress can't possibly be any worse than being a wife, so think carefully before you make your choice."

Jade flinched and looked at her feet. Sukey thought

she looked guilty, but that made no sense. Jade had nothing to repent, so perhaps she was only upset. Jeremy must have been right about Jade's feelings. She did still want him, so Sukey's acid words about marriage and freedom had drawn blood. "Unless you're truly in love," she added hastily. "Then it might be different." Her voice dropped to a wistful murmur. "I'm sorry, Jade. Just follow your heart. I'm sure you'll be happy."

God knew, *she* wasn't. Luke Wyndham was impossible. Not even remotely right for her. But after just a few happy hours together, she had started hoping—believing—that he might be. Fighting tears, she ran from the shop.

Luke followed, smarting from her accusations. He wasn't a villain, for God's sake. There was a limit to what a man should have to put up with, that was all, and his wife had persistently exceeded it.

Melanie hurried after him, catching him just outside the door. "Let her be, Luke. I don't have a doubt in the world that eventually, you'll be exactly what she wants, but you aren't there yet, and it's confusing and very painful for her."

He gaped at her. "You're saying *I'm* the one who should change my beliefs? You can't be serious!"

"But you'll have to. After all, Shelby never mentioned her loving the wrong man, so you must be the right—"

"Wait a moment. You believe she loves me?"

Melanie looked at the sky and shook her head. "Men! After last night, how can you even ask that question? But you're a work in progress, and your flaws keep scaring her off, so do try to perfect yourself quickly." She chuckled. "She'll call in Shelby if you don't, and believe me, you don't want to tangle with *her*.''

Luke didn't argue. In the face of such total gibberish, it was insane even to try. Instead, he purchased some sweets for the children, wished Jeremy good luck, and ushered everyone from the shop.

Susannah was standing on the corner, waiting mutely and stiffly while tears rolled slowly down her cheeks. All the anger drained out of him. If anyone was at fault here, it was her brother and his firebrand of a wife. They had encouraged her to run wild. Filled her with crazy notions. Tolerated illogic and superstition. Naturally she was misguided and willful.

He smiled warmly and took her arm. He would correct her in the privacy of their bedroom, he decided, but more gently than before. More patiently. They were soon piling into the carriage with their purchases, but the moment they arrived at Number One House, Sukey scooped Lexie up and mumbled that she would return the girl to her mother. Luke calmly allowed it. After all, she couldn't avoid him forever.

But Sukey had resolved to try. She knew what would happen when Luke got her alone. He would scold her, which would lead to another quarrel, which he would end by making love to her, which she could never seem to resist. She crossed through the garden, plotting her escape. She would develop a queasy stomach after dinner, she decided, and retire early. And there would be no more sharing a bed, either.

She turned into Victoria's yard just as Sir Roger Albright bounded out of the cottage. They met on the stone walkway, chatting about the attractions of Taipingshan until Lexie squirmed and demanded to go inside. Laughing, Albright took her from Sukey's hip, teased her about her fidgets, and tickled her until she giggled. It was the first time Sukey had seen the two together, and Albright's affection for the child was very clear. He probably looked forward to becoming her father.

He put her down and swatted her lightly on the bottom. "Off you go, then, straight into the house." She scampered away, and he added, "I'll make sure she finds her mama, Susannah. I'll see you at dinner, unless His Lordship sends word that he's keeping you for himself again tonight."

"Uh, yes. That is, I do hope to see you, but I'm not sure of his plans."

Albright nodded and returned to the cottage. Sukey went the other way, her mind in a total muddle. The way Lexie moved and laughed ... People looked at her blond hair and blue eyes, and they said she resembled Luke as well as Victoria, but she favored Albright even more, albeit in subtle ways.

Sukey suddenly wondered exactly when Sir Roger Albright had entered Victoria Stour's life.

She roamed the garden for the next hour, brooding about the matter. Legally, Lexie was Arthur's daughter, but what if Arthur had indeed been sterile, and Lexie was really Albright's? Luke had been the subject of scurrilous rumors, and he could quietly refute them. With no blood tie, he might not wish to support her and her mother as generously as he currently did.

But if that *was* the truth, and it did come out, then gossip would rage around poor Lexie. And Luke provided for her as much out of love as duty, didn't he? Given the type of man he was, her paternity wouldn't change that. No good could come of disturbing this hornet's nest, she decided, only harm to an innocent child.

She walked slowly back to the house, planning to lay claim to a vacant room and then change for dinner. Her hair was a windblown tangle, and her dress was wrinkled and dusty. But when she passed the parlor, she saw visitors inside—Jeremy Burns, and Jade and Kai-wing Douglas—and paused by the door. A bottle of champagne and five empty glasses sat on an end table—incongruously so, she thought, since everyone looked somber rather than happy.

Jeremy noticed her at once. "Ah, there you are, Sukey. Stour was about to toast my betrothal. I was hoping you would arrive in time to join us."

She started toward a wing chair, but Luke intercepted her and seated her on the sofa. The wine was uncorked and passed around, and Jade and Jeremy wished happiness and good health. For just a moment, Jade's face lit up. Whatever was troubling her, it wasn't her impending marriage.

Jeremy drained his glass, then set it down. "As I've told Stour, Sukey, sharing our happy news was only part of the reason for our visit. My bride-to-be has a confession to make, and I'm afraid it concerns you more than anyone. Go on, my dear."

Jade stared at the floor, looking ashamed and very forlorn. "I did not mean it to turn out this way, you must believe that, Sukey. I have enjoyed our friendship. But you were a threat to my plans, and so was Stour, so when I conceived of a way to remove you both . . ." She hunched her shoulders as if seeking to make herself smaller. "I assumed you would leave. I never expected you to save yourself by marrying. After all, you had told me you disliked him. You were always arguing. But then I watched you last week, and

I thought you had fallen in love with him, because he was forever instructing you in the most maddening way imaginable, and you never seemed to mind. It was only this afternoon, in my shop, that I realized I was mistaken. That you have been pretending all this time. In truth, you are terribly unhappy, and it is all my fault.''

It wasn't the most lucid apology Sukey had ever received, but she understood the gist of it well enough. ''You mean you're the one who hexed us at the castle? But why, Jade? How was I a threat to you? What plans did I interfere with?''

Kai-wing answered, looking even grimmer than his older sister. ''After the way our father betrayed our mother and Jeremy betrayed Jade, she came to distrust all foreigners, Susannah. You and I were growing closer, and she feared we would marry unless she removed you. Otherwise, she believed, you would leave me in the end, or fail to further my interests as a good Chinese wife should. And then there were your suspicions about the sleeping syndrome at your school.''

Sukey's head was beginning to spin. ''You mean, Jade was responsible for that, too?''

''Yes, with the help of Pearl and several of my cousins, all of whom work for taipans.'' His fingers tightened around his wineglass. ''Jade knows more about plants than anyone in this colony. How the essential elements they contain can be used to cure ailments and control behavior. How they combine in the body, so that brews administered in specific sequences at specific times can have effects they otherwise would not. Effects such as sleepwalking. Eavesdropping. Memorizing conversations, then repeating them when properly entranced. Your girls, and the handful of boys affected, were not mesmerized by a magician. They were expertly drugged by the members of my own family.''

"Who noted what they said after drinking Jade's restorative tea and passed the news along.'' Luke settled onto the sofa beside Sukey. "The goal was to obtain confidential financial information, I presume. You used it to further your business ambitions.''

"Yes, Lord Stour. I will tender my resignation—''

"But you can't," Jade cried. "It wasn't your doing, Kai-wing. I swear to you, Stour, my information proved of little use, and Kai did not know where it came from. He thought it was gossip from my shop.''

Luke coldly ignored her. She had drugged his wife and children. Spied on his private conversations. "Which were what, Douglas? To gain control of Burns and Company?''

"Not yet, Lord Stour. I still have much to learn from you. For the present, I am content to build up my capital for the future. I am not like Patrick Shaw. I would never line my own pockets at the expense of my hong.''

Luke wanted to believe that, but Hong Kong was such a den of thieves that he knew better than to be too trusting. "I'll see what our records have to show. Our losses were too high to be attributable solely to Shaw. And since I doubt bad joss was a major factor, someone else must have betrayed me.''

Sukey frowned at Jade. "*You* didn't have anything to do with the losses, did you?''

"No. My only goal—''

"What about the attack on Kilearn?'' Luke asked her. "The death of Shaw? Did you remove Kai's rivals as well as drug and spy on his behalf?''

"Dear God, no.'' Jade was shaking now. "I provided Kai with information to try to increase his wealth and power. That was all. You must believe me.''

Jeremy put a protective arm around her shoulders, then pointed out that if either Shaw or Kilearn had had Kai's talent, Luke would have appointed him the next taipan. "Only bigotry stood in Kai's way, not any human rival. Jade had nothing to gain by eliminating either man, because someone with Chinese blood could never have been named taipan.''

Luke relaxed a little. Burns was right—or rather, almost right. "Not only bigotry. We've never selected a taipan from outside the family.'' He paused. "Of course, once you marry Jade, Kai will become your brother-in-law.''

"You mean you would consider him—''

"It's not your place to ask such a thing,'' Kai snapped at his sister. "You have done more than enough mischief already.''

"The answer is yes, assuming he's cleared of any wrongdoing.'' In truth, Luke thought, Douglas could wind up richer than all of them if he weren't careful, and gain control of the hong by procuring a plurality of the stock.

"How ironic,'' Jeremy murmured. "Jade only acted because she believed the exact reverse.'' She had seen Luke as yet another English bigot, he explained, a rival who would bring so many of his relations into the hong that Kai and her sons would have no chance to become partners. Luke's tenacity in tracing the hong's losses had intensified her fears, since his investigation might uncover her subversion. So Luke, like Sukey, had become an intolerable threat to her plans.

A few bribes to the servants at Argyll Castle, however, and the pair's food and drink had been carefully and skillfully adulterated. Matters had proceeded exactly as Jade had hoped after that, except that the McClures had burst into Luke's room before Sukey even raised an alarm. But Jade insisted she had never meant a permanent scandal to result, only an uproar and a hasty departure. The gossip would have blown over in the end, she had sincerely believed, with no lasting damage to anyone's reputation.

Sukey sat tense and motionless, waiting for Luke to explode. He hadn't wanted to marry her, not at first, and he had been outraged over that business with the whore. But instead, he began to laugh. "So we were drugged repeatedly that night, were we?" He draped a proprietary arm around her shoulders. "I recall saying as much, my dear, and being soundly ridiculed for it. If I'm not mistaken, you insisted it was witchcraft. That magic actually exists."

"It would appear that witchcraft was never at play here," Kai-wing said thoughtfully. "I will inform my magician that no spell will be necessary, Susannah."

"My God, Douglas, not you, too!" Luke chuckled again. "Although why I should expect anything else from a denizen of this colony . . . So tell me, what sort of spell are we talking about?"

"One to defeat your enemies, Lord Stour. At Susannah's request, it was to be cast tomorrow night."

"Protecting me even then, were you?" He curled a lock of her hair around his finger. "I appreciate the sentiment, darling, but after last night, if you don't understand that magic is arrant nonsense—"

"You're wrong." Annoyed, Sukey squirmed away from him. "Dammit, Jade, why didn't you admit all this sooner? I could have avoided the blasted marriage."

"I am truly sorry. I believed that you loved him. But since you do not— If you haven't —That is, if the marriage can still be dissolved, perhaps—''

"Believe me, it certainly can be. Now that you've confessed, I can set the wheels in motion tomorrow morning.''

Luke was still grinning. "Well, how do you like that, Burns? She's so eager to be rid of me, she's going to recant her alibi. Leave me to the tender mercies of Captain Deane.''

She cursed under her breath. She had forgotten that little problem. "I wouldn't. You know that perfectly well.''

Indeed, Luke did. This had been a good day, he thought. An excellent day. Susannah could have cut and run, but instead, she was staying to defend him. She was stubborn and unruly, but she was also one of a kind. Honorable, loyal, and as passionate as Venus herself. In truth, Jade had done him a great service. Her scheming had delivered Susannah into his arms, with no real harm done elsewhere.

He looked at her, and realized he was falling helplessly in love with her. He had never expected it to happen, not to him, but it had, and it made him feel gloriously, exuberantly alive. God help him, he *would* have to indulge her fancies, or she would flee him the moment he was cleared.

"Uh, yes," he said aloud. "I do know that. And I'm grateful, my dear.''

"You're welcome." Sukey remembered the night before and grew even crosser. "I don't understand it, Luke. Why do you still desire me? Even if the spell of reversal didn't cure you, the spell to alienate the affections of a lover should have.'' Unless he had blundered, she realized. "You did follow my instructions, didn't you? Thought your name as you effected the spell and asked the entities to release you from your feelings?''

Luke lazed back on the sofa and crossed his ankle over his knee. ''Tell me something, Douglas. All week long, you've been mooning over my wife, but tonight, you seem almost indifferent to her. There's friendship and concern, certainly, but nothing deeper. Why is that?''

Kai looked confused by the question. ''I—I do not know, Lord Stour. I suppose there was no use craving what I could not have, or rather, what I believed I could not have.''

''And what he craves now is Sophie Hotung,'' Jade said. ''This morning, we took tea with her father, a friendly meeting about our export venture. Sophie poured. She has loved Kai forever, but she was still a girl when she left on her travels. She returned a woman, and today, he finally noticed the change.''

Luke nodded. ''Hmm. How interesting.''

Sukey studied him for a minute. He looked impossibly smug. ''You didn't,'' she said.

''I'm afraid I did. After all, I couldn't have him pining over you indefinitely.''

''But I wrote your name on the candle and the vellum. That should have been stronger than your thoughts about Kai. Anyway, if you don't believe in magic, why did you bother to cheat?''

''I believe you Americans would call it covering all the bases.''

Sukey folded her arms across her chest and glared at him. Not only did he outmaneuver her at every turn; he was a neophyte, yet he was already a more powerful witch than she was. It was infuriating.

*　　*　　*

The McClures arrived as Jeremy and his party were leaving, and were followed in short order by the members of Luke's family. Except during dinner, Luke never left her side. He was permissive to a fault, even when she spoke her mind. He had always been impeccably proper in public, but suddenly, he couldn't stop touching her—toying with a lock of her hair or fondling the nape of her neck. Her annoyance gave way to confusion, then arousal. She wasn't an expert on English earls, but she doubted they usually behaved as her husband did. She couldn't believe he was the same man who had been considered straitlaced to the point of priggishness in London.

Everyone noticed, of course. The McClures smiled but said nothing. Penny, who was leaving for a three-week tour of China in the morning, teased him unmercifully. Albright seemed quietly delighted. As for Victoria, whenever no one but Sukey was watching, she sent a disapproving sniff Sukey's way, as if to say that only a trollop would encourage a man to paw her like a groveling hunting hound. Victoria was very attentive to Albright, but still, Sukey had to wonder if she wanted Luke for herself, however illicitly.

Then again, it was probably only that three countesses of Stour were at least one too many for her taste. To be displaced was bad enough, but to be supplanted by a loudmouthed American frump like Sukey . . . And since Sukey felt inadequate to begin with, sitting there in a bedraggled dress and suffering silent contempt, she wasn't about to admit that Victoria had nothing to worry about. The woman could damned well stew, and anyway, the divorce was far from imminent. Alex had interviewed all the suspects that day, crossing swords with Deane a few times, but learned dismayingly little. None of them had regretted Shaw's death, he reported, and only two—Tex Stratton and Robert Kilearn—had exhibited the discomfort that so often accompanied guilt. But their uneasiness might have derived from shame over crimes short of murder, such as bribery, extortion, and embezzlement. Alex suspected both had defrauded Burns, and planned to delve further into the matter when he had the time. But the murder investigation would have to come first.

All in all, it was a dispiriting evening—the latest of far too many, Sukey thought as she followed Luke upstairs. She had been too eager to hear the details of Alex's investigation to claim illness and then retire, so she demanded her own room in the name of moral probity. In response, Luke took her gently by the arm, ushered her into his bedroom, and closed the door. "Morality won't be violated here tonight, and both of us know it. You made a promise to me, Susannah. Are you refusing to honor it?"

He meant her agreement to feign wedded bliss and share his room until the murder was solved. She wasn't a dolt—she assumed he had ulterior motives—but even if he did, she was trapped. She had given her word, and she couldn't break it without putting him at risk.

She snatched a nightdress out of the dresser and marched into the bathroom.

Chapter 19

Ten minutes later, Sukey was huddled under the covers, trying to ignore the fact that her husband was strolling around naked. She peeked at him out of the corner of her eye, purely to ascertain his whereabouts, and realized he was even more splendid than she had remembered. It wasn't fair.

Her heart was pounding heavily by the time he extinguished the lights and joined her in bed. "Susannah, about what you said to me this afternoon . . ."

Here it came, she thought glumly. The inevitable lecture. "I'm tired, Luke. Would you scold me about it in the morning?"

"If you like. But in the meantime, I was only going to remark that Hugh—my brother—is doing an excellent job of looking after my affairs in my absence, and there's no reason he can't continue to do so. Penny says he enjoys it. I know how devoted you are to your country, and how determined you are to carry out your work there, and I was thinking that if my responsibilities in England present a hindrance . . . The thing is, with Hugh's help, we could easily spend half the year in America. Could you be content with such an arrangement?"

Whatever Sukey had expected, it wasn't that. Throughout this whole miserable week, Luke had never given the slightest indication that he respected her beliefs and dreams. Quite the opposite, in fact. He had dismissed them.

But he wasn't doing that now. And all evening long, he had been so indulgent, so attentive. Could he be changing into her future husband? Right before her eyes? The possibility left her lightheaded and disoriented. "I don't— Why would you care about my work? Have you thought about my views? Decided I might be right?"

"It's you I care about," he said softly. "I want you to be happy, Susie."

Her heart sank. "So you still believe women are inferior."

He didn't reply for several seconds. "Not inferior, but different. The world is a harsh place. It demands strength and endurance, judgment and logic. But women are tender. They think with their hearts and not their heads." He sighed. "I know some females are exceptional, my dear. You and Penny, for example. Certain of you might be suited for some professions that are currently closed to you, such as doctoring children or designing houses. And women such as yourself, who are unusually well-educated, should probably be given the franchise. If you wish to work toward those goals, I'll certainly support you."

It was progress, Sukey supposed. A hundred feet up Mount Whitney. "But the average woman, unlike the average man, should never be allowed to vote. We'll never do everything men do, because we're too stupid, flighty, and weak. Well, tell it to the female abolitionists, Luke. The Civil War nurses. The California pioneers."

"I didn't say women lacked courage—"

"But you believe there will never be a female policeman, soldier, or judge. Or scientist or engineer or minister. That we're not capable of it. That it's against the purpose of God."

"Where pure intellect is the issue, a few might qualify for some of those positions, but if you look at history and human nature—"

"In other words, no. But millions of us will be all those things and more someday."

Luke rolled onto his side, quashing the urge to stalk around the room in frustration. There was no reasoning with the woman, at least not tonight. "Fine. I'm wrong and you're right. But you're the one whose beliefs fly in the face of logic and experience. Frankly, my dear, a man would back up his opinions with facts. He wouldn't expect me to accept his views on faith, as you do."

"But you would listen to a man's arguments and weigh them carefully. You always squelch me without a hearing."

She had him, there. He hadn't wanted to waste his time. "Point taken. You can have at me tomorrow and I'll keep an open mind, but tonight, I'm far too tired." And too tense. Too exasperated. Too aroused by her closeness to concentrate on a bloody debate. "Good night, Susannah."

"Good night, Luke." Sukey thumped down her pillow, then closed her eyes and tried to sleep. It was hopeless. Her mind was going at a breakneck pace, conjuring up arguments and wondering how Luke would react. If he truly listened . . . She began to visualize a future by his side, one that was worlds from any life she had expected to live.

She shifted restlessly. Perhaps he *was* her soul mate.

After all, hadn't he just acknowledged that the world might be gray rather than black and white? That *some* women might have *some* abilities that qualified them for roles in the wider world? It was a start, wasn't it? Besides, he was the product of an oppressive and hidebound culture. If he was slow to see the light, it wasn't entirely his fault.

And then there was this awful, unbridled yearning throbbing through her . . . She could feel him beside her, tossing and turning, probably in the same wretched state as she was. She remembered the night before—the touch of his hands on her hips, the taste of his tongue in her mouth—and the ache intensified and settled between her legs. Would she really be feeling such passion for a man she could never love?

In torment, she punched her pillow even harder. Thank God it was almost over. They would talk tomorrow morning, and she would have the answer, one way or the other. But until then, she simply would have to yearn, because she couldn't afford to tie herself to the wrong man.

She wriggled around, struggling to get comfortable, trying to blank her mind so she could relax and fall asleep. It was futile. The yearning grew worse. Finally, too miserable to remain silent, she moaned, "I can't sleep, Luke."

He turned onto his back. "Now, I wonder why not, Susannah."

Even for Luke, the tone was exceptionally withering. She deserved it, she supposed. She had no right to deny him and then complain. She thought about the incredible excitement they had shared, the exquisite relief she had experienced, and flushed deeply. It was shameless, but she wanted that again. The pleasure and the sating. Surely he would be willing, given his own restless state. But he had sounded so annoyed . . .

She licked her lips. He would never make the first move—it would violate his promise not to tempt her—so if she wanted him, she would have to ask for him. "Uh, Luke? I was wondering . . . What we did last night . . . Could we— That is, would you be interested in, uh, doing it again?"

Luke cursed under his breath. He had maneuvered Susannah into his bed for precisely this result, to make her crave the delights of marriage so powerfully that she would give in and ask for them. But never had he imagined she would be brazen enough to solicit the pleasures of the wedded state without agreeing to give herself completely.

He should have known better, of course. She had been outrageous from the start. He was burning for her, but if he succumbed to his baser instincts and obliged her, this battle could rage for weeks. "No," he said. "I'm a grown man, Susannah. I want to consummate our marriage, not fumble around like a schoolboy."

She began squirming again, which made him picture her astride him, writhing against his belly as she had the night before. "But I would touch you if you want." Her voice was soft and unsteady. "Rub you and tease you. On, uh, on your male parts, that is. Last night . . . That pleased you, didn't it?"

She knew damned well it had. He clenched his fists and remained silent, praying she would either give in or give up.

Unfortunately, she did neither. "Or kiss you there. If you would like that better, I mean." He felt her shiver. "Please, Luke. Don't refuse me. I can't bear feeling this way."

He sucked in his breath. It would never end if he

said yes. They would quarrel all day and grapple all night. "Oh, bloody hell," he muttered. He was the most wretched weakling who had ever lived. "Take off your nightdress, Susie. Come into my arms. At least we'll be able to sleep afterward."

Sukey trembled as she pulled off her gown. Luke wasn't pleased about being denied his husbandly rights, that was obvious, but surely he would be sweet and patient. He always was. She stretched out beside him, and he thrust a hand into her hair and brought her mouth to his lips, kissing her with such searing, aggressive passion that she would have panicked had she been any less aroused. And then he kneaded a breast and massaged the nipple, and her fears grew hazy and distant. She arched against his thigh and found his manhood. She wanted to fondle the smooth, hot tip of him—he had appeared to like that—but her fingers were shaking with her own need, making them clumsy and a little rough.

He moved his hand down her body, slipped it between her legs, and cupped her intimately. "Drive me harder," he groaned into her mouth. "Work me faster."

Her touch grew firmer. Her pace increased. Panting now, he thrust fiercely against her hand, but he was stroking her at the same time, teasing the core of her pleasure with a single, fluttering finger until she was so frenzied with excitement that she barely had the wit to keep spurring him. She twisted convulsively against his touch, her breathing as ragged as his was.

And then his finger stilled. His movements became violent, and his mouth, almost savage. Without a word, he pulled away her hand and pushed her onto her back. She was too dazed by pleasure and need to react. His body covered hers an instant later, then exploded against her groin. When his thrusting finally stopped, he muttered a curse and rolled away from her, leaving her shaken, empty, and aching.

She retreated to the edge of the bed. Whatever had happened last night, it hadn't happened again. She wanted to tell him so, to ask him to make things right, but he was obviously very angry, and her boldness didn't extend to criticizing his performance in bed.

Suddenly, to her astonishment, she heard laughter, a helpless and lengthy roar of it. "Well, hell, Susie, *that's* never happened to me before." He turned onto his side and pulled her casually into his arms, just as if they had been lovers for years. His chest was slick from his exertions, his male member warm and soft against her belly. "Then again, I've never felt this way before. And to think I boasted about my self-control." Still chuckling, he nuzzled her neck. "I'll never hear the end of this, I suppose, but it's only what I deserve. I *am* sorry, darling, but being in love . . . It's twice as intense. Twice as exciting. I wasn't prepared for that." He trailed his fingers down her body in that erotic, possessive way he had, then murmured, "Let me make it up to you, Susie."

She barely heard him. Her brain had skidded to a halt after the word "love." Given his depth of character, if he had begun to love her, then respect and support would surely follow, wouldn't they? But suppose the word meant something different to him than to her?

She wanted to ask him what he felt and when he had begun to feel it, but he was playing with her mouth and toying with her nipples, and suddenly it seemed supremely unimportant. She twined her arms around his neck and pressed herself against his loins. His manhood stirred as he fondled and teased her, and she parted her thighs to bring him closer. "Luke . . . The way you were touching me before . . ."

"Like this, you mean?" He eased a finger between her legs and gently stroked her.

"Uh, yes." He continued until she blindly sought his mouth. Then, kissing her deeply, he slipped a finger inside her. She stiffened for a moment—he was moving it in and out of her—then shuddered and surrendered completely. He began teasing her with his thumb, his kisses mimicking the movements of his finger, and she thought she would go mad with the torment and bliss of it.

She dug her nails into his back. "Luke . . . I can't bear another moment—"

"Good. I want you to feel the way I just felt."

It was exactly like before, yet nothing like before. There was no more teasing and no respite, only dominating caresses that drove her and overpowered her until she was a creature of pure, responsive sensation. Moments later, the splintering pleasure took her in thrall. She was drained and stunned when the pulsations finally ceased.

Luke curled up behind her, his erect manhood nestled intimately against her bottom. She yawned, too exhausted to feel any embarrassment. "Luke . . . About being in love with me . . ."

"Hush. We'll talk in the morning. Now go to sleep."

She had no choice. She couldn't stay awake.

Again and again that night, she awoke to the feel of his hands on her body, grew instantly aroused, and went willingly into his arms. It was dreamlike and muzzy, but when morning finally broke and he roused her yet again, one thing was very clear: the memory of the exquisite pleasure he had given her, and the fact that she had pleasured him back. She blushed when she recalled how—the third time, he had used his mouth, and the fourth, so had she—but the moment he stretched out beside her and teased her with his tongue, she whimpered and sought him with her lips.

She avoided his eyes after they finished, wishing it were still dark outside, but he only laughed and pulled her onto his lap. "You're going to run me ragged, my love. Leave me an exhausted shell of a man. Use me so often and so mercilessly that you'll deplete my seed, which will make it impossible for me to father those four additional children."

She forgot about being embarrassed and pursed her lips. "You're to stop crowing like a rooster after a night in the henhouse, Luke. Just because you've sated me a few times—"

"It's been six by my count."

"It could have been a hundred. It doesn't mean I'll stay with you."

"Do you have any idea of how tired I am of hearing that?" He captured a nipple, then playfully fondled it. "The moment we finish our debate, I'm going to carry you up to bed and show you what sating really is. I trust there won't be any more talk of leaving after that."

She wriggled away from him. "Only if it's incredibly wonderful. Can we eat now? I'm starved."

Luke wasn't surprised, given all the energy Susannah had expended during the night. He assured her it would be perfect, sweeter than anything she could imagine, certain it would be nothing less. It wasn't only her fiery passion that told him so, but the fact that she loved him. She had shown him that during the night with her ardor and trust, the emotion in her touch, and her eagerness to please him. Of course, she hadn't accepted it yet, but she would as soon as he convinced her of the illogic of her views, and she realized he was the husband she had been waiting for.

They had breakfast in bed, chatting about the children and the day ahead. Their debate would come first, making love would surely follow, and then dinner at the McClures and an evening at the theater. Luke assumed they would discuss Alex's progress as they dined, but when or even if the murder was finally solved no longer concerned him. All along, he had wanted the woman, not the alibi, and a few hours from now, he would finally have her.

Sukey enjoyed the meal as thoroughly as Luke did, the company even more than the food. She could no longer deny that their bodies were perfectly attuned and expected their minds would shortly follow suit. How could they not, after the night they had just shared? What would happen this afternoon was only a formality, because she couldn't imagine giving herself more completely than she already had, or to anyone but Luke. In truth, the thought of another man's touch made her queasy with revulsion.

They bathed and dressed, saw Penny off on her trip, and returned to the garden outside Number One House to talk. Sukey was confident her arguments would win the day, now that Luke had finally agreed to listen. Indeed, she anticipated a thrilling transformation. An exhilarating communion of kindred spirits.

But three hours later, when she at last ran out of words, she felt only exhaustion and defeat. The harmony they had experienced during the night had proven a cruel illusion. Luke had made progress—a thousand feet more up Mount Whitney—but not nearly enough.

Ever the scientist, he would admit only one type of evidence into the debate, the world as it currently existed. It wasn't male society's so-called restrictions that had shut females out, he argued, but their very natures. The proof was in the barriers they had managed to surmount despite male resistance. They were writers and shop owners. They worked at numerous crafts. A few had studied medicine. Some had even dressed as males and fought in various wars.

No hurdles were truly insuperable, then. One had only to compare females with men of color to know that was true. In America, freed slaves had encountered resistance just as great as females had, but had persisted until they had won, becoming inventors, judges, scientists. If women had failed to match that record, it could only be because most of them lacked the necessary abilities and temperament. And *that* was a subject on which Luke was only too willing to expound. He furnished example after example to demonstrate that the great majority of females were dependent, irrational, delicate, and totally uninterested in shouldering the civic and financial burdens of men.

There *were* a handful of exceptions, he calmly conceded. Allowances should be made; greater opportunities should be provided. Sukey, for one, was more intelligent, independent, and ambitious than the average male, though she did suffer from a lamentable tendency toward illogic. In general, however, his opinion of her sex was patronizing in the extreme.

Even more maddening, with expansive charity, he informed her he would allow her to fight whatever battles she wished, declaring that, given her obvious intelligence, she quickly would come to realize she was wasting her time. But she feared his patience would last only as long as his intense desire for her did. Then, unless he shared her views, he would listen to his male friends, who would tell him people were laughing behind his back at his henpecked state and ask him why he didn't do something to rein his wife in.

In the end, wounded and dejected, she turned back toward the house. "Well, that's that, I suppose." She bit her lip to maintain her composure. "I thought I would look for the children. Do a few lessons with them. They always seem to forget so much during vacations . . ."

"Susie, wait." He put his hands on her waist from behind and closed the gap between them. "I could have lied to you, you know. Told you what you wanted to hear." He kissed the nape of her neck, which had the same dizzying effect as it always did. "If I had, we would have made love at least twice by now, and you would be stuck with me forever. But I didn't."

That was the hardest part of all—that when it came to principle and character, he was everything she had ever wanted. "Of course not. If you had, you wouldn't be the sort of man . . ." Her voice trailed off. The sort of man she could love. Probably did love, she finally admitted to herself. Dear God, what was she going to do now?

"You'll still come to dinner tonight, won't you? And to the theater?"

"Of course." A company from England was performing *Much Ado About Nothing*, and tonight was the first show. Everyone who was anyone in the colony would be there. "I wouldn't abandon you to Deane's suspicions and a theater full of speculative eyes."

"No. You wouldn't. Your courage and generosity were the first things I loved about you." He took her

by the arm. "Come, darling. Let's find the children.
We'll instruct them together."

She gazed up at him, her eyes welling with tears.
He hadn't yet realized that love wasn't enough.
"Luke . . . After Alex finds the murderer—you won't
contest the dissolution, will you?"

"Not if you're still a virgin. Of course, I plan to tell
Alex he's not to make any progress whatsoever until
you're carrying my third child." He smiled gently.
"You're upsetting yourself over nothing, Susie. I don't
know how, but it will all work out. You'll see."

She didn't smile back. She wanted him to be right,
but given how slowly he was scaling that mountain, it
would take him years to reach the top—if he ever got
there at all.

Dinner was a quiet affair, just the two of them and
the McClures, eating and talking in the privacy of the
family parlor. Unlike the night before, however, Alex
had news to impart—and it pointed in a startling direction.

Ever since Wednesday, he had been checking
steamship passenger lists, he said. He was operating
on the theory that the attack on Kilearn and the murder
of Shaw were linked—that the same party had committed both crimes. All the prime suspects had been
in Hong Kong during the entire period, save two. Sir
Roger Albright hadn't yet arrived in China when the
first incident occurred, and Jeremy Burns hadn't yet
returned to Hong Kong when the second took place.
Since absence during one crime was compelling evidence of innocence in both, Alex had decided to confirm the men's stories.

Jeremy had told the truth. If the murder had occurred on Monday night, he couldn't have committed

it. According to steamer records as well as the testimony of his fellow passengers, he had arrived on Tuesday morning from Shanghai, just as he had claimed.

As for Albright, he had debarked in Hong Kong on December 24 from a steamer originating in England, but the boats on that route always stopped in Macao before sailing to Hong Kong, and Macao was where Albright had boarded, not England. In fact, earlier that day, Alex had received word that Albright had departed for the Orient a full month before he had stated, just two days after Victoria. According to Alex's contacts in the Foreign Office, he had never been in France at all, at least not on government business.

"That doesn't prove he's guilty," Alex continued, "because he might have had legitimate business here he didn't wish to reveal. But if that's true, I couldn't discover what that business might have been. I've sent wires to contacts in Macao and the Chinese ports, and nobody reports seeing him after late November. If he traveled during the month, it wasn't on a commercial vessel. He arrived and seemingly vanished, which isn't easy to do. But he's an old navy hand who still has many friends in the region, and it's a tightly knit group. They might have helped him."

Melanie nodded. "You mean his friends all have ships. They could have hidden him at sea and transported him where he wished to go. But assuming he came early to sneak into Hong Kong and kill Shaw, why would he attack Kilearn first? There's no bad blood between the two, is there, Alex?"

"Not that I'm aware of. I assume Shaw was his target all along—that Albright meant to kill Shaw and frame Luke for the murder. That he wrote a note to Shaw to lure him to the godown, just as he did with

Luke. Somehow, however, it fell into the hands of Kilearn, who decided to investigate. In the darkness, Albright mistook Kilearn for Shaw. He shot to kill, thought he had succeeded, and then knocked Luke out, exchanging revolvers so Luke would be found with a weapon that was missing the correct number of rounds. Albright must not have learned of his mistake until he returned here on December twenty-fourth. But he still wanted Shaw dead, and eventually, he got his way, using Luke's revolver to implicate Luke in the crime.''

Luke shook his head in bewilderment. ''But he had nothing to gain by my death or imprisonment, Alex. Hugh would have taken control of the Stour holdings, and I assure you, he would have been as generous to Victoria as I am, no more and no less.''

''Perhaps it was jealousy, then,'' Sukey suggested. ''You and Victoria *were* almost betrothed once. She's financially dependent on you, and perhaps emotionally dependent, as well. Albright might resent your importance in her life.''

Luke acknowledged that Victoria seemed attached to him, but insisted the reverse wasn't true. ''I look after her out of duty and brotherly affection, nothing more. Besides, I've always encouraged Albright's suit. He has no reason to resent me. Quite the opposite.''

Melanie shrugged. ''Jealousy is an irrational emotion.''

''Maybe not *that* irrational,'' Sukey said. ''Victoria disapproves of me. Her snubs began after that business in the carriage on New Year's, and they've grown worse by the day. She seems to love Albright, I'll grant you that, but I wonder if she wants Luke as well—as a protector and admirer if nothing else—and fears that I'll take him away in some fashion. If so— if Albright sees Luke as a rival of some sort—he might have sought to remove him." She noticed Luke was blushing, something he did only rarely. "Hmm. I've struck a nerve, I see."

"She, uh, she did pursue me rather blatantly when she first arrived," he admitted, "but she wasn't herself until very recently. Losing little Arthur unbalanced her. She was restless. Irrational. Anxious and weepy."

Sukey sniffed at the explanation. "If she was, it was only because her son was the earl and she had lost her little insurance policy. I've watched her with Lexie, Luke. She's a dreadful mother, cold and impatient. By any measure that matters, we're the girl's true parents now. She would be better off remaining with us."

"'With *us*'?" Alex repeated, looking amused. "But you said you and Luke had quarreled this afternoon. That you intended to proceed with the dissolution as soon as possible."

"It was a slip of the tongue," she muttered, but it hadn't been, not really. When she looked at Luke, she yearned for forever. She dreamed about six children and nights soaked with passion. But she wanted days full of sharing and challenge, too, and she couldn't have them, not married to Luke. It was tearing her in half.

The statement evoked a pair of knowing smiles from her friends, who couldn't have wounded her any more deeply had they slashed her to ribbons with knives. They were treating her like a child, as if her most cherished goals were only ridiculous fancies.

Suddenly, all she wanted was to change the subject. To talk about something less painful. "By the way, I think Lexie is probably Albright's," she blurted. "She moves like him. Laughs like him. And you did say something about your brother being wounded, Luke, and his difficulty in siring children. So if Albright was

in England six years ago, it would all fit.'' She saw
the look on Luke's face—amusement and disbelief—
and thrust up her chin. ''Don't tell me Victoria isn't
capable of such a thing, because her past actions say
that she is. She wanted an earl and she got one. And
if she wanted a son for greater security, she would do
whatever it took to obtain that, too.''

Luke opened his mouth to chide Susannah for insulting a member of his family, then closed it. As he
reviewed the past five years, denial gave way to slowly
dawning horror. ''I, uh, I don't recall whether Albright
was in England in early '66, but it's possible. And
what you said about Victoria as a mother . . . She preferred her son to her daughter, but she saw little of
either one. She felt children belonged in the nursery,
not the parlor, and my brother agreed. I had to adhere
to their rules when I visited Stour Hall, so I stayed
there only when my mother insisted. I did run into
Albright at Wyndham House on a few occasions, but
I can't recall even seeing him and Lexie in the same
room, much less side by side, until the day we were
married.''

''But thinking about it now, do you see a resemblance?'' Alex asked.

''She looks as much like Albright as like me, I suppose.'' He took a deep breath. ''But there's something
else, Alex. The day Arthur died . . . We were racing at
the time, Arthur's yacht against mine. Albright was a
member of my crew. The sea was a little rough that
afternoon, but not treacherous. And then a storm blew
in, and suddenly we had to fight to keep from keeling
over. I assigned Albright the helm and took charge of
the sails. I was stronger than he was, and more at ease
on the spars.'' He looked down, flushing with self-
reproach. ''Besides, that was where my brother was.

Where the boldest man always goes. I saw Arthur up on his mainmast, and I had to prove I was just as good—that I could reef a sail as quickly as he could. But the rigging was thrashing in the wind, everything was slick from the rain, and we were being tossed about like a toy boat in a bathtub. I had to battle just to keep my footing." The memory made him clammy and unsteady. How many times had he almost fallen? "Arthur had almost finished when we collided, but I was only a third of the way done. Some blamed me for the accident. They said I had deliberately dawdled. But Albright was in control of my yacht that day, and now I wonder if he and I were working at cross-purposes."

"You think Albright might have increased the pitching and rolling to try to prevent you from reefing the sail," Alex said. "That he steered you toward a crash while pretending to do the reverse."

Luke nodded. "Yes. Arthur's yacht was affected much less severely than mine was, which is why he was able to finish so much more quickly than I could. I thought it was a bizarre current or wind, but now . . . My brother and I were in far more peril than the others at the time, especially Arthur, because he was higher on his mast. If anyone stood to lose his life in a collision, it was he. The accident never really made sense to me, but if it wasn't truly an accident . . ."

"Albright could marry Victoria if Arthur fell and died. Albright's son would be the next earl. And if you died as well, and Hugh was left in charge . . . He was still an inexperienced churchman back then, and Albright could have stepped in and provided guidance."

Luke nodded again, almost numb with horror and

remorse. If he hadn't been so jealous and proud . . . If he had taken the helm that day instead of trying to show off . . . Was there no end to the tragedy his arrogance had created?

Chapter 20

~~~⌒⌒~~~

Sukey moved closer to Luke as they entered the
courtyard in front of City Hall. They should
never have come tonight, she thought, not when he
was so pained about his brother's death, but he had
insisted. His absence would only intensify Deane's
suspicions, he had pointed out, and besides, he hadn't
wanted to ruin everyone's evening.

They smiled and chatted as they made their way into
the lobby, engaging in the inevitable Hong Kong ritual
of seeing and being seen. Luke's pleasantries sounded
so forced to Sukey's ears that she wanted to take him
aside and plead with him to stop flagellating himself,
but there was no point. He already had conceded that
he had been the best topman on the yacht that day,
and Albright the best helmsman. Deep down, he understood that his decision had been the only one he
could have made. Yet he believed he should somehow
have recognized what Albright was up to and out-
flanked him, as if he could see into the minds of others
as Shelby March did. And he called *her* irrational!

A trio of men strolled up, full of gossip about
Deane's inquiry, and Luke nodded and pretended an
interest. Perhaps the interest was even real, because he

knew better than most how circumstances could contrive to damn an innocent man. Albright might look guilty as sin, but they had no proof of it, only a convoluted theory that Alex meant to pursue as vigorously as possible. In the meantime, Luke could do little beyond watch his own back.

The Gibbs arrived a few minutes later, and Martha soon spirited Sukey away to introduce her to an old friend, a recent arrival from England with two little candidates for her school. She circulated after that, answering the teasing question "And how is married life?" more times than she wanted to count. Then the final warning bell sounded and she breathed a sigh of relief. She could decently escape now, to the peace and quiet of the McClures' box. They were sitting there rather than in the Burns box, which Luke and Jeremy had given to a group of junior partners for the evening.

She was crossing to the stairs when a uniformed usher materialized by her side. "I was asked to give this to you, Lady Stour," he said softly. "I'm supposed to tell you it's a matter of the utmost confidence."

The usher proffered an envelope of rich, white paper, and Sukey tucked it into her purse. "Where did this come from?" she murmured back.

"A coolie brought it, ma'am. He said his master told him to deliver it."

She handed the fellow a coin and ducked into the ladies' parlor to examine the message. It was written in a bold, black print and read, "I must speak to you tonight. Both our futures are at stake. Please meet me beneath the trees at the edge of the Cricket Ground at the beginning of the intermission. Kai."

A little troubled, she returned the note to her purse. In the normal course of events, she would have ig-

nored such a request, but this was from Kai, who
wouldn't have asked her to sneak behind her husband's back without a good reason. It probably concerned his feelings for her, or her activities in the
realm of magic.

She walked upstairs, entering the box as the final
bell sounded. Luke was in front with the McClures,
while the others in their party—Father Alvares, Maria,
Jeremy, and a repentant and very subdued Jade—were
seated behind.

She scanned the audience for Albright as Luke
helped her into her chair. He was in plain view, standing next to Victoria in the box directly across from
theirs above the opposite side of the orchestra section.
It belonged to Major-General Whitfield, who was entertaining numerous other officials that evening, including Admiral Stirling, Captain Deane, and Chief
Justice Smale.

As the lights dimmed, Sukey leaned over the railing
to search for Kai. She spotted him slightly behind her,
sitting in the middle of the orchestra section with Sophie Hotung and her family. He suddenly looked up,
then stared into the box as if he had felt her gaze.
There was such gentle but profound emotion in his
eyes that her heart contracted.

She could imagine only one reason for such a look.
Now that he knew the truth about her marriage, he
wanted to resume where they had left off. After all, it
had been Jade who had mentioned his admiration for
Sophie, not he. Luke's magic must have failed in the
end. Kai had realized he still loved her, and longed to
learn whether she could ever return that love.

The play was one of her favorites, but she was so
distracted by the muddle that was her life that Shake-
speare's words flowed over her like so much alien

gibberish. Kai was perfect for her in every way, so why couldn't she love him as she loved Luke? When she closed her eyes and dreamed of a man's touch, why was it always Luke who was caressing and kissing her? But then, maybe *she* was the one who was destined to change, and her marriage was only a confusing detour on the road to the future. In truth, she was much too bewildered and upset to make any decisions or promises right now. She would have to explain all that to Kai.

She fidgeted for the next hour, finally growing too restless to sit still. Shortly before the end of act three, she whispered to Luke that she was in dire need of the ladies' parlor, then fled the box. A minute later she was striding onto the grass of the Cricket Ground, hurrying toward the trees.

Melanie had known from the start that something was wrong. The moment she had looked at Albright, smiling and talking at the rear of Whitfield's box, the world had begun to hum in the most unsettling way. But she had whispered her concerns to Alex, and he had taken out his pistol and placed it discreetly on his lap, and she had told herself to stop fretting. Alex's eyes had flickered between Albright and the stage ever since.

It was all the more alarming, then, that the danger should intensify the instant Sukey got up. Oddly, the menace didn't seem to be radiating around her friend, but suffusing the entire area. She squinted at Whitfield's box, half expecting to see a revolver trained their way, but her eyes were accustomed to the brightness of the stage and she could make out almost nothing. "Is he still seated?" she hissed to Alex.

"Yes. Victoria keeps wandering about, but Albright

hasn't moved since the play began. Why, Mellie? Are you feeling something further?''

"I'm not sure. It's so amorphous." She put her hand on Luke's shoulder, and the hum grew stronger. "Are you all right?"

Startled, Luke jerked around to face her, a stab of alarm racing down his spine. Melanie didn't ask that sort of question lightly. "Yes. Why? Should I have accompanied Susannah——"

"No. That is, I don't think so. I believe—I have the sense it would have put you at risk." She touched him again, trying to interpret the vibrations emanating from his body. "It feels as if you're the one in danger, not Sukey. That she's perfectly safe, yet deeply threatened in some fashion. I know that doesn't make sense, Luke, but that's what keeps throbbing through my mind."

Everyone in the box was staring at her now. She had her skeptics in this colony, but after the violence that had swirled around Luke, few were inclined to dismiss her out of hand.

Alex took a final look into Whitfield's box. "Victoria just left with Lady Smale, but the others are still seated." He turned to his guests. "According to my investigation, one of Whitfield's guests is the source of the danger Melanie senses. He wants Stour dead. Stour and I will be leaving now, but the rest of you should stay until the end of the play. Having a crowd around would make it more difficult for us to get home quickly and safely."

"I want Susannah with me," Luke said. "She's in the ladies' parlor. If Melanie would go in and fetch her——"

"By all means, Mellie can tell her we've gone, but I want her to remain in the theater. To the extent that the danger derives from your being together, you'll be safer if you're apart, and so will she.'' Alex stood. "Jeremy, Father Alvares . . . I would be obliged if you would see our wives home after the performance.''

The gentlemen somberly agreed, and Luke and the McClures strode briskly out of the box and down the stairs. Applause erupted as they reached the lobby, signaling the start of the intermission. Like Sukey, several parties of women had left early to beat the rush into the parlor, but Melanie crossed the lobby so quickly that she arrived at the door before they did.

Alex took Luke's arm to coax him out of the building as Melanie disappeared from view, but he shook his head and stood his ground. Something felt very wrong here. "No, Alex. Not until I've seen Susannah. I want to assure myself that she's all right.''

But when Melanie emerged, she was alone—and visibly uneasy. "She wasn't there. Nobody had seen her. But she was so restless during the play . . . She'll pace through the corridors sometimes, when she feels—'' She stiffened and cocked her ear, as if straining to pick up a distant whisper. Then she grimaced in frustration. "The danger . . . It's farther away now. Outside, perhaps. Maybe we should find Sukey and return upstairs. I think it's safe up there now.''

A hard knot formed in the pit of Luke's stomach. "About these strolls Susannah takes . . . Does she ever go outside?''

"She never has before, but—'' Melanie stopped abruptly, the color draining from her face. "Oh, God, Alex. The danger . . . It's so much stronger now. It's drumming all around us. All around Luke.'' She put her hands over her ears in distress. "I can't think. I can't feel the source. It's so noisy in here.''

Luke was in no mood to wait for the vibrations to

clarify themselves. All he knew was that there was a threat somewhere, and that his missing wife could be walking straight into it. He ran through the lobby and slammed outside. About a dozen people were standing in the courtyard, but Susannah wasn't among them.

He was about to yell out her name when he heard her voice, calling to someone from far beyond the plaza. "Hello? Kai-wing? Are you here?"

The sound had come from the Cricket Ground, he realized, and raced out of the courtyard onto the grass. At first, it was hard to make out much of anything in the darkness, but then he noticed something in the moonlight—a figure in a long, hooded cloak, walking briskly about a hundred feet in front of him.

He gave chase. He was perhaps fifteen feet behind when he spotted Susannah even further ahead of them. She was standing under the trees that bordered the Cricket Ground, the moonlight illuminating her bright chestnut hair.

The figure stopped, evidently unaware of his rapid advance. He saw the glint of a silver pistol, moving slowly upward in the figure's hand. He was almost within striking distance now, but he didn't dare risk a flying tackle. The attacker might fire in the act of falling and hit Susannah. He had to get between his enemy and his wife, then turn, strike, and wrench the pistol away.

To Sukey, it was like watching a very languid ballet. She was looking around for Kai when she saw someone approach from City Hall—a female with blond hair spilling out of her hood. The woman stopped and raised her arm. She was holding a gun in her hand, and the hatred in her heart was so strong that it seemed to burn through the darkness like an evil fire. And then, before Sukey could run or even duck,

Luke was suddenly there, moving at what appeared to be a torpid rate of speed. His body jerked twice, began to fall, and jerked once again.

Time snapped back to normal as the third shot rang out. Sukey was already running by then, but the woman was closer to Luke and reached him first. Victoria. She screamed, a shrill wail of anguish, then threw herself over Luke's chest, sobbing wildly. "You whore. He was mine and you stole him away. I needed him and you trapped him and you killed him. It should be you, damn you. It was supposed to be you."

Alex appeared from out of nowhere, yanking Victoria off Luke's body as Sukey flung herself to the ground by his side. She was almost numb with horror and grief. He couldn't be dead. She wouldn't allow it. There had to be at least a spark of life here to fan back to health.

She was reaching for his neck to feel for a pulse when he groaned and stirred, then went limp with the effort of moving. "Susie . . . Are you all right? Were you hit?"

Shaking with the intensity of her relief—he was conscious and coherent, thank God, and from all indications, not paralyzed—she took off her coat and tucked it tenderly around his body. She was vaguely aware that a crowd was gathering behind her, more and more spectators all the time. "I'm fine, darling." She took his hand, raised it to her lips for a kiss, and then simply held it. For his sake, she had to at least *pretend* to be calm. "You took all the bullets. I wasn't touched. Are you warm enough?"

"Yes." He shifted again, struggling to sit up. "But who—"

"Victoria. Alex is here, too. He won't let her get away." She gently pushed him down. "Please, darling, you mustn't attempt to get up. I promise you, we'll get you home as soon as we can and see to your wounds.''

"But my back . . . It's like a bloody fire . . ."

"I know, love. Now hush." She stroked his hair, slowly and reassuringly. "Your injuries could be serious, so you mustn't exhaust your strength or do anything that could put you in greater danger. Keep still and breathe deeply. It will help with the pain. I'll be right here beside you."

Alex was snapping out orders, sending Melanie home with one of his friends to prepare for the patient's arrival and instructing a pair of gentlemen to run to Victoria Barracks for a stretcher, a lantern, and some bandages. He didn't ask for a doctor, but nobody there expected him to. Between the two of them, the McClures were as skillful as any physician in Hong Kong. Everyone knew that.

Fighting panic, Sukey kept stroking Luke's hair, dabbing at his brow, and assuring him he would be fine. Had he arrived only seconds later, she realized, she would be the one lying here on the grass, perhaps mortally wounded.

Above her, she heard Captain Deane speaking, using his crisp policeman's voice. "Victoria Stour, I hereby place you under arrest for the attempted murder of Robert Kilearn, the assault on the earl of Stour, the murder of Patrick Shaw, and the attempted murders of the earl and countess of Stour."

Victoria's sobs turned to frenzied shrieks. "I didn't. It was her. Her fault. A whore, she's a filthy whore. Get those away from me, damn you. He was mine, but she trapped him with her tricks and her lust. I won't let you do that. Why isn't she dead?"

Sukey finally looked up. Victoria was kicking and

clawing as Deane struggled to get her wrists behind her back in order to put her in handcuffs. "No. Get your hands off me, you swine. I'm a countess. I won't be treated this way. She's the one you want. It's all her fault. Roger, where are you? Why aren't you stopping him? I haven't killed anyone, you stupid fool."

Deane yelled to one of his men, and between the two of them, they managed to subdue her. As she cursed and screamed, Deane barked that he would have her gagged as well as handcuffed if she didn't hold her tongue, then pulled a crumpled handkerchief out of his pocket and snapped it menacingly in front of her face. She flinched and jerked away, then fell to the ground, weeping softly.

Deane put the cloth away. "That's better, Lady Stour. I assure you, I'll see that justice is served in this matter. The chief justice will take personal charge of your case." He peered into the darkness, toward the milling crowd. "Sir John? Are you out there?"

Chief Justice Smale had been sitting in Whitfield's box, Sukey recalled, as had Deane himself. Now he called back an answer from the front of the mob. "Right here, Captain."

She realized that both Smale and Deane must have run out only moments after Luke had, but she couldn't imagine why. Unless her sense of time had gone completely awry, Victoria's shots couldn't have mustered them. They had arrived too quickly after the attack, within moments of Alex.

Smale joined Deane by Victoria's prostrate body. The two men were talking in low, confidential tones when Albright finally appeared, elbowing his way out of the crowd into their presence. He put his hand on Deane's shoulder in the manner of an old and intimate friend. "William . . . Surely, there's been a mistake here. I don't know why Victoria came out here, but obviously she was alone in the darkness. She saw shadows she couldn't identify, grew frightened, and fired in order to protect herself." He dropped to the ground and put his arm around her shoulders. "This terrible list of crimes you've laid at her feet—"

"—belong there, I'm afraid. I'm sorry, Roger." Looking grim, Deane explained that he had never suspected Stour of murder, not after that very first night. It was far too obvious that someone was trying to frame him, especially after the murder of Patrick Shaw. Any enemy that determined to remove Stour was bound to strike again, Deane said, and personally, he had feared that if circuitous means didn't succeed, more direct ones would be employed.

He walked over to Luke and knelt down by his side. "My men and I have been watching you ever since Wednesday in order to protect you. I didn't tell you because I knew it would alter your behavior, and I wanted to deflect all suspicion onto *you*, so your enemy would be emboldened to try again quickly, while I still had the money and manpower to support such a complicated operation. Tonight, she finally did. I followed you when you left your box, but I was slowed by the crush of people, so I couldn't get here in time to prevent this. I'm sorry."

"My wife . . . Your damned game of cloak-and-dagger almost got her killed," Luke said in a slurred voice.

"My suspicions were turned in another direction, I'm afraid. Again, I regret this deeply, Lord Stour."

"Regret it? You should have confided in me, or at least in Alex. If I weren't half dead myself—"

"You would want to punch me in the jaw. I quite understand."

Sukey put a finger over Luke's lips. "You're not to agitate yourself, darling. I'm perfectly fine, and you will be too, as soon as we patch you up." Unless he bled to death before they could get him home. She looked at Alex, trying desperately not to show how terrified she was. "Shouldn't they have returned with the stretcher by now?"

"The barracks are a quarter mile away," Deane reminded her. "Even at a run, it will take them a few minutes to collect everything and get back here. But believe me, Lady Stour, I've never received such an expert tongue-lashing from a man who failed to survive."

Deane had a point. Luke *was* reassuringly irate. Her fear diminished a little.

"What brought you out here tonight?" Deane continued. "Were you lured in some fashion?"

"Uh, yes. I received a note asking me to come. I thought it was from a friend." But obviously it hadn't been, and her stupidity and hubris in thinking herself so special that Kai couldn't live without her had almost gotten Luke killed. If Kai had looked sympathetic in the theater, she realized, it was only because he knew she had been trapped into marrying Luke, and felt sorry for her.

Racked with guilt, she peered into the darkness. "Kai-wing? Are you here? Are you all right?"

He answered from the rear of the throng. "Yes, Susannah. I was at the Cathedral." He sounded breathless. "That was where you instructed me to meet you. In your letter, that is—or so I believed. I have only just arrived. I am told Lord Stour was shot. That the bullets were intended for you. Were we the victims of a plot?"

"So it would appear, Mr. Douglas," Deane said.

"The letter you received was almost certainly from Lady Stour—Victoria Stour—and not your friend. She was lured here under the pretext of meeting you, knowing her husband would surely follow. I assume Lady Stour intended to kill them both. It would have been made to look like a murder and a suicide at the hands of the same madman who had struck twice before. And she almost succeeded."

Albright jumped to his feet, then said in a voice laced with hysteria, "For God's sake, William, that's utterly absurd. What motive could she possibly have had? She had nothing to gain by their deaths."

Deane returned to his friend. "Murder is a crime of madness and passion, Roger." His tone, though not unkindly, was markedly less congenial than before. "All we know for sure is that she wanted her brother-in-law dead and was willing to use almost any means to accomplish it. Perhaps he wasn't generous enough. Perhaps she resented the title that had once been her husband's, then her son's. I'm afraid we'll never learn exactly what set her off—why she came here to Hong Kong and went on a murderous rampage. Not unless she enlightens us before she hangs."

At the word "hangs," Victoria began to sob wildly, and a great gasp arose from the crowd. The idea of hanging a lady was shocking enough, but executing a countess was unthinkable.

Deane ignored the commotion. "Take her to the gaol and keep her under armed guard," he instructed two of his men. "Sir John, if you can spare the time, perhaps we can repair to your office at the court to discuss the evidence in this case, which I assure you is considerable. I believe you'll agree that Lady Stour should be indicted and tried as soon as possible. I won't have this turning into a Roman circus."

Two burly policemen took Victoria by the arms. And then Sir Roger Albright let out a cry of such raw, piercing anguish that Sukey cringed. He sank to the ground and pounded his fists against the dirt. "Why couldn't you have left it alone, Victoria? Why did you have to come to Hong Kong? You didn't need *him*. You didn't need his money. All you needed was me." He began to weep. "Why wasn't I enough? I never wanted to kill anyone, so why did you make me do it? God in heaven, why did you make me do it?"

Deane gazed at his friend and sighed heavily. "I had hoped it would be anyone but you, Roger. I truly had." He nodded at one of his officers, and Albright was pulled to his feet and handcuffed. Sukey had never imagined that the stoic William Deane could look so exceedingly pained.

Chapter 21

An hour later, Sukey could still see the blood in her mind. It had seeped through Luke's clothing into the ground, leaving obscene brown blotches on the area beneath his right arm and upper back. Though Alex had bound up his wounds with gauze, it had oozed through the cotton into the stretcher beneath as he was carried back to the house. Two of Melanie's finest white towels, boiled pure by the time they had arrived and used to sponge off his skin, were smeared with streaks of red.

Luke was lying on his stomach on Sukey's old bed now, drifting in and out of sleep. Melanie had applied a poultice to his wounds, using herbs to aid clotting, reduce swelling, numb the nerves, and fight infection. She had offered him a sedative, as well, but he had refused it, mumbling that he preferred to remain coherent.

All three bullets had struck him. One had dredged a ragged, bloody channel across his back and then emerged, while the others had left a gaping wound in his upper arm before embedding themselves deeply in his flesh. Whenever he stirred, he moaned in pain,

340

making low, terrible noises that Sukey suspected would haunt her for months to come.

She was sitting beside the bed, talking to Melanie while Alex was down in the kitchen, sterilizing his instruments. "I can't get it out of my mind. All that blood. I wish I could give him some of mine. I'm O negative, you know. Shelby typed the whole family. Lord knows why." She stroked Luke's cheek—he was so pale and sweaty—then realized what the testing might imply. "Maybe it was Luke. Perhaps we're meant to do a transfusion." The procedure was usually deadly in this era, and thus illegal—blood types hadn't yet been discovered—but it was still feasible.

Melanie pulled over a chair and sat down. "Perhaps, but we would have to manufacture our own apparatus, and none of us is any good at that sort of thing." She paused. "Shelby probably typed you because she knows she's going to need your blood one day to save someone's life, but you won't know for sure unless you ask her."

"What would be the point?" Sukey asked. "She won't tell me anything." And her silence was intensely frustrating. What good did it do to have medicine from the future at your disposal when you didn't know if you were allowed to use it? Oh, the rules were clear enough—it was for herself, her husband, and their children, to employ as she saw fit—but how was she supposed to decide if Luke was the husband in question? "Where on earth is Alex? Shouldn't he be back here by now?"

"He should and he is," Alex said, walking into the room with a tray full of equipment—medical instruments, a needle and sutures, anaesthetic, and bandages. He lowered his voice. "This won't be pleasant, ladies. Thank God we have chloroform to use."

Luke mumbled something unintelligible as Alex closed the door. "I swear to you, Mellie," he added in a lighter tone, "I can still feel every jab of your needle. Lord, you took your time that night."

Alex had been Melanie's first patient, only days after they had met. "I've improved since then. Anyway, I wouldn't have to stitch him if Sukey would only agree—"

"No chloroform," Luke murmured, the demand no less emphatic for being slurred. "You're not . . . putting me out."

Sukey grimaced. She had assumed him to be asleep, but if he had heard something he shouldn't, there was nothing she could do about it now. "But darling, if you remain awake—"

"It's *my* arm. I'll decide . . . whether it's to go or to stay. I can't make a sound judgment . . . if I'm groggy and nauseated . . . from anaesthesia."

Alex cocked an eyebrow at Sukey, silently seeking her guidance. She paled as she gazed at the wound in Luke's arm. Given its severity, the bullets might have splintered the bone and mutilated the tissue, increasing the risk of sepsis. In such circumstances, failing to remove a limb could result in death. It was in her power to save the arm by killing any dangerous bacteria, but she didn't know whether she should do so.

Unable to decide, she temporized. "We won't know what we've got until you've taken a closer look, Alex. If Luke wants to be conscious and lucid, that's certainly his right. Now can we please just get on with it?"

Melanie fixed her with a reproving look. "For God's sake, Sukey, one word from you and there would be no danger. No pain. No stitches. What are you waiting for?"

Sukey replied in a low, agitated voice, turning her back to Luke so he couldn't hear her. "None of us knows what's supposed to happen here. I don't have the right to interfere. History could be changed for the worse if I do."

Melanie pursed her lips in a silent rebuke, removed the poultice, and tossed it into the trash. Alex took her chair, then inserted a pair of long, slender forceps into Luke's arm. He gingerly examined the injury while Melanie stood by his side with a sterile towel, dabbing away blood.

Whatever hope Sukey had harbored that the procedure would be less than excruciating disappeared with the first deep probe of Alex's forceps. Luke flinched, grunted, and shut his eyes tightly. She took his hand and gently held it. The bullets were in there somewhere, but Alex had to be careful not to damage him any further, and the work was painstaking in the extreme.

He pulled out tiny pieces of bone and fragments of tissue, but no metal. No bullets. Sukey died a little whenever the pain spiked and Luke's fingers tightened crushingly around her own, but she quashed the urge to intervene. She had been lectured until she was half-deaf on this subject. Take care what you do and say. You mustn't change history. Billions could suffer if you do.

Finally, sweating with exertion, Alex sat back and swiped a sleeve across his brow. "Sukey, grab the lamp and hold it closer. If I could get a better look inside . . ."

Luke opened his eyes. "The damage . . . ?"

"I won't lie to you, Luke. It's substantial."

"Better my arm . . . than my life. I want you . . . to fetch a surgeon."

"Let's take this one step at a time," Alex answered evenly. "Let me find the bullets and clean out the wound. Then we'll discuss our options."

Sukey held the lamp almost flush with Luke's arm as Alex rooted more deeply inside it. Luke tensed in agony, growing whiter with each probe, trembling helplessly as he struggled not to move. Alex finally located one of the bullets, but the other continued to elude him. It was hell to watch. Utterly barbaric.

"Dammit, where is a neural pistol when you really need one?" Sukey mumbled, and then, unable to bear another moment of this medical savagery, set down the lamp and strode to the wardrobe. "That's it, Alex. I won't let this continue."

She pulled out a metal box, then pressed her thumb to the scanner to release the lock. Since Luke refused to be rendered unconscious, numbing him was the only alternative. If he saw things he shouldn't, it couldn't be helped.

Alex cleaned off his forceps. "Whether Melanie likes it or not, it *is* your decision, Sukey, and your point about the future is well-taken. You could be starting down a road it might be difficult to exit. So if you have any doubts—"

"Of course I have doubts. You've heard the way he talks. You know the way he thinks." She opened the box, then filled an infuser with paracaine. "But I love him. I can't stand to see him in such pain. I have the authority to end it, and I'm damned well going to use it." She strode to the bed and ran the infuser over his arm, using the technique she had seen Sarah employ on her little son when he had fallen and slashed his forehead.

She hesitated. *In for a dime, in for a dollar*, she thought, and numbed the wound in his back, as well.

Every muscle in his body slackened in relief. "What is that gadget? What medicine . . . does it contain?"

"Something that deadens the nerves," Melanie replied. "Chinese medicine is far in advance of our own. Just try to relax, Luke. There won't be any more pain."

Luke grunted and shifted his body, positioning himself to get a better look at his arm. He was obviously fully alert now, and as curious as he was bewildered. With the torment finally at an end, nothing would escape his notice.

The trio returned to work. It took Alex a few minutes, but he finally unearthed the second bullet, eased it out, and extracted the remaining debris. Then he set down his forceps and sprawled back in his chair, a somber expression on his face. "He's got a deep wound, a splintered bone, and injuries to the surrounding tissue. Despite the care we've taken, infection is extremely likely. He's weak from loss of blood and ill with a cold, which will diminish his ability to recover."

Luke grew more ashen than ever, but his voice remained strong and decisive. "Summon a surgeon. Have him cut off my arm. It could kill me if you don't."

Alex ignored him. "Which is it going to be, Sukey? Amputation or treatment?"

"It's my blasted life," Luke objected hotly. "If there's a decision to be made—"

"Sukey will make it. She has information you lack, Luke. You can argue all you like—"

"What information?"

"—but you would be wasting your breath." Alex stood, then stretched wearily. "Well, Sukey? What do we do next?"

Both prudence and principle required her to call in a surgeon. Luke would likely survive, and then history would proceed exactly as it would have if her medicines had never been brought here. Except that they *had*, and she loved him, and that was as far as her heart could see. Tonight, she could save him and keep him whole, and if tomorrow or next week, she was required to give him up, then she would carry out her duty and be grateful she had been able to help him.

"Fix him," she answered. She smoothed his hair, struggling to keep her eyes from welling with tears. "Please trust me, sweetheart. I promise you, there's no need to sever your arm. If an infection is beginning to develop, we have the medicine to cure it."

"What medicine? Where does it come from?"

Melanie's lips twitched. "Would you believe China?"

He grunted in disbelief. "Not bloody likely. What's a neural pistol, Susie? What is O negative blood?"

The man had the hearing of a cougar, she thought in dismay. "There's no point your asking questions, because I can't answer them. I wish you would stop agitating yourself. It could diminish your strength. Slow your recovery."

"And that worries you?"

"Of course it does." She returned to the metal box and removed a tube of bioglue, a cartridge of universal toxicide, and a can of Syn-skin. Then, setting them atop the dresser, she went next door to the bathroom to wash and sterilize her hands. She had smaller fingers than Alex or Melanie, so she was the logical one to repair the bone.

Luke was lying quietly when she returned, staring at the objects on the dresser. She picked them up and carried them to the night table, then sat down by the bed. The bioglue was like a putty or paste, and adhered to any solid in the body—bone, skin, ligament, and so on. With Alex exposing the injury with his forceps, she used the tip of the applicator as a surgical instrument, applying glue where the bone had chipped away, anchoring down loosened fragments, and repairing damaged tissue. The material set within seconds, then became inert and nonadhesive, dissolving slowly into the body as the injuries mended themselves.

Luke watched in astonishment as she cleaned and dried his skin, then eased the ragged edges together and sealed them with bioglue. She repeated the process on his back, then sprayed on some Syn-skin to create a smooth layer of protective bandage. Finally, accepting the inevitable, she picked up the cartridge of toxicide and held it before his eyes. She didn't want him to worry, and besides, after all he had seen, one more miracle could hardly matter.

"You're a scientist," she said, "so I'm sure you know about microscopic organisms. You've probably even studied them in your lab. Some are the cause of sepsis. The medicine in this cartridge will kill all such organisms, no matter where in your body they reside." She infused the toxicide into his left arm, and he winced. It was a painful inoculation, or so she had been told. "And now, Melanie, if you could fetch me some bandages and tape . . ."

"Coming right up," Melanie said cheerfully.

"For the sake of appearance," Luke said. "I don't actually need them. That material you sprayed on . . . It's better than any conventional dressing, I suppose."

"Yes." Sukey took the length of gauze Melanie held out and wrapped it around his arm.

"The medicine you administered . . . Will it cure my cold?" Luke asked.

"No."

"Why not? You said it fights all disease."

Sukey rolled her eyes as she taped down the gauze. "I told you, no more questions. I can't answer them."

"But *you* don't have a cold. I've been sniffling and coughing ever since I arrived in this wretched colony, and you and I have been close, even intimately close, for almost as long, yet you haven't become ill. Why not? Is there something in your metal box that cures colds, or even prevents them?"

She went to work on his back. "No," she lied.

He smiled, clearly not believing her. "If I agree that women are not only the equals of men, but their moral and intellectual superiors, will you give me a dose?"

She smoothed a strip of tape in place. "I should have thrown you to the surgeons when I had the chance," she grumbled.

The fever began toward dawn. Sukey was lying protectively by Luke's side when she first felt the heat. It wasn't unexpected; the toxicide was a cure, not a preventive, and the infection had obviously been brewing from the very beginning. The medicine would hit the germs hard, then continue to attack them for the next several weeks.

Luke began moaning in pain, so she infused an analgesic to compensate for the waning action of the paracaine, then fetched a basin of cold water and some towels and sponged him down. She kept him comfortable enough that he dozed on and off for the next several hours, but the germs in his body were obviously virulent, and they caused his temperature to creep steadily higher as the morning dragged on. She knew the fever would help his body defend itself, so she took no action to bring it down. Shelby had been very clear about that. Give medicine at 104 degrees, not any earlier.

The night before, he had pestered her with questions, but now he barely said a word. He was so muddled by heat and fatigue that even when she promised him he would recover, he didn't seem to understand. In Sukey's experience, males were the most trying of patients, but Luke was so cooperative, so utterly uncomplaining, that she could barely endure it. He believed he was in danger, perhaps even blamed her for risking his life, but he was so valiant and strong that if she hadn't loved him already, she would have fallen head over heels on the spot.

With an anguish that racked her heart, she wondered if she might be fated to have two great loves in her life: Luke, whom she would have to give up, and the paragon she had long been awaiting, the man who would stand by her side and help her with her work. If so, Shelby wouldn't have told her about the pain she was destined to suffer; the knowledge would have been too awful to bear.

She could refuse to divorce him, of course, but it wasn't just her own life at stake. If she stayed with him—if there was no second marriage and no enduring record of achievement—history might change. Women might take longer to reach their goals. It would have been the height of selfishness to put her own happiness over the welfare of so many others. So she would leave him if she had to, dissolve the marriage if he was the wrong man, but deep down, she believed something had changed between this version of history and the version Shelby had read about in her diary. She couldn't have loved this deeply, then found contentment in the future. It was utterly impossible.

*   *   *

Luke's first thought when his fever began to plunge was that he was a lucky man. Eight hours before, the last time he had checked the clock, he had felt desperately ill. Now, not only was he remarkably cooler; he was in no pain at all, which should have been impossible given the extent of his wounds.

His head was still muzzy, but he was first and foremost a scientist, so he applied logic to the situation. His wife and friends had used terms he hadn't understood. They possessed implements he had never before seen. Their medicines couldn't possibly be Chinese, because China would have conquered the world by now, with wisdom such as that. Something odd was going on.

The phrase, "I'm not at liberty to say" drifted into his mind. How many times had he heard that? He had taken it as the purest poppycock, but now he understood that these people possessed knowledge he lacked, and not just medical knowledge, either. They seemed to know facts about the future and the nature of the physical world that were far beyond the reach of accepted science. It was as unnerving as it was baffling. Where could such knowledge have come from? A hidden society like the mythical Atlantis? He longed to know the answers, but whenever he asked questions, Sukey refused to reply.

He studied her, then smiled to himself. She was dozing in an armchair beside his bed, exhausted from attending him throughout the night. What had she said yesterday evening? "I love him. I can't stand to see him in such pain." At least she no longer denied her feelings. Indeed, her speech was so sprinkled with endearments that if she had called him by his Christian name even once during the past twenty hours, he couldn't recall it.

He pulled himself up and poured himself some tea. It was truly astonishing, how much better he felt. At the rate he was going, he would be up and about within days. Susannah could protest all she liked, accuse him of badgering her and tempting her beyond endurance, but as soon as he was physically capable of it, he was going to attend to two very important matters: getting the answers to his questions, and consummating his marriage. And not necessarily in that order.

Chapter 22

The week that followed was eventful even by the frenetic standards of Hong Kong. After three days of questioning by Captain Deane, Sir Roger Albright and Lady Victoria Stour had provided what Sukey presumed would be as much of the truth as anyone would ever learn. Both were out of reach and would never be heard from again, but the crimes to which they had confessed had painted a sordid picture indeed.

Victoria had come to Hong Kong for only one reason: to seduce the man who had once loved her. She was fond of Roger Albright, but he wasn't wealthy, and Luke was. Faced with the loss of the luxury she had enjoyed as the wife and then the mother of an earl, she had seen only one way to assure herself of the comforts she believed she deserved. She would become Luke's mistress.

She had believed she would get more out of Luke as his lover than as his dead brother's widow, and besides, after she had heard so much about him from Clarissa St. Simon, he had become an itch she was longing to scratch. When she pictured the future, she saw herself as either a widow of independent means or a happily remarried woman who happened to have a generous lover on the side. She hadn't decided which.

Luke had been honest enough to admit that if it hadn't been for Sukey, Victoria's plan might have succeeded. But Sukey had stormed into his life so boldly, and disrupted it so thoroughly, that whatever lingering passion he possessed for Victoria had faded in a tumult of annoyance, desire, and frustration. The great tragedy in all this was that Victoria had refused to accept Luke's lack of interest—and that Albright hadn't recognized it until it was too late.

Albright had followed Victoria to Hong Kong within days. Understanding her completely, he had guessed her plans and was murderously jealous, especially after he had arrived there and learned that Luke was visiting her each evening. He had feared that if Victoria got what she wanted from Luke—an opulent home, a large annuity, a superior lover—she wouldn't need *him*. Not his protection, not his support, not his passion. Loving her with a devotion that amounted to obsession, it was more than he could endure.

His failed murder scheme had been more about having a weak stomach than being exceptionally clever. He had hated Patrick Shaw for seducing his sister, hated him enough to put a bullet through his head, but his feelings about Luke were more complicated. He knew Luke hadn't encouraged Victoria's scheme; on the contrary, he was an innocent target.

Because of that, Albright couldn't bring himself to dispose of Luke directly, but to attempt to frame him . . . that was another matter entirely. Perhaps Luke would hang, but a trial followed by an acquittal would be the best result of all. It would remove Luke from Victoria's world for long enough for Albright to reclaim her affections, but Luke and his financial acumen would survive. As Victoria's husband and Lexie's stepfather, Albright could only benefit from the pots of money Luke brought into the family.

As Alex had surmised, Albright had sent letters to both Shaw and Luke to entice them to the godown, and both had taken the bait. But a third man had been present that night, Robert Kilearn. As he had claimed, he had been checking inventory, but for reasons that had more to do with lining his pockets than with doing his job.

Alex, Jeremy, and Luke had been hard at work all week, studying Burns's records, and their investigation finally had borne fruit. For the past year, they had discovered, Kilearn had carefully and selectively helped himself to the hong's merchandise, then altered shipping and financial records to disguise the fact. On the night in question, Kilearn had likely been pondering what to steal next. Albright had seen him, taken him for Shaw, and fired. Kilearn had simply been in the wrong place at the wrong time.

As for Shaw, he had reacted as warily as Luke upon receiving an anonymous message. He had entered the warehouse even earlier, then hidden himself to await developments. From his perch above the designated meeting spot, he had witnessed the attack on Luke and Kilearn, and recognized Albright as the assailant. Later, when Albright had returned to Hong Kong, Shaw had coldly blackmailed him. It was his final crime in a long list of them. He had paid for it with his life.

Within days of Shaw's death, of course, Luke and Sukey had married. Albright had quickly noticed that the only woman Luke wanted was his new wife, and had been as relieved as he was delighted. There would be no need to remove Luke now. After all, Victoria allowed him into her bed each night, so obviously she cared for him. With Luke out of her reach, surely she would come to her senses and marry him as soon as she was out of mourning. He had expected them to leave Hong Kong together, then resume their previous lives.

Instead, as Victoria had watched the newlyweds together, her resentment had grown. The marriage was becoming more genuine by the day. Sukey was stealing Luke away from her. Thwarting all her plans. Her dislike of Sukey had turned into hatred and rage, finally exploding into violence.

Other than Luke, none of the parties in this tragedy was still in Hong Kong. Robert Kilearn and his liquid assets had disappeared. Everyone had known that records were being taken to Number One House each day, and that daily meetings were being held among Luke, Alex, and Jeremy. Fearing discovery, Kilearn had fled. Rumor had it that he was en route to Australia, but nobody knew for sure.

Albright was dead by his own hand. He hadn't wanted to face the disgrace of a public trial, so William Deane, in a final act of friendship, had provided him with a long length of sturdy rope with which to avoid that fate. A former seaman, Albright had been good at tying knots, including hangman's knots.

His remaining secrets had gone with him to the grave. He had vehemently denied plotting against Arthur Stour, though Luke still believed that in the midst of the storm that day, Albright had seen an opportunity to eliminate the husband of the woman he loved, and seized it. As for Luke's doubts about Lexie's paternity, neither Albright nor Victoria would have admitted to an affair, and an accusation would only have resulted in a scandal. There was nothing to be gained by having Deane question the two on the subject, so Luke had remained silent.

At Luke's insistence, Lexie was still at Number One House. She was already his ward, and he planned to formally adopt her as soon as possible. Purely for Lexie's sake—to avoid saddling her with a mother who was a convicted felon—Luke had persuaded Deane to drop the charges against her. Her actions that night had been attributed to fear and confusion, and she and her maid Alice had been permitted to depart.

She was on a steamer to San Francisco now, supposedly taking an extended vacation in North America to regain her health. But in truth, Luke had dangled out a stipend, to be paid as long as she remained abroad, and she had agreed to settle in Canada. Ironically, it was only a fraction of what she would have received had she never left England in the first place, but she was in no position to argue.

As for Sukey, she had resumed her normal activities, spending her days at her school with her students and a contrite Pearl. She hadn't started dissolution proceedings, finding the prospect of leaving Luke too painful, but she wasn't really a wife yet, either. On Sunday morning, they had returned to Number One House, and she had moved into the bedroom next door to his. He needed his rest, she had explained to the staff, and given his injuries, would sleep more soundly alone.

Each afternoon that week, she had returned to the Burns complex with Ellie and Lexie, picked up William from school, and escorted the children to Luke's bedroom, where he listened to their chatter, allowed himself to be beaten at cards, tumbled and chased them, and read to them aloud. Eventually, a few of the servants arrived with dinner, and the family ate. Afterward, Sukey took the children up to the schoolroom, helped them with their homework, and handed them over to Mei-mei to be put to bed. She and Luke always talked after that, mostly about their childhoods, their families, and their activities that day.

Her final stop of the evening was always Luke's bathroom. The same fellow who rolled around on the floor with his children—who performed calisthenics twice a day to regain his strength—claimed that his injured right arm and tender back prevented him from washing himself properly. Given the Syn-skin on his wounds, none of the servants could be permitted to assist him, so the task had fallen to Sukey.

She was happy to oblige—she enjoyed the way he closed his eyes and moaned with pleasure as she scrubbed and massaged him—but she wasn't blind to the way his manhood hardened and swelled, or impervious to the tension that always suffused the room when these sessions ended. In truth, she wasn't just bathing him, but making love to him, and though he never kissed her or touched her, he was doing the same thing back to her. Night by night, the way he looked at her and spoke to her grew hotter and softer and sweeter. But he always stood motionless as she toweled him dry, and never said a word as she helped him into a fresh dressing gown and walked out of the bathroom.

Their encounters always ended the same way. Though visibly hungry for each other, they exchanged quiet good nights and went their separate ways. On Friday, however, Luke strode out of the bathroom ahead of her, turned the key in his bedroom lock, and calmly removed it. Then he dropped it into his pocket and crossed to the bed.

Sukey's heart began drumming in her throat. Luke had an alarmingly determined look on his face. A part of her wished he would seduce her and get it over with. Trap her in the marriage for good. But having promised not to tempt her, he was far too scrupulous to manipulate her that way.

He made himself comfortable on the bed, then smiled at her. "Tell me something, Susie. Why are you still here? Everyone knows by now that you were forced into this marriage by Jade's scheming. Deane has cleared me of any wrongdoing in Shaw's death. Shouldn't you have returned to Alex's by now? Taken steps to dissolve the marriage?"

She flushed hotly and stared at the floor. "You know the answer to that as well as I do. I love you. You love me. I can't bear to leave you."

"But you're afraid I'm the wrong husband, so your solution is to keep your options open. Live here and take care of me while I recuperate, love my children as if they were your own, but remain a virgin so the divorce will be less complicated to obtain in case I fail to reform."

Her temper rose. She was in agony over this situation, and *he* had the gall to sound amused. "It's not funny, Luke. This happens to be very painful for me."

The blasted man chuckled. "And for me, as well, believe me, darling. If you would look at me, you would see that I'm crooking my finger at you. I want to undress you, preferably very slowly and temptingly. It's one of the great pleasures of marriage. Why don't you come over to the bed and let me show you?"

She finally met his eyes, but she didn't move. He was relaxing against the headboard, the very picture of lazy indulgence, supreme confidence, and pure male magnetism. Heat invaded her body, traveling from her fingers and toes to the pit of her stomach. He was right about being in love—about the way it intensified one's desire. She was only human. Wanting him so much, how was she supposed to refuse him?

She took a step forward, then stopped. "I want to, Luke, but I can't. Not until you believe that the views I hold are correct."

"I see." He unbuttoned his dressing gown and let it fall open to below his waist—a ridiculously blatant ploy, but an exquisitely effective one. She could barely tear her eyes from his manhood, which was thrusting against the fabric of his gown and threatened to escape it entirely. "The medicines and devices you used on Saturday . . . Am I correct in assuming that if you explained their workings and described the source of your knowledge, I would be more inclined to accept your opinions?"

She pondered the question. If he believed she was speaking the truth, he would. "I suppose so. You *are* a scientist. You seem to accept whatever evidence you deem credible."

He smiled gently. "Then why don't you provide it?"

"Because I'm not allowed to. That is, if you were the right husband I would be, but since you appear to be the wrong one . . ." She shook her head in frustration. "I just can't. Not until I know for sure."

"It's a Gordian knot, then. Your knowledge would reform me instantly, but you can share it only with your true husband. But I can't become your true husband because I haven't yet reformed. How do you propose we cut it?"

When he put it like that, her agonizing seemed absurd. "You want me to take a chance. You're convinced it will all work out."

"As the philosopher Kierkegaard said, there are things we can't know from our own senses, so we simply have to believe in them. Take a leap of faith." He motioned to her again, adding in a soft, coaxing voice, "Trust me, Susie. Believe in me as I believed in you, when you told me you could save my arm and cure my infection. I won't disappoint you."

He had argued her into a corner. She had asked for his trust on Saturday night, and he had given it. If she truly loved him, how could she withhold her own trust now? She took another step forward, then stopped again. But it wasn't the same at all. She had responsibilities he lacked—the weight of future history on her shoulders. What was she supposed to do? Which duty and which voice was she supposed to obey?

Finally, too confused and distressed to make a choice, she screamed out with her mind. *This isn't fair, Shelby. If you had told me nothing about my future, I would have made love with him by now, and I would have been happy. And if you had told me everything, I would have known what to do, and I wouldn't be tortured this way. Is he the one or isn't he? You have to tell me what to do!*

Shelby didn't reply, though surely she had heard. Her mind was too powerful to miss such an anguished cry. A bolt of raw fury slashed through Sukey. Damn Shelby and her stupid rules! Had she been in the room, Sukey would cheerfully have throttled her.

Fine, she snapped silently. *Don't answer me. But I love him and I want him and I'm damned well going to have him unless you stop me. And I'm not giving him up, either, so if I mess up the next two centuries of history because you refuse to talk to me, then don't blame me.* She waited a moment and heard nothing, then kicked off her shoes and marched to the bed.

Luke took the long period of silence to be a fierce internal struggle. When Susannah finally started forward, he broke into a grin. He had begun to doubt his strategy, to wonder if seduction might be the only way to break their interminable stalemate, even if it meant breaking his word as well. But his instinct to use debate had proven correct. And to think he had labeled his wife irrational. She was anything but, a female who responded most forcefully to facts and logic—a scientist's perfect soul mate.

She stopped near the edge of the bed. As usual, she was dressed demurely, in a brown skirt and jacket with a white blouse beneath, her hair tucked into a neat bun at the back of her head. He swung his legs over the side of the bed, one on either side of her body, and pulled her closer still. To his astonishment, she shrugged out of her jacket and dropped it on the floor, then pulled a pin out of her hair, and then a second and a third, tossing them atop her jacket.

He turned his attention to her blouse, quickly undoing the buttons. If he hadn't been so aroused, he would have laughed in sheer delight. He had expected to bed a jittery maiden tonight, but found himself with a provocative siren. He pulled off her blouse as her hair tumbled down, his eyes glazing with hunger as she ran her fingers through her locks in the most wanton fashion imaginable.

"You certainly do get into the spirit of things." He unbuttoned her skirt with an unsteady hand and eased it over her hips. "Are you sure you haven't been drinking?"

"Not a drop. I don't need it tonight. I love you, remember?" She stepped out of her skirt and petticoats, then slid his dressing gown off his shoulders and down to the bed, so that only his legs were still covered. "And I love touching you. Did I ever mention that?"

She ran her hands down his chest, then homed in on his nipples and fondled them with her thumbs. His self-control began to splinter as her touch grew slightly rougher. He caught his breath, all but stupefied with pleasure. "Why are you just sitting there, Luke?" she asked softly. "You promised to tempt me."

"Uh, right. I'm sorry." He eased down her shift and fumbled with the laces of her corset. "The thing is, I promised to undress you slowly, too, but I didn't expect you to be so—" He swallowed hard. She was rubbing his exposed male parts with a stockinged knee, rhythmically and seductively. "Uh, Susie . . . I wouldn't do that if I were you. Not if you want me to take my time."

Sukey wasn't worried for a moment—she knew Luke would make things perfect—but she lowered her knee and took a step backward. She loved everything about this, from the urgent passion of his hands when he touched her, to the stunned excitement in his eyes when she touched him back, to the way he blushed when she teased him. She had enjoyed being tempted and coaxed, but giving herself eagerly to a man she loved had a pleasure and exhilaration all its own.

"You mean it will be like Friday. You'll rush ahead, spill your seed, and leave me aching, but this time, you'll do it inside me. So much for your vaunted self-control." Giggling, she dropped to the floor and cupped his knees. "Perhaps this will cool you down. But if it doesn't, I expect you to spend the rest of the night making it up to me"—she tickled him unmercifully—"or pay the price."

He laughed helplessly, then retaliated, stripping her naked, shrugging out of his dressing gown, and lifting her into bed, under the covers. For a man who was convalescing, he was amazingly supple. He covered her with his body and pinned her hands above her head, then arched away. But their loins were still in contact, and his manhood was hot and urgent between her legs. As he moved gently against her, he captured one of her nipples and rubbed it between his thumb and forefinger. She moaned that she loved him, then shuddered and closed her eyes.

His fingers grew more demanding, intensifying her excitement, and she wrapped her legs around his thighs and arched into his thrusts. She had been with him often enough now that, even imprisoned this way, she knew how to please him. She moved her hips in slow, inviting circles, rubbing the core of her pleasure against his swollen member, teasingly retreating only to return more eager for him than ever. But just as the sating began to come, he released her wrists, eased downward to end the intimate contact, and kissed her. It was like an erotic drug—slow, hot, deep, and mesmerizing. She twined her arms around his neck, tightened her legs around his thighs, and clung to him.

All the willpower drained out of her. She became a creature of pure response, and the response was electric. Even when he teased her—which he certainly did, withholding his tongue from her mouth, stroking her everywhere between her legs but where she most wanted him to—there was no frustration, only the purest sort of pleasure. She was burning for him, desperate for release, but the torture was sublime. He had promised slowness and temptation, and he was delivering with a blissful vengeance.

She felt him probing her passage with his manhood, moving carefully in and out of her, and once again, she whispered that she loved him. Though breathless and dazed, she hadn't forgotten that his wedding night with Kate must have been a horror, and she wanted him to know that it would be different with her. A man as tender as Luke needed a little encouragement when it came to deflowering a virgin.

He probed more deeply, and she felt a piercing pain. He withdrew the moment she flinched, looking miles beyond the end of his tether. "I'm sorry," he said hoarsely. "Just one hard thrust and it will be over. Unless you would prefer—"

"No. Go ahead." While her passion had given way to discomfort, her heart was fuller than ever. "Have I mentioned that I love you?"

"Several times." He kissed her lightly on the mouth, then eased himself back in place. "I have the sense that when I join with you, I won't ever want to leave. I adore you, Susannah. If you're not willing to give me forever, you had better stop me right now."

"If I didn't want forever, Luke, I wouldn't be here," she answered softly.

He kissed her again, with such intense emotion that when he entered her, she scarcely minded the pain. It diminished quickly, and she learned he had been right about how it would feel. He remained there, filling her to the hilt, and she experienced an overwhelming closeness and tenderness. She wished they could remain this way forever, keeping each other safe.

Then he began to thrust again, very gently, in thrall to a need she no longer felt. She matched his rhythm, caring only about his pleasure, but somehow, when he rolled onto his back, taking her with him, then kissed and caressed her, other desires intruded. She longed to be teased. Fondled. Returned to the brink of ecstasy.

She was. Her passion intensified until she was bucking urgently into his thrusts, almost controlling him in this position, going faster and faster until their love-making became a wild and breathless mating. He kept going even as the pleasure flooded through her, which felt glorious, then stilled for a second and exploded.

They remained joined afterward, her head nestled into the crook of his neck, his hand absently stroking her back. For the first time in Luke's life, he felt that he had a home. A place of comfort, shelter, and love. Susannah could march in as many suffragist parades as she pleased, if that was the price of having her as his wife.

His manhood finally slackened and he shifted her to the side, so that her body was sprawled half atop his. "So?" he murmured. "Was it incredibly wonderful enough to end any notion of leaving?"

"I suppose so," she answered sleepily.

He didn't care for that at all. "What do you mean, you suppose so? Aren't you certain?"

"Of course I'm certain. I said 'I suppose so' because it's love that makes me feel that way, not sex." She nuzzled his neck. "Although it *was* fantastic. If you're the one Shelby was describing, she was right about that. Addictive, in fact. I probably *will* run you ragged." She caressed his slumbering member, which began to stir. "I'm already getting urges in that direction, Luke. Are you?"

He fondled her bottom, completely content now. "Umm. Though if you're at all sore . . . That is, your body isn't accustomed to making love, darling, and you're so physically passionate that I worry—"

"I'm fine." She touched his injured arm. "And you? Your wounds don't pain you, do they? Because if they do—"

"Not at all, thanks to your bioglue and Syn-skin." He rolled onto his side, so they were lying face to face.

"Speaking of which . . ." He looked her sternly in the eye. "Now that you've decided to keep me, Susannah, I suggest you tell me what those are. Where they come from."

Sukey hesitated. She knew that commanding tone and was reluctant to challenge it, but Luke was still Luke. Stubborn and backward. Perhaps she should wait until he reformed before she confided in him. *If* he reformed. Maybe he never would.

But even if he didn't, she thought, she wasn't going to leave him, even if a veritable angel dropped down from the sky. She loved him too much. If they had political disagreements, so be it. He wouldn't interfere with her work. He had promised, and if she had come to understand anything about him, it was that he wouldn't break his word.

"They're medicines from over two hundred years in the future. Shelby brought them back. She didn't want to live in the past without them. Naturally, she wanted her family to have them, too. The people of her original time weren't happy about the idea, but they let her take them. She almost always gets her way. Her mind is incredibly powerful."

Luke nodded calmly. "You're telling me that Sarah's sister is from the future." His tone was so bland that Sukey had no idea whether he believed her or thought her mad.

"She's Sarah's daughter, actually. Sarah traveled here from 2096 as part of an experiment to change the past. She was supposed to save Lincoln, but she failed. It was evidently too big a change to carry out. Anyway, she got lost in time and fell in love with my brother, and over five years later—in the future, I mean—Shelby came back to find her. Shelby isn't all that fond of the nineteenth century—it's very primitive by her standards—but she and Sarah were much too close to be parted. Since Ty couldn't go to the future—their machines can't do that—Shelby stayed in the past.''

Another bland nod. "So when you tell me what women will accomplish in the years to come, your source is actual history. Future history. That's why you're so insistent. So confident. You know for a fact that you're right.''

"Yes.''

"Hmm. Imagine that.'' He smiled, looking bemused. "I must say, it's humbling to have been proven so wrong.'' But he didn't sound humbled, only intrigued. "And your so-called magic?''

"The product of beings in a higher dimension. The physics of it won't be discovered for a century and a half. I don't understand a bit of it, but they *do* exist.''

"Do they really? How extraordinary.''

She wrinkled her nose at him. "I must say, you're awfully calm about all this. On the face of it, it's totally unbelievable. How can you just lie there and nod at me?''

"As you've said, I'm a scientist. When I'm furnished with proof of something, I accept it. It's the most plausible explanation for your medicines.'' His smile broadened. "Besides, your brother is the luckiest investor I know, and in speculative silver stocks, of all things. It's a very volatile area. I wouldn't touch it on a bet. Almost everyone who stays in the game loses money, but your brother has made a fortune. Now I understand how. When he guesses wrong, it's only for show. Sarah has told him what's going to happen. So Tyson Stone, the saintly crusading journalist, is actually a brazen cheat.''

"They give most of the money to charity," Sukey said defensively.

Luke chuckled. "I'm not criticizing him, darling. It's just nice to know that he's human, especially since I'm married to a woman who worships him. That's tough competition." He paused. "So tell me about the future."

I'll field that one, if you don't mind.

Sukey jerked into a sitting position, then yanked the covers up to her neck. "Now I know how my brother felt. You certainly do pick your moments. For someone who's totally brilliant, you seem to have a problem grasping the simple concept of privacy, Shelby March."

Geez, Suke, will you ice it? I wasn't prowling around in your head. I was just surfing the surface a bit.

Luke cocked an eyebrow at her. "That voice—"

"You can hear her?"

"Yes. When you said she had a powerful mind, it was a considerable understatement. How does she do that?"

A combination of natural talent and extensive training, Your Lordship. Listen, Sukey, this is mostly your fault. I mean, I was sitting here in Bombay, minding my own business and having a nice dinner, and you suddenly start screaming at me. What was I supposed to do? Ignore you? Naturally I kept an ear open.

Sukey turned a bright shade of red. "Dear God. How could you, Shelby? I may never forgive you for this."

Oh, for Pete's sake, I didn't listen to the play-by-play. I just know you finally got together, and that it was pretty sensational.

Luke sat up and draped an arm around Sukey's

shoulders. "It certainly was, Miss March. I take it you can pick up as much or as little as you choose. And in this case, all you wanted was the gist of what was going on, so you would know when to pay us a visit."

Exactly, and it's Shelby. I'm glad someone in the room has some common sense. I like this guy, Sukey. I mean, we know he's going to turn out great in the end, but I like him right now.

"Thank you, Shelby. The feeling is mutual."

You're welcome. You're the most balanced mixture of order and creativity I've ever sensed, Luke. I guess that's why you're so completely cool about this—about me. It's the combination of logic and curiosity. You're a nice change from the other people I've had to pop in on. By the way, you don't have to talk if you don't want to. You can just think me stuff. If you want Sukey to hear it, I'll know it, and I'll flick it into her mind.

Your powers—they're fascinating, Luke thought.

And they truly were. All of it was. A scientist's paradise. Luke was wondering what more he would learn, when a kaleidoscope of images began to play in his mind. Women in every conceivable role, from a robed judge to a police officer in male trousers to a female in an odd-looking coverall floating in front of what appeared to be stars to a woman sitting behind a desk in what he recognized as the American president's Oval Office. There were snippets of science, as well, about the nature of matter and energy, the character of the universe, and the fundamental bases of life. He sat spellbound, taking it all in, registering a sharp mental protest when it stopped.

Sorry, Luke, but there's a limit to how much I can show you. It could muck up the future if you know too much. I'll be coming to Hong Kong in a couple of weeks to sing, and we can talk more then, but in the meantime, keep all this to yourself, okay?

Of course, Luke thought. *Thank you for the look ahead. I wouldn't tamper with the future, though the activities I'll have to engage in . . .* He sighed to himself. Facts were facts and fair was fair. *Me. A suffragist marcher. Humph.*

Sukey had recovered from her embarrassment by then, and she was utterly irate. *For heaven's sake, why didn't you tell me he was the one? Do you have any idea of how much I've suffered?* She glowered at the wall. Of course Shelby did. She had read the diary. *Well, anyway, you shouldn't have put me through this. It's not as if telling me would have changed history or anything.*

Think about it, Suke. If I had told you, would you have loved him the same way? As deeply and completely? There was a poignant wistfulness in Shelby's tone. *You would have taken him for granted. Never understood what makes him so special, because you never had to fight to find out.* Amusement. *But there is one thing I can tell you. You guys are going to conceive a child tonight, but I don't know which time. You tried so hard, you didn't get much sleep. So if I were you, I'd get on with the job.* And with that, she was gone.

"And I thought *you* were a handful," Luke said with a laugh. "I don't know whether to be thrilled or terrified by the prospect of actually meeting her."

"You should be both, probably," Sukey said absently. Her mind was on what Shelby had just said. She had been right, of course. Sukey had been forced to risk everything for Luke, and it had opened a heart that had been closed tight and made it sing again. The last few months had tested her to the limit. Turned her into a different person. A better one. She couldn't regret any of that.

She rested her head on Luke's shoulder. "She's remarkable, though. She feels what people feel—the love and the joy, the pleasure and the triumph, but also the anguish, the pain, and the fear. She wants to heal the world. Truly, I feel privileged that it's my destiny to help her, even if it's only a little."

Luke looked bemused. "And my destiny, as well, it seems." He paused. "That business about rearing six children . . . It wasn't really a vision at all, I assume. Shelby knew it for a fact."

Sukey trailed her finger down his chest. "Yes. And even if we count William, Ellie, and Lexie as the first three, that still leaves three more for us to bring into the world. I believe we've been given our marching orders, darling. We had best obey them."

"I couldn't agree more," Luke murmured.

They turned into each other's arms. They evidently had a long, splendid night ahead of them, and both of them knew how dangerous it could be to tamper with the future.

Avon Romantic Treasures

*Unforgettable, enthralling love stories,
sparkling with passion and adventure
from Romance's bestselling authors*

LADY OF SUMMER *by Emma Merritt*
77984-6/$5.50 US/$7.50 Can

HEARTS RUN WILD *by Shelly Thacker*
78119-0/$5.99 US/$7.99 Can

JUST ONE KISS *by Samantha James*
77549-2/$5.99 US/$7.99 Can

SUNDANCER'S WOMAN *by Judith E. French*
77706-1/$5.99 US/$7.99 Can

RED SKY WARRIOR *by Genell Dellin*
77526-3/ $5.50 US/ $7.50 Can

KISSED *by Tanya Anne Crosby*
77681-2/$5.50 US/$7.50 Can

MY RUNAWAY HEART *by Miriam Minger*
78301-0/ $5.50 US/ $7.50 Can

RUNAWAY TIME *by Deborah Gordon*
77759-2/ $5.50 US/ $7.50 Can

Avon Romances—
the best in exceptional authors
and unforgettable novels!

THE MACKENZIES: LUKE   **Ana Leigh**
78098-4/ $5.50 US/ $7.50 Can

FOREVER BELOVED   **Joan Van Nuys**
78118-2/ $5.50 US/ $7.50 Can

INSIDE PARADISE   **Elizabeth Turner**
77372-4/ $5.50 US/ $7.50 Can

CAPTIVATED   **Colleen Corbet**
78027-5/ $5.50 US/ $7.50 Can

THE OUTLAW   **Nicole Jordan**
77832-7/ $5.50 US/ $7.50 Can

HIGHLAND FLAME   **Lois Greiman**
78190-5/ $5.50 US/ $7.50 Can

TOO TOUGH TO TAME   **Deborah Camp**
78251-0/ $5.50 US/ $7.50 Can

TAKEN BY YOU   **Connie Mason**
77998-6/ $5.50 US/ $7.50 Can

FRANNIE AND THE CHARMER   **Ann Carberry**
77881-5/ $4.99 US/ $6.99 Can

REMEMBER ME   **Danice Allen**
78150-6/ $4.99 US/ $6.99 Can

Discover Contemporary Romances at Their Sizzling Hot Best from Avon Books

THE LOVES OF RUBY DEE   *by Curtiss Ann Matlock*
78106-9/$5.99 US/$7.99 Can

JONATHAN'S WIFE   *by Dee Holmes*
78368-1/$5.99 US/$7.99 Can

DANIEL'S GIFT   *by Barbara Freethy*
78189-1/$5.99 US/$7.99 Can

FAIRYTALE   *by Maggie Shayne*
78300-2/$5.99 US/$7.99 Can

Coming Soon

WISHES COME TRUE   *by Patti Berg*
78338-X/$5.99 US/$7.99 Can